inspiration.

Enjoy –

Rick Stein

4·18·2014.

THE
DANA TWINS
AND
RELATED MATTERS

ALSO BY RICHARD STEIN

No Cause for Shame

Reasonable Degree of Certainty

THE DANA TWINS AND RELATED MATTERS

Richard Stein

Library of Congress Control Number:		2013919367
ISBN:	Hardcover	978-1-4931-2210-3
	Softcover	978-1-4931-2209-7
	Ebook	978-1-4931-2211-0

This is a work of fiction. Names, characters, places and incidents either are the product of the author's imagination or are used fictitiously, and any resemblance to any actual persons, living or dead, events, or locales is entirely coincidental.

This book was printed in the United States of America.

Rev. date: 12/09/2013

To order additional copies of this book, contact:
Xlibris LLC
1-888-795-4274
www.Xlibris.com
Orders@Xlibris.com
141576

CONTENTS

From *Number One Country Hits, 3rd edition, 1997.*

From November 1995 to January 1996, the Dana Twins, Richie and Stevie Dana, topped the charts with "Lost in Your Eyes." Following their discovery by Nashville promoter Milton Brandenburg, the two eleven year old boys from West Tennessee parlayed a sugary sweet country-pop sound, the music and lyrics of Cory Bayliss, and the skills of producer Jackson Daniels into a triple platinum recording.

1

THE BET

D R. MELVIN AARON wasn't a gambling man. Except for putting ten dollars into the betting pool at the annual Super Bowl party hosted by his brother-in-law, Milton Brandenburg, he didn't bet at all. Melvin never played poker and when he travelled to Las Vegas with his wife, as he did every four or five years, it was only to see the shows. However, whenever he was asked how he and his wife had met, Dr. Aaron announced with pride that he had won her as part of a wager that he made with Chris Calliro back when the two of them were house officers in Boston.

Dr. Aaron's wife never took exception to her husband's hyperbole even though he made it sound as if she was a trophy he had won in a Texas hold'em tournament. In truth, the start of the relationship that produced exactly one half of the Dana Twins depended on something far more serious than a poker game.

Chris Calliro possessed enough medical knowledge to be a fine physician but he wasn't one. Dr. Calliro had a palpable dislike for almost all of his patients. He hated the intravenous drug addicts who had given themselves hepatitis, the alcoholics whose drinking had led to cirrhosis, the cigarette smokers who had developed chronic lung disease or lung cancer, and the obese individuals whose eating habits Calliro blamed for their coronary artery disease and diabetes. If there had been a medical sub-specialty that excluded patients with life-style related illnesses, Chris Calliro might have been able to find a comfortable niche in the field of internal medicine. Unfortunately for Dr. Calliro, no such field existed.

In June, 1972, Dr. Calliro was assigned to complete the last month of his medical internship at Mt. Moriah Hospital on Medicine Team B. From the beginning of the month, Dr. Aaron, the Team B resident could not help but notice his intern's hostility toward his patients. After hearing Dr. Calliro complain about the patients on his service, Dr. Aaron told him, "Calliro, there are no such things as dopers, drinkers, smokers, and fatties as you call them. There are only sick people who have problems and who need care. If you can't understand that, you can't be an effective physician no matter how smart you are and no matter how much medicine you know."

Calliro shrugged his narrow shoulders and said nothing.

"Look. Why don't you just show people the same consideration that you would like doctors to show your wife?" Sharon Calliro, who frequently visited her husband at the hospital, was eight and a half months pregnant with their first child. The ultrasound had shown that it was going to be a boy.

"Unlike the dopers, drinkers, smokers, and fatties, my wife hasn't destroyed her health."

Melvin Aaron sighed and returned to reviewing the charts of the Team B patients. He noted that Dr. Calliro's diagnostic and therapeutic plans were superb. As a result, Dr. Aaron would not have acted on his intern's attitude problem if not for the two cases that convinced him that Dr. Calliro was a liability to the field of internal medicine.

The first week in June, Melvin Aaron was eating lunch in the hospital cafeteria, discussing the Red Sox dismal performance during April and May with three other medical residents, when he got a page from his intern.

"Mel, I'm in the Emergency Room. Our new admission, Nancy Hayes, is a twenty-three year old chronic alcoholic with pneumococcal pneumonia." Chris Calliro reviewed his choice of antibiotics with his resident who considered it a straight-forward case for a doctor in the last month of his internship. As he rejoined his colleagues, Melvin Aaron considered that twenty-three was young for someone to be considered a chronic alcoholic. He headed up the stairs from "The Cave," as the hospital cafeteria was known, to the Emergency Room.

Dr. Aaron found Nancy Hayes in a hallway, sitting up on a gurney; her hospital gown was drenched with sweat. He obtained the history that she had experienced a shaking chill the previous evening following which she started coughing up rust colored sputum. Dr. Aaron reviewed the x-rays and listened to her lungs. There were abnormal breath sounds at the base of the right lung, exactly where the x-ray showed an abnormality.

For the sake of completeness, Melvin Aaron asked the patient how much she drank.

"Not much. I may have a glass of wine if my husband and I go out to dinner. Champagne on New Year's Eve. That's all."

Dr. Aaron excused himself and walked to the small room where the doctors reviewed laboratory tests and wrote admitting notes. He paged Chris Calliro. "How did you get the story that our patient was an alcoholic? I didn't get that history from her."

"She denies it, but there's alcohol on her breath. It's barely noon. She's a drinker."

"Thanks." Melvin Aaron considered that his sense of smell was failing and he returned to his patient. This time he checked the mucous membranes of her mouth, assessing her breath in the process. There was, perhaps, the faintest whiff of alcohol. "Everything's fine, except for the pneumonia," he told her. "We'll start you on intravenous antibiotics. There are no guarantees in medicine, but I suspect we will have you feeling better and out of here in a couple of days."

"Great!"

"Just one question, though. I thought I smelled alcohol on your breath. Have you been drinking?"

Nancy Hayes' eyes widened. "No. I told you . . ." She paused to cover her mouth as she coughed. "The cold medicine I've been taking has a little alcohol in it. You obviously have a very educated sense of smell."

"Thank you. I thought it was something like that, but I just wanted to be certain."

As Melvin Aaron walked back to the doctor's room to write his admission note, he considered that Chris Calliro's disdain for certain categories of patients was bad enough. Now, Calliro was going out of his way to place patients into those categories. Melvin Aaron was muttering to himself when he was interrupted.

"Hello, Dr. Aaron."

He looked up and saw Tina Danashevsky, one of the Emergency Room sign-in clerks. "Hi." He waved his hand as a greeting and returned to writing his note.

The buxom blonde clerk was not deterred by the brevity of Dr. Aaron's reply. "You look unhappy. A sick admission?"

"It's not a sick admission; it's my intern."

"Calliro, right? I saw him down here with your patient just as I left for lunch." Tina Danashevsky had once hoped to become a physician. A year earlier, when she graduated college, ninety percent of positions in medical schools went to men. Despite excellent grades in the sciences, and an excellent score on the medical college aptitude test, she had been rejected by all nine medical schools to which she had applied.

"You got it. My other intern, Roger Anderson is fine. It's Calliro." He told her about Calliro labeling Nancy Hayes a chronic alcoholic.

Tina grimaced. "It's not that doctor's wives can't be drinkers, but she's married to a fourth year medical student and she's in graduate school herself."

"Calliro left that out. How did you know?"

"I looked at what she wrote on the sign-in sheets under personal history. I make it a rule to read the forms, even though it isn't part of my job description. Anyway, my lunch break is over. I have to get back to my desk. See you around."

"See you." Melvin Aaron had chuckled when Tina Danashevsky mentioned rules. The doctors were in charge of the patients, but when Tina D was on duty, she ran the Emergency Room and she enforced the rules. No more than one family member was ever allowed to accompany a patient back to the examining room. Anyone seen smoking in the waiting room was escorted out of the building by security. Tina D had worked in the Mt. Moriah Emergency Room since the summer between her junior and senior years in college and she made the ER function smoothly. Because of her efforts some of the doctors had given her a nickname, "The Blonde Bitch."

Dr. Aaron considered Tina to be a helpful resource and he had thought about asking her out. She was attractive and apparently, like Dr. Aaron, unattached. However, he had overheard her talking to one of the nurses. One of Tina D's personal rules was that she never dated medical students, interns, residents, or faculty physicians. Melvin Aaron decided to leave well enough alone.

Since labeling Nancy Hayes an alcoholic didn't affect her care, other than telling Calliro what he had learned, Melvin Aaron let the matter slide. Unfortunately, the second incident involving Chris Calliro was not benign.

A few days later, Melvin Aaron was sitting at the doctor's work station on the sixth floor home of Medicine Team B across the hall from the room of an intravenous drug addict. The patient had been admitted with a working diagnosis of an infected heart valve. Chris Calliro had no idea that Melvin Aaron was in earshot as he informed his patient of his plan.

"Mr. Dwyer, I need to draw what we call blood cultures to see if there's any evidence of infection in your blood stream. Unfortunately, your drug abuse has messed up all your veins, so I'm going to have to draw the blood directly from your heart with this syringe."

Melvin Aaron had no idea what size syringe or needle Calliro was showing the patient, but he heard the patient say "Like Hell, you are! I'm leaving!"

Calliro responded, "Well, in that case, you can sign this 'Against Medical Advice' form that I just happened to have with me and be discharged right now. Just sign right here."

Before the patient could sign the form, Melvin Aaron had bounded off his chair and sprinted across the hall into the patient's room. He explained that there were alternative places for blood to be drawn, such as the large veins in the leg. Despite his frustration, Melvin Aaron covered for Chris Calliro in front of the patient. "Dr. Calliro doesn't have as much experience drawing blood cultures as I do, and I'll take care of this. I'm certain that I can find a vein. There's no need for you to leave the hospital."

After drawing the blood cultures, a crimson faced Melvin Aaron sat Chris Calliro down in the doctor's conference room. It was all Dr. Aaron could do not to scream at his intern. "For the life of me, Chris, I can't see why you want to be a doctor when you can't stand the patients with whom you interact all day!"

"That's simple. I love medicine."

"No, Calliro, you love disease. You find it fascinating. Medicine is people, and you hate people. You don't have to love them, but I just can't see how you get any satisfaction out of doing what you do. I enjoy working with patients. You barely endure it. It's going to eat you up. Find something you enjoy doing."

Chris Calliro snorted. "I spent four years in medical school, I have sixty thousand dollars in debt, and you want me to make a different career choice? Fuck you!"

"Look, I'm not saying you should quit being a doctor. I'm saying you should do something other than internal medicine. Be a radiologist or a pathologist. Those fields don't necessarily involve interaction with patients. You're smart and you know as much medicine as any of the interns here at Mt. Moriah, possibly even more, but it doesn't matter. There has to be a better way for you to apply your education. At least think about it."

"Can I go now?"

"Look, just think of it this way. It's hard enough being sick and in the hospital without having to face the fact that your doctor dislikes you."

Sounding even more irritated, Calliro glared at Melvin Aaron as he repeated his question. "Can I go now?"

"Sure."

The blood cultures that Melvin Aaron had drawn on Calliro's patient were positive for bacteria. Marvin Dwyer stayed in the hospital, received appropriate treatment, and survived his infection. Had Melvin Aaron not intervened, the patient almost certainly would have left the hospital and died.

Melvin Aaron discussed the situation with the attending physician on Medicine Team B as well as with Frank Rice, the Chief Resident in Medicine. They offered no constructive suggestions.

"Would you want him as your doctor?" Mel Aaron asked Dr. Rice, who was scheduled to join the faculty in July.

"Of course not. I'm five feet eight and I weigh two hundred and sixty pounds. He'd consider me a fatty and we wouldn't bond. I'd go to someone else."

"That's fine. But what happens next year when he has a captive audience of patients who are assigned to him."

Frank Rice drummed his fingers on his desk. "I have no idea, and anyway, as of July 1, it's not our problem. He's taking a residency in western Massachusetts."

"So that's it? We do nothing?" Mel Aaron shook his head and looked away.

"This is your last month of residency, Mel. Don't go looking for problems you can't solve. In July, you'll start your fellowship in cancer medicine here at Mt. Moriah. I'll be on the faculty. Calliro will be somewhere else. Life will go on."

Melvin Aaron stood up and started to leave when Frank Rice abruptly changed the subject. "Hey, did you hear what the blonde bitch did now?"

Dr. Aaron winced when Tina D was called the blonde bitch.

Dr. Rice continued. "You'll love this. A sixty year old woman came to the ER last week complaining of weakness. The labs showed severe anemia and she got admitted to Medicine Team A. Despite the fact that there were no signs of iron deficiency they ran her gut."

Melvin Aaron knew that in the medical jargon, running her gut meant doing diagnostic studies to determine a source of gastrointestinal bleeding. "Where does Tina Danashevsky fit into this?"

"Tina who . . . ? Oh, is that the blonde bitch's name?"

"Yes it is."

"I'm getting there. When the in-patient team didn't find a source of bleeding, they did a bone marrow test to diagnose the unexplained anemia, and found that the bone marrow was packed with cancer. I reviewed the chart to see if any clues had been missed. The intern and resident admission notes said, 'Anemia—evaluate for blood loss.' However, the admitting card, the card that has to get turned in from the ER to the admitting office for a patient to be admitted, said, 'Anemia—suspect cancer metastatic to the bone marrow.'"

"So, Chase Alston or Arnie Glass got it right and the docs on Medicine Team A didn't read it?" Chase Alston and Arnie Glass were the medicine residents who alternated twenty-four hour Emergency Room shifts during the month of June.

"No! Chase Alston just wrote one word, 'anemia,' on the admitting card. He figured that the counts were so low that the patient had to be admitted. He didn't think about the cause of anemia at all. The blonde bitch, whatever her name is, was the one who made the diagnosis and put it on the card."

Mel Aaron smiled. "Her name is Tina Danashevsky and I don't think she's a bitch. How did she do it?"

"I went and asked her. It seems that lab tests are crossing her desk all day long and she has this book on test interpretation. The patient had more than twenty nucleated red cells in her blood for every hundred white blood cells with the normal number being . . ."

"Zero."

"Exactly. Zero. Anyway, Ms. Danashevsky told me that she knew that nucleated red cells can be a sign of myelofibrosis."

Melvin knew that myelofibrosis was a condition in which the bone marrow was replaced by fibrous tissue. "If that was the diagnosis, the patient would have had a big spleen."

"Exactly. Ms. Danashevsky read the physical exam recorded by the intern in the ER and found out that the patient didn't have a big spleen. So, she ruled out myelofibrosis. She also knew that cancer metastatic to the bone marrow can lead to nucleated red cells in the blood. When the woman filled out the medical history form she reported that she had had a mastectomy for breast cancer a year ago."

"And Tina D put it all together."

"Tina D put it all together and put the correct diagnosis on the admitting card." Frank Rice paused as if he was deep in thought. "If we could make her an intern and make Calliro a clerk, we'd probably be better off."

"Except that she didn't go to medical school and as sign-in clerk, Calliro would run people off."

"You're probably right. Look, if you think of something constructive, do it. Otherwise, just forget about it."

Since Melvin Aaron had no idea what to do about Chris Calliro, he did just that. However, that evening, as he walked home to his apartment on Brookline Avenue, he came up with a plan.

In the morning, he greeted his two interns. "Good morning, Roger. Good morning, Zero."

Dr. Calliro took a step backwards. "What did you call me?"

"I called you 'Zero.' You show zero compassion to your patients and until you change, you are 'Dr. Zero.' You're too callous to be an effective physician, and someone has to do something about it."

"Fine. Anything else."

"Actually, there is." Dr. Aaron explained that he was transferring some of Chris Calliro's patients to Roger Anderson, the other intern on the team. Additionally, Dr. Aaron would take over the role of intern for a few of Calliro's other patients. If Calliro couldn't treat patients with compassion, then someone else would be their physician.

The flaw in the plan was obvious. Chris Calliro would have less work to do and, in essence, he would be rewarded for being inappropriate. However, patient care was primary in Melvin Aaron's mind, and if it was necessary to move patients from Chris Calliro's part of the team to guarantee compassionate care, then so be it. At the time, that was as far as Melvin Aaron's plan went.

While Chris Calliro winced every time that he was called "Zero" or "Doctor Zero," he tolerated the hazing. Of note, in front of patients or their families, Dr. Aaron always addressed his intern as Doctor Calliro; he felt it would be unprofessional to do otherwise. As for Zero Calliro, his attitude remained the same.

Melvin Aaron was resigned to defeat until he saw Sharon Calliro having lunch with her husband in The Cave and overheard them discussing possible names for the baby. Dr. Aaron had an idea. It was not the most rational of ideas, but it was imaginative.

The next morning, Melvin Aaron informed Roger Anderson and Chris Calliro of his new plan. "Zero, I've been thinking about our situation. I've taken away some of your patients. Dr. Anderson is now up to thirteen patients. I'm the acting intern for five patients. You have four patients. I've given you a nickname. It hasn't changed things. So, from now on, any time you make an inappropriate or hostile remark about a patient, either in front of the patient or behind the patient's back, I'm going to take that patient away from you and make it mine. If you get down to zero patients, I'm going to make an appointment with Dr. Tarkington and recommend that he not give you credit for the year and that you repeat your internship." Dr. Tarkington was Chairman of the Department of Medicine.

Dr. Calliro thought it over. "He won't listen to you."

"Yes he will. You're leaving the program at the end of June. You have no leverage. I'm scheduled to stay and do my fellowship in cancer medicine starting the first of July. If I make an issue of your lack of professionalism, and tell him that I'm considering transferring to another program in the city unless he takes a stand about your attitude, what do you think he would do?"

Melvin Aaron would never have left his program in the lurch by walking out at the last minute, but Chris Calliro didn't want to bet a year of his life on Melvin Aaron's loyalty to Mt. Moriah. "That's not fair. You can't do that. Think of something else."

Melvin Aaron smiled. Zero Calliro had walked into his trap. "OK. Instead of my contacting Dr. Tarkington, how about you agree that if you are down to zero patients when your son is born, you'll name him 'Zero' as a lifelong reminder of the importance of showing a little professional compassion. Zero Calliro. It has a nice alliterative ring to it." Calliro was silent. "Well, what do you say?"

"I'm thinking."

Dr. Aaron expected that he would get an argument from his intern. Instead, after almost a full minute of silence, Calliro offered a response. "What if I don't get down to zero? What do I get?"

"You get the satisfaction of knowing that you have a modicum of professionalism."

Calliro frowned. "Fine. But I'll never get down to zero patients. Mr. Taylor in 606 is an alcoholic with cirrhosis. Mr. Haley in 610 has chronic lung disease from smoking like a chimney for twenty years. I may slip and say something about them, but my other two patients are Mrs. Johnson in 618 and Mr. Clark in 626. They aren't going anywhere, and I have no reason to make what you call an inappropriate or hostile comment about either of them."

Melvin Aaron suspected that Calliro was correct. Mrs. Johnson was a sixty-eight year old woman with multiple myeloma, a form of bone marrow cancer. Mr. Clark was a fifty-five year old man with terminal colon cancer. Nothing about their life styles had caused their illnesses.

From a medical point of view, Mrs. Johnson was stable and could have been discharged at any time. However, a week earlier, the social worker had informed Dr. Aaron and Dr. Calliro that there had been difficulty getting her family to arrange nursing home placement. It appeared that Mrs. Johnson would spend the entire month, and more, at Mt. Moriah.

Mr. Clark was terminally ill, but as hospice programs did not exist in 1972, and as the family could not care for him at home, Mr. Clark seemed destined to die as a patient on Medical Team B.

"Is it a deal?" Melvin Aaron asked.

"Yes. You get off my back, let me finish this rotation and complete my internship, and you say nothing to Dr. Tarkington. If somehow I get down to a census of zero patients at the time my son is born, I'll name him Zero. It's a ridiculous bet, but if it makes you happy—fine."

"Is that a promise?"

"Yes, it's a promise." The two men shook hands. "And since I will never get down to zero patients, it's not a problem."

But it would be. Because of the fact that the bet was ridiculous, word of Dr. Aaron's wager with Chris Calliro spread throughout the hospital. Though Melvin Aaron had agreed not to contact the Department Chairman, Dr. Tarkington learned of the situation and initiated an inquiry into Zero Calliro's performance as an intern. There was a consensus that Calliro was one of the smartest interns ever to work at Mt. Moriah but that because of his attitude he was a horrible physician.

With two interns on the service, Dr. Anderson and Dr. Calliro alternated the days on which they admitted patients. As June 30th was the end of the academic year, June 29th was Chris Calliro's last day to admit patients. As he had predicted, he started the morning with a census of two patients, Norman Clark and Dorothy Johnson.

At eight A.M., just as the team sat down to review their patients, Norman Clark had a cardiac arrest. Under the circumstances, there was a "Do Not Resuscitate" order on the chart. The Clark family was at the bedside; Dr. Aaron and Dr. Calliro expressed their condolences; Zero Calliro's census was down to one. Though he was likely to admit three or four patients by the end of the day, Calliro began to fumble with the set of index cards on which he kept information about his past and present patients.

At nine forty-five, just before morning rounds with the attending physician were scheduled to begin, an African-American man arrived on the sixth floor wearing an obviously expensive sharkskin suit and asked to speak to the doctor in charge. Melvin Aaron was summoned to meet with Allen Johnson, Dorothy Johnson's son. He had been in England working for the Stone Banking Trust, but now that he was back in Boston, he was prepared to take his mother home.

Dr. Aaron was pleased that Mrs. Johnson could be discharged. Patients who did little more than lay in their hospital beds were at risk of developing blood clots. "That's fine. I'll have the social workers tell you what equipment you'll need, and we'll be able to get it together over the next couple of days."

"No. You don't understand, Doctor Aaron. I spoke to the social worker before I returned from London. I've already had a hospital bed, a bedside commode, and a walker delivered to my home in Newton. I've also arranged for private duty nurses around the clock."

"Well, then I guess you are ready to take her home."

At that point, Chris Calliro arrived on the scene. "What's going on? One of the nurses told me that someone in Mrs. Johnson's family was here and that she was being discharged."

Melvin Aaron explained the situation to his intern who, recognizing the implications of having a census of zero, went ballistic. "He can't take her home! How do you know who he really is? Did you see any identification?" Calliro paused. "Is this guy an actor? Did you set this up knowing I was going to be down to one patient?"

In the brief interval since Mr. Clark had died, Dr. Aaron hadn't had time to hire an actor. While it was all he could do not to laugh at the idea, Allen Johnson was not amused. He was beginning to suspect that despite its excellent reputation, Mt. Moriah was staffed by lunatics, one of whom was caring for his mother. "Dr. Aaron, what is this man talking about? Of course, I'm Mrs. Johnson's son."

"I'm sorry, sir. Doctor Calliro has gotten quite attached to your mother during her time here. In addition, his wife is pregnant with their first child. She's due any day now, and he's a little bit nervous . . ."

Allen Johnson chuckled. "Say no more. I remember what I was like when my first child was born." By eleven AM, Dorothy Johnson was in an ambulance headed for home; Zero Calliro had no patients. Almost stammering, he called Chase Alston, the Emergency Room resident, asking him to admit someone to his service.

Dr. Alston chuckled. "All year long you've been begging me to send people home and not bother you with admissions. I admit people to the hospital when their medical condition warrants it, period." Dr. Alston slammed down the phone.

All through attending rounds Calliro kept hoping for a call from the Emergency Room informing him of a new admission. At eleven fifteen his beeper went off. It was his wife, Sharon, telling him that she had gone into labor and that, as planned, a neighbor was driving her the four blocks to Mt. Moriah. Melvin Aaron advised Dr. Calliro to keep his wife company in Labor and Delivery on the third floor. "Don't worry, Zero. It's your day to admit patients. If I get any admissions, they count as yours even if you're not here. You probably won't be at a zero census for more than a couple of hours and first time labor usually takes more than that." He paused for effect. "Of course, sometimes it doesn't . . . Zero Calliro. It does have a nice alliterative ring to it."

While his wife was in early labor, Chris Calliro called the admitting office every ten minutes to check if a patient had been admitted to his service. At a similar interval, Melvin Aaron checked in with the obstetrics nurses to see how Sharon Calliro's labor was progressing. For the next several hours there were no admissions to Medicine Team B and baby boy Calliro remained unnamed in the safety of his mother's womb.

A little after four in the afternoon, Melvin Aaron received a page from Chase Alston. "I have an admission for your team, Mel. Her name is Josie Boyd. She's a thirty-one year woman with insulin dependent diabetes. The physical exam is unremarkable. Even though she doesn't have ketoacidosis, her glucose is extremely high, it's six hundred. She needs to come in the hospital. How come you're taking the call? I paged your intern."

"His wife went into labor. He's keeping her company. I'm the acting intern and I have his beeper until she has the baby."

"Zero Calliro's wife?" The entire hospital knew about the nickname and the wager.

"Zero Calliro Senior's wife. Possibly Zero Calliro Junior's mother, if not for Josie Boyd."

"What's his census?"

"Without Josie Boyd, it's zero. With Josie Boyd, it's one."

There was a pause at the other end of the line before Chase Alston responded. "Too bad. You almost got him. There's nothing I can do. I already gave the ER clerk the admitting card to turn in to the admitting office."

Melvin Aaron trudged down to the Emergency Room to admit his patient. He examined Josie Boyd, confirmed her medical history, and reviewed her laboratory studies. He was sitting in the doctor's area starting to write orders when Tina D came up to him.

"What's wrong? No offense, Dr. Aaron, but you look awful."

"You know the bet I had with Calliro?"

"Of course."

"Well, until Josie Boyd got admitted, Calliro was down to zero patients."

"How is his wife's labor progressing?"

Melvin Aaron had quit checking when he was called by Dr. Alston. "The last I heard, delivery was imminent."

"It sounds like you came close."

Dr. Aaron sighed. "Maybe coming close will matter. I wanted to do something to grab his attention and make him realize what a horrible doctor he was because of his attitude. Knowledge and judgment are important, but there's more to being a doctor than that. We take care of people."

"Well, you certainly do. I think you're one of the best doctors here." For a moment, Tina D rested her hand on his shoulder. "Chris Calliro made it through eleven months of the year with no one doing anything because he's smart, and you cared enough to do something." As Mel Aaron shook his head, Tina D took the admitting card from her pocket. "I was supposed to walk this over to the admitting office half an hour ago. Until I do, the patient isn't officially admitted and Calliro's census is zero." She dropped the card on the linoleum floor and stepped on it. "I seem to have misplaced it. The patient has to get care, but you can do that down here in the Emergency Room for an hour or two. Maybe Calliro will be a father before one of us finds that missing card. It must be someplace." She looked around, pretending not to see it, and started to walk away.

"That's cheating. I didn't know you were that devious."

Tina D turned around. "I'm usually very direct, but I can be devious. I'm a woman; the potential to be devious comes with the second X chromosome."

"Aren't there rules about delivering the admitting card to the admitting office?"

Tina D glared at Dr. Aaron. "Don't make fun of me and my rules. And, anyway, you guys have your own set of rules." She began to quote what Melvin Aaron regarded as the intern's credo, a list of principles that he, Chase Alston, and some of the other interns had put together the year before. "Save your own humanity, then save humanity. Remember that life is a terminal condition. Take the job seriously, but not yourself. After midnight there is no such thing as an interesting admission."

He was about to say that the intern's rules were philosophical statements about the practice of medicine and not rigid constructs, but he saw no point in challenging her. She was the most interesting, attractive woman that he had met during his internship and residency. She also had a rule about not dating physicians.

Before he could say anything, she finished her recitation of the intern's rules and smiled. "In any case, I can't deliver a lost card. Let me know if you find it."

Melvin Aaron chuckled. "I'm surprised that it means that much to you."

"You've been with him a month. I've seen him down here with patients all year. It just galls me that he got into medical school and that I got turned down because I'm a woman." She usually kept her feelings about gender discrimination to herself and she waited for him to make a sarcastic comment about how men made better doctors, as if a Y chromosome had anything to do with practicing good medicine.

Instead, he said, "I know what you're saying. When I was in med school, we had ten women in a class of a hundred and six. Eight of them ranked in the top fifteen. Clearly, only the top tier of women applicants got in. The world isn't always fair."

"No kidding.' She sighed. "I'll tell you one thing. If I ever have children, it won't matter if they are girls or boys; I'm going to see to it that they get the most out of their potential. Anyway, I'm sorry to ramble on. I have to get back to my desk."

RICHARD STEIN

Dr. Aaron called the Obstetrics floor and learned that Calliro's wife had just been wheeled into the delivery room. Calliro's son would be born within the hour. Melvin Aaron slipped the admitting card into a pocket of his white coat and decided to treat Josie Boyd in the Emergency Room.

A little before five o'clock, Baby Boy Calliro entered the world. At ten minutes after five, Dr. Aaron brought the admitting card to Tina D and, together, they walked it to the Admitting Office. Only at that point was Josie Boyd officially assigned to Team B and to Dr. Chris "Zero" Calliro.

At six o'clock, the proud father returned to the sixth floor and passed out cigars. Melvin Aaron thanked his intern and turned the responsibility for Medicine Team B back to him. "How is your wife?"

"She's fine."

"How is little Zero?"

"Fine. He weighs seven pounds, two ounces, and we're naming him Anthony."

"Anthony?"

"Look, I made the bet, but I'm only the father. Sharon said that our arrangement didn't count." Actually, that was a lie. Assuming that he would never get down to zero patients, Calliro had never mentioned the bet to his wife. "You can go down to the third floor and argue with my wife if you want."

Melvin Aaron realized that there was nothing he could do. The terms of the bet were unenforceable and he knew that he had cheated by "accidentally" misplacing the admitting card. "Well, congratulations. Here's your beeper. Let's sit down and review all of our patients."

"Great. It'll be my last night on-call as an intern."

Before heading home, Melvin Aaron stopped by the ER to tell Tina D what had transpired, but she had already left for the evening. He found Tina D's phone number in the hospital directory. "I'm sorry to call you at home, but I just wanted you to know that despite everything, Chris Calliro and his wife named the baby, Anthony. His wife didn't like the name Zero. The joke's on us."

"Well, you made your point." She sounded pleased to hear from him. "That's all anyone can do. And this way, every time he calls the baby Anthony he's got to think about the wager and the fact that he needs to show more compassion. That's what really matters, right?"

"Exactly . . . Hey, would you like to get together and get a bite to eat?"

She answered immediately. "Thanks, but no thanks. I have a rule about not dating medical students, interns, residents, or faculty. Rules are rules. My life is simpler that way." As soon as she said it, she considered that she should have made an exception. He was caring, intelligent, and, as his bet with Chris Calliro had shown, he had a sense of humor. She had broken the rule about immediately delivering the admitting card to the admitting office. She wondered if she had broken the wrong rule.

Melvin Aaron thought about saying that it would just be a snack, not a date, but he decided not to press the point. "I understand. I'll see you around. I just called to let you know that they named him Anthony. Thanks for your help."

As she hung up the phone, she realized that he would never ask her out again.

The next morning when Melvin Aaron arrived on the sixth floor, he found his intern, Roger Anderson, and the Chief Resident, Frank Rice, waiting for him. Melvin Aaron asked Dr. Rice why he was on the sixth floor.

"I've been here all night, Mel. I'm the acting intern. I admitted two patients. Sit down and I'll tell you about them."

"What happened to Calliro? Did something happen to the baby? I would have come back in."

Frank Rice shook his head. "No. Nothing happened to the baby. After you left for the night, Dr. Tarkington and I came up to the floor. We had a long talk with Dr. Calliro. Dr. Tarkington sort-of fired him. That stunt he pulled with Marvin Dwyer, the patient with the infected heart valve, a few weeks ago, turned out to be the straw that broke the camel's back. Dr. Tarkington said that there was no way that he was going to send Calliro out in the world as a certified trainee of Mt. Moriah. He had been waiting until after the baby was born to say anything. Don't ask me why he waited. I think Dr. Tarkington was trying to show Dr. Calliro some compassion."

Melvin Aaron suddenly felt sorry for Chris Calliro. "Compassion? The guy put in three hundred and sixty-four days and he gets no credit for it?"

"That's why I said 'sort-of fired.' Dr. Tarkington told Calliro that he would give him credit for the year he spent here as long as he went into something that didn't involve direct patient responsibility."

Melvin Aaron realized that that meant radiology and pathology. "Look, I'm sorry you had to cover the service. You should have called me."

"I couldn't call you. Dr. Tarkington said that being on call as an intern was my personal penance for not bringing the matter to his attention after you told me everything."

"Are you in trouble, Frank?"

"No. I let something slide that I shouldn't have let slide. It's ok. I made a mistake; I learned from it."

The paranoia in medical training programs runs wide and deep. Melvin Aaron was worried that his fellowship in cancer medicine might be withdrawn. "Am I in trouble, Frank?"

"Not unless that note for you means trouble. Dr. Tarkington only had good things to say about you."

Melvin Aaron removed a white envelope from the wall of the doctor's office expecting to find a message from either Dr. Tarkington or from Chris Calliro. He read the note twice to make certain that he wasn't misinterpreting what was said.

The note read: "Rules are rules, but my rule applies to medical students, interns, residents, and faculty. Have a great fellowship year." Tina Danashevsky had underlined the word fellowship in case he missed the point. He didn't. Within a few weeks, Tina D was no longer known as "the blonde bitch." Her new sobriquet was "Mel Aaron's girlfriend." Two years later, when Dr. Aaron completed his fellowship in cancer medicine at Mt. Moriah and accepted a faculty position at Chicago Medical Institute, he and Tina got married. Although it wasn't literally true that Melvin Aaron had won his wife in a bet, if not for the absurd wager involving Chris Calliro, it would never have happened.

As a faculty member in Chicago, Dr. Aaron often told stories that illustrated important aspects of patient care. Sometimes, when he observed a health care professional demonstrating a lack of compassion, he told the story of the intern who despised patients, the ridiculous wager, the misplaced admitting card, and the baby who could have become Zero Calliro. Dr. Aaron found the story to be an effective and somewhat humorous way to illustrate that all patients have a right to be treated with compassion.

Late one evening, years after the Aarons had left Boston, Tina Aaron received a phone call at her home.

"I'm trying to get in touch with the Melvin Aaron who was a resident at Boston's Mt. Moriah Hospital in 1972? Do I have the right Melvin Aaron?" the caller asked.

"Yes, you do, but my husband can't come to the phone right now. May I take a message?" Melvin was in Washington, D.C., at the time attending a National Cancer Institute sponsored meeting on lung cancer. Tina had a rule about not providing that information to callers.

"I'm not sure he'll remember me. This is Chris Calliro. Your husband was my resident during my last month of internship at Mt. Moriah."

Tina Aaron's mouth fell open. She said nothing.

"I wanted to thank him for what he did for me. I didn't appreciate it back then, but I don't think I could be a good father or a good husband, let alone a good doctor, if I had stayed in internal medicine. I'm Chief of Pathology at a small private hospital here in Worcester, Mass. I'm much better suited to pathology."

"That's an understatement," Tina said to herself. "I'm happy you found something that you like. I'll tell Melvin you called. I'm sure he'll want to talk to you."

"That's not necessary. I just wanted to thank him. Our son is twelve today and I started thinking back to the time he was born. Do you guys have any children?"

"Yes, we have two boys. Jonah is five and Barry is three." Tina was convinced that Jonah was going to grow up to be something special—a doctor, a scientist, or maybe something so special that she couldn't even imagine it. The other day, when she and Melvin had sat down to watch a Cubs game on television with their oldest child, he had shown them how to calculate a pitcher's earned run average. However, instead of bragging about Jonah, Tina decided to be polite and ask about Chris Calliro's son. She tried to remember the boy's name, but drew a blank. She said the only thing that came to her mind. "How is little Zero?"

The line went dead. Chris Calliro never called back.

2

CAMP OJLIAGIBA

CAMP OJLIAGIBA, LOCATED on the shore of the private lake of the same name, was a summer day camp offering softball, swimming, nature study, traditional arts and crafts, and a course on Native American lore to one hundred children between the ages of eight to twelve. According to the information given to the parents of potential campers, Ojliagiba was a Native American word meaning mystical forces of nature. Many of the campers' parents were former hippies, now evolved into politically correct members of the upper middle class. They considered an official Native American name and heritage, as well as a reference to mystical natural forces, as a reason to spend an extra eighty-five dollars a week in tuition, as compared to similar camps, some of which had the temerity to use the term "Indian."

As part of the application, potential campers—actually future campers, since any application accompanied by a check was accepted—had to complete a brief personal statement as to why they wished to attend. Jonah Aaron, a precocious eight year old who read at the ninth grade level, wrote the following:

> I am interested in attending Camp Ojliagiba because I read your brochure and I want to learn in which Native American language Ojliagiba means mystical forces of nature.

Dr. Melvin Aaron and his wife Tina were not interested in either Native American lore or mystical forces of nature. However, as Jonah might otherwise have spent much of the summer of 1987 indoors, the Aarons had decided that a day camp would be a valuable experience for their son. After visiting five local camps, reading their brochures, and comparing the potential camping experiences, practical considerations prevailed. Jonah was enrolled in a four week program at Camp Ojliagiba because Tina Aaron only had to drive her son a mile and a half to catch the blue and white camp bus.

To his parents' surprise and delight, Jonah, a tall, wiry boy, revealed himself to be a natural athlete, finishing second among eight to ten year olds in the camp's version of the pentathlon—the fifty yard dash, push-ups, pull-ups, freestyle swimming, and the rope climb. Jonah enjoyed nature study under the canopy of giant oak trees that surrounded the camp on three sides, but his favorite activity was the daily session on Native American lore. Jonah had established a goal for himself, and he intended to learn the answer to his question.

Charles Gillespie, the owner of the camp, told Jonah that he didn't remember which tribe had provided the camp with its name. None of the counselors knew, nor did any of the staff.

During the Native American lore session, while the other campers worked on arts and crafts, Jonah read a book entitled *Native American Tribes of Illinois.* He learned nothing about the origin of the word Ojliagiba. When the third week of camp started, Jonah's plan was to read the pamphlets on the Illini, Miami, and Ho-Chunk tribes, all of which were native to the state. Jonah was certain that this was the week he would find his answer in his reading material. Midnight altered those plans.

Midnight was an eighteen-year-old black stallion with the bad temperament that often visits humans and animals in their later years. Charles Gillespie, the owner of Camp Ojliagiba, had purchased the horse to pull a wagon full of children around the property. Had he not done so, the horse would have been euthanized. Midnight, of course, could not tell Mr. Gillespie that he would have preferred a quiet and simple death. As in the case of many elderly humans, Midnight's wishes regarding the end of his life were unknown. What is known, however, is that Midnight took every opportunity to frustrate Curtis Jensen, the camp's seventy-two-year-old caretaker. Despite his age, Mr. Jensen had a pleasant disposition and loved both the children and the animals.

On the third Monday of Jonah's camp experience, Midnight broke free from Curtis Jensen as he was placing a harness on the animal. Mr. Jensen was knocked to the ground, suffering injuries only to his pride. Jonah Aaron was less fortunate.

According to the camp counselor who was walking twenty feet behind him at the time, Jonah was proceeding down the main camp road when something apparently caught his eye and he turned to his right almost ninety degrees. As a result, Jonah did not see Midnight charging towards him. When the camp counselor screamed, "Look out," Jonah turned toward her voice, not towards the horse, and was knocked through the air a distance of ten feet. He landed on ground which had been softened by a recent rain but which also contained numerous limestone boulders. When the counselor, Charles Gillespie's daughter Abby Jo, reached Jonah's side, the extent of his injuries was not immediately apparent. An ambulance was summoned.

Charles Gillespie understood that communication was the key to avoiding legal difficulties. Any negative event, from poison ivy to the occasional fractured limb, warranted a phone call to a parent. Mr. Gillespie called the Aaron residence and informed Tina Aaron that Jonah had been injured in a collision with a horse and that he did not know how badly her son had been hurt. He volunteered to meet Mrs. Aaron and her husband in the Emergency Room of the Highland Heights Hospital. Mrs. Aaron, on the edge of hysteria, called her husband at work and informed him that Jonah had been seriously, perhaps critically, injured.

Dr. Aaron had no patients scheduled that Monday as he had planned to review data from a clinical research study. He left Chicago Medical Institute immediately and headed home. Tina Aaron, a part-time student in Interior Design at the Art Institute of Chicago, called Camp Ojliagiba but all anyone at the camp would say was that Jonah had been taken to Highland Heights Hospital by ambulance. In the background, she heard someone saying, "You might as well tell her that his head was covered in blood."

Tina Aaron placed several calls to the Emergency Room at Highland Heights Hospital. By hospital policy, the ER clerk could only tell her that her son had arrived at 9:42 A.M. and was being evaluated. Having once worked as an Emergency Room sign-in clerk, Tina understood the rationale behind the policy. If sign-in clerks could be pumped for information, they would never get any work done and the doctors would need to keep them in the loop about patients whose conditions could be changing minute by minute. Tina's frustration grew. A non-smoker and non-drinker, she took two benzodiazepine tablets that had been prescribed for anxiety years earlier and began to gnaw her fingernails.

In the early morning hours, there is minimal traffic away from the downtown Chicago area where CMI is located and Melvin Aaron arrived home in suburban Lincolnwood less than half an hour after receiving the call from his wife. A little after ten o'clock, Dr. Aaron and Tina loaded their six year old son Barry into the back seat of the family car. They headed north to the Highland Heights Hospital having no idea what awaited them.

Melvin Aaron was a month short of his forty-first birthday. He was better than average looking, and despite having a sedentary occupation, he was only five pounds overweight. His best feature was his warm smile. That morning, he was not smiling. Neither was Tina. When she had worked in the Emergency Room, she had seen scores of people break down after receiving tragic news. She realized that she might be on the verge of becoming one of them.

As they drove to Highland Heights, Melvin Aaron held his wife's hand whenever the traffic allowed him to drive with one hand on the wheel. They said nothing. The awkward silence was finally broken by Barry who asked, "Is Jonah dead?"

Tina Aaron stared into space and said nothing.

"We don't know how Jonah is," Melvin Aaron said matter-of-factly.

Tina Aaron began to cry. "He's dead," she whispered. "A mother can sense these things. He was so smart. He could have been someone special." She began to sob uncontrollably. "You're always saying that the great tragedy in America is to grow old and outlive your mind. Let me tell you, this is much worse."

Dr. Aaron started to pull the car over to the side of the road to comfort his wife, but she shook her head and motioned to him that he should continue on to the hospital. He began to consider that his oldest son might indeed be dead. As a cancer specialist he had accepted the fact that the death rate was one hundred percent, but he had never expected to lose a child. "We don't know how Jonah is."

Silence filled the car until Barry Aaron spoke. "If Jonah's dead, can I have his baseball cards and the other good stuff?"

Melvin Aaron stifled a laugh and sighed.

Tina Aaron knew this was going to be the worst day of her life and tried to distract herself by looking at the buildings on Skokie Highway as they drove to the hospital. As they passed Old Glenview Road, she saw the Weinstein and Sons Funeral Home. She took that as an omen.

When the Aarons arrived at the hospital they barely had time to notice the antiseptic hospital smell and tell the clerk their names before they were led to the Family Counseling Room just outside the Emergency

Department's treatment area. "Please go right in. The doctor needs to speak with you. I'll go get him."

Tina Aaron was numb while Melvin Aaron experienced a wave of nausea and a sour taste in his throat. He realized that his wife had been correct. At CMI, a small conference room near the Emergency Department, like the room to which they had been directed, was where families were assembled to be informed that their loved one had died.

Tina Aaron put her hand on the doorknob and paused before she opened the door. She was certain that she was crossing a threshold into a world without Jonah, a world in which she would constantly be explaining that she had once had two children. She turned to her husband. "I'm not going in there."

"Not going in there isn't going to change anything."

She shook her head. "It's freezing in this hallway. There's much too much air-conditioning. Why do they do that?"

Actually, it was over eighty degrees where they were standing. As Tina Aaron lifted Barry up and held him in her arms, Melvin Aaron hugged both of them. He opened the door, intending to wait until they were joined by a staff physician bringing bad news.

However, as they entered the room, they found Jonah very much alive in the company of Charles Gillespie and a young woman wearing a T-shirt identifying her as a counselor from the camp. Jonah was playing with a large model airplane.

"Dr. Aaron, Mrs. Aaron, I'm Charles Gillespie from Camp Ojliagiba. I bought him the plane while he was getting his shoulder x-rayed. I hope that's ok."

Jonah's left arm was in a sling. Before running to his parents, he put down the plane and picked up a copy of an x-ray that had been taken that morning. "Look, dad. I broke my collarbone. That's the same thing as a clavicle, right?" He pointed to the fracture.

Melvin and Tina were both crying as Melvin Aaron awkwardly hugged his son. He had no problem showing affection, he simply had no idea how to hug an active boy wearing a sling. Tina was too busy muttering, "Oh, thank God, thank God," and hanging on to Barry, to consider hugging her son. Barry was contemplating all the good stuff that was not headed in his direction.

The reports that Jonah's head had been covered in blood were in error. When Jonah had collided with Midnight, he had ended up in the spot where the counselors sat on the rocks and ate hamburgers from a nearby McDonald's. His head had landed on a pile of discarded half-empty packages of ketchup.

Charles Gillespie introduced the Aaron's to his daughter, Abby Jo, and assured them that their son had not been unattended when the accident happened. "The campers were walking up the main road from the bus stop and my daughter, Abigail, was just a few yards behind him. The horse had never been a problem. What happened was just one of those unpredictable and unprecedented accidents. You have no idea how happy I am that except for one broken bone he's fine." As a parent himself, Charles Gillespie was thrilled that Jonah wasn't seriously hurt, but his use of the phrase "unpredictable and unprecedented" revealed his concern with avoiding litigation. If the accident could not have been anticipated, then the camp was not negligent. In any case, the Aarons were not litigious and they both considered a fractured collarbone a relatively trivial injury.

Tina was amused to see a big smile cross Jonah's face when Charles Gillespie spoke his daughter's name. She wondered if her eight year old son had a crush on his counselor whose age she correctly guesstimated as seventeen. As was often the case, Tina Aaron had completely misread her oldest child.

Melvin Aaron considered driving his wife and children home and then returning to his office at CMI. However, that quickly became a moot point. Jonah remembered what he had seen in the tall grass. "We have to find the dog," he told the group. "There was a little black doggie with white legs in the tall grass. I heard barking and I turned to see what was there. That's why I didn't see Midnight coming at me. We have to go make sure that it's all right. It may have been hurt."

Melvin Aaron picked up his son. "I think we have to get you home, Jonah. You need to rest. Mr. Gillespie and Abigail can find the dog, if there was a dog."

Charles Gillespie nodded. He had not been paying any attention to the discussion of the dog that Jonah claimed to have seen. Mr. Gillespie was considering—and rejecting—the option of euthanizing Midnight. He decided that the horse would never again be allowed anywhere near children. "That's right. You go home and get some rest. With that broken collarbone, I think you've seen the last of Camp Ojliagiba for this year." He turned to Dr. and Mrs. Aaron. "Of course we'll refund your entire camp fee, and on behalf of the camp, I'd like to offer Jonah a free month at camp next summer."

RICHARD STEIN

Melvin Aaron shook hands with the camp director and thanked him for his generous offer as an Emergency Room physician arrived to discuss the medical situation.

Tina Aaron had her arm around her son's shoulder. "Time to head home, Jonah."

"But Mr. Gillespie and Abby Jo might not know where to look!" Jonah was adamant. "I think the little doggie might have been hurt. I'm fine! The doggie had a collar. It belonged to someone. Think how badly they feel. We have to go find the dog!" At the age of eight Jonah had learned that he could accomplish far more by reasoning like an adult than he could by raising his voice. In his mind, tantrums were for children, like his brother, Barry.

Melvin Aaron reconsidered. Jonah had a good point. Having been away from the camp for much of the morning, Charles Gillespie would likely perform only a cursory search before returning to his usual activities. Abby Jo would likely have to get back to her group of campers. Melvin Aaron told his wife and sons that it seemed best to return to the camp and search for what was likely someone's missing pet.

Having accompanied Jonah in the ambulance, Charles Gillespie and his daughter drove back to Camp Ojliagiba in the Aaron's car. Jonah didn't object when it was Barry, smaller and younger, who got to sit on Abby Jo's lap.

Upon arriving at the camp, Mr. Gillespie excused himself, but he told the Aaron family that they could search for the dog as long as they wished. Abigail and her father both told Jonah they were looking forward to seeing him at camp next year.

Jonah led his parents to the main road and identified the spot where he had been standing when he had collided with Midnight. "It was right here, because when I turned I could see the boat dock on Lake Ojliagiba over there between those trees."

Before helping their son search for the dog, Melvin and Tina Aaron tried to visualize the accident. In a small area surrounded by a circle of rocks, they noticed food wrappers, ketchup packages, French fries, and, to their surprise, a used condom. They noted that the grass had been flattened where Jonah had landed in a small safe haven surrounded by certain death. If Jonah hadn't turned towards the dog, he likely would have landed a few feet to the right or to the left—with fatal consequences.

Jonah, looking at the rocks, was reaching the same conclusion. His father picked him up and hugged him tightly. Jonah tried unsuccessfully to hold back his tears. Tears were for babies. Suddenly he shouted, "There's the dog." Partially hidden in a rotted log was a tiny, hungry shih-tzu. As Jonah had reported, it was a black dog with white forelegs, and, indeed, the dog had a collar. A tag said "Karma, 699 Woodland Hills Lane, Highland Heights, IL." A second tag read "The Federoffs" and gave their phone number.

"Well, Jonah," his mother said, "you probably just saved the life of that dog."

Jonah said nothing. He had concluded that the dog had saved his life as well.

As Melvin Aaron learned when he called the number on the dog's tag, Adele Federoff was distraught over losing the dog three days earlier when a careless gardener had left a gate open. The Federoff home was three miles from Camp Ojliagiba. As Melvin Aaron drove to the Federoff home, he realized that to reach the spot where he and Jonah had found the dog, Karma had somehow managed to safely cross the Edens Expressway, a six-lane highway with moderately heavy traffic twenty-four hours a day. Melvin Aaron wondered how the little dog had accomplished that task. It was a mystery that would remain unsolved.

After a fitful night with little sleep, having considered that the camp was named Ojliagiba and that the dog was named Karma, Tina Aaron asked her husband if he felt that mystical forces might have been involved in saving their son's life. Jonah was after all, an obviously gifted child. "I don't know, Melvin. I saw those rocks. If he hadn't turned because he heard the dog barking . . ." She was unable to complete the sentence. "Maybe the universe has some grand design for him."

Dr. Aaron replied immediately. "Jonah and Barry are wonderful boys, but let me ask you this. If there is some grand design involved, what was the universe thinking in letting the horse get loose?"

Tina Aaron chuckled. "Good point."

While his wife drank a cup of coffee and criticized his nutritional choices, Melvin Aaron heated up two slices of cold pizza in the microwave and grabbed a banana to eat while he drove to work. He kissed his wife goodbye and left the house while his children were still asleep. Later that morning, as Jonah and Barry were eating a breakfast of scrambled eggs, pancakes, and orange juice, Tina inquired how the boys wanted to spend the day.

Jonah answered first. "Can we go to the library, mom? I want to get some detective stories."

Jonah had never read mystery novels before. He generally read biographies and books about science. "Sure. We can do that. Why the sudden interest in detective stories?"

"I think I may be good at solving mysteries."

Tina Aaron remembered the previous week's discussions about the origin of the camp name. "Oh, did you figure out which Native American tribe the word Ojliagiba came from? From what Mr. Gillespie said, I thought you never made it to the camp library yesterday."

"I didn't make it to the camp library. I didn't have to. It's not a Native American word. I figured it out yesterday when I learned that my counselor, Abby Jo, was Mr. Gillespie's daughter and that her full name was Abigail."

"So?"

Jonah shook his head. His mother could be so dense. It was obvious to him. Wasn't it obvious to her? "Abigail Jo spelled backwards is Ojliagiba. It doesn't mean mystical natural forces. Calling it 'Camp Ojliagiba' is just a hokey way to promote the camp with a name that sounds like a Native American word. Anyway, I want to read mysteries. I think I'm going to be an investigator when I grow up."

Tina Aaron lifted the camp brochure from the refrigerator door and read the name from back to front. Jonah was correct. Ojliagiba was indeed Abigail Jo spelled backwards. Tina was impressed that Jonah had figured it out. Jonah had talked about becoming a doctor, a lawyer, or an architect. She expected his interest in being an investigator would last only a few weeks or a few months. "You are going to be a lot more than an investigator," she told Jonah as she hugged him. She hugged Barry as well. "And so are you!"

Jonah Aaron was not concerned with his mother's expectations. At the age of eight he had just learned an important lesson about the value of marketing. He had concluded that the proper translation of Ojliagiba was "the right story can help you sell just about anything." It would take eight years, but the lesson would serve him—and the Dana Twins—extremely well.

3

PERSONAL STATEMENTS

A S A SENIOR in college, Eric Cain lost interest in becoming a doctor. If he had intended to become a physician, he would have submitted a serious personal statement on his application to medical school. As a general science major in the era before rampant grade inflation, Eric Cain had received mostly A's in the required pre-medical courses. His overall grade point average at South Dakota State University, SDSU, had merited election into Phi Beta Kappa. He had taken the Medical College Aptitude Test during his junior year of college and his scores put him in the top five percent of medical school applicants nationwide.

Eric never would have applied to medical school had he not read some of the personal statements submitted by his classmates. He found their pretentious dullness to be appalling. No one ever admitted that they wanted to become a doctor because they saw it as a respectable way to make a good living. Instead, his fellow students detailed a deep love of humanity and a desire to help mankind by learning, and then applying, the scientific skills needed to diagnose and treat disease. Every applicant expressed a desire to become the warm compassionate competent physician whom everyone says they want as their primary caregiver. In case that wasn't enough to impress the admissions committees around the country, personal statements often mentioned a desire to discover cures for the major maladies that afflicted mankind, an intention to win the Nobel Prize during the research elective that would be taken between their third and fourth year of medical school.

While Eric Cain was in favor of competent, compassionate care, research scared him. It wasn't that he was afraid he couldn't do research. Having taken a basic course in philosophy of science, he was afraid of what would happen if we suddenly were blessed—or would it be cursed—with a cure for cancer and heart disease. Instead of a utopia, he imagined a world full of debilitated, demented centenarians.

As he observed the cheery college seniors looking like penguins as they headed off to their medical school interviews in their white shirts and dark suits, or their white blouses and dark skirts, Eric Cain decided that there were enough physicians in the world. As a handsome man blessed with curly blond hair, blue eyes, and more than a smidgen of musical ability, he decided that he would try his hand at becoming a rock star.

While Eric Cain had the intellectual ability and the interpersonal skills to become a physician, his future success in rock music was doubtful. His college roommate, Davey Chase, had listened to Eric play with his band, The Black Hills, and had told him "You're halfway there."

"What do you mean?"

Davey Chase explained himself. "My uncle is in the music business, I've heard him say that to be a success in rock and roll you need a great piece of music and absolutely no talent. You're halfway there."

Instead of being insulted, Eric Cain said "Thanks for the advice." He began working on original compositions, trying to come up with the great piece of music that would compensate for his lack of talent. As a result, the Black Hills became the leading party band in a three state area.

Nevertheless, despite having decided against a career in medicine, as a lark, Eric Cain chose to apply to medical school. Amidst the scores of platitudinous, self-serving, boring personal statements, his application was aimed at keeping members of admissions committees awake, rather than putting them to sleep. He anticipated that the admissions committees around the country might laugh at his application and he doubted that his personal statement would lead anyone to offer him a position in a medical school class. Had he been offered a position, his intent was to turn it down.

Personal statement: In 1750 to 2000 words please explain why you wish to become a physician.

> Many individuals experience a life changing event that makes them appreciate medicine. For some individuals this involves the illness of a family member or the death of a friend. For others, the life changing event might be an accident or an experience in the military. For me, it was the wart.

I was seventeen years old and the wart was on the heel of my left foot. I knew nothing about warts. I was a junior at a suburban Chicago high school and warts were not in the curriculum. Even if warts had been in the curriculum, I might not have paid attention. School was easy and boring. Aside from playing hockey, my major interests were playing guitar and performing lead vocals in a rock band called Electra's Fathers. We compensated for our deficiencies in talent by the use of excess volume. It was a strategy that kept us in great demand on Chicago's north shore.

It was Sally Templeton who told me that what I had thought was a splinter was actually a wart. Sally was a wholesome looking strawberry blonde who dressed conservatively, spoke quietly, got straight A's, and neither smoked, drank, nor wore make-up. Her parents had once hoped that she would become a professional musician and play in a symphony orchestra. At the age of eight, however, Sally had given up the violin in favor of the bass guitar. Sally was the only talented musician in the band and was also a closet courtesan. Her father, Dr. Walter Templeton, III, was a gynecologist whose subspecialty was sexual dysfunction. Sally's home reading would have made a whore blush. At the age of sixteen, during her junior year in high school, Sally graduated from reading to practical experience. For the record, Sally did not indulge in romantic fantasies about me, and, from my point of view, she was simply my bass guitar player-with benefits.

Some people jog; some people ride mountain bikes. Sally and I had our own uncomplicated form of exercise. Some of our exercises put Sally in a position where she could see the sole of my left foot. While Sally's sex drive merely wore me out, it was her limited knowledge of medicine that nearly killed me. Sally recognized that I had a wart and that I needed to see a doctor. My fate was nearly sealed in four steps.

Step One. We drove to the office of Dr. Gerald Danforth, a general practitioner. He was chosen not on the basis of talent, but because my father, an accountant, did his tax returns, and he gave my family free medical care in exchange. Warts can be frozen off, burned off, or cut off. Dr. Danforth decided to use a new treatment that he had read about in the *Journal of the American Medical Association*. He injected the wart with a toxic chemical. As I suspect the members of the admission committee know, there is a motto in medicine that says "see one, do one, teach one." Dr. Danforth had never used the medicine, and having never witnessed the procedure, he neglected the step where the drug was diluted by a factor of ten.

Step Two: Three days later, on Saturday, Electra's Fathers performed at the Spring Fling at New Trier West High School. After the dance, I collapsed as I got in our van. Glenn and Adam, the other two members of Electra's Fathers wanted to take me to a hospital, but Sally convinced them that I just needed to sleep it off. She claimed to know what she was talking about because her father was a doctor. Glenn and Adam overlooked the facts that her father was a gynecologist and that a doctor's daughter is not a doctor. I am no longer on speaking terms with Glenn and Adam.

Step Three: Sally dropped me off at my home. My father was asleep; my mother noticed that I had a little rash and felt as if I had a fever. She decided it was nothing. My mother was not a doctor. Five critical hours were wasted. Born 1957, died 1975—almost. At five in the morning my mother found me moaning deliriously and talking about a basketball game being played on a triangular court with three baskets and three teams. I had a temperature of 106 degrees. My mother concluded that I was sick. One hundred and six is bad; at one hundred and seven—sell. I suppose I shouldn't complain. She did eventually call an ambulance, but wasting five hours with a dying teenager is unforgivable. I am no longer on speaking terms with my mother.

Step Four: The ambulance took me to a private hospital where the emergency room did a blood count and found out that I had no white blood cells to fight infection. Assuming that I had acute leukemia, which I have since been told was the most likely possibility, they sent me to Chicago Medical Institute, CMI. Had I stayed at the private hospital, I would have been dead in twenty-four hours. I was living on inertia. A body in motion tends to stay in motion unless acted upon by an outside force. Pseudomonas septicemia, infection with the Pseudomonas bacteria, is one heck of an outside force. Of course, since the members of the admissions committee are doctors, you don't need me to tell you that.

The only reason that I didn't die that Sunday morning was that the resident in the Intensive Care Unit at CMI was Sarah Pitt. Dr.

Pitt was interested in Infectious Diseases and was extremely well read. She was not as well read as Sally Templeton, I suspect, but she had read a recent article in a medical journal, and recognized my rash as a sign of pseudomonas infection, an infection that doesn't happen in normal teenagers. Of course, normal teenagers have not had their white cell count reduced to zero by receiving a ten-fold overdose of an anti-wart medicine from an incompetent primary care doctor. For the record, my family was well-off and there was no reason that my father should have insisted that I receive my medical care from an incompetent fool just because he and my father had worked out a stupid barter arrangement in order to avoid paying taxes. I am no longer on speaking terms with my father.

Sarah Pitt performed an emergency bone marrow examination. The marrow exam showed that I didn't have leukemia; I had a toxic drug reaction and overwhelming sepsis. Is there such a thing as underwhelming sepsis? Well, I guess that's one of the things I will learn in medical school, if I am accepted.

Sarah Pitt started me on gentamicin, an antibiotic, and saved my life. Dr. Pitt also did a complete physical exam and noted that I had an infection the size of a silver dollar on the bottom of my foot. Most doctors would never have examined the bottom of my foot; most doctors would have been filling out my death certificate in the morning. Sarah Pitt consulted a surgeon to drain the infection in the middle of the night; she gave me a fighting chance. Dr. Pitt is the most wonderful doctor in the world, and if she didn't have a restraining order out against me in the state of Illinois for stalking her, I would probably be dating her even though she was twenty-seven and I was seventeen when we met. However, I am a law abiding citizen and therefore am no longer speaking to Dr. Sarah Pitt.

The road to recovery was not an easy one. I developed both kidney failure and pneumonia. I spent two weeks on dialysis and four weeks on a ventilator—or perhaps it was the other way around. I can hardly be blamed for not knowing since I was in a coma for thirty-one days. During that time, my parents were told that if I pulled through I would probably be a vegetable. I have always wondered if they meant an eggplant or a squash. For what it is worth, I love eggplant; I hate squash. When I awoke from my coma, completely lucid, one of the nurses in Intensive Care said that it was a miracle. My personal opinion is that like most so-called medical miracles, my recovery simply represented an error in prognostication. Before the wart, I had been young and healthy. Given time and excellent medical care, I recovered. I don't see a miracle in that, but there is no sense arguing the point.

After two months in a rehabilitation unit, I took my final exams, received credit for my senior year of high school, and graduated. I matriculated at South Dakota State University where I have majored in biology. I even worked myself into shape and managed to walk-on to varsity hockey where I have earned a scholarship on a team that is in contention for a national championship. I had once considered trying out for basketball, but even though I am Methodist, my nickname on the basketball court was "Catholic" because my defensive skills were none, as in "nun" as in "Catholic." It was my college roommate, Davey Chase, who gave me that nickname which I find most embarrassing. I am no longer speaking to Davey Chase.

My near death experience had an interesting impact on Sally Templeton. She recognized that her limited knowledge of medicine had nearly killed me, and she was impressed with the technology that had been used to save my life. Sally Templeton decided to pursue a career in medicine in order to immerse herself in that technology. Unfortunately, when she told me how impressed she was with all the equipment that had been used to save my life, I made an immature comment to the effect that the only equipment I was interested in was hers. Sally Templeton broke off our "relationship" and quit speaking to me.

I learned a great deal from this experience. Life is precious; don't waste it. Relationships are important; choose them carefully. Doctors can help you if they are dedicated and know what they are doing; they can kill you if they don't. I want to be one of the doctors who knows what he is doing. My reason for choosing your medical school is that as of this coming July, Sarah Pitt will be joining your faculty in the Division of Infectious Diseases. There is no order of protection against me in your state and one never knows what can happen.

While I really can offer no reason that I will be a better student than any other applicant, I would like to mention that I will not be needing any of your scarce scholarship money as the malpractice settlement with Dr. Danforth put over six hundred thousand dollars in my personal bank account. Dr. Danforth is no longer speaking to my family and has retained services of a new accountant.

Respectfully submitted,
Eric Cain
South Dakota State University
Brookings, South Dakota 1978

P.S. If I am accepted to medical school, I would like to request that my admission be deferred for at least one year. My college rock band, The Black Hills, has been renamed Night Shadow and I believe that we have the potential to be successful. We will be starting a national tour the month after graduation. *Rolling Stone Magazine,* in a review of collegiate bands, has stated that we are completely devoid of talent and play the melody on the drums. We appreciated the publicity, but I respectfully disagree with their assessment. I have cancelled my subscription to *Rolling Stone Magazine.*

That personal statement was embellished for effect. The story of the wart, Sally Templeton's role in its diagnosis, the fact that Eric Cain ended up in the ICU with low blood counts, and the settlement of the malpractice suit were all true. However, Eric Cain was never in a coma; Davey Chase, the goaltender on the South Dakota State hockey team, was Eric Cain's roommate and best friend; Sarah Pitt had neither dated Eric Cain nor requested a restraining order. She had never considered an academic career and was a general internist in private practice.

Eric Cain applied to nine medical schools including the South Dakota State University School of Medicine; he received nine letters of rejection. If not for Ryan Chance, Eric Cain would never have become a physician.

In February of 1979, The South Dakota State University hockey team competed for the NCAA Championship in the Frozen Four. In the finals, Eric Cain, a defenseman, spent much of the game harassing BU's star center, Ryan Chance, a superb athlete who went on to play in the National Hockey League for seven seasons. While Eric Cain and his teammates kept a heavily favored Boston University team off the scoreboard, as the clock ran down the final minutes of regulation in the championship game, SDSU and Boston University were tied 0-0. With the game headed to overtime, a nearly exhausted Eric Cain, who had spent forty seven minutes on the ice, leveled Ryan Chance with a vicious, but completely legal check. Ryan Chance retaliated by ramming Eric Cain into the boards, drawing a two minute penalty. Eric Cain could easily have ducked out of the way of the charging Ryan Chance; he took the hit for the good of his team.

Ryan Chance's indiscretion put SDSU on the power play and with six seconds left in regulation, Eric Cain fired a slap shot from the point and scored the only goal of the game. Needless to say, he became a school hero.

There are many hockey fans in South Dakota, among them several members of the Board of Overseers at South Dakota State University. Noting that Eric Cain had applied to and been rejected by the SDSU School of Medicine, without Eric Cain's knowledge, they persuaded the Medical School Dean to award the second string all-American defenseman a position in the class entering SDSU School of Medicine that fall. When the dean met with Eric Cain to tell him the news, the dean said, "Mr. Cain, I have reviewed your application, especially your personal statement. Even though I think you have no business in medical school, I see no point in challenging the Board of Overseers. I'm glad to welcome you to the Medical School Class of 1983. If you end up graduating from medical school, I will be the most surprised man on the planet. With your attitude I expect that you will flunk out during your first year. If you want to take a year off, two years off, or your whole life off before you matriculate, it is fine with me."

Eric Cain was shocked that anyone, let alone the dean of SDSU School of Medicine, had taken his personal statement seriously. While he had been intending to explain to the dean that he had no interest in becoming a physician, he took the dean's comment as a challenge.

Eric Cain spent the next four years as the lead vocalist and rhythm guitar player in Night Shadow, a group briefly mentioned in the *Encyclopedia of Rock and Roll* as being "a weak imitation of the glitter rock band, Kiss, but with less outrageous makeup and an order of magnitude less talent." Nevertheless, Night Shadow sold over three million records and had two hits reach the Top Twenty on *Billboard,* "Thinking Big" and the somewhat oedipal tune, "A Boy's Best Friend (Is His Mother)."

Often bored on the road, Eric Cain used his free time to pen an autobiography which included, as its opening chapter, the personal statement from his medical school application. The book was a tale of sex, drugs, and rock and roll, though Eric Cain claimed to have gone heavy on the sex and to have abstained from drugs. His band mates were less discriminating. Night Shadow's drummer and bass guitar player eventually succumbed to drug overdoses.

Night Shadow, the book, presented a cogent argument that the only reason to go into rock and roll was to get laid, and that the music was incidental. According to *Night Shadow*, the number of women with whom Eric Cain had slept while on tour was somewhere between five hundred and six hundred. The true number is impossible to ascertain. While Eric Cain was scrupulously honest as a physician, he rarely let the truth get in the way of telling a good story.

In contrast to the band's relative success, following reviews which proclaimed it "a witty, satirical, raunchy commentary on life on the road with a rock-and-roll band," *Night Shadow*, the book, was a commercial failure. Eric Cain claimed, only somewhat facetiously, that it had sold exactly twelve copies.

In the fall of 1983, Eric Cain returned to South Dakota and matriculated with the Class of 1987. To the surprise of the dean and the faculty, he graduated as a member of Alpha Omega Alpha, the national medical honor society. When the time came for Eric Cain to write a personal statement as part of his internship application, he wrote the following.

I was a teenager when I first saw the classic painting by Sir Luke Fildes entitled "The Doctor," showing an exhausted general practitioner who had been up all night at the bedside of a sick child. His compassion is exemplary but if penicillin had been invented at that time, the parents would not be anxiously awaiting the outcome of their child's illness. Their child would have already recovered. Instead of spending the night at the bedside of a sick child, the physician would have been able to spend the evening with his family.

I learned the value of combining compassion with scientific knowledge when I was ill as a teenager, and a caring, competent medical resident and her team at Chicago Medical Institute saved my life. At that moment I chose to devote myself to a career in medicine.

Lacking the maturity to move directly from college to medical school, I took a brief detour to explore a career in a rock band. However, after four years I returned to medical school with a single-minded devotion to my future profession. While my experiences as manager, lead singer, and rhythm guitarist are obviously not directly applicable to medicine, I did learn to manage a team, and the stage presence which I learned on the job will likely help me as a lecturer if I go into academic medicine.

During medical school I have developed an interest in cardiology, and I have been impressed by the fact that technologic advances often make medicine more expensive, without demonstrating benefit proportional to cost. Upon completion of my medical residency, and a fellowship in cardiology, I hope to develop an automated, computerized approach to the interpretation of electrocardiograms. While physicians could of course supplement or override the computer, such an advance would be time saving, cost saving, and quite possibly life-saving. In the middle of the night, an exhausted physician, like the one in Sir Luke Fildes' painting, might be prone to error. The computerized system would be as accurate at three in the morning as it would be at high noon.

The personal statement represented both maturity on the part of Dr. Cain, as well as his ability to master the use of platitudes. His letters of recommendation were enthusiastic. His scores on the National Board exams, taken after the second year of medical school, placed him in the top three percent of students nationwide. When the CMI committee that evaluated prospective interns reviewed his application only one physician raised concerns about accepting Eric Cain into the program.

Dr. Melvin Aaron commented, "You can get the young man out of rock and roll, but are we certain we can get the rock and roll out of the young man and have an intern who isn't a disruptive force here at CMI?" The committee answered in the affirmative and because of his concerns, Dr. Aaron was assigned the task of being Dr. Cain's attending physician during Eric Cain's first intern rotation at CMI.

At the medical school graduation, the dean congratulated Eric Cain as he handed him his diploma and asked, "Where are you headed for internship? I've forgotten."

"Chicago Medical Institute. They're at the forefront of the use of computers in medicine."

"A fine program," the dean replied. "Congratulations."

Of course, as Eric Cain told the story afterwards, he hadn't answered the dean's question. After all, according Eric Cain's version of the story, he and the dean were not on speaking terms.

4

MUCH TOO CLOSE

EVERY JULY, NEW medical interns begin their careers with enthusiasm, motivation, a critical lack of experience and a limited fund of knowledge. While it is therefore easy to feel sorry for the patients who come to a teaching hospital at that time, one should also extend a measure of sympathy to the freshly minted interns and residents for whom the start of the academic year often involves a confrontation with a tsunami of responsibility. In July of 1987, the most significant confrontation that occurred at Chicago Medical Institute involved the members of General Medicine Team C.

The team, based on the eleventh floor of CMI, consisted of a medical resident, Dr. Roy Danton, and two medical interns, Dr. Eric Cain and Dr. Gail Riley. Dr. Melvin Aaron, the attending physician for the month, was responsible for meeting with the team on a daily basis to review the new admissions and provide a modicum of supervision. As a medical oncologist, Dr. Aaron was, by neces ity, very involved with managing the patients when he was the attending physician on the cancer medicine team. However, whenever he was assigned to general internal medicine, he took a more laissez-faire attitude, giving the young doctors more responsibility to determine plans for diagnosis and treatment. He felt, quite reasonably, that it gave them the opportunity to grow as professionals.

Roy Danton, the resident, was a small man from the small town of Ewan, Washington, in the eastern part of the state. He was, by far, the outstanding student at the regional high school, and, having been voted Most Likely to Succeed by his high school classmates, he came to expect great things of himself. Growing up in a small town, he had never confronted the character building experience called failure.

Roy Danton attended college and medical school at Washington State University where he graduated in the top one tenth of his class. As a child he had suffered from asthma, and he intended to pursue a career in pulmonary medicine. He had become a medical intern at CMI in July 1985; in July 1987 he was starting his third year of post-graduate training.

His fellow house officers considered Dr. Danton to be an only an average intern and a less than average resident. However, the faculty considered him to be a rising star. Although none of the papers had yet to appear in print, Dr. Danton had managed to have eight manuscripts accepted for publication in medical journals during the first year of his residency. That was six more than the number of papers accepted for publication by the other nineteen physicians in his residency group.

During his first year of residency, Dr. Danton had approached the attending physicians at CMI and had defined mini-projects that he could perform in their laboratories in his spare time, a commodity that the other first year residents working ninety to one hundred hours a week apparently lacked.

Roy Danton appeared to have a golden touch in the laboratory. As his second year of residency started, he had already been awarded a fellowship in pulmonary medicine at CMI scheduled to start in July 1988. He would have been on the fast track for a faculty position at the medical center except for the fact that there were concerns about his clinical judgment.

Like most physicians, Roy Danton was upset when patients died. Unlike most physicians, he had failed to appreciate the fact that there is a time when nature should be allowed to take its course, when patients should be allowed to die peacefully, and when further medical care represents cruel and unusual punishment. Patients who die suddenly and unexpectedly from cardiac arrhythmias may at times be successfully resuscitated; patients in whom death is the final event in a downward medical spiral almost never leave the hospital alive let alone with anything resembling health.

For that latter group of patients, a medical truism states that if one can't keep a patient alive when he is alive, one can't keep him alive when he is dead. Nevertheless, Roy Danton favored attempting to resuscitate every patient who experienced a cardiac arrest. Since the patients subjected to his personal brand of irrelevant, extraordinary care were often beyond the point of suffering, it was their families who endured most of the pain engendered by Roy Danton's inhumane approach to terminal illness.

However, despite his questionable judgment regarding end of life care, Dr. Danton would have been an almost adequate medical resident if not for the fact that he was dishonest, a trait that had not been appreciated by his colleagues or supervisors during his internship and first year of residency.

By the start of the twenty-first century, the medical literature would be easily accessible via the ubiquitous desktop computers that sprung up like weeds on the medical units of most hospitals. In 1987, however, to review the medical literature required a trip to the medical library, a place rarely seen by interns whose workloads approached one hundred hours a week. A medical resident who could quote the medical literature and cite the basis for relevant scientific principles was a treasure.

No matter how obscure the clinical problem, Roy Danton was generally able to provide his interns with a reference to a relevant medical publication. There was only one flaw with Roy Danton's medical references. They were often wrong. After the event that marked the midpoint of his July rotation as one of Roy Danton's interns, Eric Cain frequently referred to his resident as "a wise old owl." The term was meant as a pejorative term rather than as a compliment. Eric Cain always added that in the child's classic, *Winnie the Pooh*, Owl was considered the smartest animal in the forest because he could spell Saturday. Of course, as the author, A.A. Milne, had noted, Owl spelled it incorrectly, but at least he could spell it.

Roy Danton developed the habit of giving inaccurate references by accident. In April of his intern year, he quoted a paper on the treatment of lymphoma and, that afternoon, in the medical library, he found that he had attributed the paper to the wrong group of authors and had overstated their results. This was hardly a major crime. When he provided copies of the paper to his medical team the next morning, as a form of apology, he realized that no one had bothered to go to the library in order to find the publication. No one had discovered his mistake.

Roy Danton began to intentionally give incorrect references as a way of demonstrating to himself that no one was scholarly enough to check out the misinformation that he was providing. Eventually, having acquired a reputation as a master of the medical literature, he felt obligated to provide citations related to obscure facts. Some of those references were manufactured on the spot. On a medical service where interns were overworked and where attending physicians were often more interested in returning to their research laboratories than with reading a journal article, not once was Roy Danton challenged about an erroneous reference. Keeping his interns busy with meaningless tasks was both a consequence of Dr. Danton's poor judgment and a means of keeping his interns away from the medical library. That it compromised patient care did not cross his mind. As the academic year began in July 1987, Roy Danton entered a collision course with the two interns on Internal Medicine Team C.

While Eric Cain had reached CMI with a resume that included a NCAA championship in ice hockey and four years with the rock band, Night Shadow, Gail Riley arrived on Medicine Team C with more standard academic credentials. She had graduated from Harvard College and had received her M.D. from Harvard Medical School where she also obtained a Ph.D. in Molecular Biology in 1987. Like Eric Cain she had also been a member of AOA. Also like Dr. Cain, whose single publication was his embellished autobiography, *Night Shadow,* Dr. Riley had a solitary publication, her doctoral dissertation on the significance of protein tau-zeta on the malignant potential of the squamous epithelium of the lung.

At the time she began her internship, Gail Riley was an avid photographer, a cross country skier, and a lover of country music. In marked contrast to Eric Cain, the number of individuals of the opposite sex with whom Gail Riley had slept could have been counted on one hand even if she were missing three fingers. She had married one of the men, Larry Patterson, after the seventh of the twelve years that she had spent at Harvard. Larry Patterson was a brilliant man who held a Ph.D. in Physics. Like Gail Riley, he wanted no children, and he had no problem with the fact that his wife was as devoted to her work as he was to his.

Best of all, as far as Gail Riley was concerned, Larry Patterson appreciated her sense of humor. Shortly after they had gotten engaged, Larry asked her what she intended to do about her name. She replied, "Riley is a good name; Patterson is a good name; hyphenated names are a pain in the butt." She took a quarter out of her wallet and said "Heads we'll be Riley; tails we'll be Patterson. Is that okay?" They both started laughing so hard, that neither of them caught the coin when she tossed it and it had rolled into a sewer.

Gail Riley was an extremely attractive brunette. Eric Cain became fond of telling mutual acquaintances that she had been a second runner-up in the Miss Rhode Island contest at the age of eighteen. If she had entered the competition, it might well have been true, but Gail had no interest in beauty pageants. She had, however, garnered a first place award in the Rhode Island High School State Science Fair. Gail Riley possessed a charming smile, and, when she was single, had no trouble attracting and rejecting men. One of the reasons she had married Larry Patterson was that she believed that simplifying her personal life would be a major advantage in having a career.

As a medical student, Gail Riley had taken a visiting elective at CMI in the spring of 1985 and had decided to rank the institution as her first choice when entering the national matching program for an internship. Her husband had obtained his doctorate in Physics from M.I.T. a year before Gail Riley obtained her M.D., and, during his post-doctoral fellowship, he had been offered a faculty position at the University of Chicago. Dr. Riley had the option of staying in Boston, and having a commuter marriage, or applying for a position in Chicago. The excellence of the program at CMI convinced her that she could live with her husband without compromising the quality of her medical training.

In the first hour of her internship she met her resident, Roy Danton, and started to have doubts about the training she would receive at CMI. However, despite her resident's shortcomings, under ordinary circumstances, Gail Riley would have completed the month with Roy Danton as her resident and each of them would have moved on to the remaining eleven months of their respective internship and residency. That it didn't happen was in large part due to Eric Cain.

*   *   *

Eric Cain's first admission as an intern was a twenty-one year old heroin addict, with eyes and skin as orange as a pumpkin. The diagnosis was obvious—viral hepatitis. Dr. Cain had handled more difficult cases as a fourth year medical student and his diagnostic plan was simple. He would obtain a battery of serologic studies to determine which type of hepatitis was present—hepatitis B and hepatitis C were the likely offenders—and rule in, or rule out, the presence of HIV, the virus that had been identified as the cause of AIDS. The treatment plan was equally straightforward: support the patient until she could eat without having

RICHARD STEIN

nausea or vomiting, and then discharge her to the Hepatology (Liver) Clinic for follow-up.

When Roy Danton suggested that a liver biopsy be performed, Eric Cain thought that his resident was joking. Patients with severe liver disease caused by hepatitis are at risk of serious, even fatal, bleeding if a liver biopsy is done. A biopsy was unnecessary and inappropriate. Eric Cain chose not to consult the liver team who, in any case, would have vetoed the idea of performing a biopsy. Roy Danton told his intern, "Cain, This is an academic institution. You have a bad attitude. We are here to know."

Both in the hockey rink and in medical school, Eric Cain had learned to stand up for himself. "No. We are here to help patients. Tests are indicated when the benefit exceeds the risk. Unnecessary testing is wasteful and can be dangerous." Eric Cain appreciated that it is better and simpler to test for what is likely and what is critical, and then do other tests only if one hadn't found an answer. Eric Cain had devoted a considerable amount of time and effort to seducing women but he had graduated medical school near the top of his class.

Roy Danton believed in "every possible test for every possible diagnosis." He repeated the mantra when he and the two interns made work rounds early in the morning, before Dr. Aaron, the attending physician, arrived on the floor. He repeated it when they signed out their patients at the end of the day. Fortunately for Eric Cain, the policy at CMI was that only interns could enter orders into the chart. As a result, Eric Cain accepted only an occasional suggestion from Roy Danton and managed to deliver first rate medical care to his patients.

Dr. Riley was less fortunate. Having spent her final years at Harvard in the molecular biology laboratory working towards her Ph.D., she was well prepared for a career in research, but less well prepared to be an intern on an active clinical medicine service. Dr. Cain felt safe ignoring Roy Danton; he either muddled through or asked one of the residents assigned to another service for advice. Gail Riley, however, was at Roy Danton's mercy. Under the direction of Roy Danton, Gail Riley's patients were subjected to a substantial overuse of diagnostic tests and procedures.

Both Eric Cain and Gail Riley could create a list of five or six possible diagnoses for most clinical problems. However, while Eric Cain ordered tests selectively, Gail Riley, under the misdirection of Roy Danton, often ordered tests for obscure diagnostic possibilities and spent her days and nights chasing down irrelevant test results. Occasionally, one of the unnecessary tests gave a false positive result, suggesting that a condition was present when it was not and leading to further unnecessary testing.

During the first week in July, Gail Riley admitted a nineteen year old woman who was transferred from the Obstetrics service when she became short of breath after delivering her baby. Her chest x-ray showed a pulmonary infiltrate. Because the woman had bled significantly during the delivery, she had been transfused with four units of packed red blood cells. The following morning, as Eric Cain listened to Dr. Riley present the case to Dr. Aaron, he concluded that there was a ninety-nine percent chance that the woman had either fluid overload from the blood transfusions or an allergic reaction to the transfusions, an uncommon condition known as transfusion related acute lung injury.

After Gail Riley concluded her case presentation by mentioning those possibilities, Roy Danton commented that there were over a hundred causes of such an infiltrate on a chest x-ray. The first condition he mentioned was silo filler's lung. Gail Riley apologized for not mentioning the malady. To Roy Danton's surprise, instead of being impressed by his erudition, Dr. Aaron commented that "it might be best to stick to disorders that might actually be present instead of confusing the issue by enumerating irrelevant possibilities."

Despite attending medical school in the farm state of South Dakota, Eric Cain had never heard of silo filler's lung. After rounds, he picked up the textbook of medicine located in the doctor's area on the unit. Reading the single paragraph devoted to the rare condition, he learned that silo filler's lung occurs in farmers who are exposed to the nitrogen dioxide that accumulates at the top of poorly ventilated silos when they are filled with fresh organic material.

Eric Cain doubted that there were any poorly ventilated silos in the part of Chicago where the patient lived and he was willing to bet that a nineteen year old woman who was nine months pregnant hadn't climbed up into the upper levels of a silo to take some deep breaths. Dr. Aaron had apparently used similar reasoning.

Eric Cain suspected that Gail Riley's ability to synthesize information would improve over time. However, considering that Roy Danton was in his third year of training after medical school, Eric Cain suspected that Dr. Danton was both a complete fool and a hopeless case. Dr. Cain also realized that while Dr. Aaron was maintaining his distance and allowing the house staff to manage the patients, he was a knowledgeable clinician.

It was with respect to cardiac resuscitation that the differences in the experiences of the two interns were the most dramatic. Since he didn't order tests that weren't indicated, Eric Cain didn't waste hours tracking down irrelevant test results. He was able to spend time with his critically ill patients and their families discussing prognosis and the possibility of resuscitation. Dr. Cain found the discussions to be difficult, but he considered Roy Danton's strategy of resuscitating everyone to reflect laziness as well as a lack of both compassion and judgment.

Eric Cain always pointed out the long odds of resuscitation being successful and took care to mention the moderately high probability, especially in older patients, that the net result might be a near vegetative existence. When one of Eric Cain's patients died, and Roy Danton would start to call for the Code Team to initiate resuscitation, Eric Cain would point out that the patient and their family had opted for DNR status, Do Not Resuscitate.

Repeatedly, Roy Danton would ask Eric Cain, "How are you going to learn to resuscitate people if you don't resuscitate your patients?"

"Fortunately, I learned that in medical school. I took a cardiology elective. I'll do it when it's appropriate. This is not that time."

Whenever Eric Cain disregarded a suggestion, which was a frequent occurrence, Roy Danton would glare at Eric Cain and walk away. He planned on waiting until Eric Cain made a terrible mistake and then humiliate him. But, despite being a novice intern, Eric Cain made no major mistakes. Whenever his limited fund of knowledge placed him at a loss as to a course of action and Roy Danton's advice seemed questionable, he would track down Harry Falk, the resident on Medicine Team B. Harry Falk regarded Roy Danton as a fool and he was glad to offer assistance to any intern unlucky enough to have been assigned to work with Roy Danton.

As a result, things went smoothly for Eric Cain and had he chosen to go to the library instead of spending much of his scant free time talking to his patients, the situation might quickly have become even better. However, that required a more scholarly frame of mind.

On the other hand, if a patient of Gail Riley suffered a cardiac arrest, it was likely that Dr. Riley had been so busy chasing down the results of the tests that Roy Danton had convinced her to order that there had been no discussion of what to do in the event of the patient's death. As a result, an attempt would be made to resuscitate the patient. If the resuscitation was successful, in the short term, the patient would almost certainly end up on a ventilator, unable to communicate in any manner. If the blood pressure was then unstable, as usually happened, Gail Riley would be awake all night doing micromanagement of her hopeless case.

After Gail Riley honed her skills in the nocturnal management of ventilators and the use of medications to support blood pressure, Roy Danton would evaluate the patient in the morning, note that there had been no improvement, and would belatedly draw the conclusion that the situation was indeed hopeless. He would then instruct Gail Riley to suggest to the family that care be withdrawn. This left Gail Riley distressed, left the family confused and angry, and left the patient just as dead as if resuscitation had not been attempted in the first place.

Roy Danton's approach to medical care would not have led to major consequences except for one fact. Gail Riley was a beautiful married woman. Had she been both beautiful and single, Eric Cain would have attempted to sleep with her. Given the effect that exhaustion has on judgment, he might have succeeded. However, Eric Cain had a rigid moral code that stated "No Married Women—Ever." There certainly were far more than enough available single women. Gail Riley awakened Eric Cain's sense of chivalry, not his lust. Unfortunately for Roy Danton, chivalry includes the slaying of dragons.

* * *

After nearly two weeks of frustration working with Roy Danton, the act that enraged Gail Riley and energized Eric Cain occurred on the night of July 12. On the following morning, Eric Cain arrived at work and was greeted by his co-intern.

"God damn it, Eric, you won't believe what happened last night."

Eric Cain yawned, having been up much of the night enjoying the charms of a nurse who worked on the pediatrics unit. "Try me. I'll believe anything."

"Roy did it. I swear he did. I fell asleep in the Intensive Care Unit, and he woke me up and said, 'Don't worry Gail, everything will be all right.' He was standing there with a pair of defibrillator paddles in his hand, pretending I had had a cardiac arrest. He had unsnapped my scrubs and started to put the paddles on my chest."

Eric Cain's jaw dropped. "What were you wearing?"

"Scrubs."

"No. I mean under the scrubs. How bad was this?"

"I was wearing a bra. I guess it's still sexual harassment. Anyhow, I can handle a little hazing, but this was out of line. I almost wish I had had a cardiac arrest. Then this horrible internship would be over."

Most doctors would have disregarded that comment, but Eric Cain was well aware that the rate of suicide was high in the medical professions. He had observed that Gail Riley was having a horrific intern experience. "Are you serious? About wanting the internship to be over that way?"

"Of course not. If I wanted it over, I'd just quit. I haven't thought seriously about hurting myself. I have a Ph.D. to fall back on. I can always go into the lab. But thanks for being concerned. Seriously. That was nice of you, and very professional."

Eric Cain was flattered. An intern from Harvard had complimented him, the intern from South Dakota State, on his professionalism. "Where would you run away?"

"What?"

"You talked about quitting. I was curious if you had picked out a place to go before you started up your career again."

She hadn't thought about that either. "I don't know. Bermuda. I wanted to go there on our honeymoon. Larry wanted to go to Belize. We tossed a coin. I lost. I'd go to Bermuda. What about you? Where would you go if you ran away from life?"

"Acapulco."

"That was a quick answer. How come?"

There was no reason not to be truthful. "I'd go to Acapulco because every time I have been there I have hooked up with an absolutely fabulous American woman who was on vacation. If we ran off to Acapulco together, I'd be guaranteed to have a fabulous American woman."

"We're running off together?" She was laughing.

"Other than your husband, why not?"

"I'll keep it in mind. And thanks for calling me fabulous. I sure don't feel fabulous." She was shocked at how much better her mood was from a couple of minutes of chatting with Eric Cain and she could see why he was so successful with women. He was an outrageous flirt. "Seriously though, can you believe that he pulled that stunt with the defibrillator paddles on me? You're the one he hates. He says you have a bad attitude, but I'm the one he treats with no respect."

Eric Cain almost made a sarcastic comment that it was likely difficult for Roy Danton to treat Gail Riley with respect when she was, intellectually speaking, getting fucked over all day long. He thought better of it. "Of course he didn't do it to me. He doesn't know what might happen if he did. Did you say anything?"

"I told him it wasn't funny. One of the nurses saw it. She told him that if he ever did anything like that again in the ICU, she'd see to it that he was fired. A pharmacy technician saw the whole thing. She was outraged. She said she was sending an e-mail to the Chairman of the Department of Medicine. I didn't tell her not to, but I bet she won't do it. People never follow through on things like that."

"You ought to stand up to him. He's a total loss."

"I can't. And he's not a total loss. He's always giving us those references, not that I have time to read any of them. And he is really good when it comes to managing asthma."

Not knowing that Roy Danton had asthma, neither Gail Riley nor Eric Cain realized that patients with asthma were the only patients on Medicine Team C for whom Roy Danton recommended appropriate compassionate care. "Yeah, but who cares about references? I write them down, too, but I don't go to the library. Who gets to go to the library?" The implied answer was no one. "Don't worry, Gail. I'll take care of it."

"What can you do?"

Eric Cain shrugged his shoulders and walked off to see his patients. At the time, he had no answer and no plan.

Allen Minton, the Chairman of the Department of Medicine received the e-mail about the incident in the ICU and forwarded it to Dr. Richie Gold, the Chief Resident in Medicine with a brief comment saying, "Take care of this." The Chairman was a master at delegating responsibility and house staff misbehavior was the province of the Chief Resident, a third-year resident being groomed for a faculty position.

Dr. Minton noted that Annette Adams, the pharmacy technician who had sent the e-mail, seemed to have some issues of her own. In reporting what had happened to Gail Riley in the ICU she described Roy Danton as a "dangerous pervert" and a "disgrace to the medical profession who should be strung up by his private parts." Based on her description of the incident, that seemed extreme. However, Allen Minton did not meddle in other people's programs. He left Annette Adams' anger management issues to the Pharmacy Department.

Had Dr. Gold taken the matter more seriously, it wouldn't have been necessary for Eric Cain to do anything. During his internship, Roy Danton had been warned about boorish behavior toward female medical students. He had been told that the next incident might lead to a two week suspension without pay.

As in the case of the new interns and the newly promoted residents, the Chief Resident had assumed his role on the first of July. Dr. Gold knew that if he suspended Roy Danton, another resident would have to be pulled off a relatively comfortable rotation in the out-patient clinics and assigned to Medicine Team C. The Chief Resident did not want to start his academic year by generating discontent among the residents. However, he didn't want Dr. Minton to feel that he was letting the matter slide. He sent the following e-mail to Roy Danton. "You have been warned about the possibility of suspension for this type of action. Forget about suspension. If there is another incident of inappropriate behavior, or if I have any reason to doubt your adherence to the professional and ethical standards of the medical profession, your residency will be terminated. We will meet to discuss this one week from today. Please reply suggesting a time for our meeting. Early afternoon is best for me." He copied Dr. Minton on the e-mail. Had the Chief Resident been more experienced, he would have sent a copy of the note to Dr. Gail Riley. However, having been on the job for less than two weeks, he overlooked that option and, as a result, Dr. Riley had the mistaken impression that no action was being taken.

Since Gail had been on call the previous night, after a long day at CMI, she headed home a little after seven. It was Eric Cain's turn to spend a night in the hospital.

"Give your husband a hug, and come back in better spirits," Eric Cain advised Gail Riley as she left the eleventh floor of CMI.

Gail Riley couldn't manage a smile, let alone a hug. At home she explained the situation to her husband. Larry Patterson was an extremely patient man, and a good listener. He wished that he could think of something to do. Earlier that day, by phone, he had suggested that his wife talk to the Chief Medical Resident. Gail had called the Chief Resident's office and had been told by his secretary that the earliest appointment that could be scheduled was July 26, in two weeks.

At the start of the academic year, Dr. Gold had been informed by Dr. Minton that the new interns were often upset during the month of July, and that most problems, if left alone, would pass on their own, like a painful kidney stone. Richie Gold had instructed his secretary to create a cooling off period any time that an intern requested a meeting. Had he known that Gail Riley had contacted his office about the incident in the ICU, Dr. Gold would have immediately gone to Eleven West and met with her and Roy Danton. However, since Dr. Gold's secretary had no knowledge of the specific situation, she did not even inform him of Gail Riley's request for a meeting.

Feeling abandoned by the system, that night, after a quick supper, Gail and her husband went to bed. Larry Patterson hoped to have sex, but Gail fell asleep before that could happen.

At the hospital that night, Eric Cain was busy admitting Douglas McArthur. The famous general of that name had died in 1964. This Douglas McArthur was a seventy-three-year-old man with end stage cirrhosis of the liver. He had been discharged three days earlier from Medical Team B, run by Harry Falk. Dr Falk's discharge note said "Doubt we can do much. If he stays out of the hospital several weeks, or a month, then we might try to buff him up if he comes in again; if he comes in sooner, this will clearly be a case for comfort measures and a referral to hospice."

Eric Cain had no plan, but a dying Douglas McArthur started him in motion. At eight in the morning when Doctors Cain, Riley, and Danton discussed their patients, Ray Danton strongly suggested that Douglas McArthur be resuscitated when he had the inevitable cardiac arrest. There was no family to agree or disagree with a DNR plan. Eric Cain smiled and said "We'll talk it over with Dr. Aaron when he comes around at ten o'clock." Dr. Cain felt that with his own assessment and Dr. Falk's evaluation, it would be two opinions against one.

At ten o'clock, Eric Cain suggested that attending rounds start with a presentation of Mr. McArthur, who was barely clinging to life. Eric Cain presented the patient to Dr. Aaron from memory, without consulting his notes. The chief complaint was coma; the key to the past medical history was cirrhosis and liver failure. Eric Cain mentioned Mr. McArthur's hypertension, diabetes, obesity, and mild kidney failure. The family history and social history were notable only for years of alcoholism. The physical exam was remarkable for severe jaundice—the yellowed eyes and skin of liver failure, as well as ascites—fluid in the abdomen. Dr. Cain presented the laboratory data, quoted from Harry Falk's discharge summary, and concluded with a recommendation for comfort measures.

Dr. Aaron was impressed with his intern's excellent presentation. "All Eric Cain needs," he thought to himself, "is further experience and he will be a fine physician." He was embarrassed that he had doubted Dr. Cain's ability because of his brief sojourn into the world of rock and roll.

However, before Dr. Aaron could agree with Dr. Cain's plan, Roy Danton began a rambling litany discussing the reversible causes of liver failure, none of which was present. He considered what might be found if the fluid filling the abdomen was removed and sent to the laboratory for examination—an interesting physiologic point of no clinical relevance since there was no indication to perform such a procedure. Roy Danton drifted into a discussion of the microscopic findings that were likely to be observed when liver biopsies were performed in patients with alcoholic liver disease. Finally, he concluded by stating his opinion that Mr. McArthur should be treated aggressively, and that he should be resuscitated if his heart stopped.

When Roy Danton concluded, Dr. Aaron, who had been looking at his watch, offered the following comment. "You just spent eight minutes pontificating and saying nothing that was relevant."

Roy Danton's chest was tight and he had trouble catching his breath. He was not used to being criticized by an attending physician. Most of the attending physicians at CMI liked Dr. Danton as he had expanded their curriculum vitae by including them as co-authors on his pending publications. Although two of Roy Danton's studies dealt with cancer patients, Dr. Aaron had declined the proffered co-authorship on Roy Danton's projects on the grounds that he hadn't been involved with the work. Melvin Aaron was able to evaluate Roy Danton objectively; he saw Dr. Danton as a marginally competent resident whose obvious high opinion of himself was undeserved.

Before Roy Danton could defend himself, Dr. Aaron continued. "There are three reasons that we are going to do it Dr. Cain's way and go with a plan of comfort. The first is that anything but comfort care would be a futile and irrelevant waste of resources and would therefore be bad medicine. The second reason is that as physicians we always show compassion to our patients. Subjecting a patient to cardiac resuscitation when his suffering comes to an end and when there is no chance of either improvement or recovery isn't compassionate." He took a deep breath before continuing. "And the third reason we aren't going to do anything, Dr. Danton, is that while you were rambling on you weren't paying attention to Mr. McArthur. Mr. McArthur stopped breathing six minutes before you stopped talking and he was irreversibly dead by that time. Let's inform the nurses and move on . . . And keep up the good work, Dr. Cain. I always say that we should strive for excellence, and you are doing just that."

Eric Cain did not look at Roy Danton. He looked at Gail Riley and smiled. Had she not been a married woman she might have begun contemplating where on the ward she could have gotten Eric Cain alone to thank him appropriately. However, being married, she simply smiled back in return. When she went to lunch she bought a chocolate chip cookie for Eric Cain and left it at his work station with a note saying "Thank You. You are a true friend." Roy Danton had been humiliated and that was all that mattered to Gail Riley.

With most physicians, the matter would have been closed. However, Eric Cain was not like most physicians. Despite the fact that he had slept with hundreds of women, Eric Cain had never had a platonic female friend. Eric Cain was touched by Gail Riley's gesture. As a hockey player, Eric Cain had learned that when an opponent was starting to crumble under stress, that was the time to turn the pressure up, not the time to back down. Eric Cain's war against Roy Danton was just beginning.

*   *   *

That day and night Gail Riley admitted four patients and the broad smile never left her face. Roy Danton incorrectly surmised that her husband had dropped by for some afternoon delight. That was hardly the case. Gail and Larry hadn't made love since the start of internship. It was Roy Danton's mortification on rounds that had left Gail Riley glowing.

Meanwhile, Eric Cain was generating a plan. The hospital library closed at five o'clock, a fact that Eric Cain learned when he inquired, for the first time, where the hospital library was located. However, in case of emergency, one could obtain the library key from an administrator. Eric Cain considered the further humiliation of Roy Danton to be such an emergency.

Since the start of the month, Roy Danton had cited thirteen papers during discussions with his interns. Eric Cain had written down all the references. He planned to find the articles, make copies, take them home, and read them. He hoped to find something that Roy Danton had quoted incorrectly, assuming that he could remember what Roy Danton had claimed to be the important point made by each of the articles.

Unfortunately, in the two hours Eric Cain spent at the library he found only three of the thirteen articles. He concluded that the exhaustion associated with internship had kept him from taking accurate notes. He was disgusted with himself.

CMI was not located in one of the better neighborhoods in Chicago. It was a four block walk from CMI to Eric Cain's apartment. Eric was so unhappy over his apparent inability to do something as simple as accurately write down a journal reference that he started hoping that someone might try to mug him. If so, the mugger would have picked the wrong former NCAA hockey player.

After microwaving a frozen chicken dinner that included a piece of apple turnover that tasted like flavored cardboard, Eric Cain sat down and read the articles. The first paper discussed the immunologic classification of lymphoma. The second paper was on the differential diagnosis in patients with abnormal liver enzyme tests. Neither paper stated anything other than what Roy Danton had said on rounds.

Just as he started to look at the third paper, a thought crossed Eric Cain's mind. The phrase "differential diagnosis" means a consideration of the different relevant possibilities that applied to a clinical situation. When he had failed to find the references on his list, Eric Cain had assumed that he had misheard or miswritten what Roy Danton had said. That was one possibility, but there was another. He considered that he had written down exactly what Roy Danton had said, but that Roy Danton had given a wrong reference.

In his years at South Dakota State, Eric Cain had never had a resident or intern quote him an incorrect reference, let alone ten incorrect references, but it was possible that Roy Danton was consistently wrong. Eric realized that there was no way to prove if the missing references represented a mistake by Roy Danton or his mistake in transcribing what Roy Danton had said. However, Eric Cain knew he could check out any references that Roy Danton provided in the future and was going to be prepared.

While Eric Cain was at home, reaching that conclusion, overnight at CMI Gail Riley admitted a man with severe hypothyroidism, a terminal patient with AIDS, and Collette Hartsung, a woman with a bleeding ulcer. Collette Hartsung was admitted at two in the morning. Between taking Collette Hartsung's medical history, performing the physical examination, drawing blood tests, consulting the GI service to perform an emergency endoscopy, starting an intravenous line, and initiating blood transfusions, Gail Riley managed to get ten minutes of sleep—on the cot on which Collette Hartsung had been transported from the emergency room to the eleventh floor. The remainder of the night was spent taking the elevator to and from the blood bank on the main floor as Collette Hartsung required transfusions of eight units of packed red blood cells and two units of fresh frozen plasma to treat what the endoscopy revealed to be a bleeding ulcer.

By morning, Collette Hartsung was stable and Gail was exhausted when she and Eric Cain reviewed their patients with Roy Danton. Gail Riley had initiated a rational therapeutic plan for each of the new admissions, and Roy Danton had little additional to suggest regarding the management of any of them. The patient with AIDS had discussed resuscitation status with his out-patient physician and was a DNR.

Rounds with Dr. Aaron went smoothly. Despite the events of the previous morning, the mood did not seem especially tense. Eric Cain said nothing about the fact that he had been unable to track down references that had been previously provided. Dr. Riley was too tired from being up most of the night to underscore the point that her new patient with AIDS was another man in whom resuscitation would have been a futile waste of medical resources. That patient died peacefully three days later.

After rounds, Eric Cain went to the Emergency Room to work up the first of what would be his three admissions of the day. Gail Riley headed for the cafeteria. Not only had she been too exhausted to have sex with her husband, at times she had been too tired to talk to him. Today, Larry was going to join her for lunch at CMI. As she approached the elevator to head downstairs a nurse informed her that Collette Hartsung had just vomited a basinful of blood.

"Too fucking much," a depressed Gail Riley mumbled under her breath as she walked to Collette Hartsung's room to draw tubes of blood in order to check the patient's hemoglobin and to get a sample to the blood bank. As she entered the room, the metallic smell of blood mixed with digestive juices was unmistakable.

Mrs. Hartsung, a single parent with two small daughters was sweating profusely. Her breathing was shallow. Her pulse was racing. "Am I going to die?" the terrified and tearful patient who might very well be dying asked Gail Riley.

Gail Riley instructed the nurse to speed up Mrs. Hartsung's intravenous fluids. "I'll do everything I can to keep that from happening." That didn't quite answer the question, but it was the best that the exhausted intern could offer. Gail Riley realized that not only was she going to miss lunch with her husband, but on her night off she might be stuck in the hospital for much of the evening, transfusing Collette Hartsung. Since she would be on call again tomorrow night, she realized that she might be spending three straight evenings in the hospital. It was indeed much too much. After again reassuring Collette Hartsung as best as she could, Gail Riley began to call her husband and tell him to forget lunch.

She had punched in half the number when she had her epiphany. Collette Hartsung was about to get her ninth and tenth units of packed red blood cells. Ten units of blood for a single bleeding episode defined the failure of medical management and was the cutoff point for emergency ulcer surgery. Collette Hartsung was going to the operating room. Holding the blood she had just drawn in her left hand—the blood bank would need it to perform the crossmatch—Gail tossed the blood bank requisitions into the air in celebration.

Before the papers hit the ground she realized what she was doing. A thirty-four year old woman was bleeding, possibly bleeding to death, and she was celebrating the fact because it meant she could see her husband and eventually go home and get some sleep. She paged the surgeons, explained the situation to Collette Hartsung, and headed to the cafeteria as soon as the surgical resident arrived in Mrs. Hartsung's room to accept the patient in transfer.

Had Larry Patterson not convinced his wife that she was not a sociopath for appreciating the value of conversation and sleep, Gail Riley would have decided that she was losing her humanity and would have considered quitting the internship that afternoon. As it was, by the end of lunch, when she kissed her husband goodbye, Gail Riley had accepted the fact that she was a normal person working absurdly hard. Food in the hospital cafeteria was poor, but lunch with her husband had been a delicious treat, even though she couldn't remember what it was that she had eaten.

Larry Patterson had just left to return to the University of Chicago when Gail Riley noticed the cute little boy with light brown hair. His left arm was in a sling and he was smiling at her. She smiled back and noticed that the man sitting with the little boy was Dr. Aaron. She walked over to say hello.

"I assume this handsome young man is your son?"

"Yes. He was at camp and a horse ran into him. Jonah can be a handful. I've been giving my wife a break by taking him to work with me every other day."

Gail Riley introduced herself to Jonah Aaron. Pointing to his sling she asked, "Are you ok?"

"I broke my collarbone, but it's all right. The horse is dead, though. I guess I'm a dangerous man—sort of." Uninjured in the collision with Jonah Aaron, the ancient horse had died of natural causes.

Gail Riley chuckled when Jonah called himself dangerous. "Does it hurt?"

"Just a little." Actually it didn't hurt at all, but Jonah Aaron had quickly learned that appearing stoic and having "just a little pain" generated considerable sympathy.

"Are you going to be a doctor like your daddy?"

Jonah answered politely. "No! I'm going to be a private investigator. It's more interesting."

"His favorite TV shows are *Magnum, P.I.* and *Simon and Simon,*" Dr. Aaron interjected. He's been reading detective novels from sunup to sundown since he had his accident." Dr. Aaron saw that Jonah had resumed eating. By trial and error, Jonah had learned that if one bought two hamburgers, discarded the buns, and then combined the meat with blue cheese salad dressing, one had a meal that could be considered edible. "I haven't asked before. Overall, how is internship going?"

Gail Riley didn't want to badmouth Roy Danton to Dr. Aaron, and, after Roy Danton's humiliation on rounds the day before, she hoped that things would improve. "I think that I'm learning what I need to learn. I don't have enough time though. Mrs. Hartsung, the lady with the bleeding ulcer just got transferred to surgery, and I was finally going to make it to the library and look up some of the papers that Dr. Danton's mentioned on interns' work rounds. It's the first time all year I've had a chance to go the library." She showed Dr. Aaron a list of thirteen references. Her list was identical to the list that Eric Cain had taken to the library the night before. If the two interns had compared lists, Eric Cain would have realized that it was most unlikely that he had recorded things incorrectly. "I'm going to get these papers and read them tonight."

It was then that Jonah interrupted the conversation. "I can get the papers for you, Dr. Riley. My dad sends me to the library for him every once in a while. I'll get the stuff on the list and bring it to you in two hours. I'll get an extra copy for you too, dad, if you'd like."

"That would be nice, Jonah." Since Dr. Danton had cited the papers only on early morning work rounds with his interns, and not on attending rounds, this was the first that Dr. Aaron had heard about them.

Jonah reached for the list. "Do you want to make a copy before you give it to me, or do you want to trust me not to lose it?"

Gail Riley smiled. "Are you trustworthy?"

"Very!"

"Then I'll see you on Eleven West at three o'clock. Do you know where that is?"

Jonah nodded.

"In that case, I'm going to take care of loose ends with my patients. I might even get out of here early." She smiled at the thought. She might get to go home, nap, wake up, and make love. That was a very interesting thought. Larry had been so nice to meet her for lunch.

"I'll be there by three o'clock."

As Jonah said goodbye to his father and Dr. Riley, Gail Riley asked Melvin Aaron whether Jonah could really get the job done.

"He's only eight years old but he's an extremely gifted boy. I never cease to be amazed at some of the things he does." It would not be the last time that Melvin Aaron said that about his son.

Jonah Aaron went to the library and found the same three articles that Eric Cain had found and had the librarian make two copies of each article for him. Ten of the thirteen articles could not be found. The librarian confirmed that the references were incorrect. Jonah checked the journals to see if the page number might be wrong. He found nothing with the titles that Roy Danton had quoted. Jonah arrived on Eleven West at five minutes to three and located Dr. Riley at the doctor's work station. "I have three of your thirteen references." He handed her the copies. "The other references were wrong. I couldn't find them, so I had the librarian help me. She couldn't find them either. She said they didn't exist. Sorry. Here's your list back."

Gail Riley looked at the little boy standing in front of her and didn't know what to say. How could the references be wrong? She had written down exactly what Roy Danton had said. She was certain of it. If Jonah Aaron was right, Roy Danton was wrong—more than wrong. If Jonah Aaron was correct, Roy Danton might have fabricated the information. She knew that Roy Danton had poor clinical judgment, and he had certainly acted inappropriately the other night when he had pretended she had a cardiac arrest. However, this was unbelievable.

On the other hand, Dr. Aaron's son was only eight years old. Gail Riley concluded that it was more likely that Jonah Aaron was wrong. Dr. Riley wondered if the little boy had been too embarrassed to ask the librarian for help and didn't want to admit it.

Had Gail Riley not underestimated Jonah Aaron she would have told Eric Cain what she had discovered. They likely would have confronted Roy Danton at that time, and reached some sort of resolution. Instead, she simply asked Jonah, "How much do I owe you for the copies?"

"Three dollars. But you owe my dad. I charged it to his library account."

Gail Riley removed her wallet from the pocket of her white coat. "Here's five dollars. Keep two for your trouble. Give your dad the other three."

"Of course I will. An investigator has to be trustworthy." Jonah Aaron smiled with self-satisfaction.

Gail Riley smiled in return. As she returned her wallet to her pocket, she remembered that July 15 was payday and that before she left CMI she could stop by the Cashier's Office on the first floor. For her frustrating two weeks she would be receiving, after taxes and deductions, five hundred and seventy three dollars and forty-four cents.

With Eric Cain's encouragement, Gail Riley signed out to him at three thirty. She didn't mention what she regarded as a preliminary finding regarding Roy Danton's references.

*   *   *

Ella Mae Corey was a sixty-three year old African-American woman who cleaned houses for a living. She was exceptionally proud that she had been able to save enough money to send both of her sons to college. One was a minister; one was a stock broker. Sadly, one of the ways in which she had economized was by eating junk food, especially corn chips which she was known to consume a large package at a time. More than half as wide as she was tall, she had never been under the care of a physician. Unknown to her, she had had hypertension for more than a decade and late on the evening of July 15 she arrived at the Emergency Department of CMI in congestive heart failure with kidney failure. Mrs. Corey was short of breath, something that Eric Cain was able to relieve with oxygen. However, after taking a medical history and doing a physical examination, his therapeutic repertoire was as exhausted as he was.

A basic treatment for congestive heart failure is to give the patient diuretics, water pills, to get rid of excess fluid. However, given the status of Mrs. Corey's kidneys, Eric Cain doubted that the patient could urinate enough to improve her situation. The solution was simple enough, and if Dr. Cain had devoted some thought to the matter, he would have had a solution, but under the circumstances, and facing a sick patient, he did what most interns would do. He called his resident.

Roy Danton knew what therapy to initiate, but what he told Eric Cain was not the correct response to the situation. "That's an impossible combination. You need to get rid of the fluid and you can't. Just keep her comfortable like you always want to do." Then, he added, "By the way, there's this great paper on twenty-four hour stool calcium content as a predictor of survival in combined heart and kidney failure. It's in the June 1986 issue of the New York State Medical Journal. You may as well start stool collections to assess calcium." If Eric Cain wasn't going to make a typical intern error on his own, Roy Danton was going to lead him astray. That Ella Mae Corey might be harmed by this course of action did not matter to Roy Danton. Eric Cain had humiliated him on rounds and Dr. Danton wanted payback.

Eric Cain wanted to be absolutely certain that Roy Danton couldn't claim that his intern had written down the reference incorrectly. "Sure. I'll look it up. But, my pen's out of ink, Roy. Can you write that down for me?"

Roy Danton obliged. It was ten PM and Eric Cain walked over to Eleven East where he found Harry Falk and presented his predicament. Harry listened to Eric Cain present the case and responded in a manner that led Eric Cain to solve his own problem. "Too much fluid, she needs to pee. Kidney failure, can't pee enough fluid. She dies unless you get rid of the fluid."

Eric Cain interrupted, "So I guess Danton's right. She dies."

Harry Falk shook his head. "Come on. Think it through, Cain! How else can you get rid of fluid?"

The light went on in Eric Cain's head. "Got it. Damn. How did I not think of it? Dialysis. Thank you."

"No problem. That's what residents are for. Some residents, anyway."

While the Kidney Team was placing an intravenous dialysis catheter, Eric Cain tracked down an administrator and got access to the medical library. By the time Ella Mae Corey had completed her first dialysis treatment five hours later, Eric Cain had searched every journal with the word New York in the title, and had searched 1987, 1986, 1985, and 1984. The article quoted by Roy Danton did not exist. Eric Cain returned to Eleven West and discussed the prognosis with a somewhat improved Ella Mae Corey.

In the morning, when Gail Riley arrived at work and asked Eric Cain how their patients had done during her night off, he happily informed her that nothing much had happened but that Roy Danton had come up with an incorrect reference. For the first time, they compared notes and learned that each of them—Eric Cain on his own and Gail Riley through her surrogate private investigator, Jonah Aaron—had found only three of the thirteen papers. Ten of the references, now eleven, seemed to be phantoms. While Gail Riley was incensed at that fact, Eric Cain was preternaturally calm.

"You have a plan don't you, Eric?"

"Yes I do."

"Do you want to share?"

"Just wait for rounds. I have a major ambush planned." Eric Cain started whistling the first verse of a song that Gail Riley, a fan of country music, did not recognize. In 1970, it had been a top ten hit by R. Dean Taylor. It had been re-recorded by Eric Cain in the album *Night Shadow Live at the Framingham Reformatory for Wayward Women*. The song was "Indiana Wants Me" and the lyric tells the tale of a man who is on the run after killing someone who made inappropriate comments about the man's wife. The first verse begins, "If a man ever needed dying he did."

Attending rounds began at 10 AM. Dr. Aaron knew that since Jonah said that neither he nor the librarian could find ten of the references, then the references didn't exist. Dr. Aaron had decided that after the patients had been seen, he would speak privately with Dr. Danton. He intended to tell Roy Danton that making up references could not be condoned under any circumstances. One might exaggerate for effect while telling a medical anecdote, but it was no more acceptable to lie about the medical literature than it would be to fake a scientific study. He intended to tell Roy Danton that there were lines that couldn't be crossed—ever again.

As was their habit, Doctors Riley, Cain, Danton, and Aaron took positions on the four sides of a square movable chart rack. Had they been playing bridge, rather than making rounds, Dr. Aaron would have been North, Eric Cain would have been South, Roy Danton would have been West, and Gail Riley would have been East. For what Eric Cain had planned, he wanted Roy Danton on his left side. Eric Cain expected that

Roy Danton was likely to get furious and might even throw a punch at him. Eric Cain had been in enough hockey fights to know that a right handed Roy Danton standing on his left side would have no leverage if he chose to throw a punch. He would have to take a step backward before taking any offensive action and Eric Cain would have time to react.

The last new patient to be presented was Ella Mae Corey. Eric Cain gave his formal presentation of the patient in the hallway, outside the patient's room. He discussed how renal failure complicated the ability to treat congestive heart failure and mentioned that he had started the patient on dialysis. Then he turned to Roy Danton and asked, "Roy, is there anything you want to add. I'm sure Dr. Aaron would appreciate your erudition regarding stool calcium." On the top of the chart rack, he placed the piece of paper on which Roy Danton had written the name of the journal and the alleged date of publication of the non-existent article.

Roy Danton's plan to misdirect Eric Cain had failed, but he had a chance to back down, and let the matter fade away. Instead, he pointed to the piece of paper that Eric Cain had placed on the chart rack. "That journal article discusses the predictive value of fecal calcium excretion in heart failure complicated by renal failure. I can't remember exactly when it was published. May or June of 1986." He smiled at Dr. Aaron and glared at Eric Cain.

As soon as Roy Danton quoted the reference, Eric Cain took out his wallet. "Roy, I'm sure Dr. Aaron is impressed with your wisdom. However, the problem is that like most of the references you've given us this month, this reference is probably wrong. Personally, I'm tired of this nonsense! Tell you what. We got paid yesterday, and I'll bet you my salary check against yours that if we go to the library, we won't be able to find that reference. I'll let you check the following journals." He gave a list of five publications with the word New York in the title, all of which he had searched. "And I'll let you check 1984, 1985 and 1987 as well as 1986." He placed his salary check for the first two weeks of the year face up on the chart rack.

Dr. Aaron hadn't expected the interns to take any action before he had a chance to speak with his errant resident. Roy Danton began to turn pale. He realized that he had to bet and lose his paycheck in order to preserve his pride in front of the attending. He took his check from his wallet and placed it on top of the chart rack. "We'll go the library after rounds and settle this."

Eric Cain, having what he mistakenly regarded as complete control of the situation, gracefully backed down. "I'm sorry Roy. I just realized that this isn't a fair bet. You're a resident and you get paid about forty dollars more each pay period than I do. I don't have the forty dollars in my wallet to make it even." As he said this, Eric Cain opened his wallet so that only Roy Danton could see it. It contained a fifty dollar bill. Eric Cain wanted Roy Danton to know that even if his integrity was being challenged, he was being shown mercy.

As Roy Danton gave a sigh of relief, Eric Cain realized that he had overlooked one important variable. He had not considered Gail Riley's response to the situation.

Gail Riley was not quite screaming as she took her paycheck out of her purse, but she was speaking loudly. "Eric's right. It's an unfair bet. But I'm tired of your bullshit references too! And considering what happened in the ICU a few nights ago, I'll throw my check into the mix." As Dr. Aaron tried to remember if anything had ever been said about "an incident in the ICU," Gail Riley placed her paycheck on the chart rack next to the other two checks. "Now there's almost twice as much money saying you're a useless worthless liar as saying that you're not. WHAT DO YOU HAVE TO SAY FOR YOURSELF, YOU SON OF A BITCH?"

Clearly Eric Cain's plan of not forcing the issue had gone by the wayside. Only Dr. Aaron could save Roy Danton's pride and money. He saved the latter. He put a hand on the paychecks. "Look, I'm not sure that gambling on rounds is acceptable. Let's put the paychecks away." He handed the checks back to their respective owners. "A point has been made. When rounds are finished, I will speak to Dr. Danton privately about the accuracy of the references that he has provided." Roy Danton was starting to wheeze.

Dr. Aaron suggested that the team take Roy Danton to the Emergency Department to manage his asthma attack, but when Dr. Danton self-medicated himself with an inhaler and announced that he would be fine, Dr. Aaron decided that would be unnecessary. He turned to Doctors Riley and Cain. "Why don't the three of us go interview Mrs. Corey. Dr. Danton can wait here in the hall until he's breathing more comfortably."

The knowledge base of medicine is so vast that interns, residents, and even attending physicians have intermittent feelings of incompetence. Every doctor has faced a difficult medical problem and wondered if that was the case that would reveal to everyone that he or she was a fraud who had no idea what he or she was doing. Those thoughts are generally fleeting. No one is expected to know everything. The pace of medicine is such that with the help of consultants, and a review of the medical literature, clinical problems can be solved despite the fact that someone— at times, everyone—involved in the care of a patient is missing an important piece of knowledge. Errors are to be minimized, but perfection in medicine is neither required, nor expected, nor necessary.

For Roy Danton, standing in the hall outside Ella Mae Corey's room, the feelings of incompetence were overwhelming. He wondered if Dr. Aaron would fire him on the spot when he returned from his bedside evaluation of Mrs. Corey. Even if he didn't, the Chief Resident would hear of the matter. Roy Danton assumed that his residency would be terminated.

Had Roy Danton simply stayed in the hall while the team examined Ella Mae Corey, Dr. Aaron would have spoken to Roy Danton and, additionally, he would have spoken with the Chief Resident or the Department Chairman about the morning's events. Since firing a resident would have played havoc with the schedule, Dr. Gold and Dr. Minton would have found an excuse not to terminate Roy Danton's residency. Most likely, they would have taken on the challenge of improving Roy Danton's professionalism. While those efforts might have ended in failure, Dr. Danton would have remained at CMI.

Coming out of Ewan, Washington, however, Roy Danton had no experience with this magnitude of failure. He did not realize that the world would treat him with the compassion that he had, at times, failed to show others.

An essential trait to becoming a mature physician is the ability to take responsibility for one's actions. The person most responsible for Roy Danton's embarrassment on rounds was Roy Danton. However, the Team C resident had difficulty accepting his own shortcomings. As Roy Danton saw things, Eric Cain had consistently ignored his suggestions since the month had started. Eric Cain had embarrassed him with his presentation of Douglas McArthur. Eric Cain had challenged him over the accuracy of his references and humiliated in front of Dr. Aaron. Roy Danton's wheezing was subsiding, and he decided to make Eric Cain pay for what he had done.

Gail Riley, Eric Cain, and Melvin Aaron were standing around Ella Mae Corey's bed and Dr. Aaron was confirming Dr. Cain's physical examination when Roy Danton made his move. Since Doctor Riley and

Doctor Aaron were on the side of the bed nearest the door, facing the patient and the window, only Eric Cain, who stood with his back against the window, saw Roy Danton charging towards him.

The sight of a one hundred and fifty pound man racing towards him immediately put Eric Cain's mind into full hockey mode. Eric Cain had spent much of his hockey career goading opponents into taking foolish penalties. He was used to having hockey opponents take a run at him and banging him into the glass, or into the boards, that surrounded the arena where the competition was being held.

In rapid sequence, Eric's first thought was that an interference penalty would be called—one couldn't check a man who hadn't touched the puck. Then, he thought a charging penalty would be called—Roy Danton was going to have taken more than two strides by the time he hit him. Finally, Eric Cain decided it would be a major charging penalty because Roy Danton was leaving his feet and launching himself at him.

At the last possible moment, Eric Cain realized that he was about to take a hit from a smaller man, but a smaller man with a great deal of momentum. Eric realized that he was likely to be hurt in the collision. Eric Cain was quick on his feet in skates; without skates he was even quicker. Contrary to the initial rumors, Eric did not hip check Roy Danton. Had he touched Roy Danton at all, he would have absorbed some of Dr. Danton's momentum and the two men would have ended up in a heap on the floor next to Ella Mae Corey's bed. That is likely what Roy Danton expected to happen as he charged towards Eric Cain. It was the final error in judgment of his career in internal medicine at CMI.

As Eric Cain moved out of his path, Roy Danton sailed past the space that Eric Cain had occupied. Eric heard the glass crack and heard Ella Mae Corey scream as Roy Danton crashed through the window of Room 11023.

*　　*　　*

As the story is told at CMI, Roy Danton fatally plunged from the eleventh floor to the ground below. To this day, that is how Eric Cain, now a member of the faculty at CMI, tells the tale. A generation of interns and residents at CMI believe that Roy Danton plummeted to his death after being caught in a lie. It is the equivalent of an urban legend. It didn't happen.

RICHARD STEIN

When the glass shattered and Ella Mae Corey screamed, Roy Danton hung suspended in space for a brief moment—during which Eric Cain, a gifted athlete, grabbed his resident and pulled him back into Room 11023. Roy Danton sustained cuts requiring one hundred and forty-seven stitches and needed surgery to repair a lacerated radial artery. His damaged ego was beyond repair, and his embarrassment, more than his injuries, led to his taking a leave of absence from CMI. He eventually resumed his residency training at Washington State University Hospital. His career at CMI ended but not his life.

So deftly had Eric Cain moved from Roy Danton's path, that Dr. Aaron initially thought that his resident had been intending to kill himself by jumping out of the eleventh floor window. As he applied pressure to Roy Danton's wrist to stem the flow of blood, he realized that had Roy Danton intended to jump from the eleventh story window he most likely would have opened the window first.

As they accompanied Dr. Danton to the Emergency Room, Eric Cain told Dr. Aaron that if he had known there was a window behind him and not a wall, he would have broken Roy Danton's momentum. There is no reason to doubt the truth of that statement, but Eric had been facing the window as he walked into the room and it was impossible to miss. Then again, he was exhausted from being on-call the previous night and he certainly had not anticipated what his resident was going to do.

Since Eric Cain was the one who confronted Roy Danton and made the original bet, and since the outcome could easily have been fatal, the residents and interns at CMI developed the habit of referring to Eric Cain as "the one who killed Roy." Eric Cain's response to those comments was to whistle the first line of "Indiana Wants Me." The phrase "he killed Roy" became a standing joke at CMI as doctors living in the shadow of death often have a perverse sense of humor. Perhaps because of gender, the term "the one who killed Roy" was never applied to Gail Riley although it was her actions that pushed Roy Danton over the edge. Over the years, people completely forgot about her involvement in what had happened on the eleventh floor that day.

When Gail Riley told her husband what had occurred, Larry Patterson was amazed not only at the outcome, but at the fact that his mild-mannered wife had slammed her paycheck down on top of the chart rack and had challenged Roy Danton. The action was completely out of character for the reserved woman his wife had been. It was completely consistent with the assertive academic force she would become. With

Roy Danton out of the picture, as well as nearly out of the window, Larry Patterson expected that his wife's life, and therefore his own, was about to improve significantly. That is exactly what happened when Richie Gold, the Chief Medical Resident, assigned himself the role of resident on Medicine Team C.

Hours after his rising academic star, Dr. Roy Danton, had been humiliated, Dr. Minton summoned Melvin Aaron into his office. "HOW THE HELL DID YOU LET THINGS GET SO OUT OF HAND THIS MORNING?" he shouted.

Dr. Aaron had expected praise for the manner in which he had handled the situation, especially the way he had managed Roy Danton's lacerated radial artery. Applying pressure was standard first aid but internists generally didn't deal with such situations. He answered without raising his voice. "Roy Danton never gave any references on attending rounds. If he did, I would have checked them and there wouldn't have been a problem. He only gave references to the interns on their eight o'clock work rounds. I only found out that there was a problem yesterday when my son went to the library as a favor to one of the interns and couldn't find the references that Dr. Danton had given the team. I was going to take care of things after rounds."

"And what were you going to do?"

"I was going to tell him that making up references was almost an egregious an act as publishing something that wasn't true. The interns rely on information provided by their residents just like we all depend on what's published in the medical literature."

In the same imperious manner that he would have dismissed a claim that the AIDS virus was part of an anti-gay government plot, Dr. Minton dismissed Dr. Aaron's response and Dr. Aaron as well. Dr. Minton planned to meet with Dr. Cain and Dr. Riley to criticize their actions. However, before he did that, Dr. Aaron's words echoed in his mind. He realized that Roy Danton's scholarship, as demonstrated by his apparent knowledge of the medical literature, had been a sham. Dr. Minton began to wonder about the eight papers that Roy Danton had submitted for publication.

In the late 1970's and early 1980's, scandals involving scientific fraud had tarnished the reputations of several respected academic institutions. Over the next several days, Dr. Minton met with the faculty co-authors on Dr. Danton's eight pending publications. None of the co-authors had been present when Dr. Danton performed the work which he had submitted for publication. None of them had ever seen a notebook in which the results of the laboratory experiments had been recorded. Dr. Danton was unable to provide documentation that any of the eight studies had actually been performed. It appeared that Roy Danton's prodigious academic productivity had resulted from eliminating the time-consuming but necessary step of doing the work.

Fortunately for the reputation of CMI, due to typical publication delays, none of the eight articles had appeared in print by the time Dr. Minton uncovered the fraud. The eight articles were withdrawn prior to publication, sparing CMI from ignominy. However, Allen Minton never apologized to Dr. Aaron for his display of temper. In his mind, being chief meant the he didn't have to apologize to a member of the faculty.

Dr. Minton never discussed what happened that morning with Doctors Riley and Cain, and the only person who ever criticized either of them for what happened to Roy Danton was Annette Adams, the pharmacy technician who had observed the incident in the ICU. She once rode an elevator with Dr. Cain during which time she told him, "You should have let the son of a bitch fall. It would have done him good." Dr. Cain assumed she was joking; she wasn't.

The night of Roy Danton's fall from grace, Melvin Aaron was eating dinner with his family when he told the story of what had happened on the eleventh floor. Jonah reflected on his role in the episode. He had been hired as an investigator. He had uncovered a fraud. The perpetrator had been exposed and had received justice. Jonah concluded that he had natural talent as an investigator. When he was done eating, he politely asked if he could be excused from the dinner table.

"Of course," his mother replied, as Jonah left and Barry raced off with his older brother. "They're gentle boys, Melvin. You shouldn't have told that story in front of the children."

Melvin Aaron shrugged his shoulders. He felt there was no point arguing with his wife about Jonah's and Barry's sensibilities. Instead he told her about his run-in with Dr. Minton.

"You know, sweetie, CMI doesn't appreciate you, and after living all my life in Boston and Chicago, I don't appreciate the weather here. Maybe, after I complete my program in design, we should think about moving somewhere warmer, somewhere that the chief of medicine would appreciate your skills as a teacher and where the head of the cancer program wasn't a martinet like Dr. Dettman."

Melvin Aaron had often complained to his wife that Jerome Dettman's rigidity took much of the pleasure out of the practice of medicine. Still, Dr. Aaron was comfortable in his job at CMI. He began to wonder if perhaps he was too comfortable. As he got up from the dinner table to look for his sons, Dr. Aaron began to consider the possibility of leaving Chicago. He had established a reputation as a clinical investigator at CMI and it was likely that he could find a position just as good, or better, elsewhere.

Jonah had not left the dinner table because he was disturbed by the discussion. He had gone to his father's home office where Dr. Aaron kept his old college textbooks. Jonah had located a physics text and found the relevant formulas. Even though it required performing a square root, he had correctly calculated that if Roy Danton had fallen from the window, it would have taken him two point six seconds to travel one hundred and ten feet and that he would have hit the ground travelling fifty-seven miles an hour.

"You're not supposed to go fifty-seven miles an hour in a hospital zone," Jonah told Barry who repeated the comment to his parents. Melvin Aaron was impressed with Jonah's mathematical skills. Tina Aaron was appalled at her sons' sense of humor. She was so used to her sons, especially Jonah, behaving in a grown-up manner that she occasionally forgot that Jonah and Barry were only eight years old and six years old respectively.

As for Eric Cain and Gail Riley, their friendship was forged in the crucible of near-death and it endured. They routinely had coffee together; they often had lunch together. They discussed their careers, medicine in general, science, religion, sports, and politics. However, Gail Riley never discussed her marriage or things that she felt were more appropriate to discuss with her husband. Eric Cain had no problem with that boundary. She was a married woman and she became his best friend. Larry Patterson was secure enough in his relationship with his wife that he didn't mind her friendship with Eric Cain.

More than a decade later, a nurse named Candy Butler, having seen Eric and Gail having lunch together on several occasions, boldly asked Dr. Riley if she was having an affair with Eric Cain. The question was rude. However, Gail Riley had anticipated that she would eventually be asked that question and she had prepared what she thought was the perfect answer. "No," she said with a smile, "Eric and I are much too close for anything as trivial as that."

5

SLIPPERY SLOPES

"I'M WATCHING THE Bears game!"
"No, you're not!"

As with many of their arguments, the fight started over the remote control. Jared Dawson, an unemployed automobile mechanic, wanted to watch Monday Night Football. His live-in girlfriend, Debbie Branscomb, didn't. They couldn't afford a second television, and since she was the only one with an income, Debbie felt that her vote counted more than her boyfriend's. Since Jared's favorite team, the Chicago Bears, was playing that Monday night, he was comfortable disregarding her wishes. Jared was six feet two inches tall, weighed two hundred and thirty pounds, and looked like the middle linebacker he had been at St. Rita's High School a decade earlier. He had been drinking beer all day in anticipation of the opening kickoff. The Bears were going to be playing the Denver Broncos in Mile High Stadium. Debbie Branscomb didn't realize that the show she was demanding to see was a re-run that she had viewed previously.

After considerable shouting and screaming inside their apartment, Debbie Branscomb, a diminutive blonde, ran out into the hallway where she announced to the world that Jared Dawson was a worthless piece of crap and that she was tired of having him sponge off of her. That would likely have been forgiven had she not first thrown a potted plant into the television, making it impossible for Jared to watch the game in the comfort of his favorite chair.

Jared Dawson could have walked two blocks to a local tavern to watch the game. However, feeling that his manhood had been challenged, and not having an appropriate verbal rejoinder in front of the neighbors who were standing in the hallway, he instead plunged a nine-inch kitchen knife into Debbie Branscomb's back, penetrating her right kidney.

Had Debbie left the knife in place until she reached the CMI Emergency Room less than a mile away, she might have survived her wound. Instead, she pulled the knife from her flank and hemorrhaged to death while trying, and failing, to stab Jared Dawson. As neighbors called the police, Jared fled the scene in his reconditioned black 1972 Datsun 280-Z. It was a fancy car for an unemployed man, but he was an auto mechanic and had completed the work on the engine himself.

As he approached the entrance ramp to the Edens Expressway, Jared was driving fifty miles per hour in a thirty mile per hour zone. He nearly rear-ended a Cadillac El Dorado before attempting to pass it on the left. In the process, he moved into the path of oncoming traffic where he struck a Chevy Monte Carlo head-on, killing its driver.

Jared Dawson was not wearing a seat belt and he was thrown through the windshield sustaining compound fractures of both legs, a broken right arm, a shattered pelvis, a fractured skull, and a dissection of his thoracic aorta.

Jared's extensive injuries would ordinarily have been lethal. However, police responding to the 911 call at the Dawson-Branscomb apartment saw the speeding Datsun and were in pursuit when the accident occurred. An ambulance was summoned and within seven minutes of crashing his car, Jared Dawson was in the Emergency Room at CMI. The orthopedic surgery team, the vascular surgery team, the general surgery team, and a neurosurgeon were mobilized. As the injuries were acute, no one considered the option of not treating such a gravely injured individual even though there was only a miniscule hope for survival.

Once set in motion, a trauma center functions like a well-oiled machine. CMI was no exception. Jared Dawson was examined. Vital signs were taken. His injuries were assessed and catalogued. Large bore catheters were inserted below his clavicles into his subclavian veins to facilitate the administration of blood and fluids. A tube was placed into his trachea guaranteeing a safe airway. A Swan-Ganz catheter was placed into the right side of his heart to assess intravascular volume. An arterial line was placed in the left radial artery to allow instantaneous evaluation of his oxygenation. A Foley catheter was placed in his bladder. Numerous blood tests were obtained to establish a clinical baseline. A specimen was sent to the Blood Bank so that Jared Dawson could be transfused. All this

RICHARD STEIN

occurred while the Chicago Bears went ahead 7-0 on a 51 yard pass from Jim McMahon to Willie Gault.

X-rays and scans were obtained. The dissection of the aorta was determined to be the injury that took precedence over all the other problems, and the patient was sent to the operating room. The vascular surgeon had but one question after he had reviewed the CAT scan and before he took Jared Dawson to surgery, "Did anyone catch a score in the Bears game?" By then the score was 14-0; Jim McMahon had completed a six yard touchdown pass to tight end Cap Boso. Like Jared Dawson and Debbie Branscomb, the surgeons would miss the game.

During nine hours of surgery, an aortic graft was placed. The surgery took longer than expected because of the five cardiac arrests Jared Dawson experienced on the operating table. The fifth cardiac arrest, the one that led to a twenty-two minute resuscitation, was responsible for the residual brain damage. However, having committed seven hours to the procedure by that time, the surgeons were unable to surrender to reality and terminate the resuscitation after nine minutes as the anesthesiologist suggested.

While the vascular surgeons did the aortic repair, the orthopedic surgeons amputated both of Jared Dawson's shattered legs and placed a metal pin in his broken right arm. The neurosurgeons successfully dealt with a large depressed skull fracture. Jared Dawson left the operating room for the recovery room at 6 AM. Seven hours earlier, the Bears had lost to the Broncos 31-29 as John Elway rallied the Broncos for ten unanswered fourth quarter points.

Over his first twenty-four hours in the hospital, Jared Dawson received twenty-six units of red blood cells, sixteen units of plasma, and twenty-four units of platelets. Had the accident occurred in 1984, that number of transfusions might have transmitted hepatitis C, HIV—the virus of AIDS, or both. But by 1987, screening for viruses had become extremely effective, and Jared Dawson remained virus free, a triumph for blood bank technology.

As a relatively young man of twenty-seven years, Jared Dawson had no living will. He was unmarried and his parents were deceased. He had the forethought to grant power of attorney for medical affairs to his live-in girlfriend, Debbie Branscomb, but he had obviated the wisdom of that action by putting a knife into her right kidney. No one at CMI had any idea what Jared Dawson would have wanted under the circumstances and the gears of the medical machinery inexorably ground on.

By Thursday morning, the vascular surgeons, who were in charge of Jared Dawson's care, thought that the situation was hopeless. However, considering the efforts made by the general surgeons, orthopedic surgeons, and neurosurgeons, when the electro-encephalogram suggested irreversible brain injury, they were unwilling to suggest a withdrawal of care. The surgeons decided to hope for the best and to continue treatment.

When it became obvious that prolonged shock and extensive transfusions had left Jared Dawson with renal failure, the kidney specialists were consulted and dialysis was instituted. After three weeks, Jared Dawson's kidney function was back up to twenty percent of normal which was good enough to stop dialysis. By that time, none of Jared Dawson's injuries were life-threatening.

Four weeks after the accident, the surgical team decided to wean Jared Dawson off the ventilator. Even though all higher mental functions had been lost, Jared Dawson had recovered enough vegetative brain stem function to breathe on his own. The ventilator was discontinued. Jared Dawson never awoke, and everything that had made Jared Dawson who he was, was permanently gone. With no one to say "No," a feeding tube was placed in Jared Dawson's stomach.

The care that Jared Dawson received was both exemplary and irrelevant. He had survived but only if a vegetative existence can be considered survival. Like a plant, Jared Dawson could be fed and watered. His ability to react to his environment was less than that of a plant. A plant can move towards a source of light; Jared Dawson could not hope to accomplish that feat. Jared Dawson lacked the mental capacity to either hope or move.

On December 29, 1987, the forty-third day following the accident, Jared Dawson was ready to be transferred to a long term care facility. Up to that time, his hospital bill at CMI, including physician fees, exceeded two point six million dollars. As a young, previously healthy, unemployed man, Jared Dawson had no health insurance; no long term care facility would assume responsibility for his treatment. Having saved the life of Jared Dawson, Chicago Medical Institute was stuck with him. To save money, Jared Dawson was moved across the street to a less expensive long term care facility associated with CMI. Had it not been for Annette Adams, he might still be there today.

Before and during a brief marriage, Annette Adams' husband had abused her physically, the first time occurring when she informed him that she would not be taking his name when they married. That incident resulted in her suffering a broken nose and a sprained wrist. It should have been adequate warning as to what lay ahead. It wasn't. Love does not conquer all, but on occasion it conquers rational judgment. Annette Adams—though that was not her name at that time—went ahead with her wedding plans. At the wedding, for their first dance, the couple chose the old Gene Pitney ballad, "True Love Never Runs Smooth." In retrospect, "Love Hurts" might have been a more appropriate choice. Pat Benatar's "Hit Me with Your Best Shot" might have been the best choice of all, but that song was much too up-tempo for a first dance at a wedding.

Annette Adams and her husband lived in their hometown, Memphis, Tennessee, for a year after they were wed. Having suffered several broken ribs and a spiral fracture of her left arm during the marriage, she took out a restraining order against her husband when they separated. On the day he signed the final divorce decree, the man who was now her ex-husband threatened to kill her. A counselor at the women's center informed her that a restraining order wasn't worth the paper on which it was printed. "If you stay here in Memphis, the most likely outcome is that your ex-husband is someday going to be charged with both your murder and with violating a restraining order."

Annette left Memphis and moved to Chicago. Not even her parents knew where she had gone. Through the help of an attorney, her CMI name tag, and all of her other personal records, now said Annette Adams. The name was chosen because her attorney's office in downtown Chicago was in a building located at the corner of Adams and LaSalle.

Annette Adams loved her work as a pharmacy technician on the night shift at CMI. She genuinely liked the people with whom she worked and they liked her. She was happy in Chicago, and she no longer worried about being physically abused in a romantic relationship. She considered herself bisexual, but she had quit dating men. For the past ten months she had only dated women—small women.

There was only one aspect of her job that Annette Adams disliked. As part of her night shift responsibilities as a pharmacy technician, she was required to deliver tube feedings and other medicines to the long term care facility of CMI. This required her to walk alone through a tunnel that ran from the pharmacy in the main hospital to the long term care unit on the west side of Damen Avenue.

Annette Adams feared being attacked while walking through the tunnel. She was terrified that if her ex-husband somehow learned where she was working, the tunnel would be a perfect spot for him to ambush her and end her life as easily as he might snuff out a cigarette. Annette Adams' only alternative to travelling through the tunnel was to take the pedestrian overpass across Damen Avenue, an overpass that often iced over during the winter months. During the previous two winters, three people had broken their ankles traversing the walkway. One of the three was Dr. Eric Cain who had played three years of college hockey without sustaining an injury. Annette Adams decided that using the overpass was worth the risk. On her third trip across the overpass, she slipped and sprained her left knee.

In January, 1989, Annette Adams found that her trips through the tunnel involved the delivery of tube feedings prepared for only one patient, Jared Dawson. Out of interest, she read his chart. By that time, Mr. Dawson had been in the long term care facility for a little over a year. From the time of his transfer from the main hospital at CMI to the long term care unit, the chart was filled with pages and pages of notes stating nothing more than the date and two words, "Patient stable." Annette Adams learned that Jared Dawson was in a permanent vegetative state following severe anoxic brain damage during his cardiac arrests.

The morning after reading the chart, Annette Adams stayed at CMI when the night shift ended and waited for the medical library to open. She read a publication from a medical ethics conference discussing whether or not patients who lacked all higher mental functions, and who were in a vegetative state, were deserving of being treated with the respect given to human beings. The article proposed that patients in permanent vegetative states should be declared legally dead and given neither food nor water—if there were a one hundred percent reliable means of identifying patients with no chance of recovering any higher mental function. However, no such test existed then; none exists today.

The medical ethicists concluded that in the absence of a definitive test, terminating the lives of patients in a vegetative state created an ethical slippery slope. If society terminated the lives of patients in a vegetative state today, what was to prevent the termination of conscious patients with very severe mental disabilities tomorrow? Which group of individuals might be terminated after that?

Annette Adams returned to the long term care facility, read the newspaper clippings which had been placed in Jared Dawson's chart, and learned that he had murdered his girlfriend, Debbie Branscomb. Annette Adams didn't care whether or not individuals in vegetative states deserved to be treated as viable human beings. Annette Adams despised men who abused women. Jared Dawson had murdered Debbie Branscomb and Annette Adams didn't like the long walks through the tunnel. The only slippery slope that concerned Annette Adams was the dangerous pedestrian walkway across Damen Avenue.

Annette Adams volunteered to work the three to eleven shift on Super Bowl Sunday when the hospital was understaffed. No one noticed when she lingered in the long term care unit. Lethal injection as a form of execution requires a short acting barbiturate to sedate the subject, a paralytic agent to stop breathing, and a lethal intravenous dose of potassium to stop the heart. Jared Dawson was completely sedated because of his brain injury. Considering the paralytic agent to be unnecessary, all that Annette Adams needed was a syringe of potassium, something readily available in the hospital pharmacy.

The San Francisco 49ers defeated the Cincinnati Bengals 20-16 in Super Bowl XXIII when Joe Montana led his team on a 92-yard drive in the final minutes. When Montana completed a pass to John Taylor in the end zone with seconds remaining, even Annette Adams, who was not a football fan, realized that she was watching a classic moment in football history. Jared Dawson, who was in the room with Annette Adams, had no idea that there was a television in the room, that a football game was on the television, or that the game was the Super Bowl. He lacked the mental capacity to tell that he was in a hospital, that his weight had fallen to ninety-one pounds, or that he even existed, which he did—but only for a few moments longer.

Jared Dawson was found dead in his bed shortly after the conclusion of the game. No autopsy was performed. Considering his medical condition, the nurses on the long term care unit felt that his death was a blessing. Annette Adams was surprised at how little she felt. She had experienced mild nausea when she injected Jared Dawson with potassium, but that was because Jared had needed his diaper changed.

With no medications to be delivered to the long term care unit, Annette Adams no longer had to be concerned about the long walks through the tunnel. By the time that there was another patient in the long term care unit requiring her to make late night trips across Damen Avenue, it was spring.

*   *   *

In the fall of 1989, after several months working at his new job at Vanderbilt Medical Center, Dr. Melvin Aaron concluded that it was far more pleasant to deal with patients and their families in Nashville than it had been in Chicago. In Chicago, nearly every recommendation that Melvin Aaron presented to his patients had been challenged. Patients routinely requested second opinions and the practice of medicine was almost an adversarial process. At Vanderbilt, more often than not, patients deferred to his expertise. Most of his patients were referred by primary care doctors in small cities or rural areas. He was the first, last, and only cancer specialist to see the patient. As one of his folksy partners told him, "Melvin, when they come here to Vanderbilt, they realize that they have come to the head of the creek." Melvin Aaron regretted not having moved to Vanderbilt years earlier.

The only individuals who frustrated Dr. Aaron when he began practicing medicine in Tennessee were the fundamentalists who interpreted a diagnosis of cancer as divine retribution. As much as Dr. Aaron reassured them that malignancy was a biological, rather than a theological phenomenon, some patients refused to accept that their cancer "just happened" or was due to their cigarettes rather than their Lord. It took Melvin Aaron only a short while to appreciate that many southerners preferred to see themselves, their children, or their parents, as having earned divine punishment rather than accept what they regarded as the more frightening idea that the universe was not being micromanaged by Providence. He felt sorry for the individuals who saw the Hand of the Lord in every event and he did what little he could to comfort them.

Melvin Aaron was a firm believer in the randomness of the universe. The tipping point in his own life had occurred on a mountain road near Stowe, Vermont. Having four days between the end of final exams and the start of the second semester of his sophomore year at Harvard, he had accompanied four classmates on a skiing trip. A studious philosophy major at the time, Melvin was not much of an athlete. He had never skied before and would never ski again.

In high school, Melvin had contemplated becoming a physician, but his father Herbert, a respected tax accountant, had discouraged him at every turn. "Physicians understand nothing about money," his father had said, "and how can you—the son of an accountant—seriously think of becoming one of them? They make terrible investments and they have no idea what anything costs. They order tests and perform procedures without thinking of the financial consequences. If that Medicare program they're talking about in Congress passes, someday, mark my words, doctors are going to bankrupt the country."

Melvin Aaron smirked at the idea that America could go bankrupt. He thought his father was engaging in dramatic hyperbole.

To his father's surprise, Melvin Aaron considered becoming a rabbi. The Aaron family was not particularly observant; they were on the Reform side of Conservative, but Herbert Aaron regarded it as an acceptable choice for his quiet son.

Hebrew Union College, where Reform rabbis are trained, requires a bachelor's degree for entrance. After graduating as the valedictorian of Highland Heights High School, Melvin chose to attend Harvard. The ski trip with four of his classmates ended his rabbinical plans and almost ended his life.

Returning from Vermont, the Buick sedan carrying the five students hit an icy patch, fish-tailed for a hundred feet, and sailed off the mountain road toward near-certain death at the bottom of a ravine one hundred feet below. Karma, the randomness of the universe, or some higher power had other plans. Shortly after leaving the asphalt, the car struck the one and only large tree growing along the side of the road. The front tire on the passenger side burst; a wheel and an axle were badly damaged; the car stopped short of what would have been a fatal descent.

Melvin Aaron did not see his life flash before him as the car sailed off the road. Instead he thought how his parents would be disappointed that his young life had ended so sadly and he wondered what Gail Benson would have looked like naked. Then the car hit the tree and those considerations became moot. He and his companions made their way out of the Buick, having sustained no injuries. The next thing he heard were the voices of a man and a woman coming down the icy hill towards them. Seeing the car wrapped around the tree and five young men standing by the side of the road, the man said, "Praise the Lord, Martha. It's a miracle. They're all alive!"

Martha Banks and her husband Darrell owned Poplar Grove, a bed and breakfast near the top of the hill. There had once been an entire grove of poplars alongside the hill; blight had killed all but one. Darrell and Martha considered the young men to be blessed and put them up for the night free of charge.

Ordinarily, Charlie Walls, the mechanic at the local service station, did not work on Sunday mornings, preferring to sleep off his hangover rather than go to church. Hearing of the local miracle, he towed the car to his establishment and spent all day repairing the front wheel and the front axle in order to get the young men back on the road to Cambridge in time for Monday morning classes. Having been on the periphery of what he regarded as a miracle, Charlie Walls considered joining AA but rejected the idea.

Melvin Aaron saw nothing miraculous in what had happened. The car had simply obeyed the laws of physics. Upon his return to Cambridge, however, he went to the Harvard Hillel and asked the rabbi what he made of the event.

"You have seen the Grace of God first hand," the Rabbi proclaimed. "God put that tree there just to save your life."

"Did God put the ice patch there too?"

"God is responsible for everything."

"So God put an ice patch there to throw us off the side of the mountain and then he put the tree there to catch us. If that's the case, it sounds like he was really jerking us around."

"God is all powerful."

"I know that," Melvin Aaron replied. "He didn't have to toss me off a mountain and wreck a car to show me."

"Then maybe he was showing your friends, and you, pardon my pun, were just along for the ride."

Melvin Aaron didn't laugh. He considered the entire explanation that he was receiving to be intellectually appalling. "So you're saying that God was actively involved in the moment. He is more than the force behind all of nature, the force that determines when water freezes and where trees grow. He was actively involved."

"Absolutely."

"So where was He during the Holocaust? Do you think he was taking several years off, and then, Saturday night, He froze the water and He put a tree in our path just to remind us He could have done something if He had wanted to? That doesn't describe the actions of God. That describes the actions of a sociopath, and God is not a sociopath."

"It is not for us to question."

"Yes it is. God gave man intelligence to ask questions. Why shouldn't we ask questions? Plus, from your point of view, if I ask a question, it is God's will that I ask it, so how can that be wrong?" Quiet, scholarly Melvin Aaron was almost shouting; he was surprised at how angry he felt.

As a philosophy student, Melvin Aaron was quite comfortable with his question about God and the Holocaust, and he was equally comfortable with what would have been his own explanation. "God gave man free will. As a result, evil sometimes happens. Man must attempt to do good in order to save the world. He can't rely on God to intervene on his behalf."

Melvin Aaron was not comfortable with the rabbi's answer. It had confirmed his suspicion that rabbis often dealt in platitudes more than wisdom. However, he considered that a Hillel rabbi, even the one at Harvard, might not be the cream of the rabbinical crop. He began to reconsider his career choice. When he went home at the end of his sophomore year, Melvin told the story of the car, the ice, and the tree to the rabbi at his parent's congregation. Rabbi Saber, a fifty year old man who always smelled of salami and who had a short, dark beard, was very fond of Melvin Aaron, the young congregant who contemplated becoming a rabbi. Unfortunately, Rabbi Saber's answers to Melvin's questions were essentially the same as the answers Melvin had heard at Hillel.

Melvin Aaron concluded that while doctors might be ignorant as far as money was concerned, at least they were knowledgeable with respect to their own profession. Melvin Aaron wasn't certain that he could say the same for rabbis who seemed to deal in senseless platitudes. He decided that the rabbinical fraternity was one he did not wish to pledge. In the fall, when he returned to Harvard for his junior year, he continued to major in philosophy but he became pre-med. He had gone on to a career in medicine and never once doubted the wisdom of his choice.

When patients talked about God intervening in their lives, Melvin Aaron said nothing. He didn't see it as his business to talk faith or religion. However, considering all the times God had failed to intervene in the world, he found that talk almost obscene. Shortly after the Aaron family moved to Music City, a Nashville woman had backed out of her garage without looking and had run over her three year old daughter. She had told a television news reporter that she didn't understand why God had chosen her little angel to be with Him. Figuratively speaking, that entire way of thinking sent chills up Melvin Aaron's spine. He had started yelling at the television set, "Did you ever think that God put rear view mirrors on cars so that idiots like you wouldn't run over their children?"

Dr. Aaron was glad that religion could comfort people in terrible times. However, he was relieved that even in Tennessee only a minority of individuals held what he regarded as a deluded, deterministic view towards life in general and illness in particular.

Melvin Aaron saw the woman in the blue sweater as typical of the friendly attitude that patients in Tennessee and their families had toward the medical profession. The partner of the woman in the blue sweater was not Dr. Aaron's patient. He was a thirty-year-old attorney named Franklin Pangburn. He was in the hospital receiving a bone marrow transplant for aplastic anemia, a disease in which the patient simply stops making the red blood cells that carry oxygen, the white blood cells that fight infection, and platelets—blood particles that limit bleeding. The cause is almost always an immunologic disorder, though there are rare exceptions.

The twelfth floor at Vanderbilt Hospital was a twenty-four bed unit shared by the solid tumor service (primarily lung cancer and breast cancer), and the leukemia/bone marrow transplant service. Melvin Aaron spent the month of November as the attending physician on the solid tumor service. That meant that every morning he saw patients with an intern, a resident, and a fellow—an advanced trainee in cancer medicine. Technically, Dr. Aaron was responsible for the patients twenty-four hours a day, seven days a week, but with the house staff in the building full time, his evening and night-time responsibility rarely involved more than an occasional phone call.

Melvin Aaron made rounds with his team every morning at eight. While working with Jerome Dettman, the Chief of the Cancer Medicine Service at CMI, Melvin Aaron had learned to be prompt. Jerome Dettman demanded punctuality as a measure of respect and Melvin Aaron showed the same respect to his team. Like clockwork, he arrived on the twelfth floor every morning between 7:58 and 8:02. The woman in the blue sweater lived by the same schedule.

Melvin Aaron occasionally shared an elevator to the twelfth floor with the woman in the blue sweater. Rarely, if he stopped to get a low-fat blueberry muffin in the cafeteria on the way to rounds, he found himself walking down the hall from the cafeteria to the main hospital building with her. She never failed to ask about either his work or his family. She remembered that his wife was an interior designer and that he had two sons. Dr. Aaron didn't know much about the woman in the blue sweater except that she was incredibly devoted to the man in room 12004. She never volunteered any information about herself, and when he asked what she did outside of the hospital, her only response was "Let's not talk about me. I'm not the important one. It's all about Franklin."

The woman almost always wore a blue cotton sweater with one button missing. She wore blouses of all colors and fabrics. She wore skirts, she wore slacks, and on occasion she wore blue jeans. Some of her shoes looked fairly expensive. Nevertheless, she wore the blue sweater nearly every day. When it clashed with her other clothing, she carried it on her arm. As the month progressed, Melvin Aaron realized that he had never seen the woman without her blue sweater.

Once, while they were riding the elevator together, Melvin Aaron inquired about what was apparently her favorite article of clothing. Her expression didn't change. "I was wearing it the day Franklin proposed to me. I don't really like it all that much anymore, but that day was a turning point in our lives. I just want to remind him of it every chance I get."

He wondered if he ever had an article of clothing of similar emotional significance. In college, a girlfriend had knitted him a black sweater with tiny green and red threads running through it. He hadn't worn it very often, and it had been buried in a bottom dresser drawer until it had been given to charity. Melvin Aaron became lost in a reverie about the girlfriend who had given him the sweater and as they left the elevator he barely managed a "Have a nice day."

Melvin Aaron noticed that the woman wasn't wearing either an engagement ring or wedding ring to remind her of what she defined as the turning point in her life. He learned from the nurses that the woman in the blue sweater and Franklin Pangburn were divorced. It seemed logical to conclude that the divorce had been amicable.

Room 12004 was next to the Nurse's Station and was the first room on the left as one entered the Twelve North medical unit. When Melvin Aaron didn't meet the woman in the blue sweater walking down the hall or on the elevator, he invariably saw her arrive on the twelfth floor before 8:05, while he and his team stood outside 12005 or 12006 discussing their first patient.

Melvin Aaron always returned to see patients on the twelfth floor before going home in the evening. He often saw the woman in the blue sweater during those early evening visits, and he learned from the nurses that she remained with Franklin Pangburn, until midnight. Franklin Pangburn was cared for by the bone marrow transplant team and it wasn't until Dr. Aaron had been on-service for two weeks that he thought to ask one of the nurses, Linda Martinson, how Mr. Pangburn was doing."

"Not well. It's been nineteen days since his bone marrow transplant, and he's not engrafting." The phrase "not engrafting" meant that the patient's blood counts were remaining dangerously low. "His counts should have recovered by now. If it weren't for the red blood cell and platelet transfusions, his numbers would be rock bottom."

Melvin Aaron understood the implications. If blood counts did not recover, it was just a matter of time until the patent died of an infection.

Linda Martinson had been working on the twelfth floor for two years. "You know, she's the most devoted person I've ever seen, and the amazing thing is that they're not even married any more. They divorced a couple of years ago, but he got sick and she came back to be his support person. Good thing she did, because the marrow transplant service requires a care partner and he didn't have one. Having a support person is critical, especially after the transplant patients are discharged from the hospital and have to come back and forth to the out-patient area every other day."

"What about the donor? If a brother or sister donated bone marrow, why aren't they around?"

"It was an unrelated donor transplant. He has a brother somewhere, but he wasn't a match, and he couldn't come to Nashville. A perfect stranger who was enrolled in the National Marrow Donor Program was a match, and was willing to be put to sleep so that bone marrow could be collected. But that person could be halfway around the world for all we know. If his ex-wife wouldn't have agreed to be his care partner, there would have been no transplant. She's marvelous."

Just then the woman in the blue sweater stepped outside of Franklin Pangburn's room. "Excuse me, could you help me move Franklin up in the bed? He's awfully weak today."

Linda Martinson got up to help the woman who had returned to Room 12004.

"Kind of builds your faith in humanity, doesn't it?" Melvin Aaron asked. "The whole thing, I mean. A stranger donates marrow. She's divorced from him, but she comes back to help. And just now, she could be angry and frustrated about what's going on. Instead, she just asked politely for someone to help her."

"I know. Like I said, she just seems so appreciative of the care. Southerners are like that. She was working up north, somewhere, but she was born in Tennessee. I forget where, exactly."

Melvin Aaron thought about how people seemed genuinely nicer in Tennessee. Then he returned to reviewing the charts on his own patients.

Franklin Pangburn's blood counts didn't recover and two days before Thanksgiving he was diagnosed with pneumonia. Without white cells to fight infection, the pneumonia progressed despite the use of antibiotics and anti-fungal agents. His doctors wanted to place him on a mechanical breathing machine and move him to intensive care.

On Thanksgiving Day, Dr. Aaron was making morning rounds with his team when Linda Martinson drew him aside. "Can you talk to me for a moment after rounds?"

"What is it?" If there was a problem, Dr. Aaron wanted to know. He knew that he wouldn't be able to focus if he were thinking about whatever issue Linda Martinson wanted to discuss.

"The woman in the blue sweater asked to speak to you. I know Mr. Pangburn isn't your patient, but she said that you seemed kind. He's at a critical point in his care."

Melvin Aaron didn't want to butt in on someone else's patient, but he felt that if he could answer some questions for the woman, no one would mind, especially on Thanksgiving when the attending physicians were trying to get home from the hospital. After rounds, he almost left the floor before he remembered the request. It was the first time he had been inside Room 12004 all month. Franklin Pangburn looked worse than Melvin Aaron had expected. He was a large man, but the skin of his face and presumably elsewhere was loose. An oxygen catheter was in his nose, but his breathing was still labored. His skin was moist and had the sickly pale tinge of impending death. The room smelled heavily of air freshener.

"Can we step outside? I don't want to disturb him," the woman in the blue sweater asked.

"Of course."

At that moment, Franklin Pangburn groaned.

"Is there something I can do for you, Mr. Pangburn?" Dr. Aaron asked.

Franklin Pangburn shook his head. Because of his low oxygen level, he spoke in clipped phrases. "Nothing to do . . . Done bad things . . . Especially to her." He looked at the woman in the blue sweater. "God's punishing me . . . If I get better . . . Be a better person."

The woman in the blue sweater turned away from Dr. Aaron. He assumed incorrectly that she was hiding her tears. In truth, she was hiding a smile.

Doctor Aaron took the man's hand. "I'm Doctor Aaron. I'm one of the doctors who work up here on the twelfth floor. No one knows why you got this disease, sir, and all of us have done bad things from time to time, but I don't think God is punishing you."

The woman in the blue sweater looked her ex-husband in the eye. "Trust me Franklin. The Lord had nothing to do with you getting aplastic anemia."

Franklin Pangburn continued to take rapid shallow breaths. "The Lord did it."

To himself, Melvin Aaron thought, "He's one of those. It's pointless to talk about it." To Franklin Pangburn he said, "I hope you feel better."

The woman in the blue sweater motioned to the door and Melvin Aaron joined her in the corridor. "I don't know what to do," she said, as they stood next to the nurses' station. "The Transplant Team wants to put Franklin on a breathing machine, but it all seems so hopeless."

He was impressed with her stoicism. "What do his doctors say?"

"Like I said, they want to . . ."

"No. I meant about the prognosis. What do they think the odds are of his getting better?"

She shook her head. "They say they don't know. His blood counts are low, but they may have the donor give more cells for a second transplant. He might get better, but his blood counts probably won't recover in time. He's suffering so much."

"What does Franklin want? That's the important thing."

"He wants to live. But he's tired, and he wants to give up. But he doesn't want to die. Of course, he doesn't want the breathing machine, except when he decides he does want the machine." As she spoke of the options, she moved her hands back and forth.

Melvin Aaron had been through similar situations dozens of times. "I know it's hard. Just get all the facts that you can and then let him decide. I'll call his doctors and tell them you need to talk to them again. There are no easy answers."

"Thanks so much for listening. I know you're busy."

It was the only medical conversation they ever had.

The next day, Melvin Aaron saw that Room 12004 was empty. He wondered if Mr. Pangburn had died but Ms. Martinson informed him that he had been transferred to the Medical Intensive Care Unit to go on a ventilator. Dr. Aaron planned to go down to the ICU and see the woman in the blue sweater and to check on Franklin Pangburn. However, he got busy with his own patients, and it slipped his mind.

On the last day of November Melvin Aaron completed his month assigned to the in-patient service. He said goodbye to his patients and their families up on the twelfth floor. One of his partners would take over starting December first. As he was leaving the floor, Linda Martinson called him to the nursing station. "I have something for you. It's from the woman in the blue sweater. We all called her that." Wrapped in cellophane with a green or red bow on the top, the woman had baked brownies for each of the doctors and nurses on the twelfth floor.

"How is Mister . . . ?" Dr. Aaron tried to remember the name of the man in 12004. The man wasn't his patient and he didn't remember his name.

"Mister Pangburn died yesterday in the ICU. The pneumonia got worse and the doctors finally decided they were only prolonging the inevitable. They took him off the ventilator and he passed away about an hour later. The blood counts never recovered after the transplant. That's unusual, but it happens once in a while. Anyway, she came by this morning to say goodbye. To tell the truth, she actually seemed relieved. She had gifts for everybody. I missed breakfast so I already ate mine."

The gifts were personalized. Dr. Aaron's package of four brownies read "To Dr. Melvin Aaron and his family." It was signed "M. Pangburn." Dr. Aaron was embarrassed not to have learned the woman's name after all their encounters in the elevator and in the hallway. He wondered what the "M" stood for. Actually, "M. Pangburn" wasn't her name and never had been. She had refused to take her husband's name when they had married. The signature was her parting sarcastic comment.

"You know, I spend two hours a day up here making rounds before I go to the out-patient clinic. I probably spend no more than five or ten minutes inside each patient's room. I really can't imagine what it was like for the two of them, sitting behind that door, hour after hour, day after day. At least he had someone with him who cared about him."

"At least there was that."

That night, after dinner, Melvin Aaron distributed the brownies and told his family the story of the supportive woman in the blue sweater, and how she had always been so appreciative of the care her ex-husband was receiving. Jonah, who was eleven, stared at his brownie, then gave it to his nine year old brother, Barry.

"Are you okay, Jonah? I've never known you to pass up dessert," Tina Aaron asked.

"I'm fine. I'm just not in the mood for a brownie, mom."

Jonah Aaron still planned to become a private investigator. On the basis of television shows and detective novels, Jonah had created a set of basic rules to guide his future career just as his father and his contemporaries at Mt. Moriah had once constructed a credo for interns.

Jonah's rule number one was "Assume nothing." Rule number two was "Ask the correct questions." Rule number three was "Learn to shoot really well." Rule number four was "If a bad guy is using someone as a shield, and all you have is a head shot, be able to shoot the bad guy dead." Jonah, who had never even seen a gun at that point in his life, had concluded that many one hour television shows would last twenty minutes if television investigators lived by those four rules.

Rule number five was "Never accept food or drink unless you trust the source." Jonah knew that his father was impressed by the kindness of the woman in the blue sweater, but what did his father really know about her? What if she resented the fact that her ex-husband had died in the hospital? What if she had poisoned the brownies?

Jonah thought of warning his parents—and his brother—but decided that he was being silly. Just because any food from an uncertain source could be poisoned didn't mean that every bit of food from such a source was poisoned. Then again, as he had heard his mother say time and time again, rules are rules.

In the morning, Melvin, Tina, and Barry Aaron, as well as the nurses and doctors on the twelfth floor, were fine. Jonah, however, created a new rule, "Just because not everyone is out to get you does not mean that no one is out to get you." The world is a more dangerous place than most people imagine. Jonah Aaron's concerns about the woman in the blue sweater were far more reasonable than his parents would ever have imagined.

*   *   *

After years of hiding from her ex-husband, Annette Adams, a pharmacist at Chicago Medical Institute, learned that Franklin Pangburn's law firm was assigning him to its Chicago office as of the first

RICHARD STEIN

of the year. She was afraid that she might run into him, even more scared that he would see her and follow her without her knowing it. Chicago was a big city. The odds of her encountering him were small, but she was not going to go through life terrified of the face that might be lurking around the next corner. When they got divorced, he had threatened to kill her; she had moved to Chicago and lived under an alias to escape from a very real threat. She was not going to move again because of the son-of-a-bitch ex-husband who had beaten her on several occasions. She was no longer the passive girl that Franklin Pangburn had once married.

Before she married Franklin Pangburn, she had lived with her parents; now, she had been on her own for years. When she married Franklin, she had never travelled outside of the state of Tennessee. Now, she had been to China, Japan, Australia, and the Soviet Union. She had enjoyed the trips more than she had ever imagined. She was no longer limited in the ways that she had been limited during her marriage. Of course, she had also killed Jared Dawson, but considering that he had been in a vegetative state, she thought no more of that than she did about having one of her plants die when she forgot to water it.

Annette Adams decided on a pre-emptive strike. She called Franklin Pangburn at his law office in Memphis. Although more than five years had passed since she had left him, she could hear the anger in his voice. He was still incensed that she had ended their marriage and abdicated her role as his personal punching bag.

She suggested that they get together. He agreed to meet her for dinner and they met at a small seafood restaurant on the east side of Memphis. She told him that it was near her home. Of course it wasn't; she didn't even live in Memphis. She told him that she was a pharmacist at a community hospital in town; that was another lie. He had no idea that she was living in Chicago.

At dinner, Franklin informed her that he was moving up in his law firm. He was being transferred to Chicago—a major promotion. He tried to be civil, but he made it clear that he was furious that she had left him over what he regarded as nothing. She chose not to mention that what he called "nothing" involved several broken bones. Instead, she talked about how much she enjoyed being a pharmacist, how she was able to help patients by checking that medication doses were correct and by discovering drug-drug interactions that the doctors had overlooked. For the two hours that they ate dinner, she managed to hide her fear.

She ordered the same main course that he did, salmon over risotto. They split the check. He made no effort to keep her from hearing him say the word "bitch" under his breath as he walked away at the end of the evening.

She was afraid that he might try and follow her, so she took a taxi back to the airport. Instead of checking into a hotel, she spent the night sleeping at the airport gate from which her plane would fly back to Chicago in the morning. An hour before the plane departed, she called Franklin Pangburn to inform him that her stomach had been upset. It was a lie. It was her way of checking that he had been ill.

He informed her that he had been vomiting much of the night. Evidently the fish hadn't agreed with him either. She told him that it was probably an omen that they shouldn't see each other again; it had been a bad idea to get together. He agreed. She knew that she wouldn't need to be worrying about his anger much longer.

Four months later, she called to check in. By then he had been diagnosed with aplastic anemia. "How horrible!" she said. He had failed the immunotherapy treatments and the doctors had recommended a bone marrow transplant. His brother, who lived in San Francisco, wasn't a match. They were searching for an unrelated donor. On the spur of the moment she asked, "Can I be tested?"

He was surprised at the gesture. "Of course."

Working in a medical center, Annette Adams knew that the chances of her being a match would be one in five hundred thousand. She volunteered to be tested just to allay his suspicions, if there were any. She didn't match and she suspected that would be the end of it.

Six weeks later she impulsively decided to check in to see how he was doing. With over a million people in the bone marrow donor pool, a match had been found. He could get a transplant from an unrelated donor at Vanderbilt. However, that required a care partner. He would have to be in the hospital for three to four weeks, and then in an apartment across the street from the hospital for more than two months. His brother was a single father and he couldn't come to Nashville. No one in his office could take that much time off work. He didn't have a serious girlfriend. He sounded desperate. "I know I don't deserve it, but is there any way that you could travel from Memphis to Nashville to be my care partner?"

Despite the 901 area code on her cell phone, she was working in Chicago, not Memphis. She had no desire to help him. However, the thought of seeing him helpless made her reconsider. She agreed to travel to Nashville. She was not surprised when it took only two days in the hospital for him to start cursing her and for her to realize that she would enjoy watching him die. That was when she started wearing the blue sweater. She had kept it as a reminder of the first time he had hit her. It was when they had gotten engaged and she had told him that she wouldn't be taking his name after they married. There was a small spot of blood on the right cuff from the nosebleed he had given her. At the time, she had accepted his ranting that she deserved to be hit, that a man had a right to expect a woman to change her name. Now, she was paying him back in full.

Most cancer chemotherapy drugs take two weeks to lower the blood counts. If Franklin Pangburn had been diagnosed with aplastic anemia two weeks after dining with Annette Adams, either he or his doctors might have wondered about the meal they had shared together and the "food poisoning" he experienced after dining with his ex-wife. As it was, with a six week interval between his meal with Annette Adams and the development of signs and symptoms, no one would have given a second thought to the episode of "food poisoning" even if Franklin Pangburn had thought to mention it.

Unlike most chemotherapy agents, CCNU, an infrequently used oral cancer chemotherapy agent, takes six to eight weeks to have a maximal effect on the blood counts. The drug is impossible to detect at that time. Like most chemotherapy drugs, CCNU causes hair loss. If Franklin Pangburn had lost his hair at the same time he developed aplastic anemia, the doctors would have suspected poisoning. However, Franklin Pangburn shaved his head. He thought it made him look powerful. By the time he died, no one saw Franklin Pangburn as powerful. He was simply a man who beat up a woman much smaller than himself; she had had the last word.

Annette Adams had had no trouble removing a lethal dose of CCNU from the hospital pharmacy at CMI. Narcotics are monitored carefully; no one audits oral cancer chemotherapy drugs. She had dropped the CCNU in his coffee during their meal in Memphis. Neither Franklin Pangburn nor his doctors ever suspected that his aplastic anemia had been caused by a poison. No one ever suspected that his blood counts didn't recover after the transplant because of the modest amounts of CCNU that Annette Adams placed in his orange juice each morning.

By the time Franklin Pangburn died of infection, Annette Adams had become bored with sitting in the small room. She enjoyed playing the part of the loyal ex-wife. The most important aspect of the role was sincerity, and once she had learned to fake her sincere affection for Franklin Pangburn it had become amusing. Franklin had never figured it out. He died thinking that despite the beatings, she had become his devoted ex-wife.

She thought about his inane comment that God was punishing him. "No, Franklin," she thought as she rode the plane back to Chicago, "it wasn't God. It was me." She did not delude herself that's she was God's avenging angel. She regarded her agenda as hers and hers alone.

The next time she phoned her parents in Memphis, they informed her that they had read her ex-husband's obituary in the Memphis Commercial Appeal. She pretended that it was news to her and tried to sound indifferent, "I can't lie and say I'm sorry." Now that Franklin was dead, she felt safe telling her parents her address in Chicago. They mailed her a copy of the death notice.

She hadn't expected the nearly orgasmic electric rush that she experienced when she read the obituary. She realized that she had done something extraordinary. She had avenged the beatings and expunged Franklin Pangburn from the face of the earth. She was surprised how easy it had been. That night, as she tossed the blue sweater in the trash, she thought back to Jared Dawson and wondered if there was something to that slippery slope business after all.

6

THE DANA TWINS: THE TRUE STORY

"I AM GOING TO be a star. I am going to be rich. I am going to have enough money to marry Katie."

Cory Bayliss, a singer and guitar player from Poplarville, Mississippi was confident as he drove his rusted out 1982 Oldsmobile that smelled of stale beer up Interstate 65 toward Nashville. He had just passed the sign that read "You are entering Davidson County, Home of the Grand Old Opry."

It was a muggy June night in 1995 and Cory was a twenty-four year old high school dropout. He had a guitar, a dream, a drinking problem, and fifty-seven dollars to his name when he shouted to the world that he was going to be a star and marry Katie Cummings. Katie was a checkout girl at the Sunflower grocery in Poplarville and the mother of their six month old son, Austin.

It had been a seven-hour drive from Poplarville and Cory Bayliss was tired as he headed to Lightning Bug Studios to record eight songs that he had written in addition to three songs that had been previously recorded by Dwight Yoakum, Patty Loveless, and Alan Jackson. Once they were recorded professionally, he planned to take the songs around to every record label in Nashville looking for a recording contract. The tape he had made for himself in his double wide trailer hadn't opened any doors.

Cory Bayliss had prepaid two thousand dollars for the recording session, having earned the money working two months of extra shifts bagging groceries at the Sunflower. To save money, he had booked his studio time at midnight. He had arranged for the services of a sound engineer, an assistant sound engineer, a keyboard player, a rhythm guitar player, a bass guitar player, and a drummer. Cory intended to play lead guitar himself.

Cory arrived in Nashville shortly after ten PM and realized that he had nearly two hours to kill. Had Cory Bayliss been smart, he would have gone directly to Music Row and napped on one of the cots at Lightning Bug Studios. He would have awakened before midnight completely refreshed for what he regarded as his one shot at success. He would have spent the early morning hours recording his songs and left the studio with his CD. Had he done that, he likely would have met rejection after rejection. Cory Bayliss was an excellent songwriter, but his singing masked that fact. His belief that he sounded better when he was tired or drunk was just a conceit that he used to justify his drinking.

Had Cory Bayliss headed directly to Lightning Bug Studios, his songs would never have been released, he never would have become a wealthy man, and he would never have married Katie Cummings. Eventually, he would have given up his dream, held on to his bottle, and lived a short lonely life, believing that he had given it his best shot as he drunk himself into an early grave. No one would have ever heard of Cory Bayliss.

Instead, with two hours to kill before his recording session, Cory Bayliss went to a strip club on Demonbreun Avenue where the billboard outside advertised thousands of beautiful girls and three ugly ones coast to coast. The ratio was reversed that night and Cory Bayliss kept drinking beer, hoping that the more he drank, the better looking the girls would get. It didn't work. It never does.

Cory Bayliss paid nine of his fifty-seven dollars as a cover charge, paid ten dollars for a pitcher of beer, paid thirty dollars for a lap dance, and left. Having drunk the full pitcher of beer, he was outside in the parking lot when he realized that he had to urinate before driving the six blocks to Lightning Bug Studios. The bouncer at the door informed him that he would have to pay another cover charge to re-enter the strip club. Cory Bayliss had eight dollars; the cover charge was nine dollars. "I just need to use the restroom. Come on, man. Give me a break. I was just here."

"Like I remember you."

"Look, I have eight bucks. Loan me a dollar."

The bouncer responded with an obscenity. In ninety short minutes Cory Bayliss had gone from announcing to the world that he was about to become a star to begging to come inside and pee. Cory Bayliss was refused re-admission and decided to relieve himself against the side of the building.

A Nashville patrolman was in the parking lot that night waiting for his girlfriend to finish her shift on stage. When he observed Cory Bayliss urinating against the side of the strip club, he chose to act like the by-the-book policeman that he wasn't and he arrested Cory Bayliss for disorderly conduct. He considered a charge of indecent exposure, but was concerned that would label Cory Bayliss a sex offender.

Cory Bayliss begged the patrolman to show him leniency, then offered a bribe. Had Cory Bayliss had more than eight dollars, he likely would have met his date with obscurity at Lightning Bug Studios. Instead, Cory Bayliss was taken to the Nashville jail where he spent the night, thereby missing the prepaid recording session. Things like that happen more often than one would suspect in Music City—the not showing up for a prepaid session part at least.

Cory Bayliss was released in the morning, walked three miles back to the strip club to retrieve his car, and drove to Lightning Bug Studios. The day shift was already at work. No one had any information about his missed session. He decided to drive back to Poplarville. If not for his gasoline credit card, he might never have returned to Katie Cummings and his job at the Sunflower.

Ten miles out of Poplarville, he remembered that Katie expected him to cut a CD and show it around to the major record labels. There would be too much explaining to do if he showed up back in Poplarville late Tuesday afternoon. He spent the night sleeping in his car in a motel parking lot. He felt that he had hit bottom and decided that the only thing to do when one hit bottom was to have a drink. He had an emergency flask in the trunk of the Oldsmobile underneath the spare tire. At five in the morning, he arrived drunk at the trailer he shared with Katie Cummings.

"How did the session go?" she asked.

"Wonderful. The guys at the studio loved my songs. No one else did. Everyone else just shook their heads and said they were sorry. I got tired of having people tell me that," he lied. "Going door to door to the record companies was the most frustrating thing I've ever done. I don't know. I think it's time to give up the dream."

Katie Cummings started to say "You are not a quitter," but thought better of it. He was a quitter, a loser, and a pathetic drunk. But he didn't beat her, he loved the baby, and it was his trailer. She had nowhere to go. Even so, she figured that at the start of winter she would take the baby and head to Florida. She hoped her sister would take her in for a while. After Cory fell asleep she wrote her sister a letter.

Over the next several months, Cory Bayliss found that his job at the Sunflower was unbearable. It wasn't just the overwhelming sense of failure that pervaded his life. He was used to failure. It was the music. The Sunflower had started playing WNSL, the Top 40 radio station out of Laurel, Mississippi. Most of it wasn't that bad, but at least every other hour they played that god-awful song.

Cory Bayliss wasn't alive when the original version of the song had been recorded, but he knew the story because it seemed to be the only thing that the disc jockeys were talking about. "Here it is folks, the number one request song here on WNSL, for the third week in a row, those two cute little boys from Tennessee, the Dana Twins, and their remake of 'Yummy, Yummy, Yummy I Got Love In My Tummy.'"

Cory Bayliss had heard the original version by The Ohio Express. It had been called bubble-gum music back in the sixties. He regarded the remake by The Dana Twins to be sickeningly sweet. Cory Bayliss thought that it was unfortunate that the Dana Twins' father was a fundamentalist preacher who said that his sons could never go on tour. If not for that, Cory Bayliss decided that he would go to a Dana Twins concert, find them, and shoot them.

No, he wouldn't. In his heart he knew that were probably just nice little boys who sounded disgustingly cheerful. Except for the arrangements and their slight southern accent, they reminded him of the Swedish pop group ABBA, and Cory Bayliss had never liked ABBA. In any case, he knew that it wasn't the fault of the two little boys that they were a success and that his songs, the compositions into which he had poured his heart and soul, would never be heard. That was his fault and he knew it.

Katie Cummings was a month away from leaving Mississippi and Cory Bayliss, when Cory came home from work one evening and opened the mail to find the royalty check for $53,000. He knew it was a mistake. He thought about cashing the check and getting out of Poplarville, but with $53,000 on the line, he suspected that the police would track him down and that he'd go to jail. In the morning he called his publisher.

"It's no mistake, Cory. It's your royalty check. Standard royalty. Eight cents a song to the writer for each copy sold. And that's only through the end of September. There's lots more coming."

Cory Bayliss had not been a whiz at math, but at eight cents a record, it took more than twelve sales to earn a dollar. Considering the size of his check, that meant over six hundred thousand sales. None of his songs could have sold that much without him hearing about it. Well, he was hearing about it now, but he should have heard the song on the radio. "Which song of mine is selling, and who recorded it?" He knew that "Lost in Your Eyes" was his best song. It had to be "Lost in Your Eyes." But how could it sell six hundred thousand copies and not get any airplay?

"All of them, Cory. The CD by the Dana Twins has all eight of your songs."

Cory Bayliss almost dropped the phone in disbelief. He said nothing.

"Cory, are you still there?"

"Yeah. I'm here. Thanks." Under his breath he muttered, "What the f . . . ?"

Cory Bayliss and Katie Cummings loaded up Austin in the Oldsmobile and drove seven miles to the nearest Wal-Mart. There was no trouble finding *The Dana Twins*. The CD was a Blue Light Special for eight dollars and ninety-nine cents. Cory Bayliss read the list of songs off the back of the album. All of his songs were there. So were the songs by Dwight Yoakum, Patti Loveless, and Alan Jackson that he had planned to record that night in Nashville. The lead track was "Yummy, Yummy, Yummy." He could only think of one explanation. When he hadn't shown up at the recording studio, the musicians had been set to do his songs and the Dana Twins had walked in and recorded them—after recording the kind of song, "Yummy, Yummy, Yummy," that two eleven year olds would be expected to like.

He looked at the notes on the album. "Recorded at Lightning Bug Studios, Nashville, Tennessee, June 13, 1995." Each of his eight compositions had been credited to him. The check was not only in the mail, it was in his wallet.

Cory was trembling as he bought a copy of the CD, took it home and played it. It didn't take long to realize that The Dana Twins had done a far better job with his songs than he ever could have done. He looked at the cover of the CD. It showed two blonde boys wearing white sports coats and sunglasses, floating on a platform of rose petals. Those two little boys had created fantastic harmonies. He still thought "Yummy, Yummy, Yummy" was a piece of crap, but if listening to that song made people go and buy his album, technically the Dana Twins album with all of his songs, then "Yummy, Yummy, Yummy" was music to his ears. Baby Austin seemed to love "Yummy, Yummy, Yummy," clapping every time he heard the song. Cory Bayliss began to cry tears of joy.

Cory Bayliss returned to the Wal-Mart and bought a dozen copies of *The Dana Twins* to give his friends. "Lost in Your Eyes" would be the second single released off the Dana Twins album. It would reach number three on the pop charts and would stay number one on the country charts for an incredible eleven weeks. Cory would quit his job at the Sunflower, quit drinking, and start writing more songs. He eventually moved to Nashville where he would have a successful career and where his songs would be recorded by well-known country artists such as Faith Hill, Skylar Jones, and Elana Grey. In 2011, he and his co-writers would receive an academy award for the best original song from a motion picture, a song entitled "On Tour."

That night, for the first time in years, Cory Bayliss said Grace before eating. "God Bless Katie, and God Bless little Austin. Thank you, God, for looking out for me." He started to thank the Lord for his getting arrested, but remembered that Katie was unaware of what had happened in Nashville. "Lord, I don't understand your plan, but thank you, thank you, thank you. I swear I will never have another drink again. Thank you for this food and for all your blessings. Amen." He started to eat the mashed potatoes, realized they had enough money to start eating better, and then remembered whom he had forgotten.

"P.S. Dear Lord, please bless the Dana Twins and forgive me for all my evil thoughts about those sweet wonderful boys. May their lives be as blessed as You have made mine."

The P.S. wasn't necessary.

There were no Dana Twins.

There never had been any Dana Twins.

*   *   *

When Tina Aaron completed her training as an interior designer in December, 1988, she found to her disappointment that the job market for designers in Chicago was glutted. After carrying her portfolio back and forth through the slush to a succession of frustrating interviews, she realized that to put her training to maximum use she would either have to move to another city or spend years working as a designer's apprentice. She seemed destined to replace her frustration at being a homemaker with a slightly advanced form of drudgery. Melvin had long complained about the bleak Chicago winters and the short Chicago summers, but Tina doubted that her husband would leave his job at CMI on her account.

Like all relationships, theirs had evolved. She had no doubt that her husband loved her, and that she was the only woman in his life. It was just that he loved his work and he seemed to love their two boys, Jonah and Barry, a little more. She had almost resigned herself to settling for fourth place on her husband's list of priorities, and to a lackluster career, when she received the phone call from her sister in Nashville.

Mona Danashevsky, Tina's younger sister, had married Milton Brandenburg, a gentle giant of a man, shortly after she graduated from Simmons College in 1973. After false starts in advertising and sales, Milton had become a resounding success in the music business as a manager and promoter. Under Milton's tutelage, Robbie Mack, a former rock and roller, had churned out seven straight number one hits on the country charts. The Brandenburgs had three children and Milton and Mona had purchased a six bedroom home on Chickering Lane as a monument to Milton's success. In southern style, there were six colonial pillars on the front porch; magnolia trees lined the last fifty yards of the orange gravel driveway.

"Tina, is there any way you could possibly come down here and help us decorate our new home? We might have to go to Atlanta to look for furniture and fixtures, but if I have to drive to Atlanta, I'd rather drive there with you than with some snooty southern bitch of a decorator who considers me a Yankee, and who looks down on me because we're new to Nashville. I'll pay you of course." Mona and Milton had been in Nashville for over a decade, but in Music City parlance that was "new to Nashville."

"Damn right, you'll pay me," said Tina Aaron as she accepted the job.

After Tina finished what she referred to as "The Project," and even before the Brandenburg's Belle Meade home appeared in *Architectural Digest*, friends of her sister were calling Tina Aaron with commissions. She was so busy in Nashville that she thought of renting an apartment in what was becoming her home away from home, but she wanted to run it by her husband before making a decision. The problem would be what to do when he said "No." She wouldn't leave him, not permanently, but she couldn't see giving up her work. Being a designer might not be as important as being a doctor, but it was who she had become.

Melvin Aaron had seen the sketches that Tina had drawn for homes in Nashville. He had visited his sister-in-law and her husband. By Chicago standards, the Brandenburg home was a mansion. Homes were far less expensive in Music City than in the Second City. To Tina Aaron's surprise, in February of 1989, Melvin Aaron interviewed for a position in the cancer medicine program at Vanderbilt. The day he flew to Nashville, the high temperature in Chicago was twenty-one degrees. The temperature hadn't been above freezing for thirty-seven days. It was a balmy sixty-four degrees when he arrived in Nashville; the forsythia was in bloom. Despite his lifelong love affair with the Chicago Cubs and his professional attachment to Chicago Medical Institute, Melvin Aaron was ready for a change. Four months later, instead of an apartment, Tina Aaron had a home in Nashville.

The first time they drove to their house on Chickering Lane, Tina Aaron remarked that each home was more magnificent than the one before it. "Good thing we're driving in this direction, mom," Jonah had remarked. Barry laughed. Tina thought her soon-to-be ten year old son Jonah was precociously becoming an obnoxious teenager.

When Melvin decided to buy the house, Tina had asked "Can we afford it?" Their new home was forty-nine hundred square feet on three acres of land and was located half a mile from what she regarded as her sister's "estate." It was almost twice as large as their home in Lincolnwood.

"Can we afford it? Of course we can. We have two incomes, and a designer like you should have a home like this to entertain clients. How would it look if you didn't have a place like this? Plus, I want that media room. A fifty inch television will be fantastic in there."

They took out a huge mortgage on their new home, and a new lease on their marriage. In making the move, Melvin Aaron had taken a raise in rank, to Professor of Medicine, but only a small raise in pay. Fortunately for the financial status of the Aaron family, Tina's career exploded. Tina Aaron hired three assistants and her income soon rivaled that of her husband.

To keep the boys occupied that first summer in Nashville, Tina and Melvin sent Jonah and Barry to music camp. To their parents' surprise, Jonah and Barry won first place in the songwriting category for eight to fifteen year olds with a tune entitled "Dangerous Man." The chorus went as follows:

I know that you know that I know that you know that I know (drum riff) what you did last night. But I can keep a secret. I can keep a secret. I can keep a secret. You know that I can. (Boom) You think I'm a sweet boy. You call me your boy toy. But maybe, baby, maybe I'm a dangerous man.

While Tina Aaron was shocked that her sons could write music, Jonah had a perfectly logical explanation for their victory. The song was the only song in the eight to fifteen year old category that wasn't a drinking song or a cheating song. After all, it was Nashville, and the majority of the children at the camp had parents who were singers, songwriters or musicians. Additionally, Barry Aaron had a phenomenal memory for songs. While most of the other children had consciously or unconsciously submitted "original" compositions that simply put new words to old music, an immediate disqualification, Barry made certain that what he and Jonah had written was truly original. Barry believed that the song, which their cousin Brian Brandenburg called "the most annoying tune ever written," would someday be on the radio.

Melvin Aaron quickly settled in to his new position at Vanderbilt. His research activities were portable, and Vanderbilt had named him the director of a new medical school course entitled Rational Strategies in Clinical Testing. He believed that if he could constructively influence the manner in which doctors approached clinical problems, he would have accomplished something of significance.

At one time, Melvin Aaron had entertained the conceit that Jonah might be his major contribution to the world. Jonah was clearly a brilliant boy, but the Aarons had begun to doubt that he would accomplish anything of significance. Jonah still talked about becoming a private investigator, but his latest passion was his work as an assistant sound engineer in a Nashville recording studio. From Dr. Aaron's point of view, the only worthwhile aspect of that infatuation was that it kept Jonah interested in math, science, and computers.

Milton Brandenburg had learned of his nephew's interest in the recording aspect of the music business, and had given Jonah a unique Bar Mitzvah present. "Look, anyone can give you money. I'm giving you five hundred bucks, just so your mother doesn't say I'm cheap, but the real deal is this. One of my buddies owns a recording studio. I told him you're interested in a career in sound engineering. I know you want to be an investigator, someday, but there's no way a thirteen year old can do that.

Anyway, my buddy is willing to let you spend a week there this summer. Your job title is assistant sound engineer. Basically, you'll be schlepping microphones around. But when they see how smart you are, they will invite you back, and if you stick with it, you will get something out of the experience."

Jonah loved his week at the recording studio. He took summer courses at Nashville Tech and learned to operate the basic sound equipment. Like many teenagers, he knew a great deal about computers, and he soon knew more about computerized sound equipment than the senior sound engineers with whom he worked. With sound engineering becoming more and more computer dependent, Jonah's skills were greatly appreciated.

By the age of sixteen, Jonah Aaron had become a fixture at Lightning Bug Studios on North Music Row. While the sound equipment was pristine, the building was not in mint condition. The white paint on the outside of the structure was peeling. Two holes had been punched in the wood paneled studio walls by a frustrated singer named Richard Gayle. A window on the back side of the building, facing the parking lot, was broken and covered with boards. In 2001, the building would be torn down to build a restaurant, and Lightning Bug Studios and its equipment would relocate to Brentwood, just south of Music City. A plaque in the lobby of the restaurant would note that *The Dana Twins* and *Dana Twins 2* were recorded on the site.

While Cory Bayliss headed to a holding cell at the Nashville Jail to sober up and to bemoan his fate, the staff at Lightning Bug Studios was awaiting his arrival. The sound engineer at Lightning Bug Studios that night was Jackson Daniels, an Evangelical Christian who regarded his marriage vows as sacred and who would never have cheated on his wife, Mary Alice. Nonetheless, on that June night in 1995, Jackson Daniels fathered the Dana Twins.

When Cory Bayliss did not show up for his session, Jackson Daniels considered going home. However, there was always the unlikely possibility that Cory Bayliss might show up late. He had, after all, paid for eight hours of studio time. Jackson Daniels decided to spend the night working. Some new computerized sound equipment had recently been installed and Jackson Daniels wanted to experiment. The musicians also stuck around and started drinking. However, for what Jackson Daniels had in mind, he didn't need musicians—at least not at first. All he needed was a vocalist and someone who could help explain the magic of computers.

Two teenagers were present at Lightning Bug Studios in those historic hours after midnight. One was Jonah Aaron. Having two working parents, Jonah had become extremely independent. Jonah Aaron and Jackson Daniels had a simple working relationship. Jonah taught Jackson about computers; in exchange, Jackson never discussed religion with Jonah.

The other sixteen year-old at Lightning Bug Studios that night was Brian Brandenburg, Milton Brandenburg's oldest son and Jonah's cousin and best friend. Milton Brandenburg held such a jaundiced view of show business that he had told his son that he could grow up to be anything he wanted to be—except a performer. Milton Brandenburg had no reason to worry. Brian had no interest in performing, and no interest in show business. His long term plan was to become a physician like his uncle, Melvin Aaron. Brian was spending the early morning hours at Lightning Bug Studios hanging out with Jonah. School was out for the summer, and Brian Brandenburg had never been inside a recording studio until that night.

Neither Jonah nor Brian had any resemblance to the young boys who would appear on the cover of the Dana Twins' CD and on the Dana Twins' poster. Those androgynous twelve year olds with their blonde Beatle mop haircuts, white sports jackets, and Roy Orbison style sunglasses, were the picture of pre-teen innocence.

Brian Brandenburg was clean cut with dark hair and deep set eyes. He was a handsome young man, but he always looked like he needed to put on a little weight and spend some time in the sun. The weight problem was dependent on the fact that Mona Brandenburg, a full time psychologist, couldn't cook, or, more correctly, didn't cook. Every morning, the Brandenburg children served themselves either raisin bran or hard boiled eggs for breakfast. Lunch in the Brandenburg home consisted of liverwurst sandwiches and shoestring potatoes. For dinner, Mona demonstrated the extent of her culinary skills by serving hot dogs, canned ravioli, or TV dinners. Had he not developed the habit of eating at the Aarons after Melvin and Tina moved their family to Nashville, Brian likely would have been leaner. As it was, he had only one hundred and fifty-five pounds on his five foot ten inch frame.

Jonah Aaron was the better looking of the two young men and had an athletic build. He had perfected the look of needing a haircut and not having shaved in two days. He always referred to himself as a dangerous man, an appellation he first used when he was eight years old and found out that the horse that had run him over had died shortly thereafter. His parents laughed at that affectation. Melvin and Tina had fallen into the habit of making requests in the form of "Hey, Dangerous Man, would you mind taking out the garbage?"

On the other hand, Jonah's grandfather had arranged for him to get boxing lessons, as well as some martial arts training. So, when Jonah referred to himself as a dangerous man, no one in the tony suburb of Belle Meade, outside of his immediate family, ever mocked him.

Both Brian and Jonah had above average voices, but for what Jackson Daniels had in mind, their real voices didn't matter. For starters, Jackson Daniels had the two boys sing the old bubblegum rock and roll hit, "Yummy, Yummy, Yummy." His song selection was simple. He considered the original song to be so awful that he felt that there was no way he could embarrass himself if the experiment went badly. With Jonah's help, he raised the vocal an octave and a half, duplicated the vocal track to create a harmony, and—with some other machinations—created the sound that was eventually named "The Dana Twins."

By trial and error, over the course of an hour and a half, Jackson Daniels—with assistance from Jonah Aaron—perfected his technique. "Yummy, Yummy, Yummy" was, by that time, a masterpiece of computer technology. Then, using Jonah and Brian to create the starting vocal track, and making similar adjustments, he recorded the eleven songs that Cory Bayliss had intended to record. Having completed the experiment, he was ready to go home.

The musicians had finished drinking and were prepared to shut down the studio for the night. Then, they listened to the a cappella recording that Jackson Daniels had created.

"Holy shit, Jackson," Tony Mason, the bass player growled, "where did you find some ten year old kids who can sing like that walking around Nashville at night? Did they just walk in here or something? That's absolutely incredible. Why didn't you bring us in?"

"No kids. Them." He pointed to Jonah Aaron and Brian Brandenburg. "It was them and that new computerized equipment."

"That's incredible. You did that?"

"Yes I did, with the help of my Lord, Jesus Christ, and the two kids." Jackson Daniels was wearing a T-shirt that said "My boss is a Jewish carpenter."

Religion aside, the musicians were intrigued by what they heard, and stuck around to record instrumental backing to the vocals. The absence of a lead guitar player didn't matter. The rhythm guitar player did double duty and that track was added at the end of the session.

By four in the morning, twelve songs complete with instrumental accompaniment had been recorded. With Cory Bayliss not showing up, and Brian Brandenburg knowing that his father wanted him to have nothing to do with show business, the session went on the books as "Jonah Aaron Session I." It wouldn't have mattered what it was called, except for one thing.

Considering the session complete, Jonah had pulled two long elastic cords from his duffel bag and was about to start doing the daily exercises he used to strengthen the shoulder that had been injured at Camp Ojliagiba when he was eight years old. "Hey, if it's my session, how about doing a song my brother and I wrote. We have time for another song, don't we?"

Before Jackson Daniels could reply, Brian Brandenburg interjected. "No! Not that stupid 'I know that you know that I know that you know' piece of crap you and your brother wrote when you were ten years old."

That was all Jackson Daniels needed to hear. The CD sounded like it had been recorded by a couple of ten year olds; he thought that the song might be a perfect fit. "Let's do it. It might be fun even though no one is ever going to hear it."

Having gained six years of experience in the music business since his summer at music camp, Jonah added a forty-five second fade out hook that repeated the phrase "I know what you did last night—oh, yeah" eight times. With Brian Brandenburg joining in on the vocals, "Dangerous Man" became the thirteenth and final song on the CD.

Jackson Daniels thought that he had created a surprisingly professional country-pop album with arrangements that sounded as if they had been designed for Mary Chapin Carpenter. He felt he might use the technique again some time in the future. As for the cheery, high-pitched vocals, they sounded to him as if they had been recorded by the product of a mating involving the Swedish pop group, ABBA, and the American pop group the Jackson Five. He erased that image from his mind as quickly as he could.

Jonah Aaron, two decades younger than Jackson Daniels, thought that the Dana Twins didn't sound like anybody. The closest he could come was to imagine bluegrass singer Allison Krauss tying to imitate the alternative rock group, The Gin Blossoms. Considering that Allison Krauss had already won several Grammys and that the debut album by The Gin Blossoms had sold over four million copies, Jonah thought he might be sitting on something with commercial value. The more he listened to the album, the more he became convinced that he was correct.

It was summertime, and Jonah and Brian spent considerable amounts of time at each other's homes. Jonah ran into Milton Brandenburg over a dozen times in the early summer of 1995. Like scores of hopeless hopefuls, he asked Milton Brandenburg to listen to the recording.

Jonah's uncle politely refused to listen to the CD. From Milton's point of view, it was bad enough that real artists walked up to him on the streets hoping for an audition. He felt no need to humor his sixteen year old nephew who called himself a dangerous man and who had no observable talent other than the ability to attract teenage girls. Stretching to every inch of his six foot four inch frame, he told his nephew, "Yes, Jonah, I realize that it will only take me a few minutes to listen to your CD, but those are minutes that I will never have back. You may be a dangerous man, but I am a busy man."

Jonah had no response. He knew that having Milton Brandenburg promote the songs would be more valuable than anything he could accomplish on his own. He waited. For a young man, Jonah was patient. He was so patient that the recording might have achieved permanent residence in the vault of forgotten music if not for a high school cheerleader named Marnie Hubbel.

* * *

Marnie Hubbel fancied herself a singer. A rising high school junior, as a high school sophomore she had sung the lead role in the Harpeth Hills High School musical. She had been dating Brian Brandenburg since the middle of her sophomore year and he had managed to relieve her of her virginity after the spring dance. Marnie had recorded a CD at Revolver Studios on Music Row. It had been a one hour session and her father had paid five hundred dollars for the privilege of recording his daughter's voice for posterity.

Marnie hoped that Brian would persuade his father to listen to her vocal efforts. However, knowing how much influence he had with his father—absolutely none—and not wanting to make his girlfriend angry, Brian had Jonah listen to her CD and explain the situation to her.

RICHARD STEIN

"Marnie, you are very sweet, but there is nothing unique or commercial about your voice. You have a clean, clear sound. I heard you sing the role of Sandy in *Grease;* you were excellent. And, for someone your size," Marnie was four feet ten inches tall, "you have a powerful voice. But there are tens of thousands of high schools in America, and as a singer, there are thousands just like you. When you get a day job, don't quit your day job."

Jonah delivered that response very smoothly. He figured that the chance of his encountering real talent was zero, and that, therefore, it would always be an accurate assessment of the situation.

Marnie Hubbel considered what Jonah had said. "If you know what you are talking about, why don't you play something for me that you think is unique and commercial?"

"That's fair." Jonah Aaron took a copy of the CD he had recorded at Lightning Bug Studios and played "Lost in Your Eyes."

As Marnie listened in stunned silence, Brian tapped his cousin on the shoulder. "That sounds better than what we recorded."

"It is better than what we recorded. I added more of a piano track and put in a tiny bit of a fiddle track, just enough so that it sounds country but will still be able to cross over to the pop charts."

Brian's eyes widened. "You know how to do stuff like that?"

"Yeah. I figured I had nothing to lose. If it worked, it worked. If it didn't work, what the heck, I'm sixteen. It wasn't like there were any great expectations . . . It worked."

"It sounds really good. When did you do that?"

"Last Sunday, when Jackson was in church and the studio would have been shut down. I paid two musicians to come in and play. And before you ask, I didn't have permission to use the equipment. I 'borrowed' a set of keys. Investigators do stuff like that."

Marnie was impressed with what Cory Bayliss would always consider the best song he had ever written. Brian was impressed with Jonah's chutzpah.

"That is going to be a huge hit," Jonah told her.

"And when is that going to happen?"

"It will happen when the right person listens to that CD. There aren't thousands of people who sound like that. In fact, nobody else sounds like that."

"Who are they?"

Jonah had not expected that question, and he didn't want to tell Marnie that the tape represented his computer modified vocal stylings along with those of Brian Brandenburg. However, Jonah had a talent that would serve him well as a private investigator. He could make up the most outrageous stories, often on the spur of the moment, and sell them with convincing sincerity. "They're the Dana Brothers, but their stage name is The Dana Twins. My mother dragged me to this county fair in West Tennessee to look for antiques last summer. She's an interior designer you know."

"Aaron's Interiors in Green Hills? That's your mom?"

"That's my mom. Anyway, I don't know anything about antiques, so I watched the entertainment at the fair and I saw these two little boys. They were ten years old then, eleven now. I arranged for them to come in and get recorded."

Brian took Jonah aside while Marnie listened to the entire tape. "The Dana Twins? How did you come up with that?"

"Well, I didn't like Brian and Jonah. People would figure out that it's us. Your dad would have a fit. Aaron and Brandenburg had sort of a Simon and Garfunkel-ish sound to it, but . . ."

"Same thing. My dad wouldn't stand for it."

"Anyway, our mothers' maiden names were Danashevsky. That's too ethnic."

"Dana is better." Brian gave Jonah a high-five.

"Thank you. Like it or not, you are going to be a star, once your dad hears that CD."

"But he won't listen to it. And he'll never let me go into show business."

"True. To be more precise, you are not going to be a star. Your computer adjusted voice is going to be a star. Just wait a while. I've got copies made. When your folks go on vacation in a couple of weeks, I'll load up the CD player in his BMW and fill every slot with our recording. I'll make it so he can't help but hear it. I've given up on convincing him to listen to it voluntarily. Anyway, it'll be better that way."

"What do you mean?"

"It's something I learned from my father. When my dad was a faculty member in Chicago, this famous professor, Jerome Dettman, was the head of the Cancer Medicine program. My dad says that no matter what a study involved, the critical step in getting Dr. Dettman to support it was to get him to think that it was based on one of his ideas—even if it wasn't. Instead of me trying to force your dad to listen to the CD, he is going to discover the Dana Twins on his own."

Marnie Hubbel liked the bubblegum song, "Yummy, Yummy, Yummy." She loved "Lost in your Eyes." She never again asked Brian Brandenburg to help with her non-career.

Two weeks later, Milton and Mona Brandenburg left for a vacation in Hawaii. Brian's younger brothers, Terry and Joey, were sent to visit Mona's parents in Boston. Brian had the house to himself. He decided that it was time to do something he and Marnie had never done before— spend the entire night together. One of Marnie's girlfriends agreed to cover for her and tell Marnie's parents that she was spending the night at her house. Brian decided to use the master bedroom with its king size bed for the romantic evening and decorated the room with rose petals and votive candles.

Marnie was impressed with Brian's gesture. She had purchased lingerie at the Victoria's Secret store in the Mall at Green Hills and for the ten seconds that Brian saw her in the lingerie, she was truly a dream to behold.

If not for Hurricane Brenda, it would have been an evening that they would cherish until they broke up two years later when Marnie went to Auburn and Brian went to Yale. Unfortunately, Hurricane Brenda chose that night to hit the island of Maui. Mona and Milton Brandenburg, forewarned of the impending storm, had cut their vacation short.

Not wanting to bother their son, the Brandenburgs took a taxi from the airport. Hearing music emanating from the master bedroom as they arrived home, the Brandenburgs entered the master suite and found the two naked teenagers. Marnie Hubbel screamed, jumped out of bed, grabbed her Victoria's Secret underwear, and headed to the master bath. Brian Brandenburg ran after her, only to have the bathroom door slammed in his face, leaving him naked to face his parents.

Mona Brandenburg, a psychologist, was worried that this experience might leave the teens sexually traumatized. She did exactly what one would expect a woman with a doctorate in psychology to do. She turned to her husband and screamed, "MILTON, SAY SOMETHING!"

"Look at the bright side, Mona. At least now we know for sure he isn't gay."

"For God's sake, is that all you can say?"

At which time, Milton Brandenburg asked a very important question. "Why do I smell something burning?"

In the process of jumping out of bed, Marnie Hubbel had kicked the bedspread onto one of the votive candles that Brian Brandenburg had lit in what would possibly be the first and last romantic gesture of his life. The fire was quickly extinguished with minimal damage, by which time Milton Brandenburg had a more important question. "Who is dat singing? Dat's fuckin' fantastic . . . Sorry. Dat's fantastic. Who da hell is dat?" Whenever he was excited, Milton's diction regressed, and Milton was excited. "I never heard them before and I've heard everybody."

Marnie Hubbel exited from the bathroom wearing a bra and panties. She picked her clothes off the bedroom floor and began to get dressed. "Sorry."

Mona Brandenburg was yelling at her son. Milton started screaming too. "WHO DA HELL IS DAT? DERE GREAT! DERE BEYOND GREAT!"

"Me and Jonah."

With everyone screaming, Milton Brandenburg thought his son had said "Minge Ona."

"Minge Ona? Dey don't sound Japanese."

"No. Dad. Me. And. Jonah's . . . big discovery. The Dana Twins." He looked at his girlfriend, and back at his father. "Can I talk to you privately, dad?"

"Sure, but grab a towel or something."

Brain and Milton moved to a corner of the room where Brian told his father about the singer-songwriter who didn't show up at Lightning Bug Studios, how he and Jonah had done the vocals which had been adjusted by computer wizardry, and how Jonah had made up a story about the Dana Twins.

Mona Brandenburg was on the verge of hysteria. "Milton, say something. Our son has been found naked with a teen-aged girl in our bedroom. That is not appropriate behavior. Say something!"

"Brian! From now on, please entertain your dates in your own bedroom."

"MILTON!"

Milton was thinking. He didn't want his son in show business, and there was no way he could match the appearance of Brian and Jonah, especially long-haired, unshaven Jonah, to the sound on the tape. But there was no reason that he had to match their picture to the recording, no reason at all. He had a better idea. "Brian, could you call Jonah and tell him. I mean ask him if he could . . . On second thought, I'll call Jonah."

"Milton, is that all you are going to say to our son?"

"Mona," he pointed to the now empty bed, "stuff like that happens every day. Maybe not in our bedroom and not involving our kid, but it happens. Sounds like that," he pointed to the CD player, "that doesn't happen every day. That's what's important!"

Mona Brandenburg would remain frustrated with her husband's sense of values until the money started coming in. She would forgive Milton for his insensitivity when he gave two million dollars to Vanderbilt to endow a professorship in the name of her father who had dropped out of college to fight in World War II. The following year, when he gave four million dollars to the Department of Psychology at Vanderbilt and was named to Vanderbilt's Board of Trust, she concluded that the music was indeed the most important aspect of their early return to Nashville.

Mona Brandenburg was looking at Marnie Hubbel and shaking her head. "How old are you?"

"Sixteen." Wearing a teal silk blouse and sharply creased blue jeans, the tiny girl looked as if she were thirteen. "Please don't tell my parents. They think I'm at Margot Crosby's house."

Milton Brandenburg listened to "the recording." He thought that each song was better than the one before it, until he came to the end and played "Dangerous Man." After listening to Cory Bayliss' compositions, that song sounded infantile. Milton decided that it would be dropped from the eponymous *The Dana Twins* CD. "This is what Jonah has been after me to listen to all summer?"

Brian nodded.

"Other than the people in the studio, does anyone know who this is?"

"I never told anyone. Jonah wouldn't tell. You know Jonah. He wants to be a private investigator. He loves having secrets. Like I said before, he told Marnie it was two eleven year old boys."

Milton realized that his scruffy looking nephew had a natural sense for promotion. The staff at Lightning Bug Studios could be paid to keep silent. Milton knew that if it was packaged appropriately, he was listening to pure gold. Before Jonah arrived, Milton Brandenburg had found a picture of a child model on the Internet. It would be simple to purchase the rights to use the picture, convert it to a pair of twins, and make further digital adjustments. He would give the children blonde Beatle style haircuts and add some sunglasses. White sport coats would be a good touch. Thinking about what he had just seen, he would make it look as if the boys were floating on rose petals. It would be the picture of innocence.

Milton knew that Brian wouldn't be a problem. The only problem would be convincing Jonah that he didn't want to be associated with what Milton expected to be the country-pop sensation of 1995. Jonah might be talking about "The Dana Twins" when there were just voices on a tape, but when there was a hit song on the radio, and the possibility of a tour, he suspected that Jonah was going to want to be in the middle of things. Milton wondered how he would convince his nephew to turn it down. It could be such a great project if only Jonah stayed out of the way. He doubted it was going to happen. He had no idea that his plan would be rescued by a man he had never met—Eric Cain.

Jonah arrived at the Brandenburgs a little after midnight, after dropping off his girlfriend, Kelly Thompson, at her home. Kelly had never heard the CD and had no idea that Jonah had a plan to create "The Dana Twins." By that time, Milton Brandenburg had played the entire CD—twice.

"Hello, rock star," Milton greeted him as he walked in the door.

Jonah sniffed the air. "Is something burning?"

"Don't worry about it."

"OK. But I'm not a rock star or a country star for that matter. I'm never going to be one. I'm just a voice on the tape, but just to make things clear, technically, I own it. It's *Jonah Aaron, Session I*. I'm sure we can work something out."

Milton was certain that they could. "You're saying you don't want to be a performer?"

"You got that right. It's not for me." He tossed a paperback book on the table. The book was *Night Shadow* by rock-singer turned physician, Eric Cain. Eric Cain had given his autobiography to Melvin Aaron after Dr. Aaron had been his attending physician at CMI. Jonah had read nearly every book in his father's library. "I've been carrying this around since we made the tape. This guy is weird but he is absolutely brilliant. It's a great view of rock and roll, even if the book is more than ten years old. He says there's only one reason to be a rock star and go on tour—to get laid. That's not my style."

Milton Brandenburg felt he was having a surreal experience. He had discovered his son and a girl in bed, naked. Now Jonah, whom he always saw as a young ladies' man of sorts, was telling him he had no interest in getting laid. "You gotta forgive me. I've had a long flight and an unusual evening. Your objection to that life style is . . . ?"

RICHARD STEIN

"No challenge. I mean, a girl finds out you're in a band, a successful band, and she's taking her panties off before she knows your name. At least he says so in the book, and I believe him. What's the point? I mean, I'd like a girl to at least know my name and something about me before she starts taking off her clothes. It's like shooting fish in a barrel. It's too effing easy. He says it's like the whole world becomes your private whorehouse. Anyway, even with a shave and haircut, I don't think I have the right image for The Dana Twins. I'm too old."

"I agree!"

"I could tell you I want to be a star and use that to get money from you to make me change my mind, but . . . one, we're family, and two, I'm looking at this long term. I want to be an investigator, and eventually you are going need someone to hush up scandals, things like that. I don't want to piss you off. I just want a fair deal."

Milton thought that if he ever reached the point that his nephew Jonah was working as his investigator, huge rocks would be falling from the sky. He would have thought of the metaphor involving flying pigs, but even though he was a Reform Jew, he had been raised in a kosher home, and metaphors regarding pigs did not come naturally to him. Milton showed Jonah the picture he had downloaded from the Internet.

"That looks great to me. It would probably be even better if they were blonde and dressed up more. I've been thinking about this and I think that you need a grown up look that makes it clear that they're kids."

"I was thinking about white sport coats with blue jeans. I'll have them wearing sunglasses and I'll make it look like they're floating on rose petals."

"Sounds good, but what do I know? You're the promoter. I'm just the kid who's about to sign a fabulous recoding contract considering that I'm an unproven artist. I have a question though."

Milton took a deep breath. He knew Jonah had a sarcastic sense of humor. He was waiting for a deal-breaker.

"If a group has a following from personal appearances, I can see how their fans will buy their recording. And if a group has an absolutely fantastic recording, I can see how kids will buy it and then flock to their personal appearances. The Dana Twins' sound is 'interesting,' not fantastic. Without fans, how do you keep everything from going nowhere? It's sort of a chicken and egg thing with no chicken and no egg."

Milton gave a sigh of relief. "That's an excellent question. We'll get a music video out there. Not you, not Brian, someone who fits the image of the Dana Twins and have them do some interesting choreography. We'll tape it outdoors like it's a county fair with tons of audience shots, so we don't need too much of the Dana Twins. In the old days, record companies would pay to get their songs on the air. That's illegal. What we're going to do is similar but not against the law. We are going to create a regional hit. We're going to get CD albums and CD singles into the stores that report to radio stations. We'll give them a buy back guarantee. If no one buys the CD's we'll offer to take them back. Of course the CD's will sell."

"How are you sure?"

"Because we'll send people in to buy them! Once we have a small hit on our hands, radio stations will start to play the songs and kids will follow like lemmings because they will think their friends are doing the buying. Simple."

"If it's so simple, why doesn't everyone do it?"

Milton sat down on the giant living room sofa and patted the seat next to him. "Sit down. You asked the right question and that's the way to learn. First of all, if everyone did it, there would be a hundred songs in the top ten, and that wouldn't work. Second, it's going to cost nearly a quarter of a million dollars up front in promotion costs. Those costs have to be made up before we turn a profit and before you and Brian see a penny. It's in the standard contract. The point is that not everybody has a quarter of a million dollars to spend."

"Then if we have to make up a quarter of a million in costs from CD sales, because there won't be any personal appearances, I want a damn good royalty."

"Not a problem. You know, you have a good head for business and for promotions. Too bad you want to be an investigator. If you stuck around with me, I think it would someday be Brandenburg and Aaron Management."

Jonah chuckled. "Not in this lifetime."

"By the way, which song do you think should be the first song released off the album? I'm curious as to your marketing sense." Milton took a piece of paper, wrote down his answer, folded the paper, and awaited Jonah's response. He assumed his nephew was going to say "Lost in Your Eyes." It was, by far, the best song on the album.

"Well, from what you've said, I'd start with 'Yummy, Yummy, Yummy.' It'll get airplay based on nostalgia alone, and it fits the image of a couple of twelve year olds. Plus, from my point of view, it makes sense to have each song better than the one before it. If 'Lost in Your Eyes' was the first song released as a single, the Dana Twins would be on a downhill trajectory after that."

Milton unfolded the piece of paper on which he had written "YYY." Milton and Jonah shook hands. Milton was delighted that Jonah just wanted to be paid. Melvin and Tina would make certain that it happened as Jonah was sixteen and couldn't sign a contract on his own. Melvin and Tina thought it was cute that their son's vocal efforts had been adjusted in a manner that Milton felt could be commercially successful. Then the records started to sell and Melvin and Tina found the money to be a bit overwhelming.

Milton didn't even know that Jackson Daniels, an Evangelical Christian was the one who had created the sound of the Dana Twins when he fabricated the story that the boys' father, a fundamentalist preacher, did not want his sons appearing in public. The non-existent Dana Twins were on their way.

*   *   *

Jackson Daniels and the session musicians were paid both a straight fee and a royalty. They were happy to keep quiet about how the Dana Twins' sound had been created as they had a vested interest in doing so. Cory Bayliss, who received sixty-four cents for every CD sold, based on having eight songs on the album, had no idea that there were no Dana Twins. For their efforts, and for concealing the ethereal nature of the Dana Twins, Brian Brandenburg and Jonah Aaron were each paid a dollar for every CD sold. If Milton had any idea how many copies would be sold, he might have negotiated a smaller royalty. Making his teen-aged son financially independent was not his aim. Fortunately, he had the forethought to place Brian's money and Jonah's money into trusts until they were twenty-one.

Milton Brandenburg purchased a failing record label and renamed it Dangerous Man Records to produce, distribute, and promote the CD's. Jonah insisted on that name for the company when his song, "Dangerous Man," was booted from the first Dana Twins album. Under the direction of Jonah's grandfather, Herbert Aaron, a retired tax accountant, Jonah's trust purchased a minority interest in the record label.

Jonah Aaron never talked about his money or its source. At most, he said that he was "a trust fund kid." As befit a private investigator, Jonah was excellent at keeping secrets.

Milton arranged for Marnie and her friend, Margot Crosby, both of whom were excellent dancers, to lip synch the Dana Twins songs for the music videos. The camera angles and the dark glasses made it impossible to tell that the performers in the video were not the young boys on the best-selling poster and the album cover. The audience "reaction shots" in the music videos were filmed at Greer Stadium, after a Nashville Sounds minor league baseball game; no audience was present when Marnie and Margot did their impersonation of the Dana Twins.

When the videos were released, no one suspected that the teenagers in the video were girls. By agreeing to pay for Marnie and Margot's college educations, Milton guaranteed their silence. It may have been more than was necessary, but in the long run it proved to be a bargain.

Two million copies of *The Dana Twins* were sold. Between December 1995 and June 1996, two of the singles—"Yummy, Yummy, Yummy" and "Lost in Your Eyes"—reached number three on the pop charts. "Lost in Your Eyes" and three additional singles, all compositions by Cory Bayliss, reached the top five on the country listings. "Lost in Your Eyes" went to number one.

There was only one problem. Jackson Daniels, who had created the sound of The Dana Twins, had been ordained by an Internet church. He felt that Milton Brandenburg was mocking him with the story that a fundamentalist preacher was preventing the boys from appearing in public. He was happy to receive a substantial bonus for his work on *The Dana Twins*, but, despite Milton's apology, he declined to participate in the production of *Dana Twins 2*.

Fortunately, Cory Bayliss, who had moved to Nashville, agreed to write another group of songs for his favorite young singers. *Dana Twins 2* also included "Dangerous Man," as well as cover versions of some classic hits including Simon and Garfunkel's "Sound of Silence," Van Morrison's "Brown Eyed Girl," ABBA's "Knowing Me, Knowing You," and two songs previously recorded by Mary Chapin Carpenter.

Having a target at which to aim their creative arrow, Brian and Jonah, singing in falsetto voices, recorded *Dana Twins 2* with Jonah acting as sound engineer. Missing Jackson Daniels' magic touch, it sounded as if the boys were reaching adolescence and that their voices were starting to change. "Dangerous Man" became the lead track on the second album for a very simple reason. It was the only unreleased song that had been produced by Jackson Daniels using the original computer technique.

Dana Twins 2 also included a song that Cory Bayliss penned at Jonah's suggestion entitled "Each One Better than the One before It." It was a song about kisses between young lovers, not houses on Chickering Lane. Being in a mood that was both generous and sarcastic, Jonah insisted that his mother be listed as a co-writer on the song. Despite the fact that the song earned her more than a hundred thousand dollars in royalties, Tina Aaron considered her singer-songwriter son, who still intended to become an investigator, an underachiever and a major disappointment. Barry Aaron, far more appreciative of his co-writer's royalties from "Dangerous Man," did not share his mother's opinion.

There is a saying in Music City that to be a success one sometimes needs no talent, just a great piece of music and someone to produce and promote it. Milton Brandenburg had taken a non-existent group, an unusual computer generated sound, created an image, and promoted the package to the top of the charts. Overall, image may not be everything, but in the case of The Dana Twins, image was everything.

While tens of thousands of teen-aged girls hung posters of the non-existent Dana Twins on their bedroom walls and dreamed of those sweet blond boys, Jonah and Brian completed their junior year of high school. And then, as summer of 1996 approached, and with the Dana Twins riding the crest of their popularity, Milton Brandenburg nearly destroyed the myth of the Dana Twins, as well as the happiness of his family, with one overreaching act. Despite the fact that there was no way that the Dana Twins could appear in public, Milton Brandenburg decided that he was going to schedule a Dana Twins tour to coincide with the release of *Dana Twins 2*.

How did Milton Brandenburg come up with such an incredibly bad idea? There is no logical explanation except for the comment that Mona Brandenburg gave Jonah when he asked his aunt why her husband had initiated such a gloriously absurd plan. "He's a man. He never listens to me when I tell him to stop and ask for directions, either."

As mentioned in the press release, the Dana Twins tour would start in Reno, Nevada on June 13, 1996, and conclude in Nashville eight days later. Reno, Fresno, Flagstaff, Albuquerque, Amarillo, Wichita Falls, Fort Smith, Memphis, and Nashville were the scheduled stops on the tour.

A statement was made that while the father of the Dana Twins still had concerns about his children appearing in public, he had changed his mind. The implication was that Milton had convinced him with a little bit of reason and a large amount of money.

Tickets for the tour sold out within hours of going on sale. The audiences were going to be disappointed. Milton had no intention of putting Brian and Jonah on the stage. Brian had no desire to enter show business and Jonah had no desire to sing falsetto in public. He was, after all, a dangerous man. Additionally, while Jonah and Brian were handsome, they were nearly six feet tall, were dark not blonde, and their choreography was pathetic.

According to Milton's plan, the non-existent Dana Twins would vanish between Seattle and Reno and be a "no-show." The tour wouldn't happen. Tickets would be refunded, though Milton suspected that most people would hold on to the tickets as collector's items, thereby limiting his losses. Milton calculated that the disappearance of the Dana Twins would hype interest for *Dana Twins 2* and that the income gained from additional CD sales would dwarf the losses from cancelling the tour.

Milton hired a well-known Nashville investigator, Kyle Ford, to fly to Seattle with the two youngest of Milton's three sons, twelve year old Terry and eleven year old Joey. The boys' hair was dyed blonde for the trip and their tickets read "Richie Dana" and "Stevie Dana." It was five years before 9/11 and travelling under an assumed name was not difficult. Kyle Ford knew that the boys were Milton and Mona's children, but he had no idea that the boys were not the Dana Twins; he had no idea how the sound of the Dana Twins had been produced.

As Kyle, Terry, and Joey were about to leave Nashville, Milton Brandenburg notified the Seattle Post-Intelligencer that the Dana Twins had been spotted at the Nashville airport, getting on a plane bound for Seattle. As a result, the press was at the Seattle-Tacoma airport when the plane landed. Kyle Ford and the two Brandenburg children never entered the airport terminal. A limousine picked them up after they came down the steps of the plane onto the tarmac and drove them to the terminal for private planes. From there, they took a small plane that, according to the flight plan, was headed to Reno.

The pilot of that plane had been paid to file that flight plan and then fly to a private airport on the outskirts of Spokane, Washington. Milton Brandenburg had purchased the small plane and the pilot promised to dump it in Long Lake near the Spokane airstrip. The loss of the plane was a cost of doing business. Milton would never file an insurance claim for the lost plane as he quite reasonably considered that to be fraud.

According to the plan, Kyle Ford would rent a car in Spokane and drive to a resort in nearby Coeur d'Alene, Idaho where Milton and his wife Mona would have already registered. Milton Brandenburg thought it was a marvelous plan and he considered the Seattle to Reno route a stroke of genius. It was the path taken by D.B. Cooper when he parachuted from a hijacked plane with $200,000 in 1971. Milton felt that if things went well, someone searching for the Dana Twins and the wreckage of their plane might stumble upon what was left of the long lost hijacker. Milton considered that he might end up having done a public service.

Initially, Kyle Ford had felt that playing chaperone to two little boys was beneath him; he turned the job down. Then Milton Brandenburg explained why Kyle's services were being requested. "Here's the problem. My plan depends on the guy who flies the plane being dishonest enough to file a phony flight plan, but honest enough not to sell me out. I'm paying him not to sell his story to the tabloids, but what's to keep him, hypothetically, from flying Terry and Joey to God knows where, and having a bunch of his friends kidnap the Dana Twins? I'd feel a lot better if they had a bodyguard, even though the chance of trouble is small."

"Maybe you should just keep the kids out of it and announce that the father of the Dana Twins changed his mind."

"That's what my nephew Jonah said, but he's paranoid. Plus, that wouldn't drum up enough publicity. No. As long as you're there to protect the kids, everything will be fine." When Milton added a week's vacation at the Coeur d'Alene Resort to the package, Kyle Ford accepted the job. He planned to enjoy a week of sun and golf. If he got in the mood, he might even go parasailing. There would likely be some interesting single women at the resort. Even better, a resort crowd meant a rich crowd. People were likely to hear that he was an investigator and he might pick up a real case, something other than babysitting two pre-teen boys.

The plane left Nashville on June 12, 1996. The tour was scheduled to open at the Pioneer Center in Reno, Nevada on June 13, 1996, the one year anniversary of the day that Jackson Daniels had performed his computer magic. It was the day scheduled for the release of *Dana Twins 2*. Milton and Mona Brandenburg flew directly to Spokane on June 12 expecting their children to meet them just before midnight. The Dana Twins no-showed in Reno and, for practical purposes, vanished from the face of the Earth on the night of June 12. It just didn't happen the way Milton had planned.

*   *   *

Kyle Ford had always accepted that his time on earth was finite. He had served as a Navy Seal and he had worked as a private investigator in Nashville for more than a decade. He knew that he was not immune to a quick and violent death. It wasn't the dying that bothered him as much as the fact that he had so badly fumbled his final job. When the final score was tallied, he would have gotten two children and himself killed. As soon as the kidnappers established proof of life by having him speak to Milton Brandenburg, he would have outlived his usefulness. They would have shot and killed him already had The Kid not intervened and delayed the inevitable. Kyle Ford knew that a bullet would kill him, but it was the Dana Twins that would be the cause of his death.

It was one minute after midnight as Kyle Ford lay awake in the dark barn on Morgan's Ranch in Huetter, Idaho, and reflected on his life. He had been an honorable man, at least in terms of his own code of honor. He had never been financially successful, but money had never meant all that much to him. He had had his share of women, some of them very attractive. He had even been married once. It had lasted two years before she had walked out on him. He had never been injured in the military or while working as an investigator, but as far as women were concerned he considered himself badly wounded. That night, for the first time in his life, he had failed a client very badly.

He had met Milton and Mona Brandenburg on only two occasions. He didn't feel that he knew them well, but he suspected that they would never rebound from the imminent death of their two youngest sons, Terry and Joey. He had no idea if The Kid, as he called the fourth person who was going to die in the morning, really had a close family like he had claimed. With his long hair and two day old beard, The Kid looked more like a hoodlum than any of the bikers. He suspected that The Kid's family would accept his death as an inevitable event. He had to give The Kid credit, though. Thanks to The Kid, he would live until morning.

Everything had gone as planned until the small plane landed at Tightcliff Airport near Spokane. Kyle Ford quickly learned that the pilot had indeed told someone about the Dana Twins' travel plans. Three members of a biker gang greeted the plane. They shot and killed the pilot, who knew too much to be left alive, and kidnapped Kyle Ford as well as Milton Brandenburg's two sons. It all happened so quickly that there was nothing Kyle could do. As far as Kyle Ford was concerned, the only stroke of good luck had been the presence of The Kid. The Kid, had somehow heard about the Dana Twins heading for Seattle, and had managed to get himself onto the tarmac. He had wangled himself a ride on the limousine and on Milton's private plane. When the kidnapping went down, Kyle had first thought that the young man was in on the plan. On the basis of what had happened since then, Kyle had concluded that wasn't the case. The Kid was going to be killed with the rest of them, a case of being in the wrong place at the wrong time.

From the young man's point of view, however, he was exactly where he wanted to be. Jonah Aaron had joined what he considered the Dana Twins Tour to Nowhere to protect Terry and Joey Brandenburg. Jonah not only portrayed himself as a dangerous man, he believed that the world was a dangerous place and that Terry and Joey deserved protection provided by someone who took the situation seriously.

As soon as the pilot was shot, Jonah Aaron tapped Kyle Ford on the shoulder and said "Good thing I'm here to get us out of this mess."

Kyle had chuckled at the young man's bravado. "Just another idiot teenager who thinks he's indestructible," he thought.

After the pilot's body had been placed in the plane, and after the plane had been rolled into the water of Long Lake, Kyle, Jonah, and the two Brandenburg boys had been placed in the back of a pick-up truck and driven to the Morgan Ranch. While Kyle Ford expected the worst from the moment they were kidnapped, it was not until the truck drove up to the barn on the Morgan property and he saw three freshly dug graves that reality became unavoidable. The kidnappers had not been counting on The Kid being along for the ride, but as far as Kyle Ford was concerned, all four of them were as good as dead. Jonah Aaron saw the three graves too. He also saw a long length of rope and a bear trap; he saw the makings of a plan.

It had been ten at night when the kidnappers and their captives reached the barn. The kidnappers did not realize that the Dana Twins did not exist. Their information was that the Dana Twins would be travelling with their manager, Milton Brandenburg. The kidnapper's plan was to let Milton Brandenburg's family, and the parents of the Dana Twins, worry overnight about not hearing from their loved ones. They would call and make their demands in the morning. They had no idea that they had kidnapped Milton Brandenburg's sons, along with his nephew, and a private investigator.

As the kidnap victims were brought into the barn, James Halloran, the leader of the small group of bikers had a question. "Shorty, who are they? He ain't Brandenburg. I've seen pictures of Brandenburg, and I was only expecting three people."

"That's who was on the plane. You told me to bring you everyone who was on the plane and then roll it into the lake." Shorty was an ironic moniker. Shorty was six feet five inches tall.

James Halloran didn't like surprises. He walked directly to Jonah Aaron. "What are you doing here?"

Jonah Aaron had the good sense not to identify himself as the self-proclaimed security arm of Brandenburg Enterprises. "I'm Mr. Brandenburg's nephew. I was trying to connect with the Dana Twins tour."

Halloran turned to Kyle Ford. "And you are?"

Kyle Ford had expected that question and had decided on an answer during the ride from the airfield outside of Spokane. He was about to say, "I'm their bodyguard and obviously not a good one, but I can help handle the negotiations." If he had said that, he would have been killed immediately. James Halloran didn't need or want anyone else at his end handling the negotiations.

However, before Kyle Ford could reply, Jonah Aaron spoke up. "He's their father, the father of the Dana Twins. He wouldn't allow them to go anywhere without him."

Kyle Ford admitted to himself that it was a better answer. Halloran thought for a moment. If he killed the patriarch of the Dana Twins' family, he might have trouble getting money for the two boys. There was no upside to killing Mr. Dana, at least not yet. "Shorty, kill the nephew."

"Bad mistake." Jonah Aaron spoke before Shorty could raise a weapon. "Bad mistake if you do. My uncle, Milton Brandenburg, has all of the Dana Twins' money tied up in investments. He'll probably be able to pay to get them back, but there's no guarantee. Their voices are changing." Jonah Aaron pointed to the blonde boys who were appropriately terrified. "They have a limited shelf life as we say in Nashville. On the other hand, my folks are loaded. You'll get money for me."

Shorty looked to his boss for instructions.

Halloran thought it over. He and his men had been together for years. It had never been tough to kill someone just because it was necessary. It wasn't necessary to kill someone just to show that he was tough. Tomorrow it would be necessary for him to kill a number of people. Not tonight.

"What do you want me to do?" Shorty asked.

"Nothing." Halloran felt that there was no harm in keeping the young man as well as Mr. Dana and the Dana Twins alive until morning. At that time, they could show the folks in Nashville that everyone was alive, make arrangements for a ransom, and—depending on how things went—kill them all then, or wait and see what plans were made to deliver the money. It would be the height of irony, thought Halloran, if no one would raise the cash for the Dana Twins, but some rich Nashville family ended up paying for the scruffy young man with long hair.

Halloran motioned to his men. "Shorty, you, Bill, and Marty sleep here in the main area of the barn with Mr. Dana and with—what's your name?"

"Jonah."

"You stay in the main area of the barn with Mr. Dana and Jonah. Tie them up. I'm going to keep the Dana Twins in the office with me." He pointed to a corner of the barn about forty feet away from where they were standing. The office was an eight by twelve room with a large window that looked into the main area of the barn. "We don't want anyone getting loose, and trying to get help, or worse yet, trying to get away. Then we'd likely have to kill someone and we'd mess up the plan. In fact, give me your guns. If something happens, I don't want any shooting during the night."

Shorty and Bill handed over their weapons to Halloran. Marty didn't carry a gun.

Jonah Aaron smiled to himself. First, they were going to keep him alive. Secondly, they were going to try and restrain him by tying him up. Jonah had studied basic magic tricks like pulling a quarter from behind someone's ear. He knew that if you kept your wrists a little apart when someone tied you up, you had an excellent chance of getting loose. At least he hoped it worked. It had worked for Houdini. Jonah had never tried it. Then again, Houdini did it in minutes, Jonah would have hours.

While Kyle Ford was looking around trying to assess the situation, Jonah Aaron had a question. "Can I have my duffel bag to use as a pillow? There's nothing in there for you guys to worry about."

Halloran continued to do all the talking for the kidnappers. "Bill, get me the kid's bag." All the suitcases had been loaded onto the truck when the four of them had been kidnapped. The idea was to convince them that once the ransom was paid, they would be driven back to the airport and sent on their way. Somehow, the bikers had overlooked the fact that seeing freshly dug graves would destroy the comfort of that lie.

Halloran examined the contents of the bag. It contained a pair of jeans, two black T-shirts, a pair of running shoes, a roll of duct tape, the two elastic bands that Jonah Aaron used to rehab his chronic shoulder injury, a deck of cards, and a nearly full bottle of whiskey. Halloran was convinced that there was nothing that could be used to harm him or his men. He took the bottle of whisky and gave it to Shorty. "I think you guys can drink and still stay sober enough to guard a man and a boy." He handed the duffel bag to Jonah Aaron "Here's your duffel bag, kid. When you get back to Nashville you can tell them how polite we were. Sleep well." Halloran knew that there was no way that Mr. Dana, Jonah, or the Dana Twins were getting back to Nashville, but there was no point in making anyone's last night on earth any more miserable than it had to be. This was about the money, plain and simple.

Kyle Ford tried to reassure Terry and Joey Brandenburg that everything would be fine as the two frightened boys were forced to accompany Halloran to the office area of the barn. As soon as Halloran closed the door to the office, Joe and Marty tied Kyle Ford's and Jonah Aaron's hands behind their backs. The situation was not conducive to sleeping.

Unless something unexpected happened in the morning, Kyle Ford knew the situation was hopeless. He found solace in the fact that since his murder would be part of a kidnapping, the FBI would be investigating the crime. It didn't matter if it took the FBI weeks, or months, or even years. The men who had taken him prisoner and kidnapped the Dana Twins would pay for what they had done and what they were going to do. Kyle Ford had no idea how quickly they would pay.

As Halloran looked through the office window into the larger section of the barn, he realized that things could not be going better. In addition to killing the Dana family and the long-haired kid, he was planning to kill Shorty, Bill, and Marty. Having them drunk or hung-over in the morning would make it easier. Halloran had researched the music business and knew the amount of the standard artist's royalty. He had counted on a million dollar ransom for the Dana Twins, and a million dollars was a lot better split one way than four ways. Halloran had never been outside the states of Washington, Idaho and Montana. As soon as the job was finished, he was heading to Mexico.

*   *   *

Once the three kidnappers started drinking, Jonah Aaron started working on the ropes that bound his wrists, and thinking about his plan. It wasn't a great plan, but it was a start. He knew Kyle Ford had plenty of experience. Hopefully, the two of them would think up a way to deal with Halloran before they came face to face with him.

It was nearly three in the morning when Kyle Ford was awakened by someone tapping on his shoulder. It was the one he called The Kid. He had forgotten the young man's name. "Come with me I have a plan," Jonah told him. Kyle Ford noted that the three bikers were sound asleep. He followed Jonah out of the barn.

As soon as they were out of the barn, Kyle Ford spoke to Jonah Aaron. "Go for help. I'll stay here and try and think of something." He doubted that The Kid would find help, but this way one fewer person would die on his watch.

"I'm not going anywhere, but, like I said, I have a plan." The way Jonah Aaron saw it, it might end up getting them killed, but if they could find a way to deal with Halloran, they would have a chance.

Kyle Ford listened to Jonah Aaron's plan. The Kid had balls. He had to give him credit for that. But as far as Kyle Ford was concerned, the young man was out of his mind. "Run this by me again."

Jonah explained his plan for the second time. The way Jonah looked at it, the plan would take care of Halloran's three men. Unfortunately, this wasn't a video game where scoring seventy-five percent of the maximum would win a reboot and another game. Killing only three of the four kidnappers would still result in his death—which is why he needed Kyle Ford's advice. "OK. I sneak in and loosely place a noose around Shorty's neck and toss the other end over a beam. Then I climb up into the upper area of the barn, walk out on the beam, tie the rope around my waist with a slip knot, and jump down. Shorty goes flying up and breaks his neck. I land on Marty to break my fall, probably break some of his ribs, and puncture his heart in the process. We take care of Bill with the bear trap. We set it up so it snaps shut and decapitates him. Then all we have to do is figure out what to do about Halloran."

"What do you weigh, kid?" Kyle Ford asked.

"One seventy-five."

"What do you think Shorty weighs?"

"Two fifty, maybe." Jonah paused. "Oh. He isn't going to go flying up in the air, is he?"

"No. You're going to be hanging in space, or else you and he are both going to be on the ground, staring at each other. Maybe he'll choke to death. Maybe not. It's imaginative, but it won't work."

"And the bear trap?"

"Have you ever seen how a bear trap works, kid?"

"No."

"I didn't think so. It's spring loaded. You have to step on it to set it off. I can't see how we can use it to immobilize the third guy, let alone decapitate him like you planned. I think we just tie them up, and then figure out what to do about Halloran. Let's look around out here for a minute or two."

Kyle Ford and a subdued Jonah Aaron searched the area outside of the barn to see if there was anything to help them deal with the leader of the biker gang. There wasn't much, only some rope, several pieces of two by four, a piece of PVC pipe, a broom with a broken handle, and some chicken wire. Other than the rope and the two by four, Kyle Ford considered it useless garbage.

Kyle grabbed a piece of two by four. "The best we can do after we tie them up is for me to take this and stand outside the office area. You make some noise. Halloran will come out. If I hit him with the two by four before he sees me and shoots me, we're home free."

"And if he sees you, or ducks, we're probably both dead."

"Basically. You got a better idea? One that might actually work and rescue the kids in there?"

"No."

Kyle Ford and Jonah Aaron removed their shoes and entered the barn as quietly as they could carrying three sections of rope. Jonah had concealed a Swiss Army knife in the pair of shoes in his duffel bag and Kyle Ford had used it to cut the rope into sections. Kyle figured that if they were lucky, they might be able to quietly subdue Shorty, Marty, and Bill.

Kyle put Jonah's knife against Shorty's neck. "Make a sound to warn the others and you're dead." Shorty stayed silent. Kyle Ford began to tie up the larger man, until he realized why Shorty was silent. Shorty wasn't breathing. "Are those two breathing?"

Jonah, who was in the process of tying up Marty, checked for a pulse. There wasn't one. He went over to check Bill. "No."

"What the hell? Well, I guess we're in luck."

"Not luck. I think I miscalculated."

"What are you talking about?"

"I put 1000 mg of diazepam in that whiskey."

"You what?"

"No one's going to sell a seventeen year old a handgun, even in Nashville. A bottle of drugged whiskey was just about the only weapon I could think of having with me if I turned out to be right about a possible kidnapping. I know you're not supposed to combine diazepam and alcohol, but I didn't think it would kill them."

"Well, it did, and I'm not the least bit sorry."

"I'm not either. Anyway, it's their fault. They violated rule number five and it killed them."

"Explain that bit about rule number five later, if there is a later."

"OK . . ."

Kyle cut him off. "You're seventeen? You look older."

Jonah continued speaking in a whisper. "Exactly seventeen years, one month, and nine days. When I was trying to untie myself before, I was calculating how old I would be when I died."

Kyle nodded. It was still likely that one or both of them would end up dead. "For seventeen, you're not bad. Let's get set up to go after Halloran. I'll wait outside the office, and when you make noise, I'll be ready for him with a two by four. You got anything else that might come in handy?"

"Just that knife."

"You don't bring a knife to a gunfight. Keep it. You might need it. I have the two-by-four."

"OK. Can you give me a couple of minutes, though. I just had another idea."

"Want to run it by me?"

"I don't want you to laugh at me again, but I want to try something. Look, those three aren't going to give us any trouble. In five minutes I'll start making noise. Just give me five minutes."

"I'll wait." The way things were likely to go it meant five extra minutes to live. Kyle Ford had nothing against that. He hoped that the death of Halloran's men would lead to a change in Halloran's plans and that the Brandenburg boys would survive.

Kyle Ford was looking at his watch and noting that six minutes had passed when he heard a noise that sounded like a trash can cover rattling around the barn. He heard a voice yell, "Halloran, get out here. We got a problem." Kyle Ford knew that the voice was Jonah's. He suspected that Halloran would think that the voice belonged to one of his men.

Kyle Ford saw the light go on in the office area, and saw Halloran move towards the door. As Halloran opened the door, Kyle Ford swung the two by four at him. As Halloran ducked, he lifted up his left arm in self-defense. The board struck Halloran's arm and he stumbled, but he quickly regained his balance and pointed his gun at Kyle Ford. Kyle Ford knew that he was a dead man.

Suddenly, out of the corner of his eye, Halloran saw something moving towards them. The leader of the biker pack turned towards it, but before he could fire his gun, he felt a sharp pain in his neck, and he began to cough. He noticed a metallic taste in his mouth. He couldn't breathe.

From the garbage at the side of the barn, Jonah had taken two pieces of two by four, and, using duct tape, had bound them together into a cross. He had also used duct tape to attach the PVC pipe to the pair of two by fours and to attach the Swiss Army Knife to the broomstick. Jonah had fashioned a harpoon gun and its trigger mechanism was his pair of long elastic cords—the rehab equipment that he kept in his duffel bag.

While Jonah was building his weapon, he had considered where to aim the projectile. The heart seemed the best target, but Jonah wasn't certain that the harpoon could penetrate bone. He had decided to aim at Halloran's neck. It didn't give him much of a target, but it seemed like the best idea.

Jonah knew that he needed to get as near to Halloran as he could. The further Jonah was from Halloran, the less momentum the makeshift harpoon would have when it reached his target. Once he pulled the elastics back, he had started running toward Halloran. When Halloran lifted his gun to shoot Kyle Ford, Jonah fired and kept running.

Halloran had had no time to react. The harpoon sliced through his trachea, carotid artery and jugular vein. Blood sprayed over the barn. Halloran began to cough. He was drowning in his own blood. He placed his left hand on his neck. The pressure pushed more blood into his airway.

Though mortally wounded, Halloran still had the gun. However, before Halloran could fire, Jonah lowered a shoulder and slammed into him while running at full speed. Halloran fell to the ground and the gun went flying. As Jonah lifted himself off the ground, Kyle Ford picked up Halloran's weapon. Halloran was dying and it was a horrible way to die. Halloran gurgled the words "Help me."

Jonah didn't like seeing anyone suffer, but he didn't see what he could do. "Sorry. I can't do anything for you."

"But I can." Kyle Ford aimed at a spot between Halloran's eyes and fired. Halloran went limp. All four kidnappers were dead.

Kyle Ford hurried to the office where Milton Brandenburg's sons were being kept; Jonah followed behind. As Kyle untied the boys, Jonah located the cell phones and the wallets that the kidnappers had taken from them, as well as the keys to the truck.

"What happened? Did someone come and rescue us? I heard a shot." Terry Brandenburg asked sleepily.

Kyle Ford answered immediately. "We rescued ourselves." He pointed at Jonah, shaking his head in disbelief over what had just transpired. "Mainly, he rescued all of us."

"What happened to the four men?" asked Joey Brandenburg.

Jonah's mouth was dry, and no words came forth. Kyle answered, "The men are dead. It was going to be them or us. Thanks to the kid, here, it turned out to be them."

Finally, Jonah spoke. "I guess we didn't do too badly."

Kyle Ford was looking around the office. A large safe in the corner of the room caught his eye. "No. Not bad at all kid. Where the hell did you come up with the idea for whatever that was?"

"My harpoon gun? Don't you ever watch *McGyver*—on television?"

"I will now."

"McGyver doesn't like guns. I don't think he'd approve of a harpoon gun either. But, the show taught me to improvise. Anyway, after my bullshit idea with the noose and the bear trap it was nice to come up with something useful."

"Damn right it was useful, and that was one hell of a tackle. Do you play football?"

"There's no football at the academic magnet school. It wouldn't matter if there was. My parents would never give me permission to play. They'd be afraid I'd get hurt."

Kyle Ford managed not to laugh. "If you go to college someday, bulk up a little and consider playing linebacker or strong safety. You look like a natural."

Jonah shrugged his shoulders. "I have to go back and take my knife off the harpoon. I think I'll change my shirt. Want me to get you a clean T-shirt too?"

Kyle Ford realized that his shirt, as well as Jonah's, were soaked with Halloran's blood. "Good idea."

"Is there anything else you need me to do?"

For the first time since they had been taken prisoner, Kyle Ford smiled. "Take Terry and Joey and get them on the truck. I suggest they close their eyes when they walk through the barn." Jonah suspected that after hearing Kyle give that instruction, the last thing that the boys would do was to close their eyes.

Jonah Aaron led the boys to the truck before retrieving his knife from the harpoon. He got his duffel bag and went to the office to see what Kyle Ford was doing.

Kyle was examining the large safe. "It's got a touch pad mechanism. There's no way we're getting in there." He paused for a moment. "No, wait a minute. I want to try something. Can you get me Halloran's wallet? I just want his driver's license. You can keep any money you find. He sure doesn't need it anymore."

"Sure."

Jonah returned to the main barn area, rolled Halloran's corpse onto its stomach, and took the wallet from Halloran's back pocket. He took two hundred dollars for himself and returned with the driver's license. It listed Halloran's birthday as August 12, 1966. Kyle Ford tried 8121966, 08121966, 81266, and 081266. None of them worked as combinations to the safe. Nor did the number of Halloran's driver's license. What was in the safe seemed destined to stay in the safe.

"OK, hotshot. You have any ideas?" There was no sarcasm in Kyle Ford's voice. He had no idea what Jonah Aaron was or wasn't capable of doing.

*　　*　　*

"Why don't we try the date before the month?"

Kyle Ford nodded. He had served in the military but in his excitement he hadn't thought of that. He failed with 12866 and 120866.

He tried 12081966 and the safe opened, revealing stacks of bound one hundred dollar bills, and eight packages of white powder. Kyle Ford had principles as an investigator, and stealing violated those principles. However, if he left the money behind, he suspected that the money would end up in the hands of drug dealers. That was not an acceptable option. If this was as much money as he thought it was, he wouldn't be an investigator much longer. This was his retirement package. "Half of it is yours, kid."

"No, it's yours. You're the real investigator."

Kyle Ford realized that he could use all of the money. "Look. You neutralized the three guys with the drugged whiskey, and that amazing weapon you put together was fantastic. You deserve half."

"If you say so."

"I'm saying so. You know, if you had told me what you were planning, I'd have said you were crazy, and convinced you not to try. We'd probably both be dead."

Jonah Aaron thought it over. Considering his royalties from the Dana Twins CD, he didn't need the money. He was a millionaire—except that the money was being held in trust. "Tell you what. How about I keep a quarter of the money, you keep three quarters of the money, and you train me. I want to be an investigator. There's obviously stuff I can't learn in books, stuff that could get me killed if I don't know it. I need the training more than I need the money."

Kyle Ford thought it over. He could see to it that the kid got his money's worth, but he had never trained anybody. He divided the cash into two roughly equal piles. "You could use the training, but I'm not a teacher. Were you telling the truth about your family having money to pay a ransom or was that just a con to stay alive?"

"It's true."

Kyle shook his head. "Look, I'm certainly not a teacher for a rich kid who—no offense—is playing at being an investigator. Just pick whichever pile you want. They look about the same to me."

"I'm not playing." Reluctantly, Jonah put one of the piles of money into his duffel bag.

Kyle Ford took the eight packages of what he suspected was cocaine or heroin from the safe. "I'll give you a free lesson. Don't mess with drugs, Jonah, ever. Don't use them. Don't sell them. The only reason I'm taking the stuff with me is so when the cops find the bodies, they'll think that a rival gang did the dirty work. They'd never reach that conclusion if drugs were left sitting in the safe." Kyle and Jonah would slice the packages open and scatter the drugs to the wind during the ride to Coeur d'Alene. "Now, we have to take care of the bodies."

As soon as he began staging the scene, Kyle Ford was at peace with the situation. "We'll bury them. The longer it takes to find the bodies, the harder it'll be for them to conclude that this happened the night the Dana Twins disappeared. The Dana Twins will have vanished into thin air, just like Milton wants, and no one will have a clue that the Dana Twins had anything to do with this."

Together, Jonah Aaron and Kyle Ford moved the bodies to the graves. "Do we need to dig a fourth grave?" Jonah asked.

"They can share. We'll make sure Halloran gets the top spot in the double grave. It'll look like they killed three guys to get the combination to the safe, then got it from Halloran, and slit his throat and shot him as an afterthought." That was first formulation made by the forensic analysts when they discovered the four bodies. By the time they had toxicology results and the confusing information that three of the men had died from ingesting a combination of alcohol and diazepam, the Idaho Drug War was in full swing.

As he buried the bodies, Kyle Ford couldn't help but realize that it had almost been his body that would soon be rotting in a grave at Morgan's farm. Whenever he thought seriously about death, he began to think about sex. He began to estimate the odds of getting laid at the Resort at Coeur d'Alene.

Jonah Aaron was not thinking about death. He was wondering how his fantasy baseball teams had done overnight. Jonah, of course, did not need an existential analysis to begin thinking about sex. He was seventeen years old. He was always thinking about sex. He didn't like the odds of picking up the daughter of a rich couple vacationing at the resort.

The sun was just starting to come up. Kyle Ford was shaking his head. "What dumb reasons to die! Three of them are dead because they kidnapped a seventeen year old kid who gave them a bottle of drugged whiskey." Pointing at Halloran's grave he added, "He's dead because he captured the only kid on the planet who could turn a pile of garbage into a lethal weapon."

Jonah smiled. "Which is much better than us ending up dead protecting the Dana Twins."

"No argument from me." Kyle checked the barn and was certain that there was no evidence that would tie what had happened to the Dana

Twins. He and Jonah headed for the truck. "You want to drive, kid? I mean, you want to drive, Jonah?"

"You drive. I can't drive a stick shift."

Kyle Ford began to laugh.

"What's funny?"

"Nothing. You managed to do what you did, but you can't do something simple like drive a stick shift."

"Lots of things I can't do. That's why I need training."

Kyle Ford eased behind the wheel of the truck, but didn't start the engine. "You know, Jonah, you have a lot of potential, and you also have a lot of imagination. You have too much imagination. Some of your ideas could get you killed. But if you really want to be an investigator, I'll teach you what I know. Like you said, there are things you can't read in books. I think I have my retirement package," he pointed to the sack containing half of the money taken from Halloran's safe "but a little extra won't hurt. I've always wanted to buy a sports bar, and thanks to you, it's going to happen. You give me half of your share, like you offered, and I'll train you. You saved my life this morning, and the least I can do is give you enough skills to help you stay alive. I'm going to be back in Nashville in a week. Are you staying in Coeur d'Alene or are you going back home?"

"There's nothing for me in Coeur d'Alene. I'm going to go back to Nashville."

"Makes sense. We'll get together when I come back. You're probably the new breed. I bet you know a ton about computers and shit like that don't you?"

"Yeah, I do. I plan to major in math and computer sciences when I go to college."

"You have potential." Kyle smiled. "Of course, in case you haven't figured it out, potential is just a nice word for having done nothing, but you are much more than nothing."

"Thank you." Jonah wasn't certain if it had been a compliment, but he took it as one.

"Look, I'm going to take Milton's kids up to Coeur d'Alene. I have to tell him what happened. I'm going to give you full credit. It's not my style to steal anyone's thunder. Do you want me to drive you back to Spokane first?" It was fifteen minutes east to the resort. It was half an hour west back to Spokane.

"The resort will have some kind of airport shuttle, won't it?"

"I'm sure they will."

"I'll take it when it starts running in the morning. I doubt there are any planes out of Spokane until morning anyway, and there's no sense putting you out on my account."

"That'll work."

As the four of them drove to Coeur d'Alene, Jonah asked Kyle if he wanted to hear about rule number five and the other rules.

"There's nothing on the radio. Go ahead, kid."

Kyle nodded as Jonah went through his rules about assuming nothing, asking the right questions, being able to use a gun, and being able to shoot accurately in a hostage situation. "Rule number five is never to accept food or drink when the reliability of the source is unknown."

"That's the rule they violated."

"Exactly. I always thought about it as a defensive rule. I guess that sometimes a good offense is the best defense."

"No argument from me. Go on."

"Rule number six is to find a girlfriend who can shoot a gun. Rule number seven is not to have a private office because it just gives bad guys a place to find you and harass you."

"So they come attack you at home?"

Jonah shook his head. "Rule number eight is to have a surveillance system with cameras outside the door of your home. Don't have a peep hole. You can get shot through a peep hole. Rule number nine is to have a bulletproof door."

Kyle started to laugh. He thought that some of Jonah's rules were silly but his future trainee had thought of contingencies.

"Ten is not to sleep with a woman who has more tattoos than you do. Eleven is that just because not everyone is out to get you, doesn't mean that no one is out to get you. If not for that rule, I wouldn't have been in Idaho."

"Tell me the rest some other time. I'm going to concentrate on my driving."

"I'm going to try to sleep."

They completed the ride to Coeur d'Alene and Kyle and Jonah said a temporary goodbye in the lobby of The Resort as Milton and Mona Brandenburg greeted their children. Mona took Terry and Joey up to their suite. In the morning she would dye their hair back to its natural color, black, and the Dana Twins would have vanished.

Milton Brandenburg listened in amazement to the details of Kyle Ford's story while Jonah made a brief stop at the resort's business center and then went to the all night coffee shop. Jonah was on his third cup when Milton made his way over to him. "I owe you. I owe you more than you can ever imagine. Not only did you save Terry and Joey, I think you saved my marriage to your Aunt Mona. If you hadn't done what you did, I don't think she ever would have forgiven me for putting them in danger. If there's anything you want, tell me, and I'll at least think about it."

Jonah put down his coffee. "I had a lot of time to think last night, and I actually have a list."

"Go ahead. I'm listening."

Jonah cleared his throat. "When I finish high school next year I'd like you to hire me as your investigator, jack of all trades. My mom wants me to go directly to college. I want to take a year off. My dad is ok with it. He always says he's sorry he went right from high school to college to medical school, but the Viet Nam War left him no choice. Kyle's going to train me to be an investigator. If I have a job lined up, maybe my Mom won't make a big deal about my taking a year off."

"I don't have a full time investigator. I never thought I needed one. I probably don't, but you are it. When you go to college, you can even work for me part time. If there's nothing to do as an investigator, I wouldn't mind having you hanging around the business. A creative mind can never hurt in my line of work. Consider yourself hired."

"That's great, especially what you said about me being creative, and wanting to have me around. That was the second thing on my list. I think you're a fantastic promoter. You made something out of next to nothing and you made people believe in it. I want to learn how to do that."

Milton began to chuckle. "You're welcome to watch and soak up whatever you can." He paused for a moment. "It's hard to put in words, but here's your first lesson about promoting. Despite what you may think you learned from your experience with the Dana Twins, you can't make something out of next to nothing. It might look that way at times, but that's an illusion like that magic trick where you pull a quarter from behind Joey's ear. You and Brian might not be very good singers, but at the heart of every success there is always a core of real talent. In the case of the Dana Twins, the talent was the writing of Cory Bayliss and the sound engineering of Jackson Daniels—and you. Anyway, if you try to make something out of next to nothing, you will fail every time."

Jonah thought it over. "Thanks for the advice. Basically, I want just two other little things."

Milton smiled. "Go ahead. Are they really little things?"

"I think so. First, I'd like your permission to print business cards identifying me as chief of security for Brandenburg Enterprises, as well as separate cards listing me as a talent scout for Brandenburg Enterprises. I can pass for twenty or twenty-one. If I have those business cards and your permission to flash them around, my social life will improve by an order of magnitude."

"Didn't you say something once about shooting fish in a barrel?"

"This requires one-on-one talent. It's different."

Milton laughed. "Okay. I'm not sure what kind of talent scout you'll make, but what the heck. Based on your track record, the next time you ask me to listen to someone, I'll pay attention. I'll have the cards printed for you when I get back to Nashville." Milton Brandenburg began to imagine Jonah with a haircut and a clean shave, working the club scene, and telling women he was a talent scout. Milton thought that the mothers of Nashville should lock up their daughters. He suspected that Jonah had already printed the cards and was trying to avoid trouble for flashing them around.

"And the last thing. Just like you got me a job at Lightning Bug Studios, do you think you could get me a job at someplace that makes music videos. I think I've maxed out my ability as a sound engineer and since I want to work as an investigator in the music business, I'd like to know as much about it as I can."

"Sure. The best place is in North Nashville, but you wouldn't even need my help to get that. Your track record as a sound engineer would open doors for you. But I'll put in a good word for you."

"Thanks. That's it, Milton."

"Not a problem. Are you taking the hotel shuttle back to the Spokane airport?"

"Yeah. Why?"

"My bags are at the front desk. I'll ride with you. There's been a slight change in plans."

"What kind of change?"

Milton took a deep breath and let out a sigh. "I lost sight of something. When Terry and Joey and you disappeared, and I thought something might have really happened to the plane, I didn't know what to do. Someday, maybe, you'll have kids of your own, and you'll understand. The point is this. Just like I love my boys, there are kids out there that love, literally love, the Dana Twins. I don't mean that they buy the CD's. I'm talking about little girls with posters on their bedroom walls, little girls who dream of growing up and marrying Richie or Stevie Dana. They LOVE the Dana Twins! It's sweet and it's silly, and we can't kill off the Dana Twins in a plane crash and break their hearts."

"It's a little late to decide that isn't it?"

"No, it's not. There's a missing plane, but no wreckage, and no bodies. I'm going to Reno and announce that the father of the Dana Twins changed his mind at the last minute and that the Dana Twins are safe and sound in an undisclosed location. Then, I'll apologize for cancelling the tour. There are little girls who need to believe that the Dana Twins are alive, and I have to deliver that story."

"After all the effort you made to have the Dana Twins disappear? It sounds weird to me."

"Consider it your second lesson of the morning. Never forget the audience. Who are the fans? What do they need? It's not just about money and getting people to buy your product . . . Did your father ever tell you the story about the intern who hated his patients and that crazy wager he made?"

"Zero Calliro. Sure. It's the story about how he and my mother hooked up."

Milton managed a smile. "Yes, it is that, but it's also a story about the importance of compassion. Your dad and I agreed that despite the differences between what he does and what I do, being a good person in either field requires that we treat people decently, with compassion. While it's harder to become a doctor than to do what I do, it's easier to be compassionate as a doctor than as a promoter. The point is that I should have been more compassionate in thinking about the fans."

Jonah yawned. "You're very philosophical this morning. I've never seen you be so serious."

"Having two missing kids, a missing nephew, and a wife screaming at me that I took things too far can do that. Anyway, people need to believe that there are sweet little boys who make sweet music and whose father decided that they couldn't show up."

"Even if it isn't true?"

"This is show business. Sometimes, the truth is what we say it is and in this case, a lie about the Dana Twins and their father is a compassionate version of the truth. And do you want to know what's interesting?"

Jonah could barely keep his eyes open. "Tell me."

"The more I thought about this, after I found out that you and Terry and Joey were ok, the more I decided that it's a good business decision. We don't just sell music. We sell dreams. If people believe that the Dana Twins are alive, ten or fifteen years from now, we can come out with a movie about what really happened. In fact, when I announce that the Dana Twins are alive and well, I am going to mention that we have a movie under development."

"Under development? What does that mean?"

"It means I have a title."

"Which is?"

"The Dana Twins: The True Story"

Despite having been awake all night, Jonah's eyes widened. *"The True Story?* You're going to tell people what really happened in that barn in Idaho?"

"Of course not. I have no idea what the true story is going to be. I'm very flexible. It's not going to be a documentary, I can tell you that much."

Jonah laughed. "A Dana Twins movie?"

"Absolutely. We'll get a screenwriter who is as creative with ideas as Jackson Daniels is with sound equipment. Maybe it'll be an action film; maybe it'll be a romantic comedy; maybe it'll be a little of each. Even if the film doesn't make money, and it might not, we'll come out ahead on the soundtrack. Do you want to try and write a screenplay? After that thing with the harpoon gun, I don't rule out anything as far as you're concerned."

"I think you can safely rule out my writing a screenplay."

"Like I said, I don't rule out much where you're concerned." He took a long look at his nephew. "You seem a little somber. I know you're tired, but you just don't seem like yourself. Are you ok?"

"Fine. Just a little down."

"Why? You're a hero. You saved Terry and Joey—and Kyle for that matter. Are you feeling bad about killing those men? If you are, you can talk to your Aunt Mona. She's a therapist, you know—or she can arrange for someone else to meet with you."

"No, that's not it. Bad things happen to bad people. I don't feel bad about them. My basic plan was excellent, but my alternate plan was awful. What did Kyle tell you?"

"He told me you accidentally poisoned three men, and came up with some phenomenal weapon, an improvised harpoon gun, to take care of the fourth."

"That's what happened." Jonah explained about the noose, the bear trap, and his plan to jump off a beam. "I had a half-assed plan that could have gotten me and everyone else killed. We didn't need it, but if Kyle hadn't explained why I was an idiot, that's what I would have done."

"You're seventeen Jonah. Not every idea you have is going to be great."

"I guess. I just hope I don't get myself killed before I figure things out."

Milton Brandenburg put his arm around his nephew. "I hope so too. By the way, I saw you in the business center before. What were you checking out?"

"The results for my fantasy baseball teams and the time of the first morning flight from Spokane to Nashville."

"Was there anything big about the Dana Twins in the news?"

"Just that they're supposed to be opening in Reno tonight. And there was one related story. *USA Today* had a front page human interest article on this twelve year old genius, Richard Dinsmore. He's supposed to be the next Einstein or something. He's graduating from MIT today and after telling the reporter that he expects that we will have time travel or see visitors from another galaxy within our lifetime, he commented that he had wanted to get two tickets for his eleven year old sisters to see the Dana Twins. He was griping that the tour was sold out."

"That's not a problem now that there is no tour. But time travel or visitors from another galaxy?" Milton looked at his watch. "I wondered how long it would take until I heard something crazier than the story of you and the harpoon gun. It only took until four fifty-two in the morning."

Jonah chuckled.

"Do me a favor, Jonah. Find out where they live and send his sisters a couple of T-shirts from the tour that never happened."

"There are T-shirts?"

"Sure. If there were no T-shirts to sell at the concerts, all the local promoters would have known that the tour was a hoax. I even have a hundred in a box in my office. There are probably twenty thousand or so T-shirts out there. They have a picture of the Dana Twins on the front and a list of the nine cities on the back."

"I'll take care of it. What do you want me to do with the rest of the T-shirts?"

"While I stay out here in Idaho, you could contact the local promoters and offer to buy them back at cost plus shipping. I'll give you a list of who to call. I sold them at five bucks each. You can do whatever you want with them. Burn them if you want to. Keep as many as you want for yourself."

Milton Brandenburg took out his cell phone and extended it in Jonah's direction. "By any chance, did you think to call your parents and tell them you were all right?"

Jonah gave his uncle a self-satisfied smile. "I sent my Mom and Dad an e-mail. I told them everything went exactly as planned and that I was on my way home. I'm going to call them from the Spokane airport so they don't worry; it'll be morning in Nashville by then. I'll give them the details in person."

Milton put his phone back in his pocket. "That I didn't expect." Milton also didn't expect the check for forty thousand dollars that he received from Jonah later that summer. While Milton advertised himself as Nashville's Number One Promoter, he did not understand the collectibles market. Jonah, using a relatively new website called e-Bay, turned a profit of eighty thousand dollars on the T-shirts that Milton had written off as a loss.

While Milton Brandenburg and his teen-aged nephew napped on the shuttle back to the Spokane airport, Kyle Ford checked into his hotel room, showered, and counted his money. He had over $320,000 and he hadn't collected his half of Jonah's share. For a day that he had expected to be his last, things had gone remarkably well. He got in bed and set the clock radio alarm for two in the afternoon. In the process, he accidentally turned on the radio. He heard a silly sounding tune with a chorus that went:

> I know that you know that I know that you know that I know (drum riff) what you did last night. But I can keep a secret, I can keep a secret. I can keep a secret. You know that I can. You think I'm a sweet boy. You call me your boy toy. But maybe, baby, maybe I'm a dangerous man.

The melody stuck in Kyle Ford's head the entire week he was at Coeur d'Alene. It was an infectious melody that seemed to stick in everyone's head across the country. In three weeks it would be the number two song on the pop charts and it would stay there for five weeks. If not for an even sillier song called "The Macarena," "Dangerous Man" by The Dana Twins would have been Number One. As it was, the song would be the first hit off the album *Dana Twins 2*, an album that would sell nearly five million copies.

*   *   *

Karma works in unusual ways and the universe rewarded Milton Brandenburg handsomely for his concern for the young girls who loved the Dana Twins. Abandoning the story that the young blonde boys had perished in a plane crash became an immediate promotional bonanza. While some people accepted the tale that a paternal change of heart was responsible for the cancelled tour, others believed that the blonde boys had perished in a tragic accident and that a cover story was being advanced to protect the sensibilities of their young fans. Since the plane and the pilot appeared to have vanished into thin air, the failure of the Dana Twins to appear in public left the matter unresolved. The speculation helped propel *Dana Twins 2* to the top of the album charts.

In addition to "Dangerous Man," two singles from *Dana Twins 2*, "Brown Eyed Girl" and "Each One Better than the One before It", reached the top ten. A song previously recorded by Mary Chapin Carpenter peaked at number eleven. It was the final single to be released from *Dana Twins 2* and, quite appropriately, it was entitled "Quitting Time."

If not for Elana Grey, a beautiful woman with a quirky sense of humor and a flexible sense of the truth, that might have been the last time that the public heard from the Dana Twins and the Dana Twins movie might well have been "under development" forever.

When the Dana Twins had their first hit in 1995, Elana Grey was among the twelve year old girls who put a poster of the two blonde boys over her bed and went to sleep each night hoping to dream of Richie or Stevie Dana. She knew every word to every song on The Dana Twins' albums and won several karaoke contests singing their material.

To help her karaoke performance, Elana decided to master the Dana Twins' choreography. She taped the Dana Twins' music videos and played them repeatedly. Watching the "Lost in Your Eyes" video in slow motion, Elana noted that the twin on the left touched "his" right shoulder following a pirouette move. She perfected the dance move and in doing so she realized that it was exactly what she would do in order to adjust a bra strap. She wondered if the Dana Twins were girls.

Before Elana shared that observation with anyone, however, she remembered that the video had reportedly been filmed at a county fair in West Tennessee. She mistakenly concluded that Richie or Stevie was scratching an insect bite. She, of course, had no idea that while two sixteen year old boys were the sound of the Dana Twins, two petite sixteen year old girls had played the role of the Dana Twins in the music videos. Concluding that she had an overactive imagination, she thought of becoming a writer.

At thirteen, Elana Grey "borrowed" her mother's credit card and, via the internet, purchased a Greyhound Bus ticket to Nashville, a room for the night at the downtown Nashville Hilton, and a ticket to the Nashville performance that was supposed to mark the end of the Dana Twins' tour. When the tour was cancelled, Elana heard the rumors of a fatal plane crash as well as the story that Reverend Dana had derailed his sons' career. She hoped that the boys were safe, but she suspected that there was more to the story than was being revealed. She promised herself that someday she would learn the truth and tell the tale. She imagined herself becoming a private investigator or hiring one. Despite the fact that the charges on her mother's credit card were refunded, when the credit card bill arrived, Elana's mother grounded her daughter for two months.

Under what she called "house arrest," Elana phoned Brandenburg Enterprises in Nashville, and, using the same credit card, purchased a thousand Dana Twins T-shirts at the wholesale price of eight dollars each. When the bill for that purchase appeared on the next credit card statement, Elana's mother decided that her daughter was incorrigible. Elana might have been grounded forever had she not already sold the T-shirts to friends, neighbors, friends of neighbors, and neighbors of friends at the retail price of fifteen dollars each. Elana repaid her mother and also had the good sense to buy her a pair of diamond earrings.

Standing in the lobby of The Resort at Coeur d'Alene, Milton Brandenburg had scoffed at the idea of time travel, but if he had been able to journey to the future, specifically to the year 2011, he could have seen the premiere of a movie which he and his partner, Jonah Aaron, had produced, a movie that Jonah and Elana had written entitled *The Dana Twins: The True Story.*

Milton had initially expected that he would break even on the movie and make money on the soundtrack. The soundtrack was a huge success, outselling *The Dana Twins* and *Dana Twins 2* combined. The movie, which was filmed at a cost of twenty million dollars, and promoted with a budget less than half that amount, grossed over eighty million dollars for what had become Brandenburg-Aaron Entertainment. As for the version of the truth that Elana and Jonah presented in their screenplay, it is probably fair to say that people got as much of the truth as they deserved—for eight dollars a ticket.

7

WHITE SQUIRREL

DR. ERIC CAIN stood at the large picture window on the eleventh floor of Chicago Medical Institute looking over the lights of the city and the traffic moving on Lake Shore Drive. For people out in what he called "the real world," it was a Saturday night in June and a night for fun. Inside CMI, it was just another evening.

Earlier that evening, as the faculty cardiologist on-call, he had helped a second year cardiology fellow successfully place a coronary artery stent in a patient with chest pain. He had just seen a consultation on the cancer medicine service. A sixty-one year old policeman with lung cancer was experiencing a cardiac arrhythmia. Eric had made a recommendation regarding treatment, and had suggested that the patient be moved to the cardiac care unit for closer monitoring.

As he looked over the city, he tried not to think of Jerome Dettman's job offer. His personal life was the same as it had been for years, with a parade of attractive women passing through. None of the relationships ever lasted more than a few weeks. Tomorrow would be his first date with an attorney he had met while doing a medical-legal consultation.

As a former college hockey player, he followed professional hockey. The Stanley Cup Finals were underway. Colorado had just gone up three games to nothing, but he had lost interest a month ago when the Chicago Blackhawks were eliminated in the second round. Unlike most of the doctors at CMI, Eric Cain had no interest in baseball.

He looked around the empty patient lounge at the two plush sofas, the four well stuffed arm chairs, and the two card tables. Even without the Oriental rug which had been removed since the last time he had journeyed to the eleventh floor, the place had the ambience of a wealthy family's living room.

Years after the accident, the eleventh floor had become a cancer medicine unit and rooms 11022, 11023, and 11024 had been converted into a lounge. Until then, many patients had refused to be admitted to room 11023; there was a rumor that the room was either haunted or cursed. As he often did when he stood before the large window, he punched at the glass. It seemed as solid as ever. He punched the glass again, this time a little bit harder.

"It's not going to break Eric. The engineers told us that you'd have to drive an automobile into this window to go through it."

Eric recognized the voice as that of Dr. Gail Riley. "Gorgeous night. What sort of emergency brings you here?" He turned around and saw that Gail was dressed in a green suede jacket with fringe on the pockets, a matching green suede skirt, and brown knee high boots. "You look nice. Where are you coming from? Was it that Tim McGraw concert you were talking about?"

"No. Just some local band. Larry and I were just out line dancing. The Spontaneous Combustion Tour with Tim McGraw is later this summer. Faith Hill is going to be his opening act."

Eric chuckled. "Let's hear it for Tim McGraw. That's one thing I learned when I was in rock and roll. It's always great to have a female opening act." Fifty different female rock bands had opened for Eric Cain's band Night Shadow back in the day, and Eric Cain had slept with a woman from the opening act exactly forty times. He considered eighty percent a very acceptable batting average.

"Why do you assume that there's something going on between them just because they're touring together?"

"Because there's nothing else to do on the road. I told you about Iowa, didn't I?"

"The four blonde girls?"

"I guess I told you. Anyway, I'll bet you a hundred dollars that by the end of the tour, Tim and Faith will either openly be a couple, or strongly rumored to be a couple."

"Define strongly rumored."

Eric shook his head, and brought his hands up to his eyes. The tone of his voice suggested irritation, but Gail knew he was joking. "Ah, the trouble of betting with a doctor who is also a Ph.D. and who wants everything rigidly defined. OK, try this, fifty dollars says they will openly be a couple either during the tour or within a month of the end of a tour."

"You're on. Why are you convinced that people can't work together and not sleep together?"

"Because I've been on the road with a rock band, and because you and I are the only platonic friends in America. They were going to make a movie about us called *When Eric Met Gail*, but Harry and Sally got there first." He paused for effect. "Oops. Bad example. By the end of that movie, they were in bed. Speaking of which, where's your husband?"

"Larry's parking the car. I'm here for an emergency of the spirit. I wanted to say goodbye to Sarah Fahey's sons. One of the nurses paged me with the news that she wasn't going to make it until morning. I figured I better stop by." She didn't have to ask why Eric Cain was at the hospital. She knew Eric was one of the three Cardiology attending physicians rotating responsibility for the month of June. It would be unusual for him to be anywhere except the hospital on his night on call.

"How was the dancing?"

"Wonderful. For two hours, I forgot what I did for a living. Unfortunately, I am back in reality."

"Yeah, there's something almost sensual about getting an audience to drift away and lose themselves in the moment."

"You sound nostalgic. Do you ever miss it? I mean show business."

He responded more quickly than she expected. "Actually, I haven't left it. Much of what I do, running attending rounds, dealing with patients, teaching the cardiology fellows, the residents, and the medical students, I learned in rock and roll. Bedside manner is just stage presence with a very limited audience. Anyway, if I had stayed in rock in roll, by now I'd be washed up. I'd be playing clubs with microscopic crowds, so, in a way, it's no different. The pay is much better here, by the way."

Gail Riley wasn't sure if he was being serious. "I always wondered if you would go back and do an oldies tour or something."

"A Night Shadow revival? No way. Night Shadow's bass guitar player is dead from a drug overdose. Our first drummer is either homeless or dead. My lead guitar player practices law right here in Chicago. And we weren't that popular anyway. We had a few hits. A group like Styx can have a reunion. Jefferson Starship can have a reunion. The Eagles have nothing but reunions. Not us. And there's no point. I'm thirty-nine years old. Rock and roll is for guys who want to sleep with twenty year old groupies. Why else would anyone do it? No. I am out of rock and roll."

"Just wondered." To her, there was always a part of Eric Cain that seemed like a lost little boy.

He admired the way Gail looked in the suede outfit. "I might get back into country, though. Country music of the 90's is just rock and roll chord progressions of the 70's, with slightly different arrangements—a fiddle here, a piano there. And I hear the groupies are a little older and much better looking." He smiled at Gail Riley. "If I make it in country, the first thing I would do is organize an international tour. Acapulco and Bermuda."

Holding her hand to her mouth like a microphone, Gail Riley announced, "Ladies and gentleman, here he is, the former lead singer of Night Shadow, Nashville's newest sensation, Eric Cain!" She applauded her introduction.

He chuckled. "Not quite. The name Eric Cain won't cut it in country music. It would have to be Ricky Lee Cain."

"Ricky Lee?"

"Yeah. Something like that. Speaking of Nashville, I got those tickets for you and Larry."

"Fantastic! How did you do that?"

He pointed to his head. "Genius. I knew it was sold out, so I asked myself who I knew in Nashville, and I remembered that when Dr. Aaron left CMI years ago he went to Vanderbilt. His brother-in-law is in the music business and has connections to the Dana Twins. You two have seats in the third row; you owe me two hundred and sixty dollars." He handed her the tickets. "You realize that you may be sitting in the middle of a bunch of screaming twelve year old girls and their mothers don't you?"

"You're amazing! Last month I met with Mel Aaron when he interviewed for the chief position up here at CMI. I talked to him for over an hour and the topic of country music never even came up."

"Well, you and he could probably talk for hours about lung cancer and tau-zeta receptors. The only shared interest he and I have is keeping down the cost of medical care. I ran into him last year at a conference. Anyway, we had a great discussion about what it was like to live in Music City."

Gail heard footsteps behind her and turned to kiss her husband hello. "Hi, honey. Eric got us tickets to the Dana Twins in Nashville on the twenty-first." Nashville was the last scheduled stop on the nine cities in nine day tour that was days away from being cancelled.

"Hey, that's a Friday. We can make a weekend of it in Music City." He paused. "It's the weekend after Dettman's party for the graduating fellows, right?"

"Right. I wouldn't even have bothered to try and get tickets if we had to be back the next day." Jerome Dettman, Director of the Division of Cancer Medicine, held a party each June to salute the fellows who were finishing their training. After twenty-five years at CMI, Jerome Dettman was retiring as Chief of the Cancer Medicine program. There was considerable speculation as to who would assume the leadership position. Despite the fact that she had only recently been granted tenure, as a clinician with a productive research laboratory, Gail Riley was under consideration.

Just as Larry Patterson began to settle up for the tickets, a nurse entered the lounge. "Dr. Riley, Mrs. Fahey just passed away."

Gail Riley sighed, and gazed at the ceiling. "I came for her sons, not for her. She's been in a coma for two days." She began walking towards the room where Mrs. Fahey's family was awaiting her.

Eric Cain smiled at the nurse. She was a fresh face that he hadn't seen before, not that he spent much time up on the eleventh floor. With her black hair tied in a ponytail, and her face outlined by ringlets of black curls, she looked to be in her early twenties. He checked for a wedding ring and frowned when he saw she was wearing one. He had rules about getting involved with a married woman.

"Is there something I can do for you two gentleman? Visiting hours are long over. Are you lost?"

"No. Sorry. I'm Eric Cain. I'm faculty in Cardiology. My friend here is Dr. Larry Patterson, Professor of Physics. He's married to the glamorous doctor in green suede. Sometimes I just come up here to admire the view before going home."

It was 11:15, the middle of shift change. The nurse started to walk away then turned around. "Eric Cain. You're the one who . . ." She paused.

Eric Cain thought he knew what she was going to say. Based on the embellished version of the story as it was told at CMI, she was going to say that he was the one who killed his incompetent resident, Roy Danton. Actually, Roy Danton was practicing internal medicine in Spokane, Washington.

"You're the one who ducked and he crashed through the window and you saved his life. Dr. Riley told me the whole story. Nice meeting you. I have to get back to sign-out." She paused and looked at her nametag. "It says Cookie Bradford, R.N., so I guess that's who I am. Tonight, I'm not too sure of anything."

Gail's return ended Cookie's conversation with Eric Cain. "Cookie, I moved the Fahey boys to the procedure room. It's quiet there. Could you please check on them in a few minutes?" The pixie nodded and vanished. "Well, Eric, I see you met Cookie." She yawned.

"That I did. Is she playing with a full deck?"

"Absolutely. Sometimes I think they might be Tarot cards, but it's a full deck. She's got it together." Gail Riley took her husband's arm and started to leave. Then she stopped, walked back towards Eric Cain, and—even though the room was empty—began speaking softly so that there was no chance that anyone might overhear what she was saying. "You know how they say some people go into psychology or psychiatry to understand their own craziness. Well, her husband fits the bill. He's her high school sweetheart. They've been together for seven years, since she was seventeen. He's going for a doctorate in psychology and for the past few weeks he's been accusing her of sleeping around. This morning he punched her. He may have broken a couple of her ribs. She refused to get an x-ray. I gave her some pain medicine. I would have told her to go home earlier, but to what?"

Eric Cain said nothing. Part of him was worried that the pixie nurse was going to get herself killed. Another part of him was considering that her hot body might be back on the singles' scene in a short period of time.

Gail interrupted his reverie. "Her husband, like many men, is full of shit. She's straight as an arrow."

Larry Patterson spoke before Eric Cain could reply. "You have to forgive Gail. She's kind of anti-men tonight."

"Well, can you blame me, honey? Mrs. Fahey, the patient whose sons I came in to see, had breast cancer. She had three teen-aged children. Her husband stuck with her through the mastectomy, but when it turned out that the tumor had spread to her spine, he dumped her and started dating his secretary. And let me tell you, Larry Patterson, if I ever get breast cancer and you dump me for your secretary, I will personally cut off your balls!"

Larry Patterson had no interest in finding out if she was serious. Both men smiled. Only Larry Patterson spoke. "I promise not to dump you for my secretary."

All three of them knew that Larry's secretary in the Physics Department at the University of Chicago was sixty four years old, and morbidly obese. Gail yawned again, took her husband's arm, and began to walk towards the elevator. As they departed, Larry Patterson asked his wife if she had gone to see Kathy and David Hallam while she had gone to see the Fahey boys. She shook her head. Despite a night of line dancing, her trip back to CMI had left her depressed enough as it was.

*   *   *

After Gail and Larry departed, Eric Cain resumed admiring the city below and thinking about Jerome Dettman's offer. Before meeting with Dr. Dettman, Eric Cain had considered leaving CMI. His grant investigating the feasibility of computerized interpretation of electrocardiograms had not been renewed. Getting the software to work was more difficult than he had expected and in three years he had made only modest progress. Without a grant, he had little reason to remain at a research university like CMI. He had been planning to look at private practice jobs on the north shore. Now, his future was up in the air, and he had five days to render a decision.

Jerome Dettman wanted him to join the cancer program, half-time, to evaluate cardiac toxicity of various anti-cancer drugs. It was scientifically valuable work and it would give him a reason to stay at CMI. The problem was that except for the anthracycline drugs, which had been on the market for two decades, the major anti-cancer drugs that affected the heart were the compounds that Gail Riley was studying, the drugs that acted at the tau-zeta receptor. In essence, he would be working for Gail Riley. He wondered how that might affect their friendship.

Finally, Eric Cain headed towards the elevator. As the elevator door began to close, three teenagers got in with him. The youngest of the three tapped his arm. For a fraction of a second he thought he was going to be mugged. "Excuse me mister. Did you catch the score of the Cubs game?"

"They played this afternoon and beat the Expos."

"Thanks. We didn't want to have the TV on in the room. Mom hated baseball. We were pretty sure she was out of it, but we didn't want her die with baseball in the background. She used to call it 'the great drone.'"

Eric Cain realized that he was sharing the elevator with Sarah Fahey's sons. The older boy appeared to be eighteen or nineteen. The four of them silently crossed the street to the parking garage. Eric Cain turned right, the Fahey boys turned left. He didn't hear the clatter of a woman running until she was thirty feet behind him.

"Dr. Cain. Wait up." It was Cookie Bradford. She had changed out of her nurses' uniform and was wearing a cotton shirt and a very tight pair of jeans. "Boy, am I glad to see you." She was still catching her breath. "I told Gail I could use a ride home when she called on the phone to check on Mrs. Fahey. I guess I wasn't definite enough. Anyway, could you please give me a ride?"

"Sure. No problem." He unlocked his Porsche and she helped herself into the passenger side. He started to drive from the lot. "Where to?"

She glared at him as if he had suggested something improper before she realized what he meant. "You mean where do I live?" He nodded. "It's the same building as Gail. Do you know where that is?"

Eric Cain knew the way. They were three quarters of the way to Cookie Bradford's home when she broke the silence. "Dr. Cain, do you know anything about white squirrels?"

"No. Should I?"

Cookie Bradford smiled again, but somehow, her smile seemed sad. "Nobody knows. That's part of the problem." Eric Cain tried watching her and the road simultaneously. "I grew up in this small town in Southern Illinois. Olney, Illinois. Not just small, really small. To me, it was the biggest hunk of nothing you ever saw. It was the home of the white squirrels. I mean there are four cities that call themselves that, and we're one of them. There were signs all over town. 'Home of the White Squirrels.' There's a $300 fine for running one over with your car."

"I'll be careful if I ever drive there, but I'll probably never go there."

"No one ever does. Nine thousand people and two hundred white squirrels. Anyway, they're cute, but they're nothing." Her tone was bitter. "Albino squirrels. Little furry nothings. You can't play with them; they bite. And they can't do anything. They're just squirrels. The whole town's only claim to fame is that they have a whole lot of nothing." They had reached their destination. Eric Cain double parked in front. "The point is that I got out of town, but I can't get that nothing town out of me." She got out of the car. "Thanks for the ride. You know, I am just a fucking white squirrel myself. That's all I am, and all I will ever be. A fucking white squirrel." She slammed the door and ran into the building.

"That girl is crazy," he thought to himself. He was glad that she was married and therefore off limits. He wondered if it would be acceptable to have a sexual romp with a woman who looked that good if she were single and crazy. Crazy had a real downside. She could turn into a stalker. Or she could get upset when the relationship ended and kill herself—or him. He had seen the movie, *Fatal Attraction*. No thanks. He realized that he was thinking about the nurse to avoid thinking about Jerome Dettman's offer and he headed for home.

Once inside the building, Cookie Bradford slowed down and began walking towards the elevator. She was in no hurry to learn if James had returned from the library. She hoped he hadn't. What an absurd day. At breakfast James had picked a fight when she mentioned that the two interns on the cancer medicine service for the month, especially Ken Hoover, seemed very competent. How could James even think there was something between her and Ken Hoover? Dr. Hoover was married. His wife was pregnant with their first child. Ken Hoover's wife even came to CMI to join him for dinner when he was on call. Cookie had seen her waddling around in the cafeteria. How could James accuse her of being involved with Dr. Hoover? It was almost funny.

And work. Work had been crazy too. The only good thing that happened was that Sarah Fahey had died. She was out of her misery. That was life on the Cancer Unit. The best thing to happen was that someone died.

Gail was the only one who appreciated that she was a good nurse. Who else would know? She was always nervous around men, and it was easy to play dumb. Interns and residents had such fragile egos. It was easy to play up to them, easier than trying to show them that you knew as much about medicine as they did. With Gail, she was always at her best. And now Gail had called her a fool, a silly little fool, for not walking out on James. She probably was a fool, or else she was what James had called her that morning, "a fucking white squirrel."

She stopped outside the door. The apartment was quiet. Damn. Things had been so good until April. It was the goddamn dissertation. What else could it be? James had been so worried about the extension, and now that he had it, he was still worried that he still couldn't complete his work.

He had always had a terrible temper, but she had never expected that he would hit her. It was the goddamn dissertation. They'd both be better off if he dropped out of school for a while. She had told him so, but she couldn't suggest it any more. He got so angry. She couldn't say hardly anything anymore. Everything she said was wrong.

RICHARD STEIN

She turned the key in the lock. Maybe he would be home, and sorry, and apologetic like the last time. Maybe it would be nice, like it used to be. Maybe they would make love and make the pain go away. She took a deep breath and opened the door. The living room was empty. She looked in the bedroom. James appeared to be fast asleep. Maybe it was better that way. She undressed and climbed into bed without waking him.

Having gone only a few blocks out of his way to drive Cookie Bradford home, Eric Cain arrived at his thirty-second floor Lake Shore Drive condominium shortly after midnight. It was the ultimate Chicago bachelor pad. The west wall was all glass with superb views of the city. The south wall had a fireplace with a piece of stone art sculpture mounted over the mantle. The east wall contained a tribute to Night Shadow with autographed photos of the group's members, autographed guitars, an autographed drumhead, and three framed and matted autographed vinyl albums, all in mint condition. The north wall was blank; he had considered ordering custom wallpaper showing the members of Night Shadow but his decorator said that it would be overkill.

He entered the bedroom, not even noticing the mirrored walls and ceiling, undressed, and fell into bed. When he had been with Night Shadow, he fell asleep by reviewing in which of the fifty states he had had sex. By the time he quit touring with Night Shadow, the number was forty-nine. He added Hawaii to his list during winter vacation of his first year of medical school. Since that time, whenever he had trouble falling asleep, he counted the categories of women he considered off limits. There were six.

Category one was married women.

Category two was patients. A relationship with a patient was an unethical abuse of the doctor-patient relationship. The category was near the top of his list because at least once a month a female patient let it be known that she was available.

Category three was widows of patients. Some of his older cardiac patients had trophy wives that had to be seen to be believed. As widows there probably was no reason to exclude them, but Eric Cain felt there was a conflict of interest in patient care if wives were off limits and widows were fair game.

Category four was ex-wives of friends. Eric didn't have that many male friends, but good friends were hard to find. One had to keep one's priorities in order.

Category five was women looking for a serious relationship. Eric Cain would never pretend to be what he wasn't just to get a woman between the sheets. Category five included Sally Templeton, the rhythm guitar player from his high school band "Electra and Her Fathers." Sally and he had maintained a friends-with-benefits relationship during summer vacations throughout college. It had continued during the time she was in medical school and he was on tour with Night Shadow. Sally was an Assistant Professor of Cardiology at Stanford. After a long hiatus, they had started hooking-up at the annual meetings of the American Society of Cardiology. A year ago, over drinks, Sally had invited him to move to California and live with her. He hadn't slept with her that night and hadn't spoken to her since.

Category six was Gail Riley. As a married woman, she was excluded by category one. Conceivably, she and Larry could get divorced, but in that case, she would be excluded by category four as Eric considered Larry Patterson one of his few good friends. Even if Larry cheated on her and she got drunk and went looking for revenge sex—Gail was off limits.

That night, as happened most nights, he was exceptionally tired and he fell asleep after thinking of category five.

*   *   *

The yearly party at Jerome and Julia Dettman's condominium was always a tasteful celebration. The emphasis was on tasteful as the celebration on the third Saturday in June was always rather muted. Jerome Dettman, referred to affectionately, and sometimes not so affectionately, as "The Great One," demanded decorum.

As a young investigator, Jerome Dettman had led research programs that had improved survival in patients with acute leukemia. However, over the years, as Chief of the Cancer Medicine program, he had become more of an administrator and less of a physician. He saw out-patients only one half day a week. He no longer served as an attending physician on the in-patient service. He even had come to look more like an executive than a doctor. His white hair and white beard were perfectly groomed. Around the hospital, one rarely saw him in a white coat. He generally wore a designer suit and an expensive silk tie that let him fit into whatever business meeting he would be attending in hopes of raising funds to support CMI.

The cancer program at CMI received tens of millions of dollars in grant money, but unrestricted philanthropic gifts were the life blood of the program. Even at his own party, where everyone else was encouraged to dress casually, Jerome Dettman wore a sports jacket and a tie. His only concession to the festivity of the occasion was that his white shirt had short sleeves. If one didn't know that he was soon to be seventy years old, one would have guessed that he was in his late fifties.

The invitations for the party said 7 P.M. There was no such thing as fashionably late for anything involving Jerome Dettman. By the time Gail Riley and Larry Patterson arrived at 6:55, two-thirds of the guests had already arrived. As the valet took their car, Gail Riley kissed her husband's cheek. "If all goes well, next year at this time I will be chief and this party will be at our place."

Gail Riley had attended enough of Jerome Dettman's celebrations near the end of the academic year to know both the agenda and the menu. The buffet style dinner would feature Beef Wellington and Coho salmon; it would include a pasta salad, and grilled vegetables. The desert would be baked Alaska. The bar would be well stocked, but would not serve red wine. Julia Dettman's living room had white sofas and white carpets, and red wine was never served at the Dettman's. After dinner, Dr. Dettman would make some paternal, humorous comments about each of the three trainees who were completing their fellowships.

The guest list would include all eight attending physicians in the Cancer Medicine program and their spouses or dates. The senior pharmacist for the cancer center would be invited as would some of the research nurses. Patient care issues would not be discussed at the party, but medical politics and hospital anecdotes were acceptable topics of discussion.

Having said hello to Jerome and Julia Dettman, Gail Riley and Larry Patterson walked over to greet Hal Gorman and his wife, Diane. Hal was CMI's leukemia expert; he had been at CMI for over twenty years as an M.D., Ph.D., primarily working in the research lab. He was a chubby man with short curly light brown hair. "You know Gail, no matter how many times I come to one of these, I still have trouble believing that the gracious man who hosts these parties is the same compulsive, highly organized, tight-sphinctered perfectionist we work with every day."

"Why do you say that?" Diane Gorman asked. Like her husband, she was in her early fifties. She was Hal Gorman's second wife and they had been married for eight years. Her only contact with Jerome Dettman had been at the parties held at the end of the academic year.

Gail Riley answered the question. "Hal says that about Jerome because it's true. You only see him here, where he's at his social best. Jerome has one mantra." As she said the words, Hal Gorman said them along with her. "Say what you mean. Mean what you say. Be precise, or else shut up." Hal and Gail burst into laughter. "Whenever Jerome requests a private meeting with one of the faculty to review how a study is progressing, or how a grant proposal or a manuscript is coming along, he has a separate manila file folder for each item on the agenda. I finally got in the habit of bringing in a folder of my own for each topic."

Hal Gorman chuckled. "Trying to out-Dettman, Dettman. There is a bright future for you at CMI. Not many people try that."

Gail Riley laughed. "Who else ever did that?"

"The only other person who did things like that was Mel Aaron. He always matched folders with Dettman whenever he met with The Great One. He would have had a big future here if he hadn't landed a better job at Vanderbilt. He may yet have a big future here." It was widely rumored that Mel Aaron was one of the finalists for the position as chief. "And Mel Aaron did something you can't do since you're a woman."

"What?" Gail Riley's anger was evident. As far as she was concerned, there was nothing she couldn't do just because she was a woman.

Hal Gorman smiled. "Relax. This is something you really can't do. You know that Jerome has high blood pressure and has taken a diuretic for the last twenty years. Given how compulsive he is, he sets his watch alarm for ten A.M. and two P.M. so he can go to the Men's Room and urinate on schedule, just so he won't ever have to step out during an important meeting. You know how hard it is to schedule time with him. Well, when Mel Aaron was here, he often went into the Men's Room opposite Dettman's office, at 9:59 and 1:59 and stood at one of the urinals. He referred to it as his 'standing meeting with Dr. Dettman.' All of us wondered how we could rarely get in to see the man, while Mel Aaron had a 'standing meeting' with the chief. Mel didn't let anyone in on his little joke until after he left to go to Vanderbilt."

Gail Riley chuckled. "I'll have to tease Mel Aaron about that next week if I see him when Larry and I are down in Music City." Hal had swapped weekend coverage with Gail when she obtained tickets to see the Dana Twins. "I'm giving a talk at Vanderbilt on Friday, and we're playing tourist in Music City all weekend. We had hotel reservations. We figured we might as well use them even if the Dana Twins retired from show business without going on tour." Gail Riley excused herself and moved through the crowd.

Hal Gorman turned to his wife. "I think that she may be the next chief."

"Really?"

"Really! We're not a large enough program to attract a big name from the outside even though we've interviewed a few. Gail is a fine clinician and she has a lot of grant money for her laboratory work on the tau-zeta receptor. Wait and see. They haven't offered her the position yet because it always looks better to bring in someone from the outside. But, if Mel Aaron turns it down—assuming they offer it to him—they're going to end up with her, and she's a great choice. If they don't pick her, they'll lose her."

"Why do you think they'll lose her if she doesn't become chief?"

"You heard her just now. She wasn't just casually dropping the fact that she was giving a talk at Vanderbilt. She wants to be sure that the word gets out that she's interviewing for a faculty job there. As big as they are, and as good as they are, Vanderbilt would take her in a minute."

"Isn't she a little young to be chief?"

"Well, she's only three years out of fellowship, but she's an M.D., Ph.D., she has her own grant, and she has seventeen publications in major journals." He paused. "How old do you think she is anyway?"

"She looks like she's in her early thirties."

"She's thirty-nine. Plus there's direct evidence tonight that Dr. Riley is a favored candidate." Hal Gorman pointed across the room. "He's here."

Diane Gorman looked at the handsome man who was standing near the Dettman's fireplace. "Who is that? I've never seen him before."

"That's Eric Cain. He's a cardiologist, not a cancer specialist. I asked him why he was here. I thought maybe one of the cancer research nurses had brought him as her date. Dr. Cain told me that as of July 1, he is going to be studying the cardiac toxicity of anti-cancer drugs half-time, and doing clinical cardiology the other half. He's funded for three years out of Jerome's special funds for program development."

"So? I still don't get it."

"Gail Riley is the only doctor in the program who is studying a new drug that has unusual cardiac toxicities. Her drugs that bind to the tau-zeta receptor make it more likely that a patient will have a cardiac arrhythmia. Jerome Dettman is doing everything he can to support her work. He essentially bought her a half-time cardiologist."

Diane Gorman was about to thank her husband for the lesson in academic politics when she noticed the confused look on his face. "What's the problem?"

Hal Gorman discreetly pointed to a young woman with dark hair who was standing in the corner. "Cookie Bradford's here. She's a nurse on the eleventh floor. Jerome is the most compulsive man I know. She shouldn't be on the guest list."

*   *   *

Not only was Hal Gorman wondering what Cookie Bradford was doing at Jerome Dettman's party, Cookie Bradford was asking herself the same question. She had mixed emotions about accepting the position as a research nurse. She would no longer be working on the eleventh floor, caring for patients. Instead, it would be her responsibility to monitor research studies, obtaining informed consent and making certain that the study subjects obtained all the tests necessary to evaluate their response to cancer therapy. She had accepted the job because Gail Riley had convinced her that working a regular 8 to 5 job might be better for her marriage than working the 3 to 11 shift.

The new job had earned Cookie a place on the guest list, but Gail had warned her that talking about individual patients was forbidden. Cookie was uncomfortable making small talk with doctors and there were only so many times that she could say how happy she was to be a part of the research program. She was standing in a corner with her husband when Eric Cain came over and introduced his date, an attorney named Carol Bernstein, to Cookie and James Bradford.

"I guess we're the new kids on the block, Miss Bradford."

"What do you mean?"

"Well, I just became part of the lab research program, and I heard you were becoming one of the research nurses."

"Right. You're a cardiologist. I forgot about that. Sorry." She tried thinking of something to say. Nothing came to mind except "What sign were you born under, Dr. Cain?"

He wrinkled his brow. "Do you really believe in astrology, Mrs. Bradford?"

RICHARD STEIN

"Not really. I just use astrology to make conversation with the patients. Talking about their illnesses can get really depressing for them."

He nodded. "Well in that case, the sign I was born under was Hamm's beer."

"What?"

"This should be good," Carol Bernstein interjected as she picked a glass of white wine off the tray of one of the circulating waiters. "What are you talking about?"

"Hamm's beer. My mother was pregnant and in her ninth month. She and my father were at Chicago Stadium watching a hockey game when she went into labor. Since I was her first child, she thought she could stay until the end of the game before going to the hospital. She was wrong. The paramedics delivered me in front of a concession stand, under the Hamm's Beer sign."

Everyone laughed, except James Bradford, who tugged on his wife's arm so forcibly that she stumbled and almost fell as they moved towards another group.

"So you were destined to be a hockey player?" Carol Bernstein asked.

"Either that or a beer drinker."

Eric Cain was concerned by the manner in which James Bradford had grabbed his wife arm. He thought trouble might be brewing, but before Eric Cain could walk over to the Bradfords, he saw them talking and laughing with Jerome and Julia Dettman. He concluded that either he had misread the situation or that the crisis had passed.

Just then, Gail Riley and her husband made their way over to Eric Cain and Carol Bernstein. After mutual introductions, Larry Patterson asked Carol Bernstein what she did besides attending medical parties.

"I'm an attorney. Civil litigation. I defend alleged medical malpractice. That's how I met Eric. He was an expert witness for me. He was fabulous."

Gail Riley thought of Eric Cain with his tendency to exaggerate being sworn to tell the whole truth and nothing but the truth. "I can almost imagine."

"No. He was really great. He presented a very logical defense of what the doctor had done." Carol Bernstein put her hand on her date's arm. "The jury loved him. The case took seven years to get to trial and the jury was out forty minutes. My partner and I polled the jury afterwards. They said that Eric was the best part of the trial. He made the jurors understand how bad things occur even when no one is at fault."

Hal Gorman had walked over to join them, and after Eric and Hal had swapped stories about interesting characters they had known during their years as interns and residents, Jerome Dettman began the formal part of the evening—the gentle roasting of the graduating fellows and the presentation of certificates.

Driving home from the party, Larry Patterson told his wife how much he had enjoyed himself. "You know, I hate to admit it, but I enjoy parties where I get to talk to doctors more than I enjoy parties with my fellow physicists."

"That's because all that your fellow physicists talk about these days is Richard Dinsmore. The boy just graduated college and everyone in the field is quoting every paper he publishes. I will be the first to admit that I don't understand a word of it."

"He did just get his bachelor's degree, but he's ninety percent of the way towards his doctorate. Can I let you in on a little secret, sweetheart?"

"Of course."

"Half of the physics department at the University of Chicago doesn't understand him either. In fact, there are some of us who feel that his entire theory is nonsense. However, since no one has designed a way to test his major ideas, it may really be as fantastic as it sounds. Frankly, I get headaches even thinking about it. On a lesser plane, the one that we mere mortals inhabit, Melvin Aaron, the prodigal son, may be returning home. He's coming back for a second interview next week. He's going to be here at CMI while we're down in Nashville."

Gail Riley raised her eyebrows. "That's sad. Not only are we going to miss seeing him, but he might get the job here as chief. He was a co-author on that big multi-institutional lung cancer chemotherapy study and he's a first rate teacher. When I was a resident, he taught me a lot about caring for patients with lung cancer, and he was the one who taught me that whenever you give a talk you really have to know who your audience is. Otherwise, you just end up showing off what you know, and you don't teach anybody anything."

"That seems obvious."

"Yes, but plenty of people smart enough to be professors don't seem to know it. I was at Grand Rounds last week, Larry, and one of the rheumatologists gave a talk that went way over everyone's head. It was a total waste of time."

"On the other hand, you have the research grant for your lab, and he doesn't do bench research."

"True enough. Anyway, if he gets the job, he gets the job. There's nothing I can do about it at this point."

Larry knew how much being named chief meant to his wife. He tried changing the subject. "Hal Gorman was in a good mood, tonight."

"Yes, he was. I think he was relaxed because he's content with his job and isn't interested in becoming chief."

They parked in the underground garage of their condo. "Remind me again why Hal Gorman isn't a candidate for chief."

"He says that ambition messed up his first marriage. He's content being a valuable contributor to the program. That's what he told me last week in those exact words. Valuable contributor. I think he wants me to know he's valuable, in case I end up becoming chief. Of course, in my opinion, he doesn't have a lick of common sense, not that it matters. At least he's at peace with who he is."

"And you? Are you at peace with who you are?"

"Very much. It won't kill me if I don't get the job, but I think I've got a good chance to get it. I have a good idea of what changes I would try to make if I do get it—but we can talk about that some other time. There are more important things to do tonight."

"Like what?"

"Like do you want to make love to the woman who is likely to be the next head of the cancer program?"

"Depends on who she is."

"Now, you're in trouble."

"Does that mean I don't get laid?"

She kissed him on the cheek. "You're not in that much trouble, Larry."

Unfortunately, Cookie Bradford was in trouble.

"I saw the way you looked at him, Cookie. Don't think I didn't notice."

Cookie Bradford had enjoyed her evening at the Dettman's and was hoping to make love with her husband. She finished undressing and turned naked to face him. "Looked at whom? What are you talking about?"

"Cut the crap Cookie. You know who I mean. I'm talking about your new boyfriend, Dr. Cain. He didn't hire you for your brains. I should have figured you'd fuck your way to a better job."

"You can't mean that. I barely know him. And Gail got me the job. I'm working for her, not for Dr. Cain. Don't say things like that."

Affectionately, she tried to place her hands on his shoulders, and—with her hands upraised—lost her balance as he unexpectedly shoved her away. Her back struck a corner of the chest of drawers. Pain seared through her chest and tears welled in her eyes.

"No, no, no," she told herself. It was happening again. She struggled to control herself, knowing that her anger would only make things worse. "I told you I barely know him. It's the truth." She placed her hands on her hips, determined to hold her ground.

"You make me sick." This time the shove wasn't unexpected. Again she struck the chest of drawers, but this time her back crashed against its flat front. The physical pain was more bearable than her anguish over her collapsing marriage.

"Goddamn it . . . You're crazy . . . I barely know him." She was screaming between her sobs.

"Don't know him?" She was crying. He would give her something to cry about. His open palm crashed against her cheekbone. "Don't know him. I saw his car tonight. It's the same car that drove you home last Saturday. I didn't know who it was then, but I do now. You ought to tell your boyfriends not to drop you off in front any more. I'm not stupid you know."

"I don't have any boyfriends." She stopped screaming. She would try to calm him with reason. "He gave me a ride. You weren't there to pick me up because we had had a fight. Gail forgot about me. Dr. Cain gave me a ride. That's all. He gave me a ride home."

"Just a ride?" For a moment, he sounded rational.

"It was just a ride, James."

"Just a ride! A couple of minutes ago you barely knew him. Now you admit he gave you a ride. In ten minutes you'll be telling me the truth that you're sleeping with him you little slut. Why don't you admit it for once?"

"BECAUSE THERE'S NOTHING TO ADMIT! THERE ISN'T ANYONE ELSE!"

"Liar! I don't now why I stay here and put up with this!" This time the slap was anticipated. As she raised her forearm to deflect the blow, her hand brushed against his face. "So, you want to fight do you? Well, I'll show you how to fight." His fists crashed into her ribcage, tearing the breath from her chest. She fell to the floor.

"You're crazy. That's what you are."

RICHARD STEIN

To her surprise, James was helping her up. She thought it was over. Suddenly, almost before she realized what was happening, his hands were no longer under her shoulders. For the first time, ever, his hands were on her throat. In desperation, she tugged at his wrists, but the pain in her chest drained the strength from her arms. She fought for breath, but found none. She tore at his hands, and then his face, with her nails. She couldn't breathe. She realized she was going to die. If James was going to leave her, she didn't want live without him, but she didn't want to die like this. In a final effort, she tried driving a knee into his groin. She missed, but the effort made her lose her balance, and the two of them tumbled to the floor. Her head struck the night table. Everything went red, then black.

When Cookie Bradford awoke, she was alone. She could barely swallow. She coughed. Bloody mucous filled her throat. She was a nurse and the blood didn't frighten her as much as the thought that James might return—if indeed he had left. He wasn't in the bedroom. A panicked dash through the apartment convinced her that he was gone. She locked the safety latch on the front door. He wouldn't be coming back tonight. She returned to the bedroom and put on a robe.

She collapsed in her bed and began to worry that he might never come back. What would she do then? She wanted him. Not like tonight, but she wanted him the way it used to be.

Slowly, she made her way to the bathroom. Except for the pain in her ribs and the dry feeling in her throat she wasn't injured. She needed something for her pain. Pills. She would show him. She would take all the pills. She found the bottle that Gail had given her the last time James had beaten her. Damn. Gail had given her eight pills and only one was left. What a terrible idea that had been, anyway—to take pills. James would be back, and things would be better. She went to the kitchen, opened a bottle of merlot, poured herself a glass, and then another, and another.

She wanted to sleep, but despite the wine, she was far too agitated to sleep. She realized that there was only one solution. She untied her robe, lay on her back, and moved her hand to the wet softness between her legs. She began the slow familiar stroking, pretending all the while that James was doing what she was doing to herself. Her left hand reached for an erect nipple and squeezed firmly. Her pelvis responded and, almost mechanically, began a rocking motion of its own. Her breaths became deeper and more regular. Finally, her pelvis sighed and then convulsed in sad solitary ecstasy. Eventually, she fell asleep.

In the morning, the pain was gone, and with the events of the previous evening nearly forgotten, she put on a turtleneck to hide the marks on her throat and began the six block walk to CMI. She was halfway there before she realized that it was Sunday. She didn't have to work until Tuesday. She turned around.

Cookie Bradford spent most of Sunday in bed, worrying about what would happen when James returned. She spent Monday watching television, reading a romance novel, finishing the bottle of merlot, and worrying that he wouldn't ever come back. By Tuesday morning she had decided on a plan.

*   *   *

On Tuesday morning Gail Riley made morning rounds with the house staff. She was in her office, having completed a meeting with one of the Ph.D.'s who worked in her lab, when Cookie Bradford knocked on the door. "Dr. Riley, can you sign these? They're for a study patient."

"Sure." Gail scribbled her name on four prescriptions. "You didn't finish filling out this last one."

"Right. Dr. Hoover told me that you had finished rounds and had headed back to your office. I know you see out-patients on Tuesday afternoon and I figured I better to catch you while I had a chance. I didn't get to finish filling it out."

"No problem. How are things at home?"

"Not good. We had a fight Saturday night and James took off. I haven't seen him since."

"Cookie, maybe you should talk to someone. Diane Gorman, Hal's wife, is a therapist. Maybe it would help. If you don't want to see her, I'm sure she could recommend someone."

"I don't need a psychologist or a psychiatrist. I'm fine." Cookie turned and walked away.

Gail wanted to say that Cookie Bradford certainly didn't need a psychologist named James Bradford in her life, but she decided not to continue the discussion. She looked at her watch. It was twelve forty-five. Her first out-patient was scheduled for one o'clock. She went to a vending machine, got a package of potato chips, and headed to the out-patient clinic where there were seventeen patients to be seen.

RICHARD STEIN

It was nearly five o'clock and Gail was about to see the last of her patients when she received a page. She answered immediately. It was Eric Cain.

"Did Cookie Bradford quit her new job?"

"Not to my knowledge, Eric. Why are you asking?"

"I saw her a few minutes ago. She said she was leaving for the day and she told me she was sorry that we wouldn't be working together. We had chatted briefly at Dr. Dettman's party about how we were both joining the cancer research program. There was something very strange about it, but I couldn't put my finger on just what it was. I wondered if you knew anything."

"I have no idea. Maybe she's giving up on her worthless husband and going back to working on the eleventh floor. She took the job to get more reasonable hours. Look, I'm wrapping up my last patient here in clinic. I'll see you tomorrow."

It wasn't until she was writing her patient a prescription for pain medication that she realized what might be happening. She immediately called Eric Cain. "Eric, I signed some prescriptions for Cookie earlier today. She told me they were for a patient on a study. One was blank. You don't think she might have had it filled for herself and be planning on taking something, do you?"

Eric Cain thought it over. Suicide would be consistent with her comment that they wouldn't be working together. So would a number of scenarios. "I don't know. You know her. I've had all of three or four brief conversations with her in my whole life. Like I said, there was something weird about the way she was talking about us not getting to work together, but . . . What do you think?"

"I don't know. Part of me says we ought to get over to her place and make sure she doesn't do anything rash, and part of me says I'm being foolish. She told me that her husband took off after a fight on Saturday. I'm going to call the pharmacy and see if she wrote herself a prescription on the blank one she had me sign. Can you meet me in clinic?"

"Better yet, I'm done for the day. If you think she may have taken something, how about while you check with the pharmacy, I get my car and meet you in front of the clinic building? That'll be the quickest way to get to her place. If it's a false alarm, I'll just head on home."

"Sounds like a plan."

The hospital pharmacy informed Gail that Cookie Bradford had filled a prescription for thirty oxycodone pills that Gail had unwittingly written for her that morning. Taken all at once, that amount of pain medicine could be lethal. By the time Eric Cain met her at the clinic entrance of CMI, Gail was convinced that Cookie Bradford was going to be the victim of a fatal overdose.

"Come on, Gail, be optimistic. Maybe she was just too embarrassed to admit that he beat her and that she needed something for pain. That is a reasonable dose for a week of pain pills."

"I'm a cancer doctor. I can sound optimistic when I talk to patients, but I'm not naturally optimistic. She's going to kill herself, Eric. If she wanted something for pain, she could have just asked. What if she checked into a hotel and left a do not disturb sign on the door instead of going home? No one will find her in time if she did that."

Eric shook his head. "There's no point worrying about 'what ifs.' From what you told me, I'm more worried that her husband came back and asked her to quit the new job. We might get there and find the two of them going at it hot and heavy."

Gail chuckled. "That would be funny."

They rode in silence until Eric Cain asked, "How are we going to get in?"

"I have a key. I live in the same building and I take care of her plants when they go on vacation."

Eric Cain dropped Gail Riley off in front of the building. "You go see what's going on. I'll park and be right up. I'll ring her bell, buzz me in."

Her white coat flapping in the breeze, Gail raced up the steps. Over her shoulder, she shouted "It's apartment 206." She found a neighbor in the lobby, asked him to hold the door for Eric Cain, and took the elevator to the second floor. There was no answer when she knocked on Cookie's door. She called Cookie on the phone; no one picked up. She paged Cookie and heard a beeper going off inside. Gail gave a small sigh of relief. More likely than not, no matter what she had done, Cookie was inside. Gail turned the key in the lock.

When Eric Cain returned to the building he found a middle aged man standing in the doorway. "Are you Dr. Cain?"

"Yeah!"

"206."

Eric Cain was convinced they were going to find Cookie Bradford and her husband screwing. When he reached the apartment, the door was open. He heard Gail Riley yell, "Oh, no."

Cookie Bradford was lying in bed, alone and naked. Her breasts were aimed squarely at the ceiling, her legs were limply apart. An empty orange prescription bottle lay on the floor. Gail Riley tried to shake her awake. Cookie Bradford was too far gone to respond, but she was alive. Barely.

Gail checked for a pulse in Cookie's neck. "Her respiratory rate is six and I can't feel a pulse. What can we do?" Without hospital equipment, Gail Riley was as lost as any non-physician would be.

Eric Cain lifted Cookie's body off the bed and placed it on the floor. He needed a hard surface. "I'll pump; you breathe for her. Call 911 before you start!" As a cardiologist Eric Cain had run hundreds of cardiac resuscitations. As an attending cancer specialist, Gail Riley had directed only three resuscitations since residency.

As Eric Cain began chest compressions, he glanced at the empty prescription bottle. It was the oxycodone that Gail had inadvertently prescribed that morning.

"Don't die, Cookie. Don't die, Cookie. Don't die, Cookie."

"Eric, can you say something else other than 'Don't die Cookie?'"

"I always say something when I do chest compressions. Keeps me in rhythm. What do you want me to say?" Before she answered, he switched to a different mantra. "Looks great naked. Looks great naked. Looks great naked."

"'Don't die, Cookie' is fine."

"I like 'Looks great, naked,' better." With each compression, Eric Cain uttered his new mantra. "Looks great naked. Looks great naked. Looks great naked. Are these marks on her neck new?"

Gail thought back to earlier that morning. "She was wearing a high collar this morning. I don't know."

He resumed his mantra. "Looks great naked. Looks great naked. Looks great naked . . . So not only did he beat her Saturday, he choked her, and instead of being glad he's gone, she tried to kill herself."

"Isn't love funny?"

"Looks great naked. Looks great naked. Looks great naked."

"This is surreal, Eric."

"No it's not. It's just a routine resuscitation . . . Looks great naked. Looks great naked. Looks great naked."

By the time the rescue squad arrived ten minutes later, Eric Cain wasn't tired and was still muttering "Looks great naked" with each chest compression.

THE DANA TWINS AND RELATED MATTERS

The first EMT hooked Cookie Bradford up to an electrocardiogram and found that she was in ventricular fibrillation. Gail stepped away as the second EMT passed a tube into Cookie Bradford's airway and attached it to an Ambu bag. From this point on, there would be nothing for Gail to do but watch.

Eric Cain continued performing chest compressions. "Shock her at 50."

"Will do."

The first EMT applied the paddles, yelled "Clear!" and pressed the red button as soon as Eric Cain and the other EMT stepped back. Cookie twitched like a rag doll having a weak orgasm.

The EMT looked at the monitor. "Still V Fib. Keep pumping, doc."

One of the men from the rescue squad had started an intravenous line. "What do you guys want me to run?"

Eric answered immediately. "Amp of bicarb in half normal saline. Then let's shock her again. This time at 100." He had resumed chest compressions.

The EMT hung a bag with bicarbonate, let it run in for a while, set the defibrillator at 100, and applied the paddles again. "Clear!" Again, one twitch. As before, the monitor showed no change.

Eric Cain said nothing as he considered the next step. "Try 100 again."

"Clear!"

Surprisingly, this time after the shock was applied, the EKG showed a normal rhythm. The EMT felt for a pulse in Cookie's neck and smiled when he found one. Everyone gave a deep sigh of relief as one of the EMT's checked a blood pressure. "Ninety over sixty. Pulse is sixty-four. OK to roll, doc?"

"Let's wait a bit." Eric Cain watched the electrocardiogram for half a minute in order to be certain that a stable rhythm had been achieved. He took a deep breath and let it out slowly. "Yeah. Take her to CMI. That's the nearest place, isn't it?"

"You got it. You guys want to ride in back with her?"

Eric Cain glanced at Gail Riley before answering. "You have telemetry to the CMI Emergency Room, don't you?"

"Absolutely."

"Well, then you guys can handle it. I don't want to have to come back for my car. We'll see you in the Emergency Department."

The EMT's lifted Cookie onto a rolling gurney, and headed towards the elevator.

Gail and Eric accompanied them on the elevator and then walked briskly to Eric's Porsche. "Why didn't you want to ride with them? We'd have gotten there sooner. I'd have given you a ride back to your car."

"We're not needed. They'll have contact with CMI all the way. People talk enough about us anyway. If we show up together with an EMT crew, having rescued a nurse, it will be all over the hospital tomorrow. A gentleman has to look out for a lady's reputation."

"You're serious, aren't you?"

"Yes I am."

"Then maybe you should wipe my lipstick off your face."

"Did you kiss me in the middle of all that?"

"Well, that does wonders for my ego. You don't remember . . . ? No! I didn't kiss you! I was teasing just now." She squeezed his hand. "Thank you for saving Cookie. That was fantastic. You were brilliant."

Eric kept his eyes on the road as he drove back to CMI. "The only smart thing I did was pick up on her comment about not working with me any more. The rest was just routine. And anyway, we saved Cookie. Not me. Both of us . . . Hopefully."

Gail Riley picked up her cell phone and called her husband, explaining what had happened and asking him to meet her at CMI. She expected that it would be a long night. "Larry says it's ok if I kiss you once to thank you for saving Cookie."

"Tell Larry 'hi,' but save it for Acapulco or Bermuda."

Gail kissed him on the cheek and immediately wiped off the lipstick. "Acapulco and Bermuda are never going to happen. You do realize that, don't you?"

"Of course I realize it, but it's still fun to joke about it. Actually, what we should do is run off to Nashville. I could get back in the music business, and you could see all the big name country music shows you want."

"Nashville is not out of the realm of possibility for me, but I think I'd rather stay here and become chief."

"You think you're going to be offered the job?"

"I had my third interview with the Dean and the Chairman of Medicine yesterday. You are very likely sitting in a car with the next chief of the Cancer Medicine program at CMI."

"May I kiss you for congratulations?"

"No. That would be two kisses. That would be like necking. That's unacceptable. And it's still not definite. But I've let them know that if I don't get the job, I'm going to start looking elsewhere."

"You might leave?"

"I can't leave the city, not with Larry wedded to the University of Chicago. But, there are other places in town. I'm looking around at other places to gain perspective and to make them realize what they have to lose if they don't make me chief. Don't look surprised. College coaches look at other jobs just to get a bump in salary. Why can't an associate professor of medicine look at a job somewhere else to help get a promotion?"

"Makes sense. Do you mind if I turn on the radio?"

"Of course not."

The first channel was playing "The Macarena." Eric Cain quickly changed the channel and found the falsetto voices of two young boys.

I know that you know that I know that you know that I know (drum riff) what you did last night. But I can keep a secret, I can keep a secret. I can keep a secret. You know that I can. You think I'm a sweet boy. You call me your boy toy. But maybe, baby, maybe I'm a dangerous man.

"Much better!"

*   *   *

Gail Riley, Larry Patterson, and Eric Cain spent the early evening in the Medical ICU waiting area. As of nine o'clock, Cookie hadn't regained consciousness. However, attached to a respirator with intravenous lines running, she looked just like any other ICU patient. The situation no longer seemed extraordinary.

As they waited for news on Cookie, Gail turned the conversation back to the search for the new chief. "Mel Aaron is coming back at the end of the week for another interview for the chief's job. I think he reminds Jerome of himself. Mel's highly organized and logical."

Eric Cain shook his head. "He's not like Jerome. Mel Aaron has much more personality. Hey, speaking of Mel Aaron, would you mind if I told my favorite Mel Aaron story."

"What? We're sitting here in the ICU waiting area. Someone we know just tried to kill herself. We may or may not have managed to save her life, and you want to tell a funny story?" Gail looked at her husband. "Why not? Listening to you will be better than staring at the walls and at each other."

Eric Cain never needed more than minimal encouragement to tell a story. "Thanks. Anyway, this goes back to when he first came to CMI in the mid-seventies and he was attending on one of the general medicine teams."

"That's before we were interns together and he was our attending."

"I know. I heard this story from one of the senior cardiologists. You know I collect stories. Anyway, Dr. Aaron had a patient who had a cold agglutinin, an abnormal protein . . .'"

"I know what a cold agglutinin is, Eric. I'm board certified in both hematology and cancer medicine."

"Yes, but Larry doesn't know, and he's listening too. I used to be in show business. I have to reach my total audience, even if my total audience is two people." Eric held up two fingers and Larry laughed as Eric continued. "A cold agglutinin is an abnormal protein that makes red blood cells stick together at low temperature. Normal body temperature is 37 degrees centigrade. With a cold agglutinin, the patient's body temperature, even in her fingertips and toes had to be kept above thirty one degrees centigrade at all times or the red blood cells would clump together. Fatal clotting would probably occur. Well, before she became ill with the cold agglutinin, the woman had been scheduled for an elective heart valve replacement. The heart valve problem was unrelated to the abnormal protein, but it created a dilemma. Heart surgery requires that core body temperature be reduced to twenty seven degrees. That would be fatal in this patient since she had a cold agglutinin, but it wasn't a critical problem. The surgery was elective."

Gail interrupted. "Not a problem at all. All they had to do was delay the surgery until the protein went away. They usually are temporary."

"Exactly. However, the surgery was scheduled to be done by a surgical resident, and he was rotating to another institution in just three days. He wanted to do the surgery himself. Mel Aaron knew better than to argue with an angry man carrying a scalpel, so he wrote something like the following in the chart. 'The patient has a cold agglutinin and must be maintained at a body temperature above thirty-one degrees at all times. Open heart surgery requires a core body temperature below twenty-seven degrees. Doing the surgery is obviously impossible. I have tried explaining the situation to the surgical resident. However, since the surgeon is adamant, I recommend a consultation from a mathematician to identify a number that is both greater than 31 and less than 27. There probably isn't such a number, but I am told imaginary numbers exist, and I do not understand them. Perhaps a mathematician can solve this conundrum.'"

Larry Patterson, a physicist was laughing. "That is one of the most incredible things I have ever heard."

Gail was stunned. "He put that in a medical chart?"

"Absolutely. Even Jerome Dettman thought it was funny, but Dettman is so rigid that he couldn't have thought of something like that if his life depended on it. Anyway, whenever someone is faced with an impossible situation here at CMI . . ."

"They refer to it as a twenty-seven/thirty-one situation. I never knew where that came from."

"Now you do, Gail. Mel Aaron did that."

Gail Riley was silent for a moment before she turned to her husband. "That's it. They have it down to me and Mel Aaron, and it's going to be Mel Aaron. He's got a CMI pedigree; he's a solid clinician; he's done good clinical research; he's a great teacher. He may not have the grant support that I do and he doesn't have a lab, but he's going to get the job. He's personable, he's older than me, and he probably would be a great recruiter." She closed her eyes, dropped her chin on her chest, and looked as despondent as she felt. "Well, I made it to the final two, that's something at my age."

Larry Patterson took his wife's hand, but Eric Cain was suddenly very animated. "The final two? You and Mel Aaron are the final two? Are you sure about that?"

"Everyone else has been eliminated or has dropped out."

Despite the reason that they were in the ICU waiting room, Eric Cain smiled. "In that case, congratulations, Gail. If you and Mel Aaron are the final two, you're going to get the job. Mel Aaron isn't going to take it even if they offer it to him."

"How do you know that?"

"You know I called him to get the tickets for that Dana Twins concert that got cancelled? We had a nice conversation. His older son is going to be a senior in high school in the fall. His younger son is going to be a high school sophomore. Mel's wife is an interior designer in Nashville. She had trouble getting a good job in Chicago, which is one of the reasons why they left. His family is immovable. He's not going to

RICHARD STEIN

come here and have to commute back and forth. He's not going to take the job!"

"Why didn't you tell me that before?"

"I didn't tell you because I had no idea that it was down to you and Mel Aaron. I'm a cardiologist. I just joined the cancer program. I'm out of the loop as far as the academic politics are concerned."

"And Mel Aaron told you all that?"

"Basically. Despite joking about not being on speaking terms with people, everyone loves talking to me."

"You're sure about this?"

"I'm reading between the lines, but he told me that his older son and his wife don't get along and that he didn't see himself being gone during the week every week and heading back to Nashville every weekend. He's not going to take the job."

"So I'm going to become Chief of the Cancer Medicine program because some high school kid doesn't get along with his mother?"

Eric Cain was almost laughing. "Well, you made it to being one of the final two candidates on your own merits. But, basically, that's right."

"Well, thank God for bratty teenagers."

Eric Cain pretended to take offense. "Hey, don't take his mother's side! My mother used to make a big deal out of my room being a mess, and that my rock band was too noisy when we rehearsed in the garage. Also, she didn't like my high school girlfriend—who grew up to be a professor of cardiology at Stanford. Maybe you should be giving thanks that his mom is a neurotic bitch. He could be a perfectly lovely young man. God, I have to think of that kid's name."

"Why?"

"Just give me a second. It's Joshua. No, that's not it . . ." He was tapping his fingers on the coffee table in front of them in the waiting room. "Jonah. That's the kid's name. If they don't give you a named professorship, from now on I may call you the Jonah Aaron Professor and Chair of the Division of Cancer Medicine." He shook her hand, and Larry's hand as well. "Congratulations. I think it's about time I stopped joking about Acapulco or Bermuda. I've worn that one out. I need something new to take its place. Actually, I should call you the Tina Aaron Professor of Medicine, since you're getting the job because the kid's mother has issues. I like that better. Why blame the kid?"

She was going to be chief. She was almost certainly going to be chief. "Larry, Eric, I'm going to go back in to check on Cookie."

"And I'm going to go home and leave you and Larry to see how Cookie does. I was on call last night; I need to get some rest. Call me if anything happens. And if she wakes up, and asks what happened, you can skip the part about me saying 'Looks great, naked' while I did the chest compressions."

Larry Patterson congratulated his wife as Eric Cain left the waiting room. "What was that about? Looks great naked?"

"That was just Eric being Eric. He evidently repeats a mantra while he does chest compressions in order to keep in rhythm. He chose 'Looks great naked' for his mantra while he was resuscitating Cookie."

Larry Patterson looked around to see if anyone could overhear them. An elderly couple was sitting in the other end of the waiting area. He whispered in his wife's ear, "You still look great naked, yourself, and you are the most fantastic woman I have ever met or ever will meet."

"Larry, that is absolutely the nicest thing anyone has said to me in forever."

"Well, it's true. And congratulations, assuming what Eric says is right."

She sat down next to him, and he put his arm around her shoulder. "You're pretty wonderful yourself, Larry Patterson. What brought that on? Telling me how great I look naked."

"I just wanted you to feel appreciated for something other than your brilliant mind."

Gail kissed him on the cheek. "Let's go back there together and see how she's doing. You're not a doctor, but they won't kick you out if you're with me."

While Gail and Larry checked on Cookie Bradford, Eric Cain drove home to his condominium and went to bed. He made it to category six before falling asleep. At 3 AM, he was awakened by a phone call from Gail Riley.

"She's conscious and off the ventilator. The doctors say that medically she's going to be fine."

Half awake, he muttered, "That's fabulous."

"I told her what happened. I told her how you suspected something was up when she said that the two of you wouldn't be working together and how we went to her place and brought her back to life. She was upset and angry. She said we had no business interfering in her decision. She said she'd talk to me but only because she needs me to take care of her plants while she's in the hospital. She said that when she comes back to work she is never going to speak to you ever again."

"Well, at least she's alive . . . Goodnight future chairman."

"Goodnight, Eric."

He hung up the phone and fell back asleep.

*   *   *

By Wednesday afternoon, Cookie Bradford was awake, alert, and well enough to be transferred out of Intensive Care. She spent Thursday receiving the visitors who, had things gone as she had planned, would have been attending her funeral. On Friday morning, when a bed was available, she was moved to the in-patient Psychiatry Unit in order to initiate individual and group therapy.

Charles Foster, the attending psychiatrist in charge of Cookie's care, felt that it was incredibly sad that an intelligent woman would rather kill herself than live without the man who beat her and choked her, but it was nothing that he hadn't seen before. He placed Cookie Bradford on anti-depressants and arranged for out-patient follow-up before he discharged her after five days on the in-patient Psychiatry Unit. It had required a fight with Cookie's insurance carrier to get approval for the fourth and fifth days.

As Cookie was leaving the hospital, Charles Foster told her, "Remember what I said. Suicide is a permanent solution to a temporary problem. You have your whole life ahead of you. You have a job. You have people who care about you. Things will get better. Where are you going to be staying?"

"I'm staying with the Gormans for a while." Returning to her apartment seemed unsafe while James Bradford's whereabouts were unknown, and living alone didn't seem like an especially good idea. The nurses who were Cookie's good friends didn't want to deal with an angry James Bradford, in case he came looking for his wife. Fortunately, Hal Gorman, like all the members of the cancer program, had learned of Cookie's suicide attempt. Hal's wife Diane was a clinical psychologist with an office in her home. The Gorman's suburban residence seemed an appropriate place for Cookie to stay for several days.

Charles Foster thought about stating another homily, about how suicide was often a case of mistaken identity. What he meant was that people try to kill themselves because they don't really understand who they are. He was afraid that Cookie would take it to mean that she should try to kill James Bradford instead of herself. He decided to skip the homily. "I'll see you this Friday at 9 AM, and we'll talk about going back to work and returning to your apartment." On Tuesday evening, one week after her suicide attempt, Hal Gorman drove Cookie Bradford to his home on Waverly Drive in Highland Heights.

On Wednesday morning, however, Hal Gorman had second thoughts. Having Cookie Bradford stay in his home while he went to work at CMI and while his wife saw patients in her home office was not as good an idea as it had first seemed. He wondered what would happen if James Bradford managed to learn where his wife was staying. Hal Gorman didn't see how that could happen, but he couldn't rule out the possibility. He decided that it would be prudent to arrange for additional protection for both Cookie Bradford and his wife.

He remembered that Melvin Aaron, whom he had seen during the second of Dr. Aaron's two recent interviews at CMI, had a son who either was an investigator or wanted to be an investigator. Bodyguard duty sounded like the thing a young investigator would do. Hal Gorman contacted Mel Aaron and was disappointed to find out that Jonah Aaron was just seventeen and had only recently completed his junior year of high school.

"Sorry, Hal. Jonah could probably handle just about anything but . . ."

"That's ok. I'll think of something."

"Actually, I have an idea. There's a detective in his mid-forties who is teaching Jonah the ropes. He would probably be perfect for you." Melvin Aaron checked the telephone directory for Ford Investigations and gave the number to Hal Gorman. One phone call later, Hal had arranged for Kyle and Jonah to head to Chicago.

Satisfied that he had provided for all contingencies, Hal Gorman headed to CMI. Although he had gone to the trouble of hiring a bodyguard for his house guest, Hal Gorman had doubted that there was any way that James Bradford could locate his wife. He had overlooked the obvious. James Bradford had called Cookie on her cell phone and had asked to see her. Cookie told him where she was staying before she added that it was probably a bad idea for him to drop by. For James Bradford, that was an invitation.

It was mid-afternoon, and the plane carrying Kyle and Jonah had not yet touched down at O'Hare. Diane Gorman was in her home office seeing a client. James Bradford was standing outside the partially open front door at the Gorman's home. Reckless enough to tell James Bradford where she was staying, Cookie had cautiously kept the door latched as she spoke with her estranged husband.

"It's good to see you Cookie. You look great. Can I come in?"

She thought it over. "Can we just talk for a minute?"

"Sure. What do you want to say?" Now that she saw him, she was angry again. The last time they were together he had almost choked her to death.

"First of all, I'm sorry." He paused, waiting for a response. There was none. "Look, I'm your husband and I want to be with you. I'm sorry I hurt you. It will never happen again."

"Until the next time," she said under her breath. "You know, I told you it was a bad idea to come here. You're in violation of a court order. You could get in trouble." Based on the choking incident, a judge had not only issued a restraining order against James Bradford, a warrant had been issued for his arrest on a charge of felony battery.

James Bradford looked down at his shoes. "I'm not worried about that. I want to come in and talk to you."

"What do you want to say that you can't say through an open door? What do you really want to do? Hit me? Choke me? Rape me?" She was surprised at the depth of her anger.

"Cookie, I would never hit you again. Look, I want to come in. Standing here like this is too public."

"Public? We're seventy feet from the street. No one can see us. This is private. What else do you have to say?"

He swallowed hard. "Cookie, I love you."

Tears filled her eyes and a dull ache filled her body. "I love you, too."

"Then let me in."

"No!" She said it so loudly that she waited to see if Diane Gorman had heard. It appeared that she hadn't.

"Cookie, if you love me, let me in." He sounded more reasonable than he had sounded in months.

She cleared the tears from her eyes. "James, I care about you a lot, but what you did to me nearly destroyed me. I'm not going to let you do it again. I'm not going to let you do it to yourself. This was a mistake."

"Do what again? I told you I wouldn't hit you. I love you. What are you talking about?'

She didn't know what to say. She wasn't sure if she should believe him. "James, you made me feel worthless and useless. You made me feel that I was nothing. Hurting me couldn't let you have a very good opinion of yourself. Don't hurt yourself James. I'm sorry I told you where I was. You shouldn't have come here. Please leave."

"That's psychobabble, Cookie, and you know it. It's amateur psychology."

She took a deep breath. "No. It's not amateur psychology. It's professional psychiatry. I'm quoting Dr. Foster."

"Who's he?"

She waited for an accusation. She waited for him to accuse her of having an affair with her doctor. That was his usual pattern when she mentioned a man's name. The accusation never came. Maybe things were different. "He's my psychiatrist."

"You need one, you crazy bitch."

Strike one. "Oh, I need one. After what you did to me, I sure as heck need one. I need him to tell me that being married to an immature piece of shit who beat up on me because he couldn't handle his own life didn't make me a nothing. People make mistakes. My mistake was staying with you." Her chest was so tight it was difficult to breathe.

James Bradford stood back from the door and applauded. "Very good, Cookie. You're repeating what they tell you. You know you don't feel that way. Maybe someday you'll have the brains to think on your own."

Strike two. She closed her eyes in disgust, but as much at herself as at him.

"Come on, Cookie. Let me in."

She was shaking her head. "Don't you tell me I'm stupid. I have a good job and I do good work. Just because I didn't see things clearly about us doesn't make me stupid."

"Cookie, come on and let me in. I'm sorry for what I just said. I love you so much, this is really killing me. Let me in, please, for old time's sake. We had some great times Cookie."

She caught the look in his eye. He hadn't come to talk, or to apologize. He had come over to get laid, like nothing had ever happened. "Goodbye, James." She closed the door.

"Cookie. Cookie! COOKIE!" He was knocking at the door.

Reluctantly, she opened the door again, but left the latch closed. She peeked through the small opening. "Yes, James."

RICHARD STEIN

"You know, you're giving up the one guy in your life who ever really loved you. I know I didn't show it at the end but I really loved you. And we had a lot of good times. A lot of good times. I am sorry."

She was trembling.

"I know I hurt you, Cookie. I have no excuse. It was my fault, not yours. I know that. Let me in. Let's talk about it."

He looked so sad and so helpless. He looked like the young man she had fallen in love with when she was seventeen years old. She closed the door so she could undo the latch and let him in. Under her breath she started murmuring, "It's going to be different. It's going to be different."

And it was, but only because when Cookie Bradford closed the door completely so she could open the latch, James Bradford interpreted the move not as a surrender, but as a rejection. It was more than he could take, and he began his tirade. "You worthless little bitch. Just because you're cute you think you're something. Who the hell do you think you are? Don't you realize this is your last chance? Don't you know that if you turn me down, no one is ever going to want you, not really want you, you little slut?"

Her hand was on the latch as she listened through the door in a state of shock. Strike three. She shuddered. She had come so close to letting him in. She felt ashamed and dirty. She was furious, but more at herself than at James.

James was yelling at her through the closed door. "Tell the truth, Cookie. Besides me, what's the longest you've ever been able to hold on to a guy? Two weeks? One week?"

There was no answer. She had met him when she was seventeen years old and there had never been anyone else. She ran to the kitchen where she had left her purse. Earlier, while Diane Gorman was seeing a client, Cookie had taken a self-guided tour of the Gorman home. She had found the loaded gun that the Gormans kept in the master bedroom night table. She took the gun from her purse and returned to the front hall.

"Cookie. You're my wife. I'm coming in."

She heard his body slam against the door. Again and again his body lunged against the door. The hinges and the latch held as she returned to the front foyer. "James, stop that."

Diane Gorman had heard the noise in the front hall. She had left her client and she was dialing 911 on her cell phone.

Cookie Bradford was terrified. She sat down on the floor of the foyer, pulled the hammer back on the revolver, and pointed it at the door. If

James knocked down the door, he was going to have a big surprise waiting for him. Again and again, she heard him crash into the door. She was going to end it once and for all. She waited for James to come crashing through the door.

While Cookie sat silently, gun in hand, Diane Gorman addressed James Bradford. "Mr. Bradford, this is my home, and I have called the police. You are in violation of a restraining order, and I suggest you leave immediately."

Before James Bradford could respond, his wife informed him what was waiting for him inside the Gorman home. "James, I want you to know that I have a gun."

The pounding stopped. James Bradford doubted that his wife would shoot him, but he wouldn't bet his life that she wouldn't. The police were a potential problem. Cookie Bradford and Diane Gorman walked from the front foyer to the dining room window and saw James walking to his car. Cookie ran to the bathroom and began to vomit. For several minutes she lay on the cool tile floor, wondering what she would do if James was out of her life. When she returned to the front hall Diane Gorman told her that James had driven off.

"Are you ok, Cookie?"

"I think so . . . I almost let him in . . . I'm sorry . . . I am such an idiot." She buried her face in her hands.

Diane Gorman shook her head. "You are not an idiot. Love and lust sometimes make people do things that aren't very smart. Do you want to talk about it?"

"Not right now. Maybe later."

The two women opened the door. The bottom of the door was slightly scuffed, where James had kicked it, but there was no significant damage. The two women sat on the front steps and waited for the police.

The police, even in small suburbs like Highland Heights, Illinois, take domestic violence calls very seriously. In addition to the threat that James Bradford posed to his wife, the police knew that violent spouses were capable of turning their anger—and occasionally their weapons— on the police. Officer Janeway informed Diane Gorman and Cookie Bradford that the police in Highland Heights would be on the lookout for James' white 1994 Chevy Impala. He explained that other than that, there wasn't much that they could do. Before he left, Officer Janeway advised them to call if there was any further trouble. There would be two more calls to the police from Waverly Drive that day.

RICHARD STEIN

*　*　*

Diane Gorman couldn't decide what upset her most, the fact that Cookie had told James Bradford where she was staying, the fact that Cookie had found the loaded gun, or the fact that Cookie had told Diane that she felt safer keeping the gun in her purse rather than returning it. When Hal came home Diane was going to give him holy hell for leaving a loaded gun where their temporary house guest could find it.

Frustrated by the situation, and the fact that Cookie didn't want to talk about anything, Diane Gorman chose to sit in her home office while she awaited her next client. Cookie Bradford decided to take a nap, but she was too agitated to sleep. She thought about calling Dr. Foster at CMI but changed her mind. The episode with James had left her sexually aroused. She lay down on the bed, unsnapped the top button on her jeans, and lowered the zipper. She slipped her hand inside her panties. This is why some people let sex mess up their lives she told herself. The obvious, inescapable truth was that it was so damn much fun. And if what she was doing felt good, the real thing was much better. The problem was that with James out of her life, if he was out of her life, there was no one to fill the void, not only the void in her life, but in her fantasies. She couldn't get off unless she could pretend that a man was doing what she was doing to herself.

She thought of Dr. Foster, her psychiatrist. He was nice. Her pelvis began rocking. But he was married. The movement stopped. She was probably in love with him. Most patients love their psychiatrists. She assumed he wouldn't mind that she thought of him while she let her fingers play with her fun button. And it felt so good. She had even heard that some psychiatrists screwed their patients as part of therapy. What a dumb idea. She would end up telling him about what she was doing and be embarrassed. She needed another image.

Eric Cain. He had a girlfriend, but he was cute. Getting involved with him would mess up her job. But he was cute. And he was single. And Cookie was cuter than his girlfriend. She had heard that Eric Cain never got involved with married women, but it seemed like she was going to be single in the near future. Her hips began a rocking motion, speeding up tempo in time with her probing wet fingers. She began to concentrate on the job at hand, and on Eric Cain. He wouldn't abuse her; he would simply sleep with her and leave her. Next time, she'd have to think of someone else, for now she could think of Eric Cain.

Before she reached orgasm, the doorbell rang. She could hear that Diane Gorman was on the phone talking to a client. James must have come back. She made herself a promise. James Bradford would never touch her again. He would never hit her again. She would kill him first.

The doorbell rang again. Cookie's breathing had almost returned to normal. Her purse was lying at her side. She picked it up and went to the door, taking the gun from the purse as she walked. She looked through the peep-hole and saw two attractive men. The older one looked to be in his mid-forties and he had a small moustache. She guessed that the younger one, with long hair and an apparent two day growth of beard, was about twenty. Each of them was carrying a duffel bag. "Where were you guys when I needed a fantasy," she said to herself. She felt herself getting wet again. As she had done with James, she opened the door slightly but left the latch on. "Can I help you?" she asked.

"I'm Kyle Ford. This scruffy young man is Jonah Aaron. We're here to protect Cookie Bradford. Is that you?"

Unless there were two young brunettes with large chests staying at the Gormans she obviously was Cookie Bradford, but it seemed reasonable to ask. Jonah had been exposing Kyle to his basic rules. Kyle had his doubts about Rule Number Six, concerning the need to have a girlfriend who could shoot a gun, limiting the need to rescue her. Kyle thought Jonah watched too much television. However, Rule Number One, "Assume Nothing," made perfect sense.

"I'm Cookie Bradford. In the flesh." She checked to see if she was presentable. She put the gun down next to her purse on a small table near the door while she zipped her jeans. Then she undid the latch, and opened the door. "Come on in." Almost unconsciously, she picked up the gun back up.

Kyle and Jonah entered the front hall of the Gorman home. "Would you mind putting that gun down?" Kyle Ford asked.

She didn't even realize that she was holding the gun. She placed it back in her purse and shook hands with the two men. "Good to meet you." She hadn't washed her hands since her aborted exercise in self-satisfaction and she smiled at the thought. She wondered if it would be ok to have a fantasy about one of her bodyguards. On second thought, why should it be a fantasy?

Kyle Ford would have had to be blind not to notice that Cookie Bradford was attractive. Her breasts were pushing against the fabric of her shirt. Her nipples were erect. The jeans were incredibly tight. He remembered what he had told Jonah about being a bodyguard. Do the fucking job, and the job is not fucking. Never let it get intimate. Kyle Ford had every intention of following his own advice. Still, he couldn't help but admire her figure. He hoped that Jonah had the good sense to stay out of her bed during the time they were in Highland Heights. "Is that gun loaded?"

"Goddamn right it is!"

"You know, you really shouldn't have a gun when you're upset," Kyle Ford told his client.

She said nothing.

Kyle Ford continued. "The problem with having a gun is that you have to be prepared to shoot it, to kill someone if necessary. If you wave a gun at someone, they may feel it's necessary to try and kill you. Overall, having a gun is not a good idea. Please give me the gun."

Cookie Bradford looked Kyle Ford in the eye. What he said made sense. "I think I'll keep it. If you were him, I mean if he came back, I would be ready to shoot him. I was sitting in the front hall before when he tried kicking the door in. I'd have shot him if he came in."

"What?" Kyle Ford's eyes widened. "He came here? How did he find you? Dr. Gorman told me that there was no way that he could track you down."

"He called me on my cell phone and I told him where I was . . . I know. Not smart." She confessed to being about to unlatch the door when James began trying to kick it in.

"That makes our job harder, but so it goes." Kyle Ford thought it over. Maybe she would have shot James Bradford. More likely he'd have taken the gun away from her and killed her with it. "Is it your gun or the Gormans' gun?"

"It's their gun. I had nothing to do so I was looking around the house and I found it."

"Are there any other guns here?"

"I have no idea."

"Well, I have a gun, and since we're here now, and we're the ones hired to protect you, do you mind giving that gun to me."

She thought it over. She knew how to fire a gun. "Have you ever shot someone?"

"Yes."

"Ever kill someone?" she asked.

"Rarely. So has Jonah."

Cookie Bradford looked at the younger of the two men. He looked extremely dangerous. Jonah nodded at her without smiling as she looked him over. She had the feeling that he was looking right through her. She turned back to Kyle Ford. "I think I'll keep the gun anyway. If James comes back, he'll be focused on you. He'll never know what hit him."

Kyle Ford chose not to argue. If James Bradford returned and Cookie had a gun, Kyle worried that Cookie might shoot him in order to protect her husband.

Diane Gorman, who had completed her phone call, welcomed Kyle and Jonah, and agreed to walk them through her home. The back door was solid wood with no glass partitions. Kyle Ford and Jonah Aaron checked that all the windows in the house were locked. Someone could always try breaking in a window, but they would be heard. Plus, the home had an alarm system. Kyle checked the location of all the bedrooms. When he came to the guest room where Cookie was staying he walked in. There was no adjoining bathroom where someone could hide. There was a window air-conditioner preventing the window from giving easy access to the room. "You're safe in here, even at night."

As they finished the tour Cookie Bradford asked "Anything else you'd like to see?"

It was a perfectly innocent statement, but her tone suggested that she was willing to disrobe. He wasn't certain if she intended a double entendre or if she just naturally talked that way. "No, just go back to doing what you were doing when I got here. We'll walk around the outside of the house, then sit in the den." Cookie Bradford smiled as she remembered what she had been doing when Kyle Ford rang the bell.

After convincing himself that there was no place to hide around the Gorman home, Kyle Ford came back to the front door and knocked.

"Who is it?"

"That's good, Cookie. Always check. It's me, Kyle Ford."

"Where's your partner?"

"He's not my partner. He's someone trying to learn the business. But to answer your question, he's out scouting the neighborhood."

She let Kyle Ford into the Gorman's home, walked him to the living room, and sat down next to him on the sofa. "Do you know anything about white squirrels?"

"I have no idea what you're talking about."

"Nobody knows about white squirrels. See, I grew up in this small town in Southern Illinois. Olney, Illinois. Not just small, really small. To

RICHARD STEIN

me, it was the biggest hunk of nothing you ever saw. It was the home of the white squirrels. I mean there are four cities that call themselves that and Olney is one of them. Brevard, North Carolina, Marionville, Missouri, and Kenton, Tennessee are the others."

"I live in Tennessee and I never heard of Kenton."

"I have no idea where it is either. If it's like Olney it's probably in the middle of nowhere. That's the point. Nothing towns with nothing but albino squirrels. Nothing! Nothing! Nothing!"

Kyle Ford could only shake his head. His job was to guard an agitated woman who had invited the man who had tried to choke her to death to come and visit her. In addition to that, she might be suicidal. Well, what had he expected? He knew that he best be on the alert. His experience with the Dana Twins had convinced him that a simple job that didn't look dangerous could get him killed. "Would you like to take a walk? It's a beautiful day. We shouldn't be a prisoner inside just because your husband's been here once looking for you."

"Good idea. Do you have your gun with you?"

He opened his jacket to show her the gun in his shoulder holster.

"I think I'll leave the gun in my purse, and leave my purse at home. I think I'm safe enough with you." She gave Kyle Ford her best smile. James had always accused her of fooling around. She never had. She wondered if she was ready to start making up for lost time and decided that was a bad idea. She resolved that she would avoid sexual relationships until she had her head together. Well, almost together. Maybe for a year. Well, at least for a couple of months. She could take care of things on her own. If the doorbell hadn't rung and interrupted her, she would have done just fine.

As she placed her purse on a table in the front foyer, Kyle Ford breathed a sigh of relief.

*   *   *

Since Waverly Drive had no sidewalks, Kyle Ford and Cookie Bradford walked in the street. Kyle was surprised that in such an expensive neighborhood the homes were on such small lots that they seemed ready to bump into each other. He had researched the community on the Internet before leaving Nashville, and he knew he was looking at homes in the $600,000 to $900,000 price range. Even with his Idaho retirement package, he knew he could never afford to live in a place like Highland Heights. In Nashville, he could purchase something similar, on a two acre lot, for less than half the money.

Although he found Cookie Bradford attractive, Kyle Ford wasn't even looking at her as they walked. He was scanning for trouble. Not only was there no trouble, there wasn't much of anything. A few children were riding bicycles; an older woman was watering her lawn. Other than that, the street was empty. It was just a quiet suburban neighborhood on a lazy summer day. Kyle doubted that James would show up again, but he noted that with utility poles and trees lining the street, he had adequate protection if James' white Chevy Impala came bearing down on them. He also had backup. Jonah was somewhere in the area, but Jonah was unarmed.

Kyle and Cookie had walked about a quarter of a mile and had just crossed the intersection of Waverly Drive and Woodland Hills Lane when a loud whistle mobilized his attention. He heard a car gunning its engine and turned to see the white Chevy coming towards them. He grabbed Cookie Bradford's arm and pulled her towards a utility pole twenty yards away.

As they moved to safety, the car swerved towards them and hit the pole head-on. The air bag deployed. Smoke billowed from the car. James staggered from the driver's seat, a pistol in his right hand. He had injured his left ankle in the crash and he hobbled towards them. He intended to inform his wife that he was going to kill her and her new boyfriend, but before James could utter a word, Kyle Ford grabbed his right wrist and twisted. Kyle put his left hand above James' elbow and kicked him away from him using his right leg. Kyle heard James' arm snap as the gun fell harmlessly to the ground. The fight was over before it started. "Stay down if you don't want to get hurt any more than you already are." Kyle Ford had drawn his gun and was pointing it at James Bradford's head.

James Bradford moaned in pain. He wasn't used to fighting anyone larger than his wife. A former Navy Seal who stood six feet two inches tall was out of his league. James wasn't getting up and he wasn't shutting up. He alternated between screaming at Kyle Ford for breaking his arm, complaining about the pain in his ankle, and cursing at his wife.

Kyle Ford grabbed James' right wrist and twisted. He suspected that the pain in James' broken arm was excruciating. "Shut up, or I'm going to twist harder."

James Bradford screamed in agony then sat silently, waiting for the police. Responding to the 911 call, the Highland Heights police arrested

James Bradford. He would be charged with attempted murder for trying to run down his wife and Kyle Ford. Because of his injuries he was taken to Highland Heights Hospital instead of jail.

Cookie Bradford began to cry as she watched the police take James Bradford away in their patrol car. She was sobbing as she and Kyle Ford walked back to the Gorman home.

"Cookie, are you ok?" Kyle asked her.

"I guess so. He wasn't hurt too badly was he?"

"Depends on what you mean by that. The way he was carrying on, I think he may have broken his ankle in the crash, and I broke his arm to make him drop the gun."

"Did you have to do that?"

"Well, I could have just shot him and maybe killed him. He was coming at us with a gun in his hand, but I didn't see any point to doing that."

"Poor James."

"Yeah. Poor James." Kyle Ford considered that if Cookie Bradford had been carrying her purse, she might have used her gun to defend her husband. As far as Kyle was concerned, the sooner he could get out of Highland Heights the better.

As for Jonah Aaron, after he had whistled to warn Kyle, he had watched Kyle disarm James Bradford. Once the police arrived, Jonah knew that Kyle didn't need his assistance. The job was over. He went back to the Gormans' home, told Diane Gorman what had happened, and changed into running clothes to go for a run.

Diane Gorman was waiting on the front porch for Kyle and Cookie when they returned. "Jonah told me everything. What's happening with James Bradford?"

Cookie looked down at the ground as Kyle answered. "Among other things, he's facing a number of charges including attempted murder. He's going to the hospital, but he's under arrest. I suspect he's not going to be getting out for a while. I'll check with the police later and find out exactly what's happening. I think that Jonah and I are going to be heading home in the morning or later tonight if we can catch a plane. If James Bradford gets released any time soon, Jonah and I can always head on back if you want us."

"Speaking of your partner . . ."

Kyle Ford interrupted her immediately. "He's not my partner. He's a seventeen year old kid that I'm trying to train."

Diane Gorman wondered why Kyle Ford resented having Jonah referred to as his partner and realized that to do so was to put Kyle on equal footing with a teenager. "Sorry. In any case, he said he was going to run a couple of miles. He told me to tell you that he had his cell phone with him in case you wanted to leave right away." Diane Gorman turned to Cookie Bradford. "Cookie, it's your life, but considering what's been going on lately, I think you have to consider that you are better off without James."

"I need to forget him."

"Good idea. But it's easier said than done."

"He always said I cheated, but I never did. It's his problem, not mine."

"Do you want to come in my office later and talk about it?"

"Not really."

The doorbell rang. It was Diane Gorman's last client of the day. "Maybe we'll talk later."

"Maybe." Cookie Bradford headed to her room. Kyle Ford sat down in the recreation room in front of the television. He found a re-run of *Magnum, P.I.* and had settled in to watch when he heard Cookie Bradford calling him. "Mr. Ford. Could you come here a minute, please?"

He found her sitting on the edge of the bed, a blank expression on her face. "I made a decision. Good sex will help me forget James." She started unbuttoning her blouse.

Kyle Ford shook his head. "Keep your clothes on. That's not part of bodyguard duty." He moved towards the door. The woman was attractive, but one didn't have to be a psychologist to know that she was an emotional mess.

"But you're not my bodyguard anymore. I don't need one now that James is in jail. Consider this a bonus." She had removed her blouse and reached behind her back to unfasten her bra. Her breasts popped free.

"Look, you have enough problems already and I don't want to make them worse."

She stood up and grabbed his belt, pulling him towards her, pushing her breasts into his chest. "Yeah. Old man like you. Probably couldn't get it up anyway."

"Old man? I am not an old man."

"Show me." She imagined what it would be like to have sex with someone other than James. Thinking about it had her so wet that her panties were drenched. As she began to remove her jeans, she imagined Kyle Ford pounding his way into her.

Kyle Ford realized that his job as Cookie Bradford's bodyguard was over and that she was extremely attractive. He also realized that she was mentally unstable. "Two out of three isn't bad," he told himself. "Do you know what I'd like?" he asked.

Whatever he wanted, she would oblige. "What?"

"What I'd really like to do is get cleaned up and take you to dinner. Maybe we could get to know each other a little better before . . . before we think about getting to know each other a little better."

She paused to think it over and crossed her arms in front of her chest before speaking. "OK. I'll let you be a gentleman. That'll be nice." She smiled to herself. It was going to better than nice. Much better.

*   *   *

As he lay in the bed at Highland Heights Hospital, waiting for the pain shot to kick in, James Bradford marveled that someone had broken his arm in a fight. The police had informed him that the man he had assumed was his wife's boyfriend was, in fact, her bodyguard—a former Navy Seal. He knew that Seals were trained to run covert missions and to cut throats or snap necks of enemy sentries. He was glad he had stayed down when he had been ordered to do so. Surgery was scheduled for the morning and the orthopedics team had assured that with physical therapy, his arm would be as good as new in six weeks.

As for his legal situation, he had met with an attorney and they had decided on a strategy. Since he had been staying in a motel after nearly choking his wife to death, he had never been served with the restraining order. Therefore, violating it was not a problem. As far as choking his wife was concerned, he told his attorney that it had never happened. In any case, he doubted that Cookie would testify in court. Even if she did, and even though his attempt to run her over would buttress her credibility, a jury would likely regard her as a crazy woman who had overdosed on pills.

His attorney had suggested that he plead to a reduced charge of attempting to do bodily harm. He had, after all, been brandishing a weapon. Since Cookie hadn't been injured, and since James had no criminal record, the attorney believed that he would get probation. As James fell asleep, he decided that if that happened he would put it all behind him and get a divorce. It was fine with him if his wife wanted to screw around.

And that was exactly her intention. After Kyle had left her bedroom, Cookie Bradford showered and dressed for their date. She put on the sexiest underwear she had brought with her and a pink dress that flaunted her cleavage. She looked in the mirror, admiring what she saw. She was positive that Kyle Ford wouldn't reject her after spending the evening admiring her.

There was only one problem. She kept coming back to the fact that the only one who ever cared for her was James. Without James, her life was totally pointless. She was just a fucking white squirrel like James had said. She was nothing. James had said she was a cheater. She was still married to James and she was about to become a cheater. If James was right about that, he might be right about everything. Tears filled her eyes.

Cookie knew that there was no future with Kyle Ford. He would leave for Nashville in the morning. She suspected that her life was on the verge of becoming a series of meaningless sexual encounters. She knew that men found her attractive. She would have no trouble finding men to share her bed, but James was right. How long would anything last? Screwing Kyle Ford, having sex with anyone, would likely feel wonderful, but it would be pointless. Her whole life was going to be pointless. Did she really want to live like that?

She walked to the dresser, took the gun from her purse, and impulsively put it in her mouth. Dr. Foster had said that suicide was a permanent solution to a temporary problem. Well, it was a solution, and her problem wasn't temporary. James was out of her life and he wasn't coming back. A permanent solution was a comforting thought.

She pulled back the safety on the gun and put her finger on the trigger. She took a deep breath and let it out. All she had to do was squeeze the trigger and her problems would be over. The pills hadn't worked, but that was because Gail and Eric had raced to the rescue. No one was going to come to her rescue if she pulled the trigger with the gun in her mouth.

Before she pulled the trigger, she realized that splattering her blood and brains all over the walls and carpets of the Gormans' guest bedroom was no way to repay their hospitality. She removed the gun from her mouth, placed it back in her purse, and walked out into the backyard. It was a beautiful evening. The smell of charcoal from a neighbor's grill filled the air. She thought of the expression that the Klingon used to say on Star Trek. "It's a good day to die." She sat down next to an oak tree. "How fitting," she thought. "Just like a white squirrel, I am going to end up dead at the base of an oak tree."

She saw Kyle Ford talking to Diane and Hal Gorman at the side of the driveway. Kyle was wearing a jacket and tie. He looked handsome, but that was no reason to change her plan. She could hear Hal Gorman talking about the big announcement at CMI. Gail Riley had been named Chief of the Division of Cancer Medicine. Cookie was happy for Gail. Despite what Cookie had said the morning after her first suicide attempt, she wasn't angry at Gail as much as she was guilty about having tricked Gail into signing the prescription. She wasn't angry at Eric Cain as much as she was embarrassed that he had found her naked. She thought about leaving a note to tie up those loose ends, but decided against it. She didn't want to go back in the house to find a pen and paper.

Cookie saw the young man who had accompanied Kyle Ford standing there next to the three of them. She didn't remember his name. She waved at Kyle, Diane, Hal and the young man. They waved back. They were looking right at her when she took the gun from her purse and placed it in her mouth. Hal, Diane, and Kyle began rushing towards her. The young man just stood there.

She wondered what she would hear when she pulled the trigger. She realized that she might hear noise for a split second before the bullet tore apart her brain and her mind ceased to exist. She wondered if she would feel anything.

Kyle Ford stopped five feet in front of her. "Cookie, think it over. You have a lot to live for. You're a beautiful woman. People care about you. There's no reason to do this. There has to be a better way."

She took the gun from her mouth and looked him in the eye. "You don't know me. You know nothing about me. You have no idea what I'm feeling."

Kyle Ford thought that saying something was better than keeping silent. "Cookie, my wife left me seven years ago. At first, I thought that I couldn't go on. I can't say that I don't still hurt, but I'm glad I'm still around. Please don't do this."

Cookie Bradford looked around her. Hal Gorman's shirt was drenched with sweat. His wife was crying. The young man was on the phone. Cookie wondered if he was calling 911. What could anyone possibly do for her after she pulled the trigger? She put the gun back in her mouth. She had heard somewhere that when the trigger is pulled, there is a click before the explosion. She decided to concentrate on hearing the click. When the bullet fired, her brain would be mush. There would be nothing left to hear the explosion. She closed her eyes as tightly as she could and pulled the trigger. CLICK.

* * *

Cookie Bradford heard Diane Gorman scream. Confused at being alive, Cookie opened her eyes. Kyle Ford, Diane Gorman, Hal Gorman, and the scruffy young man were standing in front of her. Kyle Ford was still talking to her. "Cookie, please put the gun down."

She pulled the trigger for a second time and a third time. CLICK. CLICK.

She stood up and looked at Kyle Ford. It was his fault. He was the one who had beaten up James. She looked him in the eye as she pulled the trigger for the fourth, fifth, and sixth time. CLICK. CLICK. CLICK.

Kyle took the gun from her hands and began yelling at Hal Gorman. "You let a suicidal woman into your home and you left a gun where she could find it! What the hell were you thinking?"

Hal Gorman shook his head. "I'm sorry. After the kids were grown and out of the house, I stopped locking up the gun. We always talked that we would keep it in the safe if we ever had grandchildren, but since we don't . . ." his voice trailed off.

Diane Gorman glared at her husband, put her arm around Cookie Bradford, and walked her into the house.

Kyle Ford turned to Hal Gorman. "I think it would be a good idea if she were back on a psychiatric unit."

For the first time since Cookie Bradford had come outside, Jonah spoke. "I already called 911."

Hal Gorman sighed before speaking. "You know, with her going to the hospital, and her husband in jail, we obviously don't need a bodyguard. You certainly earned your fee Mr. Ford. Just send me your bill; I'll take care of it. Thank God you took the bullets out of the gun, Mr. Ford. I would never have forgiven myself if she had killed herself.

Kyle Ford chuckled. "I didn't take the bullets out of the gun. I hate to admit it, but I had my mind on other things."

Jonah took six bullets out of his pocket and counted them as he placed them in Hal Gorman's hand. He looked at his watch. "If we leave

RICHARD STEIN

now, Kyle, we can get the rental car back and catch the eight thirty plane to Nashville."

Kyle Ford and Jonah Aaron shook hands with Hal Gorman and walked to the car. "Nice work, Jonah. Did you check that she didn't have access to any other bullets when you left the gun in her purse?"

"I talked to Diane Gorman when I came back to the house after you neutralized James Bradford. She said that there were no other guns in their home and that while the gun was kept loaded, all the other bullets were locked in a safe in the master bedroom."

"And you left the unloaded gun with Cookie Bradford because . . . ?"

"Why not? I thought we would talk to Dr. Gorman about it when he came home. I wanted to be sure he realized what a careless thing he had done. As long as it was unloaded, and she didn't have access to bullets, I figured it didn't matter."

The two men were now seated in the car, but Kyle hadn't started the engine. "There's a lesson here—an important one."

"Yeah. Don't leave a loaded gun where a suicidal woman can find it."

"No. There's a more important lesson." He paused to be certain he had Jonah's full attention. "You meet a lot of vulnerable, disturbed women when you are in this line of work. Don't get involved with any of them. It's a lot easier if you have a girlfriend. Otherwise a woman like that can be hard to resist. Of course, if you have a girlfriend, or a wife, a woman like that can be real poison."

Jonah thought it over. What Kyle was saying was obvious. Then again, he had to wonder what would have happened if Cookie Bradford had come on to him. "Did a woman like that break up your marriage? You said that . . ."

Kyle chuckled. "No. Unfortunately, I made the mistake of marrying a woman like that once. She hired me to investigate her husband. She thought he was cheating on her. He was. At the time, I wondered why anyone would cheat on a woman like that. She was smart, sexy, and beautiful . . . Over time I learned that she also was very needy. She didn't trust anyone. She always thought that I was cheating on her when I went on the road. I wasn't. She needed to be told all the time just how beautiful she was. All women need that to some degree but she needed it all the time. She ended up leaving me for her hairdresser. He was a jerk, but he was always in town." Kyle paused, saw that Jonah was listening intently and continued, "Anyway, I'm probably not the best guy to give advice about women."

"It sounds like good advice. Maybe I'll make it a new rule. 'Don't get involved with desperate vulnerable women.'"

"It would be a good rule, but don't you already have a couple of rules about women?"

Jonah nodded. "Number six is to have a girlfriend who can shoot so you don't waste time having to rescue her. Number ten is not to sleep with a woman who has more tattoos than you do. I heard that when I was eleven years old; it sounded cute."

Kyle laughed. "Do you have any tattoos?"

"No."

"Well I got five when I was a Navy Seal. That rule might work for me, but considering the number of women getting body art these days, you may want to reconsider that one. Anyway, I can tell you one thing about women. Where women are concerned, partner, it's easier to know what to do than to actually do it . . . Why are you smiling?"

"You called me partner."

Kyle Ford smiled. "Yeah, I did. You have definitely earned it."

*   *   *

It was three A.M. and Eric Cain was staring out the window of his condominium, looking at what little traffic was moving along Lake Shore Drive. He rarely had trouble sleeping, but this night, after Hal Gorman had called to tell him what had happened, he couldn't fall back asleep. He kept thinking of Cookie Bradford. He wondered if she would try again until she succeeded in killing herself. Gail had once told him that Cookie had been with James Bradford since she was seventeen years old. Apparently, Cookie couldn't see the possibility of life without him. Eric Cain didn't claim to know much about love, but to him, that wasn't love, that was either a confusion of lust with love, or fear of change.

Eric Cain had been with hundreds of women, and none of them had been that important to him. For him, the end of a relationship just meant moving on to someone else. Often there wasn't even a relationship that came to an end. The majority of women he had been with were one night stands. Carol Bernstein, the attorney he had been dating for a few weeks, was intelligent and attractive, but he knew that if she were struck by lightning tomorrow, he would simply move on to someone else—likely within days. From what he knew of himself, he probably would try to pick up a woman at the funeral.

RICHARD STEIN

He thought of Gail and Larry. He was certain they had spent the night celebrating Gail's success. He wondered what his life would be like if had someone in his life on a permanent basis to share his successes and failures.

Since high school, the only woman he had ever cared about on a long term basis was Gail Riley, and that was because their relationship wasn't sexual and never would be. He wondered if he was he even capable of a long-term sexual relationship with anyone. He decided to find out. He was thirty-nine years old. Things were going to change—as soon as he was forty. That would be in seven months. That would be soon enough. There was no reason to rush things.

That night he added a seventh category to his list of women who were off limits—Cookie Bradford. The woman looked great naked, but if she resumed working at CMI, he would give her a wide berth.

8

FAMILY MATTERS

TINA AARON WAS thrilled that her husband had decided to turn down the position as chief of the cancer program at CMI. Moving back to Chicago would have meant starting over as a decorator and she wasn't about to do that. If Melvin had taken the job, they would have had a commuter marriage, and neither one of them wanted that; she certainly didn't. Last night, they had gone to dinner at F. Scott's in Green Hills then come home and made love to celebrate Melvin's decision. As far as Tina was concerned, the only remaining problem in her life was Jonah.

Jonah ranked third in the rising senior class at the academic magnet school. While his sabbatical working for Milton Brandenburg was a year in the future, Tina worried that Jonah wouldn't attend college. After what had happened in Idaho, she was terrified that her longhaired son, who always looked in need of a shave, would become a hoodlum, or land in jail, or worse.

Two weeks had elapsed since Jonah had returned from rescuing Terry, Joey, Kyle, and himself in Idaho, and *Dana Twins 2* had already sold three million copies. The royalties were supposed to be going into a trust fund and although Milton Brandenburg had promised Melvin and Tina that he wouldn't advance Jonah any money, Jonah seemed to have a large supply of cash at his disposal. A new flat screen sixty-two inch television had shown up in the Aaron's media room; an expensive collectible from the 1985 Chicago Bears Super Bowl Champions arrived at the Aaron home every few days; Jonah was driving a new black Lexus sports car that he had paid for in cash.

The Aarons wanted to know if Milton knew the source of the money, but Milton was incommunicado. After Idaho, Milton decided that he needed what he called "quality time with my family" and had taken Mona, Brian, Terry, and Joey on a month long excursion in Europe.

Jonah was spending most of his time with Kyle Ford learning to fire a gun, pick a lock, hot wire a car, do surveillance without being seen, and to engage in hand to hand combat. The Aarons had sent Barry, who all but worshipped Jonah, to Melvin's parents in Florida lest Barry spend the summer under his brother's influence. As far as Tina was concerned, the only thing worse than having one underachieving son become an investigator was having two underachieving sons become investigators.

For Melvin Aaron, turning down the position as chief at CMI had been a difficult decision. Considering the favorable weather and the lower cost of housing, he much preferred living in Nashville to living in Chicago. At Vanderbilt, he had an excellent clinical practice, superb colleagues, and a major role in the medical school teaching program.

On the other hand, he had been caring for patients with lung cancer for more than two decades and it was wearing him down. Determining whether a patient should receive surgery, radiation, chemotherapy or a combination of treatment modalities was a technical task that had become second nature over time. It was the unavoidable eventual conversations with families about whether a patient should receive additional treatment or be referred to hospice that were difficult. A position that carried more administrative responsibilities and fewer clinical obligations was appealing.

Dr. Aaron's reputation as a clinician and a teacher had garnered respect from the CMI search committee. More importantly, as far as CMI was concerned, he had coordinated a national clinical trial on lung cancer. Despite the fact that he did no laboratory research, he had been offered the position as chief. He was flattered, but the more he studied the situation, the more he realized that building a program at CMI would be more difficult that he had first imagined.

CMI was a small program and, other than Gail Riley and Hal Gorman, none of the cancer specialists at CMI had a national reputation. The budget for expansion was limited and without a major commitment to salaries and space, recruiting was going to be difficult. After listening to him weigh the pros and cons of the job at CMI, Tina had summarized the situation perfectly. "Melvin," she had told him, "the problem is that anyone talented enough to help you improve the program at CMI isn't likely to be foolish enough to risk their career by accepting a position there." Still, despite Tina's getting to the heart of the matter, if not for the friction between Jonah and his mother, Melvin's ego might have gotten the best of him. As it was, he had decided to leave the headaches to Gail Riley. He chuckled at the irony. Gail Riley was a superb clinician and researcher, but she had become chief of the cancer program at CMI because Cory Bayliss had been arrested for peeing on the side of a strip club and had missed a recording session leaving the voices of Jonah and his cousin Brian to become the computer adjusted sound of the Dana Twins.

As he showered and shaved, Melvin thought about how random events could change the course of one's life. His friend Morrie Weinberg had bought his daughter a Chevy Corvette for her sixteenth birthday. Two weeks later she had taken a curve on Chickering Lane too fast and had hit a tree at seventy miles an hour. That had been the end of Melanie Weinberg. It had also been the last sober day of Morrie Weinberg's life.

Connie Johnson, one of the decorators who worked for his wife Tina, had a daughter, Marie, who had gotten pregnant at seventeen. She wasn't going to marry the father, not that it would have mattered, and she was keeping the baby. He imagined the loud thudding sound of all the doors closing on Marie Johnson's future.

The course of his own life had been changed by a patch of ice and a lone poplar tree on the road back from Stowe, Vermont, and, of course, there was Jonah and his night at Lightning Bug Studios. By helping a senior sound technician play with computerized sound equipment, Jonah had accomplished the financial equivalent of winning the lottery.

Melvin Aaron thought about what he had been like back when he had been seventeen. He wondered what he would have done if he had come into several million dollars at that age. Would he have devoted twelve or thirteen years to college, medical school, internship, residency, and fellowship to become a cancer specialist? He doubted it. He wondered what Jonah would do now that he never had to earn another penny as long as he lived.

While Jonah was adamant about taking a year off after he finished high school, Melvin believed his son was sincere about his plan to attend college. Jonah had the grades to go anywhere, but Melvin Aaron expected that his son would stay in Nashville to remain on the periphery of the music business. While everyone else's children seemed to be moving away, Jonah was likely to be staying in Music City. Considering the conflict between Jonah and Tina, Melvin saw that as having both an upside and a downside.

RICHARD STEIN

On his way to breakfast, Melvin Aaron knocked on Jonah's door. There was no answer. On the previous day, Jonah and Kyle had traveled to Highland Heights to work on a case. Melvin and Tina expected that Jonah would be gone a week or so, but Tina said that she thought she had heard Jonah come in late at night. If Jonah was back, Melvin wanted to find out how the trip had gone.

Melvin did a double take when he reached the kitchen. The room had the aroma of toast and scrambled eggs and at the kitchen table a well groomed young man was eating his breakfast. "Do I know you? For a second, I thought it was Barry." Jonah had cut his shoulder length hair to a conservative length and he was clean shaven. Considering the effort that Jonah had devoted to looking dangerous, Melvin Aaron was stunned.

"Good morning, Dad. I hope you like my new look. I suspect Mom is going to love it."

"What's the occasion?"

"I didn't think I had to look that way anymore just to seem dangerous. I had Kelly Thompson come over late last night to be modern day Delilah. She actually did a pretty good job, don't you think?"

"Are you and Kelly back together?"

Jonah shrugged his shoulders. "We hooked up. I wouldn't call it 'together.' I don't think she would either."

Melvin Aaron started to say something, reconsidered, then said it anyway. "May I give you some advice about women?"

"Join the club. Last night in Highland Heights, Kyle was giving me advice. Go ahead."

Melvin Aaron paused as he tried to remember the name of the intern in the story he was about to tell. "I've told you about the set of principles some of us created when we were interns at Mt. Moriah, haven't I?"

"Several times."

"One of the principles is 'At the end of internship, any woman looks great.' The point was that internship was such a horrible stress, being on-call every other night in those days, that when it ended you felt fantastic. Whomever you were dating, if you weren't too exhausted to be dating anyone, often got credit for making you feel great. Sammy Morris was an intern with me. He had his vacation at the end of June, the last two weeks of our internship year. On the first day of July he showed up back at Mt. Moriah for his residency married to this girl from the Philippines whom he had met in Las Vegas. She spoke about six words of English. It lasted all of two months."

THE DANA TWINS AND RELATED MATTERS   ~205~

"You're saying that after what happened in Idaho, I'm going to start feeling better and that I shouldn't give too much credit to Kelly."

"Essentially."

Jonah nodded but said nothing.

"Did you tell Kelly about Idaho?"

"Of course not. It's impossible to explain what happened without talking about the Dana Twins and I can't do that. I have an agreement with Milton. I can only tell you and Mom. Mom hasn't taken it well." Jonah made a motion that resembled pulling back on the elastic bands and firing a harpoon. He looked at the stairs to be sure no one was going to overhear what he was about to say. "Joey and Terry are alive. I'm alive. Kyle Ford is alive. Four people are dead. Anyway, I looked in the mirror this morning, and I still thought I looked very dangerous. Then again, I know what happened and I know at whom I am looking when I look in the mirror."

Mel Aaron chuckled. "I find it amazing that you can do what you did, and still make the effort to use good grammar."

"There is no excuse not to use good grammar. Would you really find things less amazing if I said that I know who I'm looking at?"

"OK, Mr. Dangerous Man. How was Highland Heights?"

"I can't talk about it. You're a doctor. You know about confidentiality. If you want to know what happened, call Hal Gorman. But, if it makes you feel any better, I saved a woman's life yesterday." Jonah knew that telling the story would involve talking about Hal Gorman's leaving a loaded gun where a suicidal woman could find it. He regarded that as the type of embarrassing information that an investigator was paid to keep to himself.

Melvin Aaron chose not to pursue the matter. He would consider calling Hal Gorman when he got to work. "Any plans for the day, now that you are looking more presentable?"

"Other than go shopping at the mall and buy some clothes to go with the clean cut look, not really. I think I'll just hang out with Kelly." He pointed upstairs.

Melvin Aaron sighed and shook his head. "Jonah, your mother is not going to be happy with you having an overnight guest . . . I'm not particularly pleased, either."

Jonah shrugged his shoulders. "Mom's not happy about a lot of things."

The conversation was terminated by the arrival of Kelly Thompson. Kelly stood five feet eight inches tall and, to Melvin Aaron's medical eye, appeared to have neither body fat nor muscle mass. She wore her black hair in bangs. Without makeup, she projected casual innocence. She was wearing an extra-long Dana Twins T-shirt barely long enough to cover her bottom. Melvin Aaron hoped that she had at least put on panties or the bottom half of a bathing suit. He wasn't going to make an effort to check.

"Good morning, Dr. Aaron. It's nice to see you again. And don't worry. Jonah had me call my folks last night and tell them where I was staying. They would have been worried that I'd been kidnapped or something if I hadn't called." Jonah winced at the word kidnapped as Kelly continued. "Your son is a very thoughtful young man."

"But not of his mother's feelings," Melvin Aaron said under his breath as Tina Aaron entered the kitchen.

"Hello, Kelly. How are you this morning?" The iciness in her voice thawed as she noted that Jonah had not only cut his hair but was clean shaven as well. Pretending that she didn't know that Kelly had been an overnight guest, she continued. "You got over here bright and early this morning I see." She turned to her son. "Is Kelly the reason you cleaned up your act?"

Kelly answered for Jonah. "No, Mrs. Aaron, I don't think I was. But I was the barber. What do you think?"

Tina Aaron looked over Kelly's handiwork. "You have obvious talent as a beautician. Where are you going to school in the fall, Kelly?"

"I'll be a freshman at Bryn Mawr. I'll probably go to law school after that."

Tina Aaron managed a smile. "What a shame. The world has far too many lawyers as it is. But that is a very good haircut. You may be missing your true calling." Tina Aaron quickly calculated that the girl she had always referred to as "that little slut" would likely be off to college in six or seven weeks. "Did Jonah tell you that he has become even more committed to being an investigator instead of something respectable like a doctor? In fact, Jonah believes that he already is an investigator instead of a young man living with his parents." She glared at Jonah. He pretended not to notice.

"Jonah told me about his plans. I think it's cool. No offense, Dr. Aaron, Mrs. Aaron, but just like there may be too many lawyers, the world has too many doctors. The cost of health care is bankrupting the country. In a way, Jonah deciding not to be a doctor is a form of national service."

"How patriotic of my son," Tina said, her voice dripping sarcasm.

Melvin Aaron had to smile. Kelly could dish it out as well as take it. She was a year older than Jonah, and had been a year ahead of him at the academic magnet school. Melvin Aaron looked down at the newspaper to keep his wife from noticing that he was smiling.

Tina Aaron conceded temporary defeat. "Kelly, I assume you are going to be here hanging out at the pool today. Do you and Jonah intend to join us for dinner? I'll pick up an extra steak to grill before I come home if you are."

Kelly looked at Jonah for guidance before responding.

"Probably, Mom, I worked yesterday. I'm sure Dad told you. One of Dad's former colleagues called and wanted to hire a bodyguard. Dad deflected it to Kyle and Kyle had me go with him."

Tina Aaron exhaled slowly. She was upset that her husband took Jonah's desire to be an investigator seriously. "Kelly, may I give you some woman to woman advice?"

"Sure, Mrs. Aaron."

"Someday, you are likely to start a family of your own. Early on in each pregnancy, I suggest that you determine the gender of the child and consider carefully whether or not you want to have sons. Life as the only woman in a home with three boys—and I'm counting you as one of the boys, Melvin—can be very difficult."

Melvin Aaron stared at his wife. They had gone over this ground many times. "You know, if he is going to be an investigator, I think you'd want him to be trained enough to do it well and do it safely."

"We're not having this discussion now. Here! Read this!" She handed Jonah a copy of TIME magazine opened to the section on science. Weighing her words carefully to avoid any mention of the Dana Twins in front of Kelly Thompson, she told him, "I know you think you're hot stuff for seventeen, but that boy is younger than you are and he is really doing something."

Jonah looked at the article. "Richard Dinsmore? So what?"

"You didn't even look at the article. Do you even know who he is?"

"Of course I do, Mom. I've already had advanced placement math and physics. Plus, I read that article on the plane coming back from Chicago. He's supposedly this generation's Einstein but with better hair, terrible glasses, and the complete absence of all those centers in the brain that determine personality."

"He's a teenager who is really doing something instead of you with your . . . with your work at that music studio and your plan to become an investigator."

"What exactly is Richard Dinsmore doing, mom? He hasn't done anything. He's got a theory about time travel and spaceships traveling near the speed of light that maybe fourteen people on the planet understand, and which no one can prove or disprove since no one can build a large matter-anti-matter engine." Having read the complete article the night before, Jonah had his mother at a disadvantage.

"What are you saying?"

"I'm saying that it may be a great scientific advance or it may all be nonsense. Science requires verification, and at this point in time there's no way to verify it. It could all turn out to be bad science fiction."

"He's right about the verification part," Melvin Aaron chimed in.

Tina Aaron glared at her son, "I don't like science fiction and I never watch it, but it doesn't matter." She clipped a picture of Richard Dinsmore from TIME magazine, and placed it on the door of the refrigerator. "I bet that you are just as smart as he is, and that he simply applied himself. That will be a reminder of what you could accomplish if you hadn't made a career choice that guaranteed that you would be an underachiever!"

"Whatever."

Melvin Aaron thought that comparing Jonah to Richard Dinsmore was a low blow. Jonah was exceptionally bright, but Richard Dinsmore was a genius.

Having felt that she had made her point, Tina kissed her husband goodbye. "I'll get breakfast at the Donut Den on my way to work. And I do like the new look Jonah. You know, in case you're concerned about it, you still look dangerous."

"It's the eyes, Mrs. Aaron. He looks right through you. I think it's sexy." Kelly poured some orange juice into a plastic cup and headed out to the pool.

As she got in her car, Tina began counting the days until Kelly would be leaving for college. Unless Jonah got her pregnant, God forbid, that would likely be the last they saw of Kelly Thompson.

Milton Aaron leafed through the paper before leaving. "Your mother loves you very much. She's just very frustrated."

"Look at page 8, dad."

Milton Aaron opened the newspaper. "Twenty-two dead in Idaho drug war. I assume that's the story you wanted me to see?"

"As they say on rock and roll radio, 'the hits just keep on coming.' Twenty-two." By the time the killing stopped, the death toll in the Idaho drug war would reach thirty-one known dead including James Halloran and his three associates.

Melvin Aaron finished reading the story and looked up at his son. "It says that the drug war is about some missing drugs . . . You're not dealing drugs are you? That's not where your money is coming from, is it?"

"Of course not! I've got more sense than to do anything like that. There were drugs and money in the safe at the barn where they took us. Kyle and I kept the money. We considered it reimbursement for our inconvenience. We couldn't exactly do it the American way and file a lawsuit for damages. We scattered the drugs along the highway as we drove to Coeur d'Alene. Thanks for being concerned."

"How much money are we talking about?"

Jonah smiled. "There was about six hundred thousand dollars in the safe. Kyle and I split the money and now I'm giving him half of my half to train me."

Melvin Aaron thought it over. "I suspect your mother would disagree, but it sounds like a good investment to me."

"Thanks. I'm glad someone takes me seriously."

Melvin Aaron pointed to the newspaper and the story about the Idaho drug war. "It's hard not to take you seriously. Have a good day, son. Stay safe."

Jonah spoke without looking up from the sports section. "Take care, Dad. By the way, Hal Gorman asked me to tell you that Gail Riley was going to be the new chief at CMI. I almost forgot."

"I knew that already. I spoke to Dr. Dettman yesterday. But thanks for telling me."

"You're welcome."

Melvin Aaron paused as he headed for the door. "I have to ask you something else. You're seventeen, but you're a whiz in math and science. How did you ever make a mistake and miscalculate what the effect of that diazepam and alcohol mixture would be? Did you intend to kill them?"

Jonah looked his father in the eyes. "The simple truth is that they drank a lot more than I expected."

His father let out a sigh. "In a way I'm relieved, but I'm also a little scared for you."

Jonah shrugged his shoulders. "To tell the truth, I'm a little scared for me, too, but I really think I can pull off being an investigator. I figure I'll be smarter and more imaginative than most investigators. That should help. And if I can't do the job, hopefully I'll quit before anything bad happens. This is Nashville. No matter what, I can always try making it as a songwriter. I did pretty well the first time."

"That you did."

"And Milton is talking about making a movie about the Dana Twins someday. Maybe I could do something with that if things don't work out. When I take the year off to work for Milton, I'm hoping to line up a part-time job working at a North Nashville studio where they make music videos."

"Whose idea was that?"

"Mine."

It was the first time Melvin Aaron had heard Jonah express doubts about becoming an investigator. He suspected that if he pushed the matter Jonah would get defensive. "It's good that you're keeping an open mind."

Jonah saluted him and headed out to the pool and to Kelly Thompson.

That evening, Jonah found a gift on his desk, along with the following note.

Jonah—

I spoke to Hal Gorman and was most impressed with what he told me about you. I hope you are as proud of what you accomplished yesterday as I am. But, just as I didn't end up becoming a rabbi, which was my intention when I was in high school, you may become something other than an investigator. It may be wise to have a backup plan, which is why I bought you this book.

You probably know that your mother once wanted to be a doctor. She didn't get into medical school because the deck was stacked against women in those days. One reason she is hard on you is that she doesn't want to see you deny yourself the opportunities that she was denied because she was a woman. For all of our sakes, please cut her a little slack.

Dad

The gift was a book entitled *Writing a Screenplay*. Jonah read the first few pages, then went to his desk and picked up a stack of index cards that he hadn't examined in several years.

Rule Number Twelve advised against taking cases for friends who hadn't been seen in many years as they probably intended to take advantage of the past friendship.

Rule Number Thirteen was "Except in rare circumstances, do not accept an open police case; all you can do is get in the way."

Rule Number Fourteen was "Never promise someone you're going to solve a crime or a problem when you don't really know if you can deliver." Jonah had learned that from his father who made a point never to tell patients that he would cure their cancer, only that he would do his best.

Rule Number Fifteen related to cashing checks as soon as they were received so that a client couldn't stop payment if they became irritated by his approach to a problem. Jonah wondered whether he needed to keep that rule. He decided that just because he didn't need the money didn't mean that he intended to spend his life working pro bono.

Rule Number Sixteen was "Going into a situation blindly and stirring things up so that the bad guys come after you and try to kill you is not a viable long term strategy."

On a blank card Jonah wrote, "Rule Number Seventeen: Whenever possible, have a Plan B."

He put the index cards back in the top drawer of his desk, along with the note from his father, and logged on to e-bay. For Father's Day, Jonah had gotten his dad a mint condition Chicago Cubs scorecard from 1952. That was the year that Jonah's grandfather had first taken Jonah's father to a baseball game at Wrigley Field. Melvin Aaron had loved the gift.

Jonah placed a three hundred dollar bid on a mint condition Cubs-Tigers World Series program from 1945. His father had a birthday coming up in August, but Jonah would give it to him sooner with a note saying "Just for being my Dad."

That night, just before she went to sleep, Tina Aaron knocked on her son's bedroom door.

RICHARD STEIN

"Come in."

She saw that he was reading. "I just wanted to say good night, Jonah."

"Good night." Jonah didn't even look up from the book.

Day by day, Tina was becoming more resigned to the fact that she would never have a reasonable relationship with her son. She assumed that the book was something about guns or surveillance. "What are you reading?"

He turned towards the open door. "It's a book on how to write a screenplay. I'm working on my backup plan in case being an investigator doesn't work out."

Tina managed not to smile. She did want Jonah to realize how pleased she was that he had a backup plan. "That sounds interesting."

"The author says you have to set the scene before you write the dialogue. I have no idea how to do that. Since you're a fantastic decorator, if I tried to write something, would you be willing to help me out by putting a description of the setting into words?"

Tina Aaron looked around the room. "Why don't you pretend that this is the first scene of your play, or your movie, and describe this place and see how you do?"

"If I wanted to do that . . ." He realized that he sounded angry and stopped. "Sorry . . . Just give me a few seconds . . ." He looked around the room, planning what he was going to say before he began. "Here goes . . . A young man sits at a desk in what is obviously his bedroom. The room is tastefully decorated in masculine shades of teal and beige. The bed is unmade. On the wall are two posters. One is an autographed poster of the 1985 Chicago Bears Super Bowl Champions. The other is an autographed poster of the Dana Twins." He smiled before continuing. "An attractive woman stands in the doorway. She is too old to be his girlfriend; she is probably his mother. She is very uncomfortable. Her arms are folded across her chest, her stance is erect. She speaks."

Tina unfolded her arms when Jonah commented on her posture. "I don't know what to say."

"That's ok. We're not doing an improvisation. The example in the book ended that way, with the words 'she speaks.'"

Tina laughed. "That was good. The description was fine. I'm glad to help you, but you may not need me."

"But I was describing something I was actually seeing, and I didn't get across that the room showed expensive good taste."

"Thank you." She looked around the room. "Well, you could comment on the Frank Lloyd Wright style lamps on the night stands, and the Scandinavian designer bedroom set. And, by the way, I like the way you framed those posters with a light colored wood to match the furniture. Most young men would have used a black frame or just taped them to the wall."

"Thanks. I learned from you."

"But I suspect that as a writer all you would have to do, Jonah, is say something like 'designed fashionably with expensive taste' and the set designer, or whatever they call it, would have to take care of the details. I don't know anything about screenplays, but I doubt that the writer has to be that specific."

Jonah nodded his head. "In that case I may not need your help in writing the screenplay as much as I need you to be the set designer when I make a movie."

They both began to laugh.

"Well, Jonah, if you ever make a movie or if you ever have a room you want decorated, just ask me. I'd be glad to help by giving it the feel you want."

"Thank you. I'm not planning to do anything right now, but when I do . . ."

"Just let me know."

"I will . . . But don't hold your breath, mom . . . And thanks."

"Goodnight, Jonah." She closed the door to his room and headed to the master bedroom.

Tina Aaron doubted that Jonah would ever ask for her help with a real project, but it was the first conversation that they had had in weeks that hadn't degenerated into an argument. She climbed into bed and slid next to her husband. "Melvin, are you awake?"

"Not really."

"I just talked to your son . . . our son . . . He's reading a book on writing a screenplay. He asked me if I would help him with set design if he ever got around to writing a script. I'm sure he never will, but it was nice of him to ask."

Melvin Aaron mumbled something into his pillow.

"What was that?"

"I said, 'With Jonah, never rule out anything.'"

When Jonah graduated high school and began working for Milton Brandenburg, he took a part-time job at a North Nashville studio that filmed music videos. Overhearing a director complain that all music videos were starting to look the same, Jonah suggested that his mother be hired to do set design. Working in the music business, Tina developed a reputation for giving videos an expensive look without breaking the budget. She also found a new clientele.

In response to the increased work load, Tina hired two additional assistants and expanded her Green Hills showroom into the building next door. When a music video on which she had worked, "What the Future Holds for Us" by Calliope, won the Country Music Association award for Video of the Year, Jonah began referring to Tina as his overachieving mother.

However, even though Jonah entered Vanderbilt in the fall of 1998 after his senior year of high school and his year working for Milton Brandenburg, his mother continued to regard him as an underachiever. The picture of Richard Dinsmore remained on the refrigerator door in the Aaron kitchen.

9

FORTY-SEVEN

THE EXPANSION OF the cancer medicine program at CMI was a difficult, slow process. Two years after Gail Riley had become Chief, the program had added only one new faculty member and three new cancer research nurses, one of whom was Candy Butler. Lying on the floor near the bank of elevators, the twenty-four year old platinum blonde wasn't at all certain what had happened. She remembered walking off the elevator and the next thing she knew the man in the white coat was reaching for her hand.

"I am so sorry. Let me help you up."

"Did I trip?"

"No. It was my fault entirely. I guess I get a two minute minor penalty for interference."

She couldn't help but notice how handsome he was, especially when he smiled. She also noticed how well dressed he was, wearing a lavender shirt and a matching tie under his white coat. His grooming was immaculate. She wondered if he was gay. "An interference penalty? That's hockey talk isn't it?"

"Yes it is. I played back in college. Are you alright? I really slammed into you."

Now that she was standing, she realized that she wasn't hurt. She also realized how tall he was. She was five-five. He was at least nine inches taller. She looked at his name tag and realized that her gaydar had missed by a mile. She had been at CMI long enough to know of Eric Cain's reputation as a ladies' man. "What happened?"

"I got off the elevator on the wrong floor. The patient I was coming to see is on ten, but I got off on eleven. When I caught my mistake I turned around quickly and . . ."

"And I had my head down reading a memo, and you wiped me out."

"Basically."

They spoke simultaneously, "Did you see that highlight on ESPN?"

They laughed.

Again they spoke simultaneously, "Larry Parks, the running back from LSU . . ."

She pointed at him as she chuckled. "You go first."

"Larry Parks. That was a real wipe-out. I'm more of a hockey fan than a football fan, but that was something. One minute the announcers were talking about his chances for winning the Heisman Trophy, and how high he would go in the first round of the NFL draft . . ."

"And the next minute he's returning a punt and wham, there goes his ACL and his MCL."

"Both ligaments? I didn't hear it was both."

Candy Butler loved impressing men by knowing more about sports than they expected. "I heard it on ESPN this morning. Both ligaments. They were wondering if he would ever play at the same talent level again. You know, Vanderbilt hasn't won a game yet this year, but they're in the Southeastern Conference and they obviously have some really good players on special teams."

"It was a heck of a hit."

"Of course, Vanderbilt still lost 24-13. Same old Vandy."

He couldn't help but see that she had a beautiful smile and a bit of an accent. "You sound like you're from the South."

"Tennessee. A little town called Kenton. But I didn't go to UT, or Vanderbilt. I went to a community college fifty miles northeast of Knoxville—Walters State." She couldn't think of anything else to say, so she extended her hand, "I'm Candy Butler."

He noticed that she wasn't wearing a wedding ring. "I'm Eric Cain. It's nice to meet you. Looks like I didn't do any permanent damage. You still look very beautiful."

"Thank you." She was about to say "If you think I look good now, you should see me naked," but decided against it. She saw that he was admiring her figure. She guessed that he was trying to figure out if her breasts were natural or man-made. That was her secret, for the time being.

"Look, I have to run and see that patient on the tenth floor, and I suspect you have to get back to work, but the Blackhawks are playing New Jersey Saturday night and seeing how you're interested in sports, I was wondering if you'd like to go with me. It would be my apology for knocking you down."

"Yes! I'd love to!" She knew next to nothing about hockey, but her divorce had recently become final and she had decided that it was time to start dating again. She took a slip of paper from her purse, wrote down her phone number, and handed it to him. "Call me during the week to make arrangements and I'll see you Saturday."

The entire time he was seeing the consult on the tenth floor, Eric Cain's mind kept drifting back to the blonde nurse. He was still thinking about her when Gail Riley found him in the cafeteria for their Monday morning meeting over coffee.

"Earth to Eric. You look distracted."

"I guess so. I was thinking about this nurse of yours that I literally ran over in the hall this morning. I ended up inviting her to go to a hockey game with me."

"Candy Butler. The real cute blonde with the big boobs. I already heard about it. She's your type."

"I have a type?"

"Actually, your type is attractive, unmarried, and having two X chromosomes. She's divorced, by the way."

He thought it over. "That probably is my type. Anyway, how are you this morning?"

"I'm fine. With two boys under the age of two, there's always a sense of relief in going back to work on Monday morning." Gail chuckled. After she had been appointed Chief of Cancer Medicine, she and Larry had changed their minds about not having children. "We have a potential faculty member coming in for an interview this week. I'm working on my National Cancer Institute grant. I have a paper I want to finish before I go onto the in-patient service November first. Then there's always the clinical research. I'm fine. Just a little busy. Hey, are you paying attention to anything I'm saying?"

"Of course I am. Your children are fine; recruitment is ongoing; you're working on a grant and a paper; the drug research is progressing. You're busy. I'm just thinking about that nurse though."

Gail sighed. "I went up on the floor this morning to see one of my patients and Candy Butler was asking about you."

Eric Cain smiled. "Really? What did she say?"

"Well, she had seen us together in the cafeteria a couple of times, and wanted to know if we were having an affair. I thought she was just being nosy, but I told her we were very good friends, that we had been good friends for a very long time, and I told her we were much too close for anything like that." Gail squeezed his hand. "Then she told me about literally bumping in to you and that you had asked her out. She said she didn't want to cut in on my territory if we were an item."

"Attractive. Sports fan. Considerate. I like her even more."

"I told her that if she was interested in you, that she should go for it, that it would be hard to do better."

He chuckled. "Considering my track record with women, I'm not sure that's true, but it's kind of you to say that. Did she say anything in response?"

"She said 'forty-seven' and walked away."

"Forty-seven? What the heck does that mean?"

Gail shrugged her shoulders. "I have no idea."

*   *   *

Candy Butler knew a great deal about football, but almost nothing about hockey. Eric Cain was years beyond the point where he enjoyed explaining the basics of the game, let alone its subtleties, to a novice. Candy Butler found him condescending. She also found him attractive and if she hadn't had to work Sunday morning she likely would have gone to bed with him anyway. Instead, when the game was over she asked to be taken home, and the date ended with a handshake. She assumed he would never ask her out again.

She would have been correct, except for the fact that several months later, a nurse who worked on the Trauma Unit came down with the flu and had to cancel a date with Eric Cain the afternoon of a Bruce Springsteen concert. Eric Cain got the bad news while he was at the eleventh floor nursing station completing a consultation. He was trying to think of whom he could ask at the last minute when he saw her. Truth be told, he had forgotten her name.

"Excuse me, could you do me a big favor."

She smiled. Doctors were always asking nurses to get them things, as if they had nothing better to do than wait on the doctors. "What do you need?"

"Look. I'm sorry to ask at the last minute, but a friend I was taking to the Springsteen concert tonight just called to tell me that she has the flu. It's no fun to go alone. I'm sure an attractive woman like you has other plans for the evening, but if you don't, I would really appreciate it if you would let me take you."

Her eyes brightened. "Of course I would. That's fantastic. Forty-seven. Thanks so much for asking."

Her enthusiasm was for Springsteen more than it was for him, but he decided that perhaps he had misjudged her attitude after their hockey date. He didn't ask what she meant by forty-seven.

To his surprise, he found that he enjoyed her company as much as he enjoyed Springsteen. At the end of the evening they returned to his condo where he got to show off his Night Shadow memorabilia and tell her about his experience in the world of rock and roll. This time, she didn't mind that he was a bit self-absorbed. She found him fascinating and would have gone to bed with him had she not had to work the following morning. She made it clear that she was interested in him and was hoping he would ask her out again. When he asked her to dinner the following Saturday night, she re-arranged her schedule to be off on Sunday.

He took her to Le Francais in Wheeling, a half hour north of the city. It was widely regarded as one of the finest restaurants in the Chicago area and it was a place he reserved for special occasions. Over the Chilean sea bass topped with caviar he asked her what she did when she wasn't working at the hospital.

"I take writing classes. I've been working on a novel on and off since I was seventeen years old, and it's finally starting to get somewhere."

"Do you want to talk about it, or is it private?"

She looked him over for a long moment before answering. "It is private, but I'll talk about it. It's about a woman who grows up in a small town where everything conspires to make her think she's nothing. It's about how she gets beyond it by leaving town and re-inventing herself. Unfortunately, that involves cutting herself off from some of the people who really matter to her."

"Interesting. How does it end?"

She smiled and returned to her food. "You'll have to buy the book—if I ever finish it and it gets published."

He laughed. "I'll do that. What's it called?"

"*White Squirrel.*"

He almost dropped his fork. "What did you say?"

"*White . . . Squirrel.*" She said the words slowly and distinctly, thinking that she had confused him by running them together. "I was born in this sweet little town that called itself 'The Home of the White

Squirrel.' I was even Miss White Squirrel when I was sixteen . . . Is something wrong?"

"No. Nothing. A couple of years ago, we had a nurse from southern Illinois who came from 'The Home of the White Squirrel.' The title of your book brought back memories."

"Olney, Illinois. That's where she must have been from. There are a number of places in America that call themselves 'The Home of the White Squirrel.' Olney, Illinois is one of them."

"You're from the one in Tennessee, right?"

"That's right." She was impressed that he had remembered. "Anyway, some people come out of towns like that decide that they are nothing because the town is nothing; other people decide that the town is just where they are from, it isn't who they are. Some people, like me, saw the good in that sweet little town, but put it in the rear view mirror just the same." She didn't see much good in her hometown, but she knew that most men didn't like women with a negative attitude. As much as she despised Kenton, she never referred to it as anything other than a sweet little town. She flashed her best smile. "I was the oldest of three girls. I left and I have never looked back."

"What about your sisters? What paths did they take?"

There was something about him that made her want to tell him the truth that she was estranged from her family. However, she realized that if she did that, it would simply delay her having to lie to him. She took a sip of wine while she thought it over. He would inevitably ask why she had no contact with her family and she couldn't tell him that her father had periodically raped her when she was a child. Who would want to date a damaged woman like that? And she certainly wouldn't admit to having worked as an escort to earn the money to pay for nursing school after she left home at seventeen. Instead, she decided to tell him the same lie she had been telling everyone for the last six years. "My entire family, including my two sisters, died in a house fire. I was out babysitting or I would have ended up burned to a cinder as well." As she pretended to wipe a tear from her eye she decided that it wasn't a lie. It was simply a borrowed story. When she was fourteen it had happened to a girl her age from the neighboring town of Dyer.

"How tragic."

She nodded her head. "It was very tragic. But, like they say, 'When life gives you lemons, make lemonade.' Money can't replace the love of a family, but the insurance paid my tuition to nursing school." Tears welled up in her eyes.

"Are you ok?"

"Just thinking about my little sisters." While she despised her mother, she loved her sisters. They were now sixteen and fifteen and while she hadn't had any contact with them since the day she left home, she knew they were doing well and that they didn't have to worry about being raped by daddy. He had taken ill around the time she had left home. If he hadn't died, she likely would have stayed in Kenton looking out for her sisters. "Funny how things work out sometimes," she thought to herself.

He put his hand on hers and when she smiled he left it there. Since they had been discussing white squirrels, he told her the story of Cookie Bradford, her abusive husband, the suicide attempt, and the resuscitation.

"That's a nice way of telling the story. You have a knack. I like the way you changed things around."

"Changed what around?"

She laughed and pointed her index finger at him. "In your version of the story, you were the one who wrote the prescription. That was chivalrous of you to take responsibility. Gail Riley once told me about signing a blank prescription and having a nurse write for what almost became a lethal overdose. I assume it's the same story."

"Yes it is." Many of his stories were embellished for effect. Few people ever caught him at it.

"What ended up happening to her, the girl from Olney?"

"You know Hal Gorman, don't you?"

"Sure. He was the attending physician on the eleventh floor two months ago."

"Well, a week after the resuscitation, she was discharged from the psychiatric service, and she went to stay with Hal Gorman and his wife. No one knew where her husband was and considering that he had almost choked her to death, the Gormans thought it would be safer for her than going back to her empty apartment."

"That was nice of Hal and his wife."

"Yes it was. Unfortunately, Hal kept a loaded gun in the house and she found it. Cookie Bradford's husband came after her and he had a gun. I'm sure that one of them would have ended up killing the other one, but, despite leaving the gun where she could find it, Hal had the good sense to hire a bodyguard. Before there was any gunfire, the bodyguard managed to disarm the husband and beat him up pretty bad."

"So it worked out ok?"

Eric Cain shook his head. "Not quite. Cookie's husband had been her high school boyfriend. They had been together for years. Later that evening, when she realized that the relationship was over, she put Hal's gun in her mouth and right in front of Dr. Gorman, his wife, and the bodyguard, she pulled the trigger."

Candy straightened up in her seat. "Oh, my God. What a horrible way to die, especially after you had saved her life."

Eric chuckled. "Oh, she didn't die. The bodyguard had a young partner with him, some kid he was training. Sometime during the day, the kid had removed the bullets. Sorry. I forgot to mention that."

She knew that he had intentionally omitted that detail to make the story more exciting. "What happened after that?"

"She got re-admitted to psychiatry and when she got out, she wanted something less stressful than the cancer unit at CMI. She went back to Olney and took a job working with a family physician. She also started volunteering at a women's shelter, helping women who were trying to leave abusive relationships."

She realized that she would probably enjoy doing something like that herself. She would think about it. "As I said before, I like the way you tell a story." Suddenly, she closed her eyes, dropped her face into her hands, and spoke without looking up. "It just hit me. When I saw that stuff at your place last week, it didn't register." She looked up as she continued. "You're the one who wrote the book, *Night Shadow*. I read part of *Night Shadow* back when I was fifteen. Sex, drugs, and rock and roll. I loved that book but my mother took the book away and burned it . . . That wasn't what caused the fire, by the way, in case you were worried."

He admired the way she could joke about what had obviously been the most horrible experience in her life. "Sex and rock and roll. I stayed away from drugs."

"Good plan. And what do you do now, when you're not practicing medicine or going to hockey games or rock concerts?"

If he told the truth he would have said, "Seduce attractive women." Instead, he began talking about the high cost of health care and segued into a description of his research into automated, computerized approaches to reading cardiograms. After losing his grant two years earlier, he had continued the research at his own expense. The project had yet to bear fruit.

By the end of the meal it was clear where the evening was headed so they skipped dessert and went back to his condo where they spent the night. He was surprised by her sexual energy. In the morning, when he cooked her breakfast she told him that it had been a perfect date. "Forty-seven."

"You said that when we were having sex. What does that mean?"

She thought about telling him, but thought better of it. "I'm sorry. I'm not ready to talk about it just yet." She recognized the disappointment in his eyes. "It's something good, but as close as I feel to you, I'm embarrassed to talk about it."

He wondered if it meant that he was the forty-seventh man with whom she had slept, but he remembered Gail Riley telling him that Candy had said "forty-seven" the day that he had knocked her down by the elevators. He doubted that that was the meaning.

Instead of taking her home, they returned to bed. He liked talking to her—she was as intelligent and witty as any woman he had ever known—and he loved the sex. He was forty-one; she was twenty-four and she made him feel like he was seventeen. When he told her that he felt he was having sex with the Energizer Bunny, she started to say "I get that a lot." Instead, she managed to blush and say, "I don't know what other women are like, but I guess I was blessed with a healthy sex drive." When he inquired how she had gotten to be so good in bed, she laughed and told him that she was "a natural" and that she hadn't been with all that many men, a statement that was true if and only if one considered a number upward of a thousand as not that many.

"In any case, past is past," she told him. "All that matters is the present and the future." He was happy to agree, especially when the present consisted of her kissing her way down his abdomen, taking him in her mouth, getting him hard one more time, and climbing on for a ride. Since the time she was sixteen, Candy had regarded sex as an orgasm hunt, and that night and morning she concluded that if the hunt was regulated by a game warden, she might be arrested for going over the legal limit.

In his entire life, Eric Cain had never been with a woman so comfortable with her sexuality. He decided not to pursue the issue of her sexual past. She never asked him about the women who had preceded her in his bed. Of course, she had read *Night Shadow* and she knew from Gail Riley that Eric Cain had been with hundreds of women but had never been in a serious relationship.

After they had been dating for several months, he began to wonder if the feelings that he had for her were love. He had never been in love and he had suspected that he might be incapable of loving anyone. He was tired of going from woman to woman and he enjoyed being with her, both in and out of the bedroom. He especially enjoyed her stories about growing up in Kenton, Tennessee, even if he had trouble separating the ones that were true from the ones she had dreamed up for use in her unpublished novel. It didn't bother him; after all, the stories he told were rarely the literal truth.

It was about that time that she asked him where he saw the relationship going. He realized that he had never been in a relationship that had survived long enough for the question to be asked. "Where do you want it to go?" he inquired.

She answered directly. "I don't know. I've never been in a relationship that lasted this long."

He knew she stretched the truth at times, but that was hard to accept. "I'm confused. What do you mean you've never been in a relationship that lasted this long? We've been dating for six months. You were MARRIED for two and a half years. You told me that much even though you never talk about it."

She laughed. "That wasn't a real relationship. Morristown, Tennessee, where I went to nursing school, was a small town. One of my professors was gay and in the closet. He was afraid people would find out, so he asked me to marry him. I liked the idea because it gave me status as a faculty wife, and guys never hit on me. It gave me time to study."

"So you were celibate for two and a half years?"

"Of course! He married me for appearances' sake. It wouldn't have been a good appearance if I was dating other men." In truth, she had been extremely discreet and only seen other men when she was out of town. However, she saw no reason to advertise her adulterous past, though, from her point of view, it wasn't adultery since it really wasn't a marriage.

While they hadn't discussed past relationships, he couldn't help but want to know more about her. "Why did it end? I'm just curious. You don't have to talk about it if you don't want to."

She sighed. "Not a problem. He got his Ph.D. and decided to leave sweet little Morristown and go into practice in the big city of Chicago. That's how I ended up at CMI. Anyway, up here, no one here gives a damn if you're gay. There was no reason to stay married." That was part of the truth. The other part was that Bradley Butler was only ninety-nine percent gay. Shortly after they had arrived in Chicago, they had shared a sexually intimate moment. Afterwards, she had attempted to augment the closeness by telling him about being sexually molested by her father and about being the school slut when she was in high school. She also told Bradley about working as an escort for two years to earn the money to pay for nursing school. By then, Bradley had stopped listening. He had decided that there was no point in staying married for appearances' sake when, at any time, his bride might be revealed to be—as Bradley had called her—"the whore of Babylon." Almost on the spot, he had walked out and filed for divorce.

Candy had decided that no matter how long she stayed with Eric, he would never know her sexual history. "Anyway, Eric, like I said, this is the longest I've ever been in a relationship. I'm getting hooked on you and I want to know what you see as our future." She expected that he would say that he was having fun and that there was no reason for it to go anywhere.

He thought it over. "Frankly, I have no idea where it's going. If it keeps going well, there's no reason we shouldn't get married, someday, if that's what you want—unless you want children. Having a wife would be one thing, but having children—I don't think so. By the time any child of mine was a teenager, I'd be almost sixty. Anyway, I just don't see myself as father material." He paused. "You're not pregnant are you? That's not why we're having this discussion is it?"

She laughed. "No way. I had a tubal ligation when I was eighteen. There's knowing you don't ever want to have children, and then there is KNOWING you don't ever want to have children."

"How come you were so definite at eighteen?"

Candy felt her heart pounding. She was getting into very uncomfortable territory. "Relationships are hard enough as it is. If one has children, they become even more difficult. If and when I get married, I really want it to work." It almost sounded reasonable. The truth was that she was terrified that if she ever had a daughter, her husband might molest the child just as her own father, a seemingly respectable preacher, had molested her. Her mother had allowed it to happen. She knew that if she had a husband and he ever molested their daughter, she would stand up for her child and kill the son of a bitch. It was better to remain childless and never let it become a possibility.

She saw that he was mulling over what she had said so she added, "Plus, I got pregnant at sixteen and had an abortion. I decided I wasn't going to go through that ever again." Except for her disastrous moment of post-coital bliss with Bradley Butler it was as much of the truth about her past as she had ever shared with any man. As much as she enjoyed being with him, she decided that if he continued to push the matter, she would walk out the door, and possibly out of his life.

Instead, he said, "I'm sorry you had to go through that . . . I think it's a good thing that neither one of us wants kids." He realized that in some ways they were better matched than he thought. He gave her a kiss, which led to another kiss, which led to them having sex on the living room rug and to her muttering "Forty-seven, forty-seven, forty-seven." A week later he asked her to move in with him and she accepted the offer. With the exception of a groupie who had spent a week with him on the Night Shadow tour bus in 1982, it was the first time he had ever lived with a woman.

A week later, she gave him as much of her unpublished novel as she had finished. He was surprised at how well she wrote, though he realized afterwards that he shouldn't have been. He knew that she had read more than ninety-five percent of the women he had known.

Two years later, Eric Cain married Candy Butler, who, in the process, became Candy Cain. At the wedding, Gail Riley, who was matron of honor, made the following comment to her husband. "I know they really care about each other, but there's something I can't get out of my mind. Considering that Eric sees himself as a bad boy ex-rock-and-roller and that part of him wants people to think of him as a modern day Peter Pan, what better choice is there than to marry a woman who now has a stripper name and resembles Tinkerbelle with a boob job?"

Larry Patterson's response was less philosophical. For her second wedding, Candy Butler Cain had chosen to get married in a black dress that was cut below her navel. The front was held together by three large silver rings. Looking at Candy in her wedding gown, Larry gave the following reply. "I don't know if there's a better match for Eric somewhere, but considering those large silver rings and her breasts, I was thinking that her center of gravity might be in front of her feet. Of course, as a physicist, I realize that's impossible."

At the wedding, during their first dance together as husband and wife, Candy remarked that the day was a forty-seven.

"What exactly does that mean? You don't have to tell me all your secrets just because we're married, but I'd like to know."

She gave him a sheepish smile. "I should have told you a long time ago. I just didn't want you to know how silly I once was . . . When I grew up in Kenton, despite the fact that it was a sweet little place, my total aim in life was to get out of town. At the southern edge of Kenton, on Highway 45W, there's a sign that says 'Jackson 47 miles.' When I was ten years old, I decided that if I could just make it to Jackson, life would be perfect."

He was gazing into her eyes and smiling as she continued. "The truth is, Eric, one carries their problems with them. There is no magic place where all of life's problems vanish into thin air. Looking back, I think it's sad that I grew up having no higher aim in life than just to travel those forty-seven miles, but forty-seven became my code word for everything being perfect." She kissed him. "Jackson, Tennessee is not paradise, but for me it was the first step in the right direction. Being with you is my idea of forty-seven."

He kissed her and they were embarrassed by the applause from the assembled guests. "I love you very much and I'm sorry that your family can't be here to share this day with you." He didn't need to add that their absence was due to their dying in a fire. That was understood.

"They've gone to a better place," she replied.

The comment surprised him because he knew that she didn't believe in any kind of afterlife. He assumed that the excitement of the day had rattled her, and he didn't press the point. In truth, from reading the society pages of the Chicago papers, Candy Butler Cain knew that her mother had remarried and moved north. Candy's mother and her two younger sisters were living in a spacious suburban home far better than anything Kenton, Tennessee had to offer. Candy doubted that she would ever see her mother or her sisters again and she wasn't going to backtrack on her original story of what had happened to her family.

Candy Cain's story-telling skills rivaled those of her husband. Although she rarely told the tale, one of her favorites was her version of how she and Eric Cain had met. According to Candy, after her first brief marriage had ended, and she had taken a job at CMI, she had asked Eric Cain to write her a prescription for an antidepressant. She had told him that it was a refill and that she couldn't get in touch with her regular physician. According to her story, she had taken the pills in an overdose attempt. Fortunately, Eric had realized that he might have made a grave mistake, had gone to her apartment, had convinced the superintendent to let him in, and had saved her life.

That story was, for the most part, the description of how Eric had saved Cookie Bradford. In addition to claiming that the first time that their lips touched was when Eric was giving her mouth to mouth resuscitation, Candy Butler Cain always included the fact that Eric's mantra while doing chest compressions was "looks great naked." She often added the detail that as a devotee of strawberry flavored sexual lubricants, she had "drowned her private parts in the stuff" before she overdosed since she figured that otherwise her body might smell pretty rotten by the time it was discovered. She claimed that she could always get her husband turned on by eating a strawberry in front of him. In truth, she could get him turned on by eating just about anything, if she did it in an erotic fashion.

The story of how she had met her husband was, like the story that her family had perished in a tragic ``fire, something that she had borrowed from someone else's life because, like a perfect hand me down dress, she liked the way that it fit. When she was eighteen and dating for dollars in Memphis, she had attempted suicide. Eric might not have saved her by doing a cardiac resuscitation, but considering the course of her life prior to meeting him, what he had done for her was equally dramatic in its own way. Furthermore, both she and Cookie Bradford were from towns that called themselves "The Home of the White Squirrel." Synchronicity counted for something.

And, she was an aspiring writer. Writers deserved some literary license. From her point of view, it wasn't a lie at all.

10

I PUSH THE BUTTON
AND IT GOES

I N A SMALL three bedroom apartment in Warwick, Rhode Island, single parent Nora Dinsmore did her best to provide for her twin girls, Bethany and Laura, and her son, Richard. Fortunately, scholarships paid for her brilliant son's graduate school education and while money was not hemorrhaging out, neither was it flowing in.

Nonetheless, Nora Dinsmore, who worked as a research assistant in a cancer biology lab, complained to her son on almost a daily basis. "Richie, what good is all that nonsense about time travel or travel at the speed of light? Those two boys are no older than you and they are making their family wealthy."

"Those two boys" were the Dana Twins, Bethany and Laura's favorite singing group. In addition to having posters of the two androgynous blonde boys over their beds, Bethany and Laura put a poster of the Dana Twins on the outer door of their bedroom just to annoy their brother. Richard Dinsmore resented having his life's work called "nonsense;" he resented the fact that his mother called him "Richie" instead of Richard; most of all, he resented being compared to two boys whose total IQ, he incorrectly suspected, was less than his own.

In 1998, Richard Dinsmore obtained his first salaried position as the youngest Assistant Professor of Physics in the history of MIT. Two years later, sixteen year old Richard Dinsmore had a psychotic episode and was admitted to Mt. Moriah Hospital. Nora Dinsmore was devastated. The doctors informed her that her son might spend his life in and out of hospitals. Nora Dinsmore realized that since his creative mind was all he had, not being able to trust his mind, not being able to tell reality from delusion, was the worst possible thing that could happen to him. She prayed that he would get better—for his sake. She had grown up poor, and if the family was destined to be poor, she knew she would somehow get by.

Although Tina Aaron had never met Richard Dinsmore, she read the news of the physics prodigy's illness with a sense of personal sadness. She decided that perhaps it wasn't so bad that her son Jonah was destined to be an underachiever. If Richard Dinsmore was a pertinent example, too much complex thinking might be bad for people's brains. Jonah, who had walked on to the varsity football team at Vanderbilt, was happy, well liked, and was making excellent grades. Other than the fact that he intended to be a private investigator, he was a fairly typical college student. Without ceremony, Richard Dinsmore's picture—which had spent four years on the refrigerator door in the Aaron home—was removed and tossed in the trash. Tina phoned her son who was a sophomore at Vanderbilt.

"What is it, Mom? You never call. Is something wrong?"

"No. Nothing's wrong. I just wanted to tell you that I love you."

"Love you too, Mom." There was silence at both ends of the line. "Thanks for calling."

Two months later, Richard Dinsmore left Mt. Moriah on an authorized home visit and vanished. Six days later, he was found naked in a farmer's field on the outskirts of Kiev, Ukraine, in what had once been the village of Rikney. The Nazis had destroyed the village and slaughtered its mostly Jewish inhabitants during World War II.

Because of the military potential of Dinsmore's scientific theories, Lowell Huntington, a psychiatrist on the staff of the Central Intelligence Agency, was flown to Kiev on Air Force Two in order to meet with the young man. The interview took place at the Kiev City Jail in a small conference room that smelled of tobacco and sweat. After introducing himself, Dr. Huntington asked the obvious question. "How did you get from your mother's apartment in Warwick, Rhode Island to a field in Rikney?"

"I didn't."

"But you were on a home visit from Mt. Moriah Hospital's Psychiatric Unit and you were found naked in a farmer's field on the outskirts of Kiev, Ukraine. That is correct, isn't it?"

"Of course it is. But I didn't come from Warwick, Rhode Island. I came from the future. I came from the year 2055 to be exact."

"So it's not true that you were a stowaway on a trans-Atlantic flight like the Ukrainian authorities told us?"

Dinsmore shook his head. "They couldn't explain my presence, so they made that up. I came from the future."

Lowell Huntington had read Dinsmore's hospital records from Mt. Moriah. While Richard Dinsmore's research dealt with time travel and travel near the speed of light, the delusions he had previously shared with the psychiatrists at Mt. Moriah had included no mention of being a time traveler. Dr. Huntington had considerable experience dealing with delusional schizophrenics, but none as intelligent as Dinsmore was reputed to be. "Okay. You came from the future. How did you get there?"

"By living fifty-five years in what was the present, one day at a time. How else would one get to the future? Time travel is a one way road. One can only go backwards!" Dinsmore paused. "If my tone just now was disrespectful, I apologize. As I have grown older, I have become less tolerant at times."

"Apology accepted, but I have to ask, you look to be about sixteen years old. If you came from the year 2055, wouldn't you be," he looked down at Dinsmore's dossier and made a quick calculation, "seventy-one?"

Dinsmore nodded. "I was seventy-one on January 1, 2055. I look sixteen because time travel backwards in time makes one younger."

Huntington took a deep breath. "Why is that? Why did you become younger?"

"I'm not certain why. And before you ask, that's why I was naked. Although the clothing I was wearing when I left the future was supposed to be authentic clothing from the twentieth century, it turned out not to be the case. The clothing had been manufactured after the year 2000 and it had a negative age, so to speak, when I appeared in the past. Of course, it's the present for you, but both the present and the past for me. Anyway, I can't explain why I became younger. Obviously, it works that way."

"Obviously." Dr. Huntington paused as he decided to try another tack. "So if you are from the future, then somewhere back in Rhode Island, there is another one of you walking around, right?"

Dinsmore shook his head. "No. No. NO! When I arrived here in the past, the other version of me ceased to exist. Two of the same person cannot exist in the same space-time."

Lowell Huntington considered asking why that was true, but thought better of it. He realized that he should have brought a physicist with him to assist in the interview. He decided to keep asking questions until he

RICHARD STEIN

found a logical inconsistency in the delusions. Over the next hour and a half Dinsmore told him of the arrival of aliens from a planet called Rikenny in the year 2020. He informed the CIA psychiatrist that the alien leader was a woman named Noraa. Dinsmore claimed that the similarity between the name of the alien leader and his mother's name was simply a coincidence, that his mother's name was pronounced NOR-uh while the leader of the aliens was no-RAH. He stated that the time machine had been set up in the former location of the town of Rikney as an ironic choice based on the name of the alien planet. Dr. Huntington reached the more logical conclusion that Dinsmore was weaving his life experiences into his delusional system. After hearing Dinsmore's story of a dystopian planetary future, he arranged for the physics savant to return to the United States.

Dinsmore was re-hospitalized at Mt. Moriah and a transcript of his interview with Dr. Huntington was forwarded to the hospital to assist the doctors in dealing with their patient. Two months later, after he had been placed on high doses of anti-psychotic medications, Richard Dinsmore was discharged to be followed in the out-patient clinic. Though his non-tenured appointment at MIT was not renewed, Yale University offered him a teaching position.

Instead of being assigned to teach a graduate seminar or an advanced physics course, tasks for which he felt extremely well suited, Dinsmore was given what he regarded as the odious task of teaching Introductory Physics for Pre-Medical Students. He knew that no one taking the course had a serious interest in physics. However, the Medical College Admission Test, the MCAT, had a section on Physics, as if physics had anything to do with the practice of medicine. Having spent time in hospitals, Dinsmore thought that future patients would be far better served if their doctors were required to take a course in psychology or even an acting class that taught them how to pretend to show compassion.

Every Monday, Wednesday, and Friday, Richard Dinsmore walked six blocks from his apartment to the Physics Lecture Hall on the Yale campus. On the Friday morning before the midterm exam, the foliage had started to turn autumn colors and there was a faint smell of burning leaves in the air. "I haven't seen as beautiful a fall day since . . . 2049," he thought.

Sedated by his anti-psychotic medications, he barely managed to smile at the custodian who let him in the rear entrance to the building.

Richard Dinsmore ascended the stairs to the stage, stood behind the podium at the left side of the auditorium, looked not at his audience, but at the American flag at the right side of the room, and without making eye contact with a single student, and without recognizing a raised hand from a confused student, of whom there were many, gave a fifty minute lecture without once looking at his notes.

He concluded the lecture with the same words he used to conclude every lecture. "If you have any questions, the answers are in the handouts." The handouts were superb and would eventually be compiled into Dinsmore's best-selling text on college physics.

After every other lecture, Dinsmore had immediately left the building through the same rear entrance by which he had entered the lecture hall. On this morning, however, he took four steps and stopped in his tracks. "I almost forgot. I have two important announcements." He returned to the podium. "First, I have a special handout. It's called 'Report from the Future.' None of the material is on the exam, but you should read it anyway. It describes the future of the planet. I think you might find it interesting."

"Report from the Future" contained much less detail than was present in Dinsmore's interview with the CIA. In a mere six paragraphs it described a series of disasters that Dinsmore hoped mankind could avoid. Dinsmore had attempted to publish his warning in a scientific journal. In the absence of data, the manuscript had been rejected by each of the eleven editorial boards to which it had been submitted.

"The second thing that I wish to say is that I know many of you are worried about the midterm exam on Monday." The lecture hall filled with the sound of hissing as the students responded to the mention of the upcoming test. "I have decided to have a review session. It will be right here in this classroom, tomorrow, Saturday at 1." Before the students could even think of asking if the session might be scheduled at a time that wouldn't conflict with the varsity football game between Yale and Fordham, Dinsmore was out the back door on the way back to his apartment.

Despite his mental illness, Dinsmore was a competent physics teacher who gave challenging exams. As it turned out, the students in Physics for Pre-medical Students would perform significantly better on the physics section of the MCAT during the year that Dinsmore taught the course than in the previous year or in the following year when Dinsmore had moved on to other activities. However, after reading "Report from the

Future," and after the median score on the midterm was 42 out of 100, many of the pre-med students in his class concluded that they were being taught by a lunatic and began to worry about their ability to perform on the MCAT. Thirty-seven of the fifty students in the class petitioned the physics department to assign another professor to teach the course. Richard Dinsmore would have gone from being one of the most famous scientists on the planet to one of the most obscure, if not for the thirteen students who wrote letters requesting that Dinsmore remain in charge of the class.

The chairman of the physics department conducted a review of the situation and found that the average fall midterm exam score of the students who supported Dinsmore remaining in charge of the course was 97. The average exam score of the students wishing to have Dinsmore replaced was 35. Without further investigation, the department chair concluded that Dinsmore was reaching the brightest students in the class and that the complaints represented the sour grapes of the pre-med dullards who could not comprehend a real science such as physics. The truth was more complex.

Since many students in Physics for Pre-medical Students had dates for the Yale-Fordham game, only thirteen of the fifty students in the class had attended the review session during which Dinsmore spent two hours working through four obscure problems which he claimed were the key to the course. The thirteen students left the review session as frustrated as they had entered it, perhaps even more so as they had missed a 36-27 Yale victory. However, on Monday morning, they arrived at the exam and found that it consisted of four problems, the solutions to which depended on the material emphasized at the Saturday afternoon review.

The thirteen students who had attended Dinsmore's Saturday review received exam scores ranging from 92 to 100. The next highest grade in the class was 49. Since Dinsmore's final comment at the end of the Saturday review session had been, "This went well; I think I'll do this again before the first semester final," the thirteen students decided that Dinsmore was to be cherished, not fired. They also decided that since application to medical school was highly competitive, they would not tell their fellow students about Dinsmore's rewarding review session.

Knowing of the petition submitted by more than half the class, and unaware of his thirteen member fan club, Richard Dinsmore feared he was about to lose his teaching position. He began to sink deeper and deeper into depression. For him, every day was cloudy and grey. Indeed, many fall days in New Haven are cloudy and grey, but on the sunny days, Richard Dinsmore didn't notice the sunshine. He never noticed the little girls playing hopscotch across the street from his apartment. He didn't even notice the cute nannies bundled up in their sheepskin coats walking strollers towards the park. Richard Dinsmore felt that the fate of the universe rested squarely on his shoulders and he was reaching the conclusion that he was not up to the task.

Fortunately for Richard Dinsmore—and for humanity in the unlikely case his tale of time travel was not a delusion—in addition to writing a petition of support, the thirteen grateful Yale students decided to invite Richard Dinsmore to go to the movies with them. At 6:30 one November evening, they knocked on Richard Dinsmore's door and extended an invitation to the stunned physicist.

Richard Dinsmore looked at the ten men and three women and wondered if they were mocking him. However, he took the invitation at face value. Until that moment, Richard Dinsmore had rarely watched television. He had never read a work of fiction. He hadn't gone to a movie since his mother had taken him to *Back to the Future III* in 1990, when he was six years old. "Why should I go to a movie?"

"Well, you mentioned in class the other day that you hadn't done any research since you returned from Ukraine. You said that you thought your medications had blunted your mind. We thought maybe this would help stimulate your imagination. Worst case scenario, it might cheer you up. If you're not doing research, you can't be that busy."

Richard Dinsmore had no desire to see a movie, but he realized that his students were correct. He had nothing better to do. He had nothing to do at all. He had prepared his lectures for the entire academic year, including six hundred pages of handouts, during the last week in July. "What do you suggest we go to see?" Dinsmore's voice was devoid of enthusiasm.

"We're going to see '*Harry Potter and the Sorcerer's Stone.*'"

"Who's he?"

"Professor, you may be the only person on this campus who has never heard of Harry Potter. You need to expand your horizons and see where it leads."

To his surprise, Richard Dinsmore sat spellbound throughout the movie. As they walked out of the theatre he turned to his students and said, "Thank you. That was fun. Even though I knew it wasn't a true story, and even though it violated eleven laws of physics, two of which

RICHARD STEIN

won't be discovered for another decade, I'll never think of witches and wizards and magic in the same way ever again. Thank you."

The students invited their professor to go for a beer with them. He declined, telling them that while he had drunk beer when he had been in the future, and had been of legal age, he was only seventeen and didn't want to get them in trouble. Twelve of the students went on their way, but one student stayed behind to speak with Richard Dinsmore.

The student was Brian Brandenburg. Like everyone else who read "Report from the Future," he doubted that a word of it was true. However, it didn't matter to him if Richard Dinsmore had or hadn't travelled through time or if aliens were really going to land on Earth on September 5, 2020, as Dinsmore claimed. The truth was irrelevant. Brian knew an interesting story when he read one, and he had an idea.

As an English major, Brian was enrolled in "The Power of Cinema in American Culture," an elective taught by Warren Tanner, an eccentric Hollywood director who was taking a year's sabbatical at Yale, his alma mater. Tanner's use of cocaine was prodigious and he went through wives like the average person went through automobiles. However, despite the messiness of his personal life, Warren Tanner never went over budget on a film and while the projects he accepted were incredibly diverse, every movie he made turned a huge profit.

Brian thought that with the help of Richard Dinsmore—and possibly the assistance of Warren Tanner—it might be feasible to expand "Report from the Future" and turn it into a motion picture. He didn't imagine a Hollywood-type production like the Harry Potter film they had just seen, or the films that Warren Tanner had directed; he imagined a small independent film.

Brian was about to celebrate his twenty-first birthday and gain access to his trust fund, more than seven million dollars that he and Jonah Aaron had each earned, essentially, from one night and one afternoon's work serving as the recorded voices of the non-existent Dana Twins. However, the Dana Twins had been Jonah's idea. Before he entered the world of medicine, Brian wanted to show his father and his cousin that he could come up with something equally creative.

As Jonah Aaron's best friend, Brian had spent considerable time at the Aarons' home and was familiar with Melvin Aaron's favorite saying: "Don't outlive your money; don't outlive your mind." The first part of the homily came from Herbert Aaron, Melvin's father, who was an accountant. The second part was based on a lifetime of practicing cancer medicine. While dying of cancer was often tragic, the slow progressive deterioration of patients with Alzheimer's seemed far worse to Melvin Aaron. In Richard Dinsmore's "Report from the Future," the disasters started when aliens brought a so-called wonder drug that cured cancer and heart disease. The result was a pandemic of senile dementia. Eventually, everyone dies of something; eliminating cancer and heart disease meant a long life but not a long healthy life. "Report from the Future" resonated with Brian Brandenburg and he decided to pitch his idea to Richard Dinsmore.

"You know, professor, you were just saying that you will never look at wizards or magic in the same way ever again. What if we take your story, 'Report from the Future,' and expand it into a movie? If we do, maybe we can alter the way people look at aliens and gifts that seem too good to be true. Maybe we can change that depressing future you wrote about. Well, it's your past, but it's my future, but it doesn't have to be the future, because we'll change the future." Brian paused to think over what he had just said. "But I have to ask, if we change the future will you still come back from the altered future so that you'll be here now to change the future?"

Brian closed his eyes and bowed his head. He was sorry he had started talking about the paradoxes that made it clear that time travel was absurd. He was afraid that Richard Dinsmore might be offended by his attitude.

Richard Dinsmore simply smiled and said, "It will be fine. I'd show you the equations, but you'd need seven more courses in mathematics and physics to understand them."

"I'll take your word for it, sir."

Dinsmore nodded. "Good . . . But, let's say I went along with this idea of yours, how would we make it into a movie. I've written twenty-three scientific papers. I don't know how to write anything else."

"That's ok. All you'll have to do is tell me a little more about what happened, I mean interesting details about life in the future, and I'm pretty sure that I can turn it into a movie."

Richard Dinsmore narrowed his gaze. Richard Dinsmore's mother had taught him to be suspicious of strangers. It had proved useful when he was going through school as the youngest person in any of his classes. In those days, fellow students were always pretending to be his friends just to embarrass him. He didn't see why it should have changed just because he was a member of the faculty. He wondered if the whole evening had been a set-up for Brian Brandenburg to swindle him. "It takes a lot of money to make a motion picture, doesn't it? If you're trying to con me out of my money, I don't have much."

"I don't need your money. With your help I can come up with a script. Between my cousin Jonah, myself, and my father, I think I can come up with the money." At this point, Brian hadn't said a word to anyone about the project, but he assumed that they would go along. "We'll have enough money to make an independent film and my father is a promoter in Nashville. He can get us access to a place in Nashville where they film music videos . . ."

Richard Dinsmore began to shout. "YOU'RE GOING TO TELL THE STORY OF THE GREATEST DISASTERS IN HUMAN HISTORY AND YOU'RE GOING TO MAKE IT A MUSICAL?"

People leaving the theatre turned around to stare at them.

Brian spoke quietly. "No, sir! I didn't mean it that way at all. There is a studio in Nashville that usually makes music videos. We can film our project there. That will keep costs down and still enable us to get a final product that has a professional look. If you go along with the project, I'll line up a first rate director. Plus, I know this kid in Florida who is a whiz with computer graphics and he can do the special effects. If you join in on the project, I'm sure we could get it shown at science fiction conventions, and enter it into a bunch of film festivals. We'll reach a thousand times as many people as would read 'Report from the Future.' And that's another thing. We have to change the title."

"To what?"

"*Angels from Rikenny*. It's catchy and it's meant to be ironic considering how mankind first regarded the aliens and what happened later."

"You've got that right. At first we thought they were angels. Then we thought they were devils. The simple truth is that they were aliens."

"Look, I'll level with you. Frankly, I don't see how time travel is possible, but I think that behind that little handout you gave the class you have more ideas and a great story to tell."

For the first time since he claimed to have returned from the future, Richard Dinsmore saw a narrow ray of hope. "More ideas? I have fifty-five years of ideas."

Brian winced when Dinsmore reiterated his claim that he had returned from the year 2055. "Do any of those ideas involve a love story or big explosions? If we want people to come and see it, we might need both."

Richard Dinsmore walked over to a bench near the entrance to the theatre and motioned for Brian to sit down. "As for explosions, yes, but I'd rather not talk about it. And there is a love story. The leader of the Rikennians was a woman named Noraa. She fell in love, I mean she will fall in love, with the scientist that the Earthers sent, will send, to try and learn about Rikennian technology . . . Heck, what I'm trying to say is that they sent me to meet with Noraa and it ended tragically. I left it out of my report."

Brian Brandenburg shook his head. Working with the professor was going to be a challenge. "You left people out of your report almost entirely, sir."

"I guess it would matter if it's a movie and not a scientific report. Just one thing, though. If making a movie is a way to change the future, how do I know that you are the right person to make my story into a movie?"

Brian had expected this question. "I've been writing screenplays for years. I'm really good at it." The statement was an outright lie, or, as Milton Brandenburg would have called it, a promotional necessity. Why would anyone work with a young man who had never written anything that had ever been produced? While Brian had borrowed Jonah's book on screenplays, the only relevant skills that Brian had mastered were using the correct format with the proper margins.

Since Richard Dinsmore didn't ask any additional questions, Brian continued. "If you tell me more about the future I'll get back to you with a script."

As one might have expected, Richard Dinsmore, who had twice been hospitalized on Mt. Moriah with a diagnosis of paranoid schizophrenia, was not the most trusting of individuals. "I've told you enough already. Let's see what you can come up with on your own. Get back to me on it, Mr. Brandenburg."

A few days later, Brian Brandenburg informed Jonah Aaron of his abandoned plan to make a movie out of "Report from the Future." "In order to move ahead, I have to figure out the details of his delusions so that he'll tell me enough additional details to make a film. Other than the fact that it's fucking impossible, there's no problem."

Since the day Tina Aaron had placed Richard Dinsmore's picture on the Aaron family refrigerator, Jonah had followed Richard Dinsmore's career. "Actually, there is no problem. When Dinsmore got to Ukraine, the CIA interviewed him. There must be hackers at Yale. Have them hack into the CIA computers, download his interview with the CIA, and you'll have your script."

"Good thinking. How long could someone go to jail for that little stunt?"

"I don't know. Thirty years, I suppose, but I wasn't being serious." Jonah chuckled. "I think you're at a dead end."

"How do you manage to say such outrageous stuff like suggesting that I hack into the CIA with such a sincere tone of voice?"

"I'm planning on being an investigator. That sometimes requires telling people absurd things as if they came chiseled on the back of the Ten Commandments."

"Well, you've mastered the skill. I really thought that you meant what you said about the CIA. With that ability to fake sincerity, did you ever think of a career in politics? You'd be a natural."

"No thanks. I have zero interest in politics, but I have an idea. If I can get you a copy of Dinsmore's interview with the CIA, what's it worth to you?"

"Money? Why do you need money? You made seven million dollars for by being one of the voices of the Dana Twins."

Jonah feigned indignation. "Hey, that's how you made your money. You're forgetting the fact that I was an assistant sound engineer and that I also wrote 'Dangerous Man.' Anyway, as an investigator, I want the money on general principle. I charge five hundred dollars a day plus expenses."

"You're going to charge me?"

"Were you planning on giving me free medical care for life once you graduate medical school?"

"Good point." Brian thought it over. "OK. I'll pay your standard fee. What percent of the film can I put you in for? I think that the whole movie can be done on a budget of six million dollars. I was figuring on putting up three million and I figured that you or my dad would kick in the other half."

Jonah began to laugh. "I wouldn't put a penny into this project. I plan on being an investigator and I think I almost have enough money to last me the rest of my life—unless I throw it away on crazy ideas like this."

Brian had to admit, at least to himself, that Jonah was being reasonable. "OK. How about this? Instead of a fee, if you buy into the film, let's say at least ten percent, which would be six hundred thousand dollars, I'll give you an extra five percent of the gross."

Jonah considered the offer. "I probably won't end up buying into the project, but I do feel bad charging you money. Just agree to pay my reasonable expenses and give me an option to buy fifteen percent of the film for six hundred thousand dollars and it's a deal."

"Deal!"

Jonah Aaron was about to become the highest paid investigator on the planet—on two planets, if one counts Rikenny.

*   *   *

Hacking the CIA was something Jonah would not have dared to attempt. However, it was public knowledge that Dinsmore had been re-hospitalized on the psychiatric unit at Mt. Moriah when he returned to the United States and Mt. Moriah was at the forefront in the development of the electronic medical record. Jonah considered it likely that the CIA had forwarded a copy of their interview with Dinsmore to the psychiatrists at Mt. Moriah Hospital.

Jonah suspected that a hospital computer system would be an easy target for a hacker. He was wrong. "What do you mean you can't break into the system?" he asked. "You once told me that any computer that connects to the Internet can be hacked." Jonah, who was special teams captain on Vanderbilt's varsity football team, was tossing a football in the air as he spoke.

Brett Phillips, Jonah's roommate, looked up from his computer. "That's right, but Mt. Moriah's medical record system doesn't connect to the Internet. They have a closed Intranet, for medical records. Intranet not Internet. There's a huge difference. Their system is more secure than the computer system that runs the electrical grid or the American banking system."

"But if the system at Mt. Moriah doesn't connect, how do I get the information?"

"Easy. Go to medical school. Become a doctor. Get an internship at Mt. Moriah. Doctors at Mt. Moriah have complete access to their medical record system."

"Is there a simpler way?"

"Well, you could go to Harvard Medical School. Their third year students have access to the medical record system at Mt. Moriah. That would save you two years."

Jonah thought it over. "How do you know all this?"

"Because the webpage for Mt. Moriah Hospital is on the Internet and it contains all this public information on how secure their medical records system is. They want patients to think their private data is safe, which it is."

"Shit! So there's no way to get the data from the outside?"

"It is absolutely impossible!"

For a few moments, Jonah thought about taking that as a challenge. Then he realized that if Brett Phillips, who had applied for a job with Homeland Security's office of counter-cyber-terrorism, said it couldn't be done, it couldn't be done. "OK. Then I know what I have to do."

"What?"

"Become pre-med. Graduate Vanderbilt. Get into Harvard Medical School. Get access to the system . . . My Dad went to Harvard Med. I bet they give preferential treatment to legacies. Then again, maybe I could take some sort of elective at Mt. Moriah as a first year medical student and cut two years off the project."

"You're kidding . . . aren't you? I can never tell."

"Of course I'm kidding." Jonah laughed and tossed the football at his friend who, despite his surprise, managed to catch it.

"So, what are you really going to do?"

"Go to Boston, get some menial job at Mt. Moriah, and play it by ear. I'll probably steal someone's ID, log into the system, and get what I need."

"That's a lot easier than going to medical school."

"I would think so."

Just before Thanksgiving break, Jonah flew to Boston. He got the job that his mother had held thirty years earlier, Emergency Room sign-in clerk. The only difference was that he took a position on the night shift in order to work when the ER was understaffed.

As expected, the job did not afford him legitimate access to patients' medical records. Only doctors had a security code. He had hoped that he could borrow a doctor's ID to get into the system. Jonah had hung around hospitals all his life and he knew that doctors left their white coats unattended all the time.

Unfortunately, Jonah soon learned that access to the medical record system required a doctor to type in a special code name—his or her so-called "MoriahNetID"—and a password. Jonah developed a Plan B.

On Jonah's fourth night at the Mt. Moriah Emergency Room, he was on a break when he observed a medical intern completing admission orders on her patient who had suffered a heart attack.

"Is it an interesting admission?"

She looked up from the computer. "Only if the eighteenth heart attack of my month on cardiology is somehow going to be more interesting than the first seventeen." Despite the late hour, she managed a smile.

"I can imagine. My father's a cancer specialist and nearly everyone he treats has lung cancer." Jonah smiled back and saw that she was looking at his ID and determining his status, more correctly his lack of status, in the health care system. Because of his good looks, the fact that his ID said "Jonah Aaron, Patient Service Representative" did not end the conversation.

"I'm being unfair. To the cardiologist doing the cardiac catheterization and placing the stent, it's probably interesting. To me, the intern doing the work-up, getting the history and physical on the chart, checking the cardiac enzymes and looking at the EKG, it's less exciting."

He smiled. "You know the concept. If it's work, the intern does it; if it's fun, the attending does it."

"Where did you hear that?"

"From my father. He did his training here at Mt. Moriah back in the seventies."

"Then you know the classic rules for interns. Number six is that there is no such thing as an interesting admission after midnight. It's hard to learn anything when you're exhausted." She looked at her watch and yawned. "It's two fourteen in the morning." She pointed to the yellowed typed pages taped to the wall of the physician's area ten feet away from where she was seated. "It's been up on the wall for a quarter of a century." She began quoting the list. "Save your own humanity; then save humanity. In the end, the protoplasm declares itself. Life is a terminal condition. Take the job seriously but not yourself."

Jonah interrupted her. "I've heard my father say each of those things from time to time when he's had doctors over to our house. I never realized that they were something classic here at Mt. Moriah."

"They are. We had a medical ethics symposium when I was a second year student at HMS and we spent a couple of hours discussing the rules."

"HMS?"

She leaned back in her chair. "You're not from around here, are you?"

"What gave it away?"

"HMS is Harvard Medical School. Everybody from around here knows that."

He extended his hand. "I'm Jonah Aaron, Nashville, Tennessee. I'm an undergrad at Vanderbilt."

"Melinda Cohen." She shook his hand. "I assume you're pre-med and that's why you're working here."

To himself, Jonah said, "Assume nothing." He shook his head. "No. My father says that the most interesting thing about medicine is solving problems. I just like solving a different kind of problem. The idea of getting eighteen of the same thing in a month doesn't interest me."

"So what kind of problems do you like?"

"It varies—a little of this, a little of that."

Melinda Cohen turned to the computer and completed the order set on which she had been working. Before she could say anything, a nurse entered the work area. "Dr. Cohen, Mr. Francis in Exam Room 2 is having runs of ventricular tachycardia."

Melinda Cohen stood up, took three quick steps toward the exam room and headed back to the computer.

Jonah held up his hand. "Don't worry. I'll shut down the computer for you. GO SAVE A LIFE!"

As Melinda Cohen and two Emergency Room physicians scurried towards Exam Room 2, Jonah moved over to the abandoned computer terminal. He typed in Richard Dinsmore's name, pulled up Dinsmore's electronic chart, saw that it contained a document labeled "Transcript of Kiev Interview 03-03-2000 (Outside Report)," and saved it to a memory stick. Only then did he sign Melinda Cohen off the computer.

Though the offense was never noted, Melinda Cohen had technically committed a Grade I security breach, leaving a computer terminal without signing off. It was an offense that could have earned her a warning. Jonah, on the other hand, had committed—in her name—a Grade IV security breach, gaining medically unnecessary access to confidential material. It was an offense that could have led to suspension, if it had been discovered, which it wasn't.

At the end of his shift, Jonah returned to his hotel room and began reading Richard Dinsmore's interview with the CIA. Several parts had been redacted by the CIA before the material was sent to Mt. Moriah, but Jonah was content with what he had obtained. He e-mailed a copy of the document to Brian Brandenburg, enclosed a bill for his expenses, and called Mt. Moriah to quit his job due to "pressing personal matters."

The transcript of the CIA interview provided Brian with substantial insights into Richard Dinsmore's delusional system and provided him with the foundation for a working script. As Brian was enrolled in Warren Tanner's film elective, he asked the director to review his work. Despite weekly prodding by his student, it took Warren Tanner nearly three months to get around to reading the screenplay. Finally, on a snowy weekend when his cocaine connection had been arrested and his Yale grad student girlfriend had dumped him, he settled down with a bottle of Chivas Regal and read Brian's screenplay in its entirety. When he finished, he phoned Brian and asked if they could meet in his office on Monday afternoon. Jonah Aaron flew in from Nashville for moral support. He had read Brian's screenplay and remained indifferent to the possibility of investing in the project.

As befit a successful movie director, Warren Tanner's office was a comfortable room with a desk, four chairs, and a sofa. Tanner sat on the edge of the desk and motioned for Brian and Jonah to take a seat on the sofa. He handed the screenplay, which now contained numerous comments in red ink, back to his student. "It's an interesting concept, Mr. Brandenburg, but it's so depressing that if it was filmed that way, it would bomb. You can't have things go from bad to worse and then conclude it with civilization on the verge of extinction and the world government sending a time traveler into the past to fix things."

"But that's Professor Dinsmore's delusion and it sets up the sequel."

Warren Tanner chuckled. "It would be a sequel to a movie that no one saw, which means no one would see the sequel. But you don't have to worry about the sequel since you'll never get a studio to put up the money to film this." As he shrugged his shoulders, he saw that Brian's chin had dropped to the point that he was almost staring at the floor. "Don't be so disheartened. I've taught courses on writing a screenplay and I've seen a lot worse. Do you plan on being a writer?"

"I'm pre-med."

"A wise idea."

Brian's throat was so dry that he could barely speak, but he managed to blurt out the only facts that would make Warren Tanner reconsider. "I have three million dollars of my own money committed to the project and I can raise the other three that I need. Plus, I know a place in Nashville where a low budget project like this can be filmed."

"Nashville? Nashville!" Warren Tanner had come to New Haven to avoid the stresses of Hollywood and it hadn't worked out particularly well. He had never been to Nashville. "Even with a number of changes and paying me my fee to direct it, it could be made for six million. And you have the money?"

Brian nodded.

"And you have someone to do special effects?"

"A computer graphics whiz down in Florida."

Warren Tanner began to pace the floor, stopping every few moments to either nod or shake his head. Finally, he seated himself behind the desk, took a deep breath pursed his lips, and sighed. "We might be able to salvage your script and it would be fun to try. I love science fiction and I've never done a sci-fi film, but there are some major problems." He ticked them off on his fingers as he spoke. "First, we need more details about that dystopian future you present. We need to know more about the aliens and their culture, even if it doesn't directly relate to the plot. Authenticity is often in the minutiae."

Brian Brandenburg interrupted. "With this script, Professor Dinsmore will talk to me and tell me more about his delusions and his aliens."

"Good. That should solve that problem. Second, we need to have "a look;" we don't want to be a cheesy imitation of every sci-fi movie ever made. We need a first rate designer who hasn't seen a ton of science fiction movies, who would be willing to work on the problem, and who would be original."

Jonah spoke for the first time. "My mother is an interior designer and . . ."

Warren Tanner waved his hand from side to side as he rejected the idea. "No. Houses are one thing. Sets are another. It's completely different designing something to look good on film compared to designing a room to live in."

"Does being set designer on over two dozen country music videos count?"

"Your mother has done that?"

"Not only has she done it, she's very good. She's the one who designed the sets for Calliope's video, 'What the Future Holds for Us.'"

"I saw it! Those sets were fantastic! Your mother hasn't seen a ton of science fiction films that would bias her, has she?"

"My mother hasn't even seen *Star Wars*. If we hire her, the future won't look like any future anybody has ever seen before in a movie."

Warren Tanner was licking his lips and barely suppressing his excitement. "Third, we need to at least consider a way that the time traveler can save the world in this film not in the next one. I have an idea but I want to sleep on it. Fourth, we need some kind of running joke to lighten it up. If we can do that, we might have a hit. I like to think I can do anything, but I'm terrible at writing humor and I have to protect my reputation as a man who never makes a movie that fails to turn a profit. Injecting humor may be the biggest problem."

Jonah Aaron and Brian Brandenburg spoke at the same time. "The Dana Twins."

Warren Tanner narrowed his eyes and wrinkled his nose. "What the hell are you talking about?"

Brian explained. "The Dana Twins are light hearted fluff and there are numerous places they can be worked in. The monitoring station that's scanning the solar system for aliens can have a Dana Twins poster on the wall. The security chief who has to lead the aliens to safety after they land on Earth can talk about rescuing the Dana Twins from their avid fans during their last world tour. Towards the end of the movie we can have a billboard in the background advertising a Dana Twins concert as if they had become the biggest thing on Earth." Brian pointed to his cousin. "Jonah wanted me to put it into the script, but I left it out."

Brian Brandenburg's father believed in synergy, using one project to promote another. Jonah's idea meant that *Angels from Rikenny* would be promoting the movie about the Dana Twins—if there ever was one.

Warren Tanner had a blank expression on his face and had clasped his hands together as if he were deep in thought. Finally, he smiled. "It would almost work. The idea that the Dana Twins would have any lasting popularity is ridiculous and that's what makes it a brilliant comedic idea. The problem is that a low budget film like this can't afford any lawsuits. We have the right to satirize, but if we use the Dana Twins, I'm afraid those cute little blonde boys and their crazy fundamentalist father are going to sue our asses. There's no way we can use the Dana Twins unless we get a release and no one knows how to find them."

"Are you sure about that?" Jonah asked.

Warren Tanner scowled. "Well . . . No."

With a perfectly straight face, Jonah announced "I work as a private investigator, Mr. Tanner. I'm sure that within a week I could track them down and get a release to use their names and likenesses in this film. I've heard a rumor that they live up in the hills in West Tennessee. It might be risky going up there. It's moonshine country, but I think I can handle it. I only charge five hundred dollars a day plus expenses. On a six million dollar project that's nothing."

Warren Tanner turned to Brian Brandenburg. "You're the one who's going to be the producer. You're the one paying the bills. What do you say?"

Brian Brandenburg was laughing so hard tears were rolling down his cheeks. "Sure. West Tennessee isn't the safest place in the world, but Jonah is a very dangerous man."

*　　*　　*

One week later, Brian Brandenburg arrived in Richard Dinsmore's office with a copy of the revised screenplay. Before he read it, Richard Dinsmore asked, "I told you that there was a meeting between me and Noraa when the Rikennians arrived on Earth. What dialogue did you come up with?"

Brian looked Richard Dinsmore in the eyes and tried to sound as serious as possible. "Well, you were sent to see what could be learned about Rikennian technology. In this script, the scientist asks Noraa how her matter-anti-matter engine works. That's the only possible basis for travel near the speed of light."

"Please continue."

"Well, the scientist hopes that the aliens will share their technology. Instead, Noraa says 'I don't know how it works. I just push a button and it goes.' We figured she would be a pilot, not a theoretical physicist, and that's what she would say. I mean, I can't explain how the internal combustion engine of my car works. I just turn a key and it goes."

Richard Dinsmore was dumfounded. "That is exactly what she said. Mr. Brandenburg, She said, 'I push a button and it goes.' I am supposed to be smart, but you are a genius."

Brian handed Professor Dinsmore a copy of the screenplay. "We added in a number of things to make it marketable, but we didn't change the core concept."

Richard Dinsmore began turning the pages of the revised screenplay so rapidly that Brian was certain that he was only pretending to read the words on the page. After only seven minutes of leafing through a ninety-nine page screenplay, Dinsmore looked up. "It's accurate in places where it needs to be accurate and imaginative in ways that—I guess—will make it entertaining. There is one major error. On page 26, you gave the aliens last names. Rikennians don't have last names; there are no family units on Rikenny. That's important. It's one way in which they are alien."

Brian waited for Richard Dinsmore to say something else. Finally, he did.

"It's good. I'll be happy to work with you and to add some more details."

"Like what?"

Before Richard Dinsmore answered, tears filled his eyes. "There was a second wave of aliens in 2050. That was a real disaster. I left it out of 'Report from the Future' so there was no way for you to know about it." That part of Richard Dinsmore's delusions had been redacted by the CIA. "And you know how they say that Eskimos have something like forty words for snow."

"Yes."

"Well, the Rikennians are very free, sexually speaking. Sex is for pleasure. They live so long that they don't plan on long term relationships. They have thirteen words for orgasm, based on duration and intensity, and not a single word for promiscuous, unfaithful, or slut. Those concepts are truly alien to them."

Brian's eyes widened. "I'm sure we can work that into the film."

After several further revisions, the final result was a shooting script that Warren Tanner agreed to direct for a straight fee of eight hundred thousand dollars. With Warren Tanner on board, Jonah invested in the project as did Milton Brandenburg and Melvin Aaron.

Jonah, Brian, and Milton also purchased a majority interest in a North Nashville studio. They felt that the studio would make a profit even if did nothing but continue to make music videos. However, they realized that the opportunity to produce an occasional film had an incredible upside. The studio was renamed Ojliagiba Studios which Jonah explained to his partners was an Indian word for "the right story can help you sell just about anything."

When Brian graduated from Yale, he enrolled in medical school. Jonah graduated from Vanderbilt, put his career as an investigator on hold, and spent every day on the set with Warren Tanner, managing the project and learning everything he could about film-making. Tina Aaron was hired to design the sets and a cadre of actors, many of whom had limited experience, was assembled. Barry Aaron, who started taking acting lessons the day that his brother and Brian Brandenburg announced their intention to make a movie, was one of them. He played the role of a CIA operative, had twenty spoken lines, and acquitted himself quite well.

To the shock of Brian, Jonah, and Warren Tanner, Richard Dinsmore auditioned for the role of the lead. After watching Dinsmore emote, Warren Tanner said, "It's uncanny. You watch him in the role and his obvious discomfort isn't a negative factor. It actually helps him convince the viewer that he has been to the future, seen horrible things, and that he has traveled back through time to save the world. Frankly, I think he believes it. He's absolutely perfect for the part."

Richard Dinsmore began to foresee a future with sunshine. He imagined children having fun, like the little girls who were always playing hopscotch across the street from his apartment. He noticed the nannies and he began to date one of them. As he told his collaborators, there was no reason for him to be uncomfortable around women. Even though he was only a teenager, he had been married for fifteen years in a future that he hoped would never happen again.

*   *   *

Angels from Rikenny was filmed in 2002 and 2003 at a total cost of 5.8 million dollars. Starting in the fall of 2002, scenes from the film were previewed at science fiction conventions around the country. Attendees at DragonCon, IndyCon, and San Diego's Comic-Con declared it one of the highlights of those conventions. The special effects and the futuristic sets were considered to be outstanding. A major Hollywood studio, whose CEO was a science fiction fan, was interested in promoting and distributing *Angels from Rikenny;* his studio purchased fifty percent of the film for five million dollars.

At the May, 2004 premiere of *Angels from Rikenny,* Melvin Aaron took Brian and Jonah aside and told them, "Gentlemen, I loved it.

However, I assume that the Dana Twins were not part of Richard Dinsmore's delusions."

Brian nodded. "Good guess! The majority of the good ideas were Warren Tanner's. Dinsmore didn't really contribute much."

Jonah interrupted. "Except for his great acting job portraying a time traveler."

Melvin Aaron sighed. "His acting was excellent, and all things considered, I believe that you have saved the world."

The two young men looked at him as if he were from another planet. "You're not seriously suggesting that Richard Dinsmore came from the future and that by making the movie we have warned the world about the arrival of aliens, are you, dad?"

Melvin Aaron laughed. "Of course not, Jonah. But there is a saying in the Talmud, 'Whoever saves one life, it is as if he has saved the whole world.'" He pointed to Richard Dinsmore. "I was thinking about him." Richard Dinsmore was standing twenty feet away, talking to one of the actresses who had appeared in the movie. "I can't help but think that if not for you guys, he probably would have killed himself by now. He had an extremely dismal vision of the future. He felt he had to prevent it. He didn't see how he could. If not for you guys and your imaginative version of things . . ." He pointed a finger at his head and made the motion of pulling a trigger. "Bang."

Brian Brandenburg shook his head. "Damn. If I've already saved the world, I've peaked. My entire career in medicine may be an anti-climax."

Melvin Aaron chuckled. "I doubt that very much, Brian. But you gentlemen need to excuse me. I'm going to find my other son, the actor, and my brother-in-law."

As Dr. Aaron walked away, Brian pointed to Richard Dinsmore who was still talking to the actress. "Have you ever seen Richard so happy?"

"Never. Let's go over and talk to him. I need him to sign something. One of the networks wants him to host a television show called *Science for Non-scientists*."

"You're joking! My friends at Yale say that he still spends every lecture looking across the stage and not out at the students. How could he possibly host a TV show?"

"You just build a studio like a lecture hall, put the lectern at the left side of the stage and put the camera on the right side of the stage. It will appear he's looking out at the audience at home."

RICHARD STEIN

"Now I know you're kidding. This is another one of your outrageous . . ."

Jonah took the contract out of his pocket. "One million three hundred thousand a year for twenty-two shows, less ten percent for me and ten percent for your father. Considering that we didn't pay him that much for being in the film, this is going to help set him up for life. Your father was thrilled by the way. He said that after years of representing country singers, including two who didn't even exist, he was honored to represent a man who might win the Nobel Prize someday."

"Let's get Richard to sign the contract, and then let's find Barry."

"Let's look for Barry, later. The first reviews are coming in."

*　　*　　*

Critics thought that *Angels from Rikenny* presented "a sobering but believable vision of the future with enough plot twists to make the movie a roller coaster ride between desperation and elation." It was considered a work of genius, specifically the genius of Warren Tanner.

The meaning of the film was in the eye of the beholder. Most people saw it as a commentary on a death denying culture and the failure of society to recognize that death must occur for life to continue. Many saw it as a serious examination of quantity versus quality of life. Some saw *Angels from Rikenny* as a statement that costly advances in medical science might bankrupt the country. In a similar vein, the movie was seen as a demonstration of how the mindless devotion of resources to the care of the terminally ill could endanger the future for everyone. Still others observed Earth's view of the aliens, as depicted in the movie, and saw the film as a parable critiquing anti-Muslim prejudice after 9/11.

There was, however, a consensus that the movie was imaginative and entertaining. Promoted as "science fiction even for people who don't watch science fiction" and "time travel for people who don't believe in time travel," the low budget movie grossed over seventy million dollars.

Richard Dinsmore stopped claiming to have been to the future though he occasionally joked about being a time traveler. Nora Dinsmore was so excited that her son had become a functional human being again and that a character in the movie had been named after her, that she legally changed the spelling of her name to Noraa.

Jonah planned to continue working part-time as an investigator. It was something to do until another movie project landed in his lap—if one ever did—and considering what he had earned from his four days at Mt. Moriah Hospital, he considered the pay to be excellent.

For Melvin Aaron, taking care of patients with lung cancer had become extremely frustrating. Over the course of his professional lifetime, improvements in chemotherapy had only extended the average survival of lung cancer patients by a few months. It seemed to him that everyone who smoked thought that someone else would get lung cancer and that they wouldn't. As he sometimes thought to himself, somewhere, someone else had been thinking the same thing and that other someone had turned out to be correct. He realized that the money he would make from his investment in *Angels from Rikenny* would enable him to retire from the practice of medicine much earlier than he had planned. He and his wife began studying brochures for photographic safaris to Kenya and Tanzania.

Paradoxically, Tina Aaron had used art deco stylings from the 1930's to create a futuristic look for *Angels from Rikenny*. Her sets had earned her an academy award nomination for best production design in a motion picture. She lost to *Phantom of the Opera*. Nevertheless, Jonah and Brian had given her what she considered the opportunity of a lifetime. She would never again refer to her oldest son as an underachiever.

RICHARD STEIN

11

ELANA GREY AND JONAH AARON'S *THE DANA TWINS: THE TRUE STORY*

IN 2004, ELANA Grey moved to Nashville and within a year of her arrival she recorded "(She Thought She Could) Fly." The song was produced by Jackson Daniels at Lightning Bug Studios for the Dangerous Man label. The CD cover showed Elana, a gorgeous young woman with long red hair, wearing a white blouse and a low cut pair of jeans. The photo revealed more cleavage and bare midriff than was usually shown on a country recording.

The CD single contained the following brief liner notes written by Elana herself:

> Nineteen year old Elana Grey, a newcomer on the Nashville scene, was born in Cody, Wyoming, and was raised in a trailer park by her grandmother, Lucinda White, who home-schooled her and made certain that Elana obtained her G.E.D. before she headed off to Music City to visit her friend, Skylar Jones, the country music darling from Bozeman, Montana. The day of the tragic suicide that is the basis of this song, a chance meeting led Elana, Skylar, and Jonah Aaron to compose this tribute.

The country ballad, backed by a jangle rock arrangement somewhat reminiscent of the Dana Twins, topped both the country and pop charts for more than two months, winning the Country Music Association award as Song of the Year for 2005.

According to what has become a Music City legend, Elana arrived in town on a red-eye flight planning a brief visit to Nashville. Skylar, who had been voted Most Promising Country Music Newcomer three years earlier, was already well along the road to stardom and heartache as Skylar's live-in boyfriend, Rickey Stone, the lead singer of her back-up band, Two in the Morning, was an alcoholic.

As the tale is told, Skylar drove to the airport to greet Elana, using the trip as an excuse to leave her tenth floor condo and avoid another tearful door-slamming argument with Rickey about his drinking. Skylar returned with Elana in tow and the two young women were in the lobby waiting for an elevator when a thunderstorm caused the power to be lost in the gentrified gulch area of Nashville where Skylar lived.

The lead story in the news that April morning involved a young woman who had leapt to her death from the Caruthersville Bridge as it crossed the Mississippi River at the Tennessee-Missouri border. Stranded in the lobby and waiting for the power to resume, Skylar and Elana began to compose a song about missing the signs that someone was contemplating suicide and about the suffering experienced by those who were left behind. Unable to find a hook to the song, they were about to abandon the project.

According to Elana, at that moment, Jonah Aaron, who owned a ninth-floor condo in the building, arrived home and gallantly volunteered to carry Elana's suitcase up the stairs. During that trek, Jonah contributed the classic hook, the words "She thought she could fly" sung to the notes ACGBC. While Rickey Stone slept off a hangover, Skylar, Elana, and Jonah completed writing the song in Skylar's condo. By three o'clock that afternoon, Elana was in the studio recording "(She Thought She Could) Fly." As stated on the CD, background vocals were performed by Skylar Jones, Jonah Aaron, and Brian Brandenburg—the only time that the two young men whose voices were the sound of the Dana Twins were ever credited for a vocal performance.

When Rickey Stone realized that his drinking not only threatened his relationship with Skylar but that it had also cost him the opportunity to participate in writing a CMA award winning song, he joined AA. Noted songwriter, Cory Bayliss, became his sponsor. Fortunately for Skylar, her stormy years with Rickey had generated enough material for an entire career's worth of lyrics.

It is a sweet story—except for the suicide at the Caruthersville Bridge—and parts of it are even true. There was a power failure in Nashville the morning of the tragedy at the bridge and residents of the Infinity Building who were in the lobby waiting for the power to resume that day have confirmed that Jonah, Skylar, and Elana walked up the stairs. Skylar, Elana, and Jonah wrote the song and the tune's success was a major reason that Rickey Stone gave up drinking.

However, Elana did not arrive in Music City that morning. She had been living in Nashville for several months when she recorded "(She Thought She Could) Fly." Additionally, she was not a nineteen year old with a G.E.D. She was a twenty-two year old college senior who had been elected to Phi Beta Kappa honor society. Elana did not consider that to be a viable image for a country singer.

At the nationally televised CMA awards show, Elana accepted the trophy for Song of the Year wearing a low cut white jumpsuit and gave the following speech:

> "Thank you all so very much. I love you. I guess I should be jumping up and down, but my song concerns the death of a young girl who was just a few years older than I am now when she tragically took her life. Out of respect to her memory, I want to remind people that there are suicide hotlines and that there is always another option." Then to keep the evening from becoming somber, she added, "Plus, if I jumped up and down in this outfit, my boobs would fall out."

Elana covered her mouth in mock embarrassment as the audience burst into laughter. After screaming the words, "We won!" she cemented her carefully manufactured reputation as the hottest young redhead in country music by kissing Jonah, who, as co-writer, was up on the stage with her, in such a passionate manner that the master of ceremonies remarked that he hoped they would get a room before they decided to celebrate.

As a solo act, Elana Grey was a one-hit wonder by choice; she never recorded a follow-up song. When she returned to the recording studio four years later, it was as part of a duo. Recording under the name Just Two Gurlz, Elana and Skylar churned out an up-tempo country song entitled "Two Pitchers of Beer."

By that time, Elana had become a screenwriter. Her first writing success was the television series, *Jonah Slammer,* a comedy-drama broadcast on the Country Entertainment Channel. It presented the weekly adventures of a depressed Nashville homicide detective who hoped to become a star in the world of country music. Rickey Stone, a talented actor when he was consistently sober, starred in the title role. Elana's second success was *The Dana Twins: The True Story.*

Filmed at Ojliagiba Studios in Nashville, *The Dana Twins: The True Story* was a musical that satirized the conventions of romantic comedy. Cory Bayliss, Elana Grey, and Skylar Jones wrote the songs. Two of them, "On Tour" and "Two Pitchers of Beer" charted in the Top Ten. "On Tour," based on Eric Cain's ramblings in *Night Shadow*, received an Academy Award nomination as the best original song from a motion picture.

*　　*　　*

In the opening scene of *The Dana Twins: The True Story,* "Nashville, June, 1996" appears on the screen. Brady, a man who identifies himself as the manager of the Dana Twins, interviews Sarah, a social worker, on the patio of a Nashville restaurant. Brady wants Sara to chaperone the Dana Twins on their upcoming tour. When Sarah asks why he needs a chaperone for the Dana Twins, Brady informs her that the Dana Twins are not the cute little androgynous pre-teen boys that they have been portrayed as being on their album covers and posters. Brady informs Sarah that the Dana Twins are two eleven year old girls.

When Sarah inquires why this was kept a secret, Brady tells her that most records are bought by pre-teen girls and that those girls would never buy recordings made by young women.

Sarah calls Brady an idiot, grabs the pitcher of beer that is on their table, and pours it over his head. As she starts to walk away, Brady offers her five thousand dollars to accompany him and the Dana Twins on their tour. He says that without her help there won't be a tour and that there has to be a tour because he's broke.

> "What happened to the money you got by managing the Dana Twins?" Sarah asks.
>
> "I literally pissed that money away," Brady replies.
>
> In an angry tone, Sarah replies, "You FIGURATIVELY pissed it away, not LITERALLY pissed it away. I was an English major in college and I hate it when people make mistakes like that."

"No, I literally pissed it away, but you really don't want to know the details," Brady responds.

Reluctantly, Sarah accepts the five thousand dollars and the job as chaperone. She tells Brady she will meet him at the airport. Not knowing Brady's true situation at this point, she calls him an exploiter of young children, picks up a second pitcher of beer from an adjoining table, and dumps that over Brady's head before walking away.

At this point, we seem to have moved into the present as the audience sees that second pitcher of beer has been taken from a table where Elana Grey and Skylar Jones are seated. The two women are dressed fashionably in black jumpsuits and purple scarves. Pointing up to a billboard advertising a multi-platinum album by Taylor Swift, Elana says, "As if young girls won't buy records by a female singer. Still, that was a waste of good beer."

> Skylar replies, "We could write a song about that."
> "Hell, I could write a movie about this," says Elana Grey.
> "It should be a musical. Let's make sure we have actors who can actually sing."
> "In Nashville?" Elana replies. "Not a problem."

Elana and Skylar then break into song.

> We were shooting billiards when you walked into the hall.
> And we knew your pretty boyfriend was heading for a fall.
> You slapped him and you told him that you knew he was untrue.
> Then you went and gave him a sudsy beer shampoo.
>
> Chorus:
> We agree that boy's a cheater; we agree that boy's a jerk
> And we all know it girl, it just isn't gonna work.
> But let us make just one thing absolutely clear
> That was a sad pointless waste of two pitchers of beer . . .

As predicted, it wasn't a problem finding actors who could sing. Brady was played by Rickey Stone. Sarah was played by Lee Graham, who had sung in Nashville clubs before landing a role in the feature film, *Angels from Rikenny.*

When the movie resumes after the musical interlude, we have returned to 1996. A private plane carrying the Dana Twins is seen landing at a small airstrip which, according to the signs, is twelve miles from Reno, Nevada. Sarah and Brady think everything is fine until a gang of neo-Nazi skinheads kidnap the girls and announce that they are going to hold them for ransom. The heavily tattooed neo-Nazis shoot and kill the pilot of the plane, since he knows too much; they abandon Sarah and Brady in the desert. The songs "He Knew Too Much" and "(We're) Food for the Coyotes" are sung by Brady and Sarah. The skinheads do not perform any musical numbers. Singing generates empathy and there is no place in *The Dana Twins: The True Story* for any empathy toward the kidnappers.

Abandoned in the wilderness, Sarah and Brady collaborate to engineer a multi-step rescue of the two young girls. The fate of the skinhead kidnappers follows the premise that once someone tattoos a swastika on himself, he can be killed in the most grotesque manner and the audience will laugh. In this case, the phrase "most grotesque manner possible" includes a hanging, a decapitation using a plow blade, being crushed by an anvil dropped from the upper level of a barn, and being fatally injured by a bear trap. These deaths are not by design and result from the fact that Sarah is extremely clumsy.

Before addressing how they might rescue the girls from the fifth and final kidnapper, Sarah asks Brady whether or not he has any suggestions about the major problem in her life, the fact that all of her boyfriends turn out to be losers. In the up-tempo song, "And This One," Sarah opens her wallet to show Brady the pictures of her ex-boyfriends as she describes her failed relationships.

She starts by telling Brady about her boyfriend who lived as if his cell phone was attached to his ear, and who broke up with her by sending a text. Next, she tells Brady about the man who left her to go back to his prior love—to whom he was still married. She concludes with the tale of a man she met in a bar—who disappointed her by proving to be an alcoholic. Having detailed these failures, as well as others, Sarah asks Brady, "What do you think?"

"Well, unlike you, I don't have a college education," Brady replies, "but all these relationships have one thing in common." Brady then sings a ballad entitled "Could the Problem Be You?" He points out that in each case, Sarah has overlooked something obvious. "Whenever you make a romantic decision, your brain seems to be in the off position."

After she thinks it over for approximately five seconds, Sarah says that she has never looked at it that way and she responds by singing "Time to Go."

> We'd been together for three years, and few words were said.
> I got up slowly, and I walked away from the bed.
> Told him as much of the truth as he needed to know
> There's no need for making speeches, when it's time to go,
> It's time to go.

As the verses in the song progress, the relationships get shorter and shorter, decreasing from three years to three months to three hours. The audience and Brady learn that Sarah has slipped into a series of unsatisfying one night stands.

At this point, before they plan the elimination of the last kidnapper, Brady decides that since Sarah has been self-disclosing, it is time to tell her "the true story" of the Dana Twins. It is shown in a black and white format, as if it represents a historical documentary, and it includes the story of Cory Bayliss, the singer who didn't show up for his recording session, Jackson Daniels, the sound engineer interested in computer experimentation, two unnamed boys who provided vocals for the Dana Twins albums, and two girls who performed in the music videos because, as Brady says, the two boys who did the vocals on the CD "just plain couldn't dance." To emphasize that this is the true story, the music video from "Lost in Your Eyes" is shown frame by frame in slow motion demonstrating that one of The Dana Twins adjusts a bra strap during the second pirouette move.

Brady's story is accompanied by a montage of songs from the first Dana Twins album performed by a band of male musicians. Although they are identified on their drumhead as The Dana Twins, the band is Rickey Stone's band, Two in the Morning. Neither Jonah Aaron nor Brian Brandenburg, appears as part of the group.

Having completed his story, Brady informs Sarah that the two girls being held by the one remaining kidnapper are not the Dana Twins nor are they the girls who performed in the music videos. They are Brady's nieces. Their parents are divorced and their mother, Brady's sister, lives in Reno. Brady is delivering them back home after a visit to Nashville to see their father. "I didn't exploit any children like you said back in Nashville. The sixteen year old singers became multi-millionaires. The girls who performed in the music videos will get college paid for. My nieces were paid good money just to get on a plane in Nashville and pretend to be the Dana Twins as part of a ruse designed by the real promoter."

After Brady sings "I'm Not What You Think," Sarah asks him who he is, if he isn't the promoter. Brady confesses to being "the guy who didn't show up for the studio session that led to this whole fiasco. When I told you I literally pissed my money away, I was accurate. I got arrested for peeing against the side of a strip club and missed my prepaid recording session. The promoter who masterminded this entire hoax had pity on me, and tracked me down. When he found out I'd be flying my sister's kids back to Reno in June, he saw a perfect ending to the Dana Twins' story. The kidnapping was not part of the plan. The Dana Twins and their plane were just supposed to disappear since the two teen-aged boys who recorded the songs couldn't possibly go on stage and convince the world that they were the Dana Twins."

Sarah comments that she always wondered why the Dana Twins' tour was scheduled to start in Reno and now she understands. After reprising "Two Pitchers of Beer," this time with an apology, Sarah inquires why Brady didn't tell her the truth in the beginning. Brady confesses that it's because he thinks she is hot and he didn't want to admit to being nothing more than a failed alcoholic country singer. He proudly shows her his one year chip from AA. She then tells him how impressed she has been with his heroism. The movie being, in part, a romantic comedy, and Sarah having confessed to her history of one night stands, the audience isn't at all surprised by what happens next. Ironically, Sarah exposes less flesh in the sex scene than in the action scene which follows.

There is still work to be done, however, as the fifth kidnapper has Brady's nieces whom he believes to be The Dana Twins. In the final rescue attempt, things go badly at first. The kidnapper captures Sarah, rips off most of her clothes, and has a knife to her throat when Brady picks up a broken broom handle. Inspired by love, lust, and the needs of the plot, Brady runs toward him. Sarah breaks free but Brady is stabbed before he can injure the kidnapper. The situation appears dire, but the two little girls retrieve the broken broom handle. As the leader of the neo-Nazi pack laughs at them, they whistle the chorus from "Dangerous Man" and put the broom handle right through one of his eyes, killing him and rescuing Brady, Sarah, and themselves.

Brady's wounds are not serious and now that Brady's nieces have been rescued, the world needs to be told why the Dana Twins are not going to appear in concert. Brady and Sarah realize that they can't tell the world about a kidnapping; the children who are fans of the Dana Twins might have nightmares. Upon thinking it over, they realize that they can't claim that the Dana Twins perished in a plane crash, as per the original plan; the fans of the Dana Twins would be heartbroken. As Brady and Sarah walk through downtown Reno singing "We Need a Story," they literally trip over a homeless person with a long beard. They have an epiphany and hire the man to play the role of Reverend Dana.

Reverend Dana gives a musical press conference in the presence of Brady's nieces who are dressed up in white sports coats and made to look like young boys. Played by legendary country singer, Robbie Mack, The Reverend announces that his sons will not be touring because the world of popular music is the devil's domain. He explains that it is fine for his sons to be a studio band, but he forbids them to go on the road where, in his vivid R-rated fantasies, teenaged harlots are seen seducing his children.

My boys accuse me of ruining their lives,
Of destroying their lives,
They say I'm controlling and fussy.

The problems not me, it's the girls, you see
There is a word for them
And the word is hussy.

And slut . . . And trollop . . . And whore.

My boys say I'm standing in their way
That they should sing and play
And perform in Reno tonight.

The thought of that makes my soul grow cold.
They're only twelve years old,
The whole thing would be Satan's delight.

Chorus:
They have been in the studio and they've been well paid.
Been well paid, been well paid, been well paid,
But they're not going on tour, not going to get laid.
To get laid . . . to get laid . . . to get laid . . .

Having created a myth to explain the disappearance of the Dana Twins, Brady, Sarah, and the two girls join the girls' mother, Joanna. Upon being reunited with her children, Joanna musically tells Sarah "Divorce is a bitch; find a guy who is a keeper." Sarah looks at Brady, and though they have known each other for all of three days, she gives the impression that she thinks she has. Of course, this conveniently overlooks the fact that, according to the script, Brady is a broke and unemployed alcoholic who urinates on the side of buildings and has no prospects for getting a job unless there is a market for the ability to decapitate neo-Nazis, mangle them with bear traps, hang them from the rafters of a barn, or crush them with an anvil.

However, since the movie has entered the land of romantic comedy, it is best to neglect those facts, just as it is best to disregard the fact that Skylar Jones and Elana Grey, who appeared in the opening scene, were pre-teens when the Dana Twins disappeared in 1996. In the spirit of romantic comedies, it is best to accept the premise that with the help of a good woman, Brady will turn his life around.

Brady decides to stay in Reno and visit his sister. Sarah realizes that since the girls are kidnap victims and have taken a life, they could benefit from some counseling. However, before going off with Brady, she turns to the audience and sings "It's Only Sex," implying that the future with Brady is not as secure as would be expected in a typical romantic comedy. To underscore this, the song has the same music as Brady's song about Sarah making romantic decisions with her brain in the off position. Nonetheless, everyone is happy—except for the neo-Nazi skinheads who have all been killed.

As for telling the entire truth about the Dana Twins, the movie ends where it began, on the patio of a Nashville restaurant. Skylar Jones and Elana Grey are sitting with the producers of the film. The older one is Milton Brandenburg, a man who—even before the success of *The Dana Twins: The True Story*—had become a nationally recognizable figure. The younger man is his partner, Jonah Aaron.

Elana Grey begins the conversation by stating, "We've told the audience that there were no cute blonde twelve year old boys, and that the Dana Twins were actually two sixteen year olds whose voices were adjusted by a creative sound engineer."

Skylar Jones chimes in "And the audience now knows that there was no plane crash and no fundamentalist father who wouldn't let them go on tour. They had to disappear because they could only get the Dana Twins' sound in a studio using a computer."

Elana, who has known the identity of the Dana Twins for years, interrupts. "But the question is this. Can we end the movie without telling who the Dana Twins really were? I was thirteen when the Dana Twins were at the peak of their popularity and Skylar was twelve. We want to know. The audience wants to know. You were their manager. Do we get a final scene where we can reveal that part of the truth?"

Milton Brandenburg points to the script in front of him and announces, "Save it for the sequel. If you want an additional scene, you can show the neo-Nazis being buried. The guy who got decapitated can be buried in a coffin with a bowling ball bag on top. The guy who got hit with the anvil can be buried in a coffin the top half of which is flat as a pancake. Otherwise, this is it."

As Elana and Skylar frown, Jonah Aaron gets the last spoken line of the movie. "Look, hopefully, we've given the fans enough good music and enough of the truth to send them home happy. It's ok to keep some secrets."

At that point, Skylar and Elana pick up on the phrase "keep some secrets" and, in falsetto voices, they burst into song, singing the Dana Twins' biggest hit.

But I can keep a secret, I can keep a secret. I can keep a secret. You know that I can. You think I'm a sweet boy. You call me your boy toy. But maybe, baby, maybe I'm a dangerous man.

As the two women begin to giggle over the lyric calling them dangerous men and boy toys, and as a confused movie audience begins begin to wonder if this final scene is supposed to be sending the subliminal message that Skylar Jones and Elana Grey were the Dana Twins, the screen goes black, "Dangerous Man" plays, and the closing credits roll.

THE END

EPILOGUE

WHEN MELVIN AARON became a physician, he hoped to make a major contribution to the field of medicine. During his thirty plus year career at academic institutions, he published sixty-one scientific papers and co-authored fourteen textbook chapters. He encouraged doctors to treat patients compassionately and to approach clinical problems in a logical manner. He received several teaching awards from medical students and medical residents and countless letters from the families of grateful patients.

When Dr. Aaron retired from the practice of medicine shortly after the success of *Angels from Rikenny,* his philosophy remained much the same as it had been when he was in training at Mt. Moriah. "Treat people compassionately; take the job seriously, but not yourself." With the perspective that comes with age he has added, "While we all believe that we are the hero of our own life's story, in the grand scheme of things we may turn out to be bit players in someone else's tale." Melvin Aaron has no regrets that his major claim to fame is that he is the father of noted television and film producer Jonah Aaron.

While the story of the Dana Twins might suggest that one can create something out of nothing, like a magician pulling a quarter from behind the ear of a child, that is an illusion. At the heart of every success there must be a core of true talent. The fact is illustrated by the autographed poster of the Dana Twins that hangs over the mantle in the family room of Milton Brandenburg's Belle Meade home. It bears the "signatures" of Richie Dana and Stevie Dana, signed by Jonah Aaron and his cousin Brian. However, the poster is also signed by Cory Bayliss and Jackson Daniels, the men whose talent gave rise to the Dana Twins.

Also of note, on the wall to the left of that poster is a nineteenth century illustration that Mona Brandenburg purchased for her husband after he sent their young sons, Joey and Terry, on an airplane ride to Seattle, a trip that would have led to the death of the two Brandenburg boys if not for their cousin, Jonah. The drawing shows Rumplestiltskin, the fairy tale dwarf who could spin straw into gold. At the end of that story, Rumplestiltskin's overblown ego engenders his destruction. The illustration serves as a constant reminder to Milton Brandenburg not to take things too far. Despite Milton's comment to Elana Grey and Skylar Jones in the final scene of the movie, there will be no sequel to *The Dana Twins: The True Story.* Everything has its limits, even in Music City, and, as Sarah sings in the movie, "When it's time to go, it's time to go."

ACKNOWLEDGEMENTS

THIS WORK OWES its existence to too many people to thank properly. However, I wish to acknowledge my "beta-readers" whose helpful comments are much appreciated. Loretta Saff's advice was so substantial that I consider her my honorary editor which means that she can take credit for much of what is good about the final manuscript while she is responsible for none of the flaws. My wife, Adele, looked at so many versions of this work that it is amazing that her head isn't spinning on its axis. Jan Bowers, Molly Stein, Debra Brodsky, Monica Stein, Lynetta Alexander, and Bill Henry also made helpful comments along the way.

My late father, Melvin Stein, is responsible for the mantra "Don't outlive your money; don't outlive your mind," the latter half of which is at the core of *Angels from Rikenny*.

My friend Darrel Bengson, a true outdoorsman, explained the operation of bear traps to me thereby helping me—and one of my characters—out of a difficult situation.

Thanks also go to my associates in the Vanderbilt University Division of Hematology and Oncology whom I consider some of my closest friends. They had to pick up the slack when I semi-retired to become a writer.

A final shout-out goes to Eric Wolf of Wolf Mastering in Nashville who reviewed the parts of the novel dealing with recording studios. If the Dana Twins ever record again, Eric is the man I want preserving their work on vinyl.

Edwards Brothers Malloy
Thorofare, NJ USA
December 13, 2013